A

Question

of

Counsel

A QUESTION OF COUNSEL (The Republic 1)
By Archer Kay Leah

Published by Ashborne Stardust Press

Second edition, October 2019
First published by Less Than Three Press, 2015

Cover designed by Natasha Snow Designs; www.natashasnowdesigns.com

Map designed by Raelynn Marie

Print ISBN 978-1-9992029-5-8

Content Notes, Warnings, and Disclaimers

A Question of Counsel contains some explicit content, all of which is meant for adult readers.

This story touches on several serious matters, including mental health issues, domestic abuse and violence, and depictions of emotional and physical situations that could bother some readers. This includes references to the recent loss of a parent due to terminal illness, grief, depictions of PTSS/PTSD (post-traumatic stress syndrome/disorder), anxiety attacks, and the use of alcohol as a coping mechanism resulting in mild alcoholism. The references to domestic abuse and violence include psychological, emotional, physical, and verbal abuse, as well as references to exploitation.

This story also contains violent situations, a kidnapping, references to human trafficking and the trafficking of children, non-consensual touching and sexual harassment, and references to the deaths of family members. Finally, this story includes references to homophobia, bigotry, and depictions of misogyny.

Please note the story uses gender-neutral pronouns for certain characters (*vem, vir, ne, they, them, their, hir,* and *hirself*). These are not mistakes: they are the chosen pronouns of those characters.

To my partner, Cris.
There's more than just a little of us in this telling.
Thank you for the encouragement, putting up with my
ridiculous hours, and listening to me babble about
imaginary people doing weird things. Most of all,
thank you for understanding. You, my Stitch, are
irreplaceable. xoxoxo

And to Megan, Sam, Sasha, and everyone at Less Than
Three Press. Not only did you give this story and every
one after the chance to get up and get out there, you
inspired the entire series and the many rabbit holes to
come (and are there EVER a ton more to come!).
You're amazing and I love you all. Thank you for the
wonderful years and the fantastic support! I literally
couldn't have done any of this without you, and I
wouldn't have had it any other way.
<3 <3 <3

A Question of Counsel

THE REPUBLIC BOOK 1

ARCHER KAY LEAH

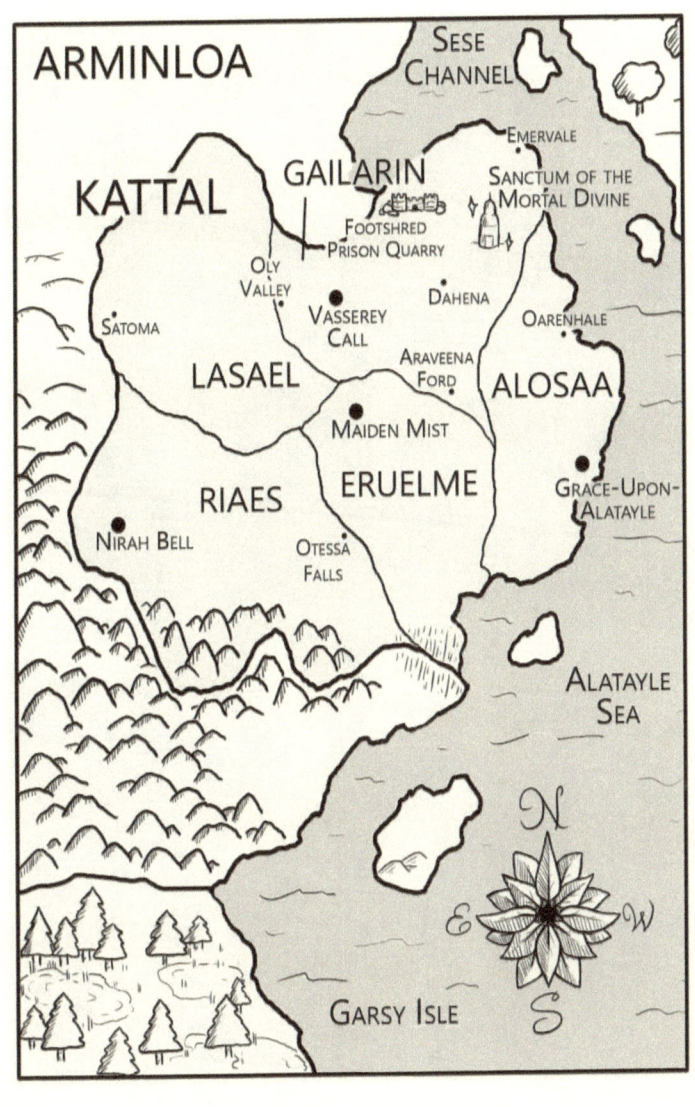

Chapter One

Dead father. Imprisoned brother. Could it possibly get any worse?

"Of course it could," Aeley Dahe answered to the silence, throwing her knife before even uglier truths bit back. The blade ended up where it should have: lodged near the centre of the wood target on the dark red wall of the study, its black hilt with blood-red and gleaming gold bands sticking out with every cry of violence inside her.

Hit something. Rage against the waning days. *Something.* She needed to do *something.* She wanted to punch it down, cry it out, scream for it all to stop—just *stop.* This was never the plan, never the future she had envisioned. And every last bit of what had been was long gone, sent down into ashes with her father; a loss she could never recover, the shards of what remained of their dwindling family nothing more than blood-crusted dirt under her feet.

But no, it could always get worse. Always.

I could be just as dead. Whatever that was worth.

Not to deny the acrid taste that thought left, Aeley leaned back against the creaking desk and pulled her knees up under her fern-green gown, gaze straying towards the windows. Light spilled across the room in bright colours, the large stained-glass panes entirely too cheerful for her to want them in one piece anymore. Once beautiful, once delightful, once a pretty comfort—they may as well have been blacker than any bottomless abyss for all she cared. Sure, she was alive, at least the last time she checked, but survival was all she had managed so far, not that it counted for much against the demands of duty. *Though some could say being the Tract Steward is almost like being a moving corpse. Our life isn't our own.*

Glancing at her father's proud, painted image above the door, Aeley let her head thunk against the desk once, then a second time to punish herself for the first. Without looking away from the painting's empty gaze, she sought the decanter of gaffa nectar with one hand, her fingers snaking across the floor to the thick glass vessel. More and more since her inauguration, she understood why her father appeared ragged and worn in his older years, worried eyes weighted with shadows, his hair a dull silver-grey where it had once been dark blonde like hers. She was only twenty-eight, but would the weight of responsibility age her faster?

Aeley sipped the sweet liquid from the decanter, comforted by its cool familiarity.

Eleven weeks.

Her father died eleven weeks ago, only days after the first of summer—and she had counted every damn day since.

Some of them she had barely gotten through. Some of them she was still trying to get through, the problems they brought rolling over from one day to the next, no resolution in sight.

Was that the measure of her life now? To merely tumble through the days, praying for resolutions that would never come and counting how many she survived?

It was far from a life. No, it was more of a life sentence in a gilded cage, wrapped in a title she had never wanted but already had to defend, spilling blood in the process and losing three of her guards. Her friends. Her family. They were gone now, passed on to the Realm of the Dead to do whatever the dead did.

She raised the decanter to her father's portrait, the silent toast coming with relentless fatigue, the pull of tears too dried up to flow, and memories she needed to drink into oblivion. There were too many memories, the unwelcome in a constant collision with the nostalgic, all pressed between remorse and grief.

Officially, she had been Tract Steward of Gailarin for all of five weeks, elected by the people to be their leader and represent their interests in the Republic of Kattal's grander affairs—a fact that still stunned her, as terrifying as it was humbling. There was too much space to mess it all up. She was a fighter, not a politician, not really. Politics had been her father's specialty; hers was putting dents in expensive weapons and making appearances at the usual social functions.

Though she was a politician now, or playing at being one at least, one of five Tract Stewards in Kattal, expected to uphold the highest levels of law, order, and governance, worrying over the price of crops, tract taxes, and how to get through meetings without completely annoying everyone else. Granted, she had more than five weeks experience at it, having been Acting Tract Steward for the first six weeks after her father's death, bringing the grand total to three months. Before that, she had assisted her father with his work, trained under his tutelage, then stepped in when he was too ill to do anything in his last few weeks.

But the first of summer... The worst truths had hit hard that night, with him confined to bed, too sick to chew even the smallest morsel, mouthfuls of water coming up almost as much as they stayed down. They had forgone the customary dinner and fancy celebrations for the Feast of Valaster and kept to themselves, sequestered in privacy with Aeley at Korre's bedside, willing him to not leave yet. To keep fighting. She would have fought on his behalf if she could have; if the Goddesses had been kind enough to swap their bodies. Not that he would have let her: even to the end, he refused to let her get away without taking care of herself, mustering a glare as only a parent could to make her feel bad enough to eat and rest and do anything that was not sitting there dying with him.

If only she could have been left alone in peace and quiet after the night he slipped away for good. Everything hurt that night, grief translated into such deep pain, the aches spreading from head to heart and hitting nearly every muscle on the way to agony. No amount of throwing things and crying had helped. They just made the aches worse.

Yet the worst of it—the absolute *worst* of it— came eight weeks later. Just *eight bloody weeks* after losing her father, her damned cursed brother, Allon, had flipped every proverbial table and brought the world crashing down around their family again. Out of jealousy, out of rage, out of self-importance. Aeley doubted any of it had anything to do with love, and certainly nothing of the sort had been spared for the memory of their father and his life's work as Tract Steward.

No, Allon had raged on through his anger at Aeley and taken it out on the people, attacking a village in Oly Valley and kidnapping innocent people for no other reason than to assert his control and delusional power over everyone. He wanted to be Tract Steward bad enough to destroy lives, including his own.

If he had wanted Aeley's attention, he had it in full then, every bit of it tied together with the abysmal depths of her loathing.

He was High Council's problem now, though his stench lingered everywhere, both of their family's estates harbouring ghosts of times long gone. Aeley and Allon had never gotten on well, that much was true, but this...

It had run her into hiding. She needed to admit that, that this sitting around, wanting to get full-on drunk in her study for the umpteenth time in weeks, was hiding.

But what was she hiding from more: everyone else or everything inside her head?

Most days the line blurred so badly she could barely see straight, no matter if she was drunk, hungover, or some variation of sober. Memory was a fickle bitch, and she'd had enough of it. Ever since Allon's attack on Oly Valley, she drank almost as much as she dreamed about chasing him through the damaged estate. Explosions constantly rocked the world in her mind, especially when she was surrounded by total silence. The awful sound of exploding walls haunted her sleep, waking her and leaving her feeling caked in the stickiness of blood and dust, ruins surrounding her with limp bodies, attesting to the destructive force that was Allon's snap of unadulterated rage.

Nowhere was safe, not when she carried the most frightening things with her. So little could be trusted, even her own judgment. Sometimes she would stop in an empty corridor and wait to feel the earth shake beneath her, expecting to hear Allon's taunts or feel the air move as he charged her down, laughing—always laughing. It was far from how she expected to spend her first months as Tract Steward.

And here I thought it'd be easier after helping Father do everything towards the end. She snorted and took another drink. *Winning the vote was the easiest part. No one in their right mind voted for Allon. Complete traitor. Not my problem now, though—he belongs to the High Council. I'm done.*

Images of Allon in a dark, rank cell raced through her mind. Rumour from the High Council indicated his punishment would be a life of labour, slogging at rocks in one of the republic's quarries. It was only fair, she figured, seeing as he intended to kill citizens of Kattal. He would spend the rest of his life serving them instead, his sweat and need for attention spent on providing for the homes and livelihoods of others.

So why did she still believe his resentment and unpredictable schemes were far from finished?

Reaching behind her with her free hand, she pulled a second knife from her belt and glanced at the wall. Beige wood planks covered the wall from floor to ceiling, crudely painted with yellows, whites, and reds. Moments like this justified having it.

She stood and placed the decanter on the floor before turning towards the target. With a breath in, Aeley steadied the blade and focused on the bright red circle midway down the target. Allon's face came to mind, and with a breath out, she threw the knife.

The blade hit close to the circle with little resistance but got stuck in the wood above her previous attempt—not her best, but at least the knife made it that far. Throwing made her feel better. It was more helpful than admitting that fighting Allon's guards and arresting him left her shaken. People would think her incapable instead of the composed, stalwart leader they expected. Appearance and perception meant everything.

Retrieving the decanter, she stared at the target. The colours blurred as she drank, the glass doors and dark wood of the bookcase to the right of the target a looming shadow at the edge of her vision, serving as a reminder of her father. His books, statuettes, and precious, breakable trinkets—she kept them in the bookcase, locked up with her nostalgia and the disturbing underlying desire to break things.

A loud knock on the door made her jump and sputter, spraying the nectar onto the floor.

"Yes?" Aeley called and held one wrist to her mouth. She stopped before her wet lips brushed the fabric. Making a mess of one of her nicer gowns was not the best idea, especially with dinner so close. As host, she needed to remain clean and prim as much as she could. Hurriedly, she drew her fingers along her lips until they felt dry.

"Cook says dinner will be served shortly," a muffled voice answered.

Aeley sighed. *Naturally.* She placed the decanter on the cleared section of her desk and tugged her belt back into place. After smoothing her hair and her skirt, she retrieved one of her knives, sheathing it before opening the door.

Haydin smiled, the wrinkles around his dark brown eyes more pronounced. "I thought I'd escort you." He winked as he bowed from the waist and added a playful flourish of his hand, the balding spot in his white hair coming into view. His deep blue shirt and short jacket with elegant silver embroidery looked immaculate as usual, his loose black pants tucked tightly into black ankle-high boots.

Every bit the perfect gentleman... with that extra little spark of mischief.

"And I can't help but accept. What girl could resist your charm?" Aeley slipped her arm around his, noting the slight tremble in his frail body as they strolled towards the dining room. As steward of the Dahe estate, Haydin's official responsibilities revolved around managing the household, ensuring everything was in order and functioning as well as it should.

But to Aeley, he was family, much more like an uncle who had helped her father for most of his life—for all of *her* life. Without any other living relatives to turn to, she clung to Haydin's steadfast nature and that calm, collected way he kept everything under control. "What would I do without you?" she murmured, leaning her head on his shoulder.

Haydin patted her hand and chuckled, his tone low and soothing. In that moment, it was as if she walked with her father again.

"And Cook," he muttered. "That's who can resist me. My charm is as welcome as a gnat where she's concerned. There's a cake pan with my name permanently etched into it, and not one bit of it has to do with baking."

Aeley failed to stop the snicker that came out, then the full-on laughter as Haydin glared at her—a soft glare, one that knew how ridiculous his halfhearted feud with Cook was even after twenty years. She almost reminded him of how often Cook kept him going when he seemed rundown and tired enough to finally pass along his resignation, wooing him back to duty with flaky pastries and nostalgic strolls in the garden. Or how every time Cook took sick or felt like death, Haydin courted her wellbeing with every comfort he could think of, sparing no expense, all the while wearing such a deep, worried frown until Cook was on her feet again.

But Aeley kept quiet, keeping him to herself for a few moments longer. She needed to hold on to what family she had left, guard them, cherishing whatever time they could spare. If her parents had taught her anything, it was that much. And Allon... he only impressed that upon her even further, his vengeance a threat to everything she needed to protect.

Once they entered the dining room, however, the warmth of their shared familial moments died.

A dozen guests filled the modest room, standing in small groups engaged in discussion around the long table, already enjoying the drinks and food the kitchen staff had set out, silver platters gleaming against the pristine white tablecloth. Three gold candelabrums stood along the centre line of the table, each forged in the shape of a gently twisting tree with four branches and thick white candles. Bright orange and yellow wreaths encircled the candelabrums, small violet berries and bright blue tendrils peeking out from among the leaves and petals, a festive complement to the colourless glass dinnerware. Other candles sat on the short ledges along the walls, casting a soft light over the dark red hue of the wood panels. Shadows danced between the spaces, playing chase-and-catch as the movement of bodies swept the flames every which way.

Everyone stilled, silence falling as they realized Aeley was there. The various earthy golds, rich greens, dusky blues, and vivid reds of their clothes were a wash of colour against the darker backdrop—almost like a painting, one to match her father's portrait in the study, though she would have rather avoided both of them altogether right then. There were too many gazes to contend with when she could barely stomach looking at herself. Mirrors offered such cold reflections as of late, the judgment they captured almost as degrading as her nightmares. If she could have shattered them all without feeling even worse, she would have.

A few of the guests stared at Aeley quizzically as she drifted through, still holding Haydin's arm, all but counting the steps to the other side of the room. Only one gaze accused her of running and hiding: the seasoned glare of Mayr, Head of the Guard for the Dahe family and their estates.

The worst part was that he was right.

Aeley looked away. Mayr had things to say, but they needed to wait. As much as she loved him, she would never get through dinner if they started up that gods-awful path. When she raised her hand, he fell into his chair and threw one arm over the curved back, his head tilted. With his long, dark hair over his shoulder, the black tattoos around his neck were obvious, making him stand out among the others.

"Please sit," she said, gesturing to the table.

Grateful as the others sat with only a few words of greeting before continuing their chatter,

Aeley took her seat at the head of the table. Haydin lowered himself into the chair to her left, while Mayr occupied the chair to her right, their presence lending her strength, though both could make just about any awful situation bearable. After her father, they were her greatest supporters, family to the last.

Where Haydin was more like an uncle, Mayr was her best friend, though she had always taken to him like a brother. If anything, he was the loving, compassionate brother she never had, one that refused to suffer Allon gladly. More than a couple dozen times, he had broken up fights between Aeley and Allon, only to back Allon up out of the room without a single touch. In those moments, Allon had proven how much he loved to fight but never when it came to Mayr, and never when it came Pellon, Aeley and Mayr's mutual best friend and second-in-command of the Dahe Guard. Whenever they were around, Allon valued self-preservation above all else, protecting his very breath over defending his convictions.

Perhaps it helped that they had spent their adolescence together, the four of them constantly in each other's space with Aeley, Mayr, and Pellon gravitating towards one another, forming bonds strong enough to withstand the uncertainty in their futures, even now when they were at their strongest. Allon had never fit into the set, never cared, only pushed their patience and tested their limits, gathering more than disdain to add to his motivations. Even so, he had paid attention to them, enough to know that while Aeley would always be backed against the bounds set by their father, Mayr and Pellon were loyal in their protection of the Dahe household, whom they considered family as much as she did.

Allon, however, had set himself apart from that family, bit by miserable bit as the years carried on, distancing himself from that protection and loyalty. In most cases, he had verbally denied the attention, keeping counsel with his own friends and comrades, well away from the main estate there in Dahena Village, the official family seat of the Dahes. Instead, Allon had run off to Oly Valley, claimed the smaller estate for himself with Korre's relieved approval, and hidden from everything. Not that Aeley had wasted time on mourning that particular loss: any day without him nearby was one where she could breathe without feeling as though she would snap anytime he spoke or even sauntered into the room, silent with that cocky smirk on his face.

And now...

The walls—they were blowing to bits, heavy grey-white stones flying through the air to slam against anything still standing... or anyone. The quietest weapon, one she never saw coming, exploding with a vengeance, taking out the unsuspecting and leaving them dazed, if not dead. And that sound—the deafening booms, the ringing in her ears, the muffled cries that bounced from here to there, hers among them. Dust and plaster and chunks of stone rained down as they ducked, ran, hid from the assault. Destruction. Utter destruction with Allon somewhere in the estate, hiding, laughing, running from Aeley. He would pay. He needed to pay—

Aeley snapped out of the images, skin tingling with the memory of sickening grit and bruises that had disappeared but never really left. Laughter. Someone's laughter had saved her just then, a deep, throaty interruption she could have listened to for several more moments, dragging her battered mind across the floor just to sit beside it. Hide behind it.

Luinn Janate-Roye—that was who she had to thank this time, another one of his laughs putting her at ease. He sat near the opposite end of the table, second seat in on the right, between Magistrate Tarne and Priestess Kee. The bright reds and oranges of Luinn's long, greying hair were difficult to miss, particularly against the vivid white fabric of his elaborately embroidered long coat and shirt. The hues were as jovial as he was, reflecting the passionate spirit within.

When he smiled her way, his green gaze passing on a subtler delight, Aeley lifted her chin and attempted to share in that smile, a slow-to-burn calm willing to broker peace with what ailed her. As the staunch patriarch of the Janate-Roye family, one of the Grand Families of Kattal best known for their wealth of knowledge, riches, and keen sense of survival through any conflict, Luinn was a stalwart ally, dependable and firm in resolution. He had stuck by her father for all of Korre's term as Tract Steward, then, to Aeley's relief, he had pledged his family's loyalty to her, recognizing the succession of leadership without any disagreement. His composure and general ease made Aeley's transition into her role a bit smoother. If the other Grand Families kicked up a fuss, she could at least rely on him to weigh the situation with a cool mind and steer his family away from unnecessary dissent.

On the other hand, Luinn's relationships to the other Grand Families were not to be overlooked or taken for granted. He held sway throughout the republic, a fact she never wanted to abuse, but use… maybe a little… if she could figure out how to do it without being mistaken for a toddler playing with puzzles at the foot of a massive throne.

Beside Luinn, at the very end of the table, Priestess Kee shared in his laughter, the layers of her shimmering red robes and veil both eye-catching and intimidating. She radiated with joy as she spoke to Luinn and the guest across from her: Winiah, one of the chattiest, most sought-after metalsmiths in Dahena with soft brown eyes, a warm black-brown complexion, and a charming lyrical tone that seemed to pull everyone to them like a friendly flame on a cold night. Whatever they spoke about failed to carry over the other voices around the table, which was a shame because all three of them appeared to be having a marvelous time.

It was almost worth Aeley dragging her chair to the other end of the table to get in on the cheer, though more than etiquette kept her in her place: Kee's sharp, dark eyes and stern features were hard enough to stop someone in their tracks for just about any reason—a valuable asset, given Kee's position as Overseer of the closest Temple of the Four, the temple on the outer border of Dahena, only a short ride away from the estate. Aeley had met with Kee several times, mostly about Korre's illness and death, with Kee and her fellow priests conducting the funeral rites. Kee had been a blessing then, her ease with taking control of the situation releasing Aeley of the anxiety she tried to ignore. Since then, she had met with Kee to discuss tract matters, what with Kee's expansive knowledge of the republic and how it functioned. She was an ally worth keeping at whatever cost, though Aeley suspected that was how the temple felt about Kee in general. They had elected her as Overseer for a reason, placing her in charge of their temple, acting as their collective voice and protector.

The others around the table were also allies Aeley hoped to keep on her side, including four magistrates and Gavis, a kind, sweet-tempered importer and exporter of various items with the softest hazel gaze but a strong-willed knack for striking bargains and successful deals. Korre had called upon Gavis to tend to several commerce matters over the years, both for tract affairs of various degrees and smaller personal needs. Korre had trusted Gavis, putting faith in vir abilities to do things right, and Aeley intended to honour that understanding.

The magistrates, however, were a different matter altogether, one she would have to tread around with careful steps and prudence... if not completely undoing the sensitive relationships by being herself and letting the fighter in her do the talking, which would not be pretty at any length. She needed to behave when it came to the magistrates, not run headlong into disaster.

Magistrate Dreca was her immediate concern. Having governed Dahena Village for the last fifteen years, he knew the village inside and out. What went on was his personal concern, and he liked to air those concerns with her on a near-daily basis, his tone usually harder with her than it had been with Korre. Whether it was because he was twice her age, seeing her as nothing but a child, or he simply respected Korre more, Aeley kept her tongue around him, not sure of how to win him over. Maybe it was meant to be a permanent thorn in her stewardship, a constant challenge to test her wits.

Perhaps it was for the best, given his colleagues at the dinner, all of them seated at the latter half of the table: Tarne, Pergill, and Calohe, magistrates of towns and massive, sprawled districts further away from Dahena and its surrounding villages. Despite their varying ages—Pergill being the youngest, ten years older than Aeley, and mildly boisterous relative to his peers—all three magistrates seemed intent on putting Aeley through her paces. They often made demands she could not meet with what resources she had, paired with deadlines that even Korre would have scoffed at and pushed hard to change. The only difference being they would have relented to Korre, his experience outdoing theirs and their respect hanging on his promises.

She had far too much work to do there—

"Do you honestly think they'll respect you?" Allon yelled, kicking the side of the cart, forcing it to jostle and creak in protest. "You think they'll see you as anything more than the little girl clinging to her father's pocket? As anything more than a brutish little brat with a sword and cold hands?" Chains rattled, metal scraping wood as he dragged across the cart bed, knees taking abuse. Fresh blood trickled from his broken nose, the crooked angles and mortality at home on his bruised and battered face. "You're not good enough, when will you clue into that? You're only going to fail, worthless and bitter—an old maid dying on the pyre, dispensable and useless."

Mayr charged towards Allon, jumping over the side of the cart and shouting obscenities as he punched Allon in the face. One shout, another, all cutting through the violent rocking of the wooden cart, wheels squealing as they rolled forward, the horse seeming to take it as a sign to move. As Allon screamed over his broken arm, guards raced to stop the horse from running off and taking the cart with her.

The fists stopped. Allon crumpled over in the cart, arm cradled tightly to his chest in the makeshift sling. Blood streamed from his nose and new cuts on his cheek, green eyes dark enough to get lost in the dirt and grime smearing his face. His gaze crept towards her, swollen lips parted as he struggled for every ragged breath. "You'll go down in flames, mark my words," he snarled. "Everything—every damned thing—will crash and you'll come running to me. You want respect? Try licking it from my boots, little filth, and save us all. Go out gracefully. You won't like the heartache coming for you. You'll scream holy bitch before the end—"

Silence. That eerie silence fell, Allon's dead weight thudding on the cart bed, skull cracking on the wood, Mayr sneering at the body and flexing his fingers—

"Ae."

She knew that voice, that gentle call, but dragging from the memory this time was like trying to wade through a pit of solidifying rock-filled mud and only budging enough to knock a leaf across the surface.

The hand on her wrist had better luck, pressure gradually increasing around her arm.

Aeley blinked, Mayr's face coming into focus. The cleanliness of his face and worried gaze pushed past the image of him locking itself back up in her head.

"You all right?" he whispered, leaning close enough to play his breath on hers, his grip still on her wrist.

"Fine." Aeley pushed him back. "Just business as usual, please? Don't make this into something it isn't." She forced a smile, her mouth uncomfortably dry. "Dinner. I just want a nice dinner. We can do that, right? Eat? Drink? Be merry? Bet on who's going to leave here on two feet or none?"

Mayr watched her with a restrained frown. "Dinner it is," he said softly. "And Pergill. My bet's on Pergill, two feet. Calohe on none."

The darkness clinging to Aeley's aches and anguish tumbled out in a wicked laugh. "Oh, you'd like to think, wouldn't you?" She pointed at the table, her voice lowered. "Luinn, two feet, in a circling argument with Tarne, no feet, over Tarne not knowing which way home actually is."

Mayr chuckled and shook his head, then sipped from his goblet, his focus still on her.

Ignoring him, mostly to avoid the nausea of painful reminders, Aeley smiled at Vant instead, a stout man with a short grey beard and thinning grey-blond hair sitting next to Haydin. Vant had served as her father's solicitor for the majority of Korre's life, handling everything from personal legal matters to tract business, particularly correspondence and presentations to and from the High Council. He managed a small team of younger solicitors from the region, all vying for his tutelage, though most of the work went through him when it came to Tract Steward business.

To Aeley's relief, Vant chose to remain as her family's solicitor. The fewer people she needed to replace, the better, though his skill with difficult issues was invaluable. She hated legalities, and she hated writing documents even more, the coordination of the body parts involved in the process not anywhere near as elegant or eloquent as she needed them to be.

Reaching for the glass goblet in front of her, Aeley finally allowed her gaze to wander to the young woman beside Vant.

Her hand stopped, fingertips brushing the side of the goblet. For a moment, she could only stare at the soft curves of the woman's face, framed by loose, brown curls. She appeared to be Aeley's age, if not younger, and everything about her was easy on weary eyes, her face not done up with paint like many of the other people Aeley knew.

When the woman's glance met hers, Aeley blinked and held tight to her goblet. While familiar, no name came to mind. *Surprising, since she's beautiful.*

Aeley bit her tongue on that thought. *How* could the *only* question she could think of right then be *Why didn't I notice her sooner?*

Clearing her throat, Aeley watched Luinn while she drank, straining to hear his discussion with Winiah. As her attention pulled towards the unnamed woman, she forced her focus to the furthest end of the table.

The chatter grew louder as the kitchen staff served the meal, and temptation joined the chaos, poking at Aeley with the clear demand to ask Vant about his companion—a demand she denied, as much as it annoyed her. *Other than getting me into trouble, he's busy chatting up the rest of the table, anyway.* Instead, she fought to focus on Haydin, Gavis, and Dreca as they spoke about business in the weeks to come, but that damned straying in the other direction...

Over the din, she heard her name. Everyone hushed and faced her.

Aeley's cheeks warmed. "Sorry?" She ignored Mayr's subdued laughter, his quiet snort not escaping her.

Kee's smile was kind and comforting. "It appears I caught you at an in-between moment. I apologize for pulling you from your thoughts." She swept strands of her black hair across her forehead, then brushed back the edge of her glimmering red veil, its intense hue vivid against her tan skin. "Even we priestesses are not blessed with perfect timing. Well, the rare few are. I was blessed with the gift of catching everyone by surprise," she added with a light laugh, winking at the magistrates.

Aeley shook her head. "It's not your fault. I'm just sorry I didn't hear you the first time."

"No matter. Everything comes in our own time. It keeps our patience at the ready." Kee's amusement remained as she waved Aeley's apology away. "I was merely wondering how you are these days? The last we spoke, you were optimistic, though I understand things have been... unsettled. The Temple sends you nothing but good wishes at this challenging time."

"Yes, well..." Aeley pushed food around her plate with her spoon. Allon was not worth dinner talk, not when he lived for every freedom inside her head. "I'm fine," she said and straightened, forcing a smile. "But thank you for your concern, Priestess, and please convey my gratitude to the Temple. I'm sorry I haven't visited recently, though I will soon. I know this dinner doesn't fix that, but I'm hoping they'll be pleased to know the people are being taken care of, despite what's happened. I've been visiting the villages, making sure they have everything, and helping with some of the harvesting and building—"

"Well-appreciated," Dreca interrupted, drawing only slight nods from the other magistrates. He grinned and raised his goblet towards her, amber-brown eyes bright if not a little too cheery for her liking. "The people thank you for your fine hospitality. Just like your father."

"Just what I keep telling her," Vant added.

With a brief look at Vant, Aeley's gaze slid to the woman next to him. Had she even spoken one word since they sat down? She could have dominated the conversation by that point and kept every eye on her, no less than most of the women Aeley knew. Instead, she watched the others, offering nothing of herself in words. Her face and constant fidgeting betrayed her, however.

Has things to say, but doesn't say them. Unable? Too scared? Or is she a servant stuck in the habit of being quiet? She can't possibly be from one of the Families. If she were, she'd have made certain I knew her name from the moment I stepped in. She'd be looking for favours. Playing on Vant's status. Something.

Pulling her thoughts together, Aeley smiled at Dreca. "And I appreciate your appreciation. I've tried to maintain the standards. There's no reason to undo what my father set forward for this tract."

"Though you're adding your own to it," Luinn said, leaning forward and tapping the table, the nearby candles giving his dark tan complexion a golden glow. "You've gotten Council to send soldiers in to help, something your father rarely did."

"And they actually haven't destroyed anything," Dreca added. He looked pointedly at Mayr before taking a drink.

Before Mayr could respond with a verbal attack to accompany his glare, Aeley cleared her throat. "Yes, I've been trying to get everyone to work together. Common goals for the good of the republic. Keeps us strong, I figure."

She glanced at the woman again, a slight shiver racing through her. Why could she not stop looking? Her control was better than that. Her focus... she needed to pay attention to her food, to the politics, not that pretty face. Though at that moment, she mostly needed her body to quit with the games and simmer down. The longer the situation went on, she only got warmer, her cheeks feeling more flushed—all of it a distraction she did *not* want.

The mercy she hoped for came quicker than expected: one of the young men working as household staff entered the room, his knock on the open door drawing all attention to him.

"Merek," Aeley greeted with a sigh of relief.

Merek jutted his thumb towards the corridor behind him. "Someone's come for you."

When a tall man slipped into the room beside Merek, Aeley wanted to duck under the table. He was a messenger from the High Council, going by his unkempt traveling clothes and brown cloak with the green shield and golden bearcats embroidered along its hem. In his hand was a scroll, fastened with yellow cord. Yellow meant a serious request from the Council that would have to be met quickly.

The messenger crossed the room in the silence and held out the scroll, letting go only as Aeley accepted. "You are to read it and respond accordingly," he said, his voice rough.

Before she could say a word, the messenger left the room as brusquely as he had entered. Merek rushed after him.

"Wonder what that's all about," Haydin muttered.

Aeley resisted the urge to say "I don't know," which would have been one half of a lie. The shivers creeping through her sensed what was coming, that sense of *knowing* caught between slithering and crawling down her arms, its spindly legs pushing doubt aside. She pulled the cord away and read the scroll.

The High Council wanted her to attend Allon's hearing in three days, putting her in the same room as him.

You bastards.

Being near him made her sick. Even if they did not suspect that much, they should have damn well tried for some common decency. Compassion and sticking to their word would have been better.

Aeley said nothing as she rolled up the scroll and tied it shut, then slipped it into her lap and continued eating. Everyone wanted to know what it said. They wanted to discuss it, to poke their noses into her business.

Meanwhile, she could barely say her brother's name.

As she glanced at Mayr, she paused. He watched her with narrowed eyes, his fist pressed to his mouth. When she forced a hint of a smile, he shook his head. He always read her emotions better than she could talk about them. While she was good at hiding things from the others, he knew how to extract the truth from her, no matter how much she wanted to lie.

"So?" Luinn said.

Aeley waved her hand. "It's nothing worth sharing. They just need some papers. We correspond so much I'm considering asking them to move in. We've certainly got the space." She turned to Vant. "It seems I'll need your help again. Tomorrow, if you can. The Council wants the response sooner, not later, and it could use your fine touch."

Without waiting for Vant's acknowledgement or looking at his companion, she focused on her meal. The food tasted sour, right down to the gaffa nectar still in her goblet. The pleasant dinner was ruined, and the mindless chatter occupying the remainder of the main course did nothing to lift her spirits. Not even stealing glances at the beautiful stranger helped.

I probably won't sleep for days now. Thanks, Council.

The desert course would be just as agonizing, Cook's efforts ruined before the dishes could even leave the kitchen. Everything was coming up as appetizing as rust.

I can't do this.

Aeley stood, her patience spent, mostly with herself. Sharing a home with Allon had been bad enough, but living with the ghost of his damned selfish ego was even worse. "I'm sorry to run off before the final course," she said, forcing the words out as nonchalantly as she could, "but I'm afraid I have something to see to. You're welcome to stay and continue. Tonight was meant for you, so don't feel you have to leave. Stay as long as you'd like. Haydin will see to anything else you need. I just need to... do something."

Before anyone could question her, she clutched the scroll and her skirt, then hurried around the table. On her way past Vant, she glanced down to the woman next to him.

In one clumsy step, she fell to the floor.

Haydin was the first to offer his hand to help. Fumbling to stand and cursing under her breath, Aeley pushed up from the ground and brushed off her skirt without assistance. *The summons.* Where was that awful scroll? It should have been on the rug, but—

"Here," a quiet voice said.

Aeley looked down to find the scroll in the pale hand of the stranger. "Thanks," she murmured, accepting the parchment. Their fingers touched, one quick moment of skin sliding along skin.

Almost instantly, she drew away to disguise the tremble in her arm, but not without noticing how grey the woman's eyes were: dark, like the sky during a late-afternoon storm.

A beautiful distraction—one Aeley could not afford. If she stayed any longer, she was bound to make another foolish mistake.

Goddesses, save me.

Aeley rushed from the room. The night was nothing like she had planned and far from what she needed.

"Ae!"

Aeley refused to stop. Heavy boots pounded the stone floor behind her.

The steps slowed as Mayr caught up. "Seriously, that's it?" he asked. "*That's* how you thought you'd get out of that whole thing?"

"I have something to do."

Mayr snorted. "Right, just as much as I believe it, I'm sure." He poked her hand. "Just as much as I know this thing isn't nothing. You went almost white when you read it. What's it say?"

"It says you need to mind your own."

"Aren't you just the joy of the four Goddesses?"

"Mayr—"

"No. Unless you're going to tell me what this is, you don't get to use my first name. It's Head Guard if you're just going to lie to me."

Aeley stopped in the middle of the corridor and sighed. Fight him. She could do that. Besides, they were sparring partners. That had to count for something, weapons or not—

"Yeah, you're being cute and all, but I'm not giving this up, so you can stop with the sighing and the huffing, and don't even begin stamping your foot." One hand around her elbow, Mayr's tender grip helped keep her steady. "Don't make me steal that thing. I've known you since we were kids, Ae. Something's wrong and you're being stubborn. Again. Just tell me. I can't help if you don't talk to me."

She considered her options. It was better if no one else knew what was happening. To have received the summons in front of her guests was humiliating enough. She did *not* have to share the details.

But Mayr was family. He already knew what had happened in Oly Valley. Goddesses alive, he had been right there beside her during the entire ordeal, making sure she returned home still breathing. If anyone deserved to know their fight with Allon was not yet done, it was him. If anything, he *needed* to know. She owed him that much and a thousand other truths to come.

Aeley sighed. "Not here. Come on." She pulled him through the halls to her study and pushed him into the room before slamming the door. On the way to her desk, she tossed the scroll at him.

"What? You're going to make me read it?"

"Always something," Aeley grumbled and spun around. "They want me to go *there*, to Council, to watch *him* receive his ultimate

41

judgment—and that's after they said I wouldn't have to."

Mayr leaned against the wall. "No, they said you *possibly* wouldn't. You slipped in that extra—"

"Mayr!"

He threw up his hands. "Fine. If it bothers you that much, don't go."

"I can't." Resignation crept through her, the words hard to spit out, let alone swallow their meaning. "The councilmen are expecting me to help them put Allon away permanently. He's a danger to everyone. His men caused so much damage. I hear some of the children they captured are still terrified—that isn't how I want things to be. We can't disappoint them and let him off easily."

"So then go."

"I don't want to."

"Ae, choose one." Mayr's tone softened as he approached her. "I'll back you on any decision, but you're going to have to choose *one*. Either you're the perfect Tract Steward or you hide. Of course, if you hide, Allon wins, and then what good is your superiority?"

Part of her wanted to throw the decanter at his head. Just when he was being sweet, he hit her with the blunt truth.

"Don't say it. You hate me."

"You have no idea," Aeley muttered.

"Yeah, but nowhere near as much as you could." Mayr grinned and ran a hand through his hair, pulling it over his shoulder. "Then again, you also don't look at me like you did that girl. I saw your face. I recognize it from those rare times you've shown an interest in someone. Found something you like?"

Her face warmed. "No. I was just trying to figure out who she is."

"By the Four, you're a terrible liar."

"And you're just asking to be kicked from the guard," she teased, poking his chest.

"Feisty. Be careful—someone might just find it attractive enough to want to marry you."

Snorting, Aeley swiped the decanter from her desk and peered out the windows into the night. In the distance, the bright sliver of the moon shone above the horizon. "Don't you have some rounds to do or something?"

"Sorry. Some ridiculous friend invited me to dinner then made me stand around, reminding her who she is." Mayr held out the scroll. "She's trying to kick me out instead of seeing how much I want to help."

Again, he was right. "I hate you," Aeley mumbled, accepting the scroll. Through her father's death, Mayr had done what he could to fill in the gaps of her sanity and give her someone to grieve with—someone she could turn to in her worst moments without worrying about being hurt worse. But he had always been there for her well before that, ever since they were kids. He protected her when she neglected to take care of herself.

Mayr gripped her slumped shoulders. "I'll go with you," he said softly. "Won't be that bad. Then you'll never have to see him again, ever. Neither do I, and if I do, he'll get my fist in his face more permanently. I'll hang his skull on my wall. You know how sparsely I decorate."

Aeley laughed quietly. "Fine. We'll go. Three days, they said."

"Good. Now if you don't mind, I need to get back to work."

He tapped her chin before leaving. Once the door closed, she held up the decanter. "Just you and me, now."

Not long after she took a sip did images of the stranger at dinner fill her thoughts, lingering with a hint of pleasure. Was there something more than what she had told Mayr? She had never made a habit of staring at women, no matter how pretty they were, and she certainly never shuddered at their touch. What did it matter the woman's eyes were a cool, stormy grey Aeley could have gotten lost in for days, or that she looked so lovely, so warm to the touch, that Aeley wanted to run her fingers over her to know how she felt?

Dammit. Maybe Mayr was right about that, too.

Chapter Two

Well, that was one way to breathe livelihood into dinner.

Lira sipped her glowberry mead, her glance flicking from one guest to the next as they traded comments and theories, chasing after Aeley's escape with curious stares. And here she had thought *she* would be the one most likely to raise a brow or two—at least when she was not completely disappearing into the background, tempted to say something but opting for silence.

Or something close to it, anyway. Aeley saw through that forced wall of nothingness, or so it seemed. Her gaze had constantly strayed to Lira with questions haunting her brown eyes, not one of them spoken aloud, oddly safeguarding that same silence. Aeley was usually more vocal than that. *More 'forget you, world' and less 'obedience is a virtue,'* which was one of the few reasons Lira was still sitting there, enduring the overly long stares of Luinn, who kept misplacing his unvoiced opinions in her direction. Yes, she was quite aware of who she was, and no, she did not need his attention—she needed his eyes to crawl back inside his head and stay there, along with his oh-so-helpful thoughts.

Aeley. She was there for Aeley. That was all.

"Well, then," Vant muttered. He cast Lira a sideways glance, his goblet in one hand as the other wiped at the tablecloth with his lace handkerchief, dusting breadcrumbs over the fresh drops of black wine—an action that clearly served little purpose other than to keep his hands busy. His frown only added to his agitation. "It looks like tomorrow's plans have changed. Should I apologize or toast you?"

Lira snorted softly. "If it means not being at home, I'm all too happy about it."

"Mmm," Vant answered, somewhere between agreement and distraction. He looked at the dining room doorway for the umpteenth time.

"Worried?"

Vant's focus turned back onto her, his brow furrowed. "A little. She usually receives Council missives without so much..." His scowl deepened. "The word fails me, to be honest. She can try to brush it off, but something about it..." He shrugged and stuffed his handkerchief into the pocket of his soft green short coat. "She acts as though it was a red-cord missive, containing something that ought to be tossed into a fire, or shredded to bits at the very least. Not the first time, but not her standard response. Well, perhaps burning it is. And the shredding. Actually, any kind of destruction, really."

Not doubting it for a moment, Lira laughed and leaned back, holding her goblet close as she swirled the pink mead gently and watched the others. After years of observing people from her side of the silence, she agreed with Vant's assessment that something had Aeley on edge. Aeley might have waved the matter away, but there was nothing she could do to retract her initial reaction: the immediate cloudy expression, the disgust that passed across her face at such a minute scale it was easily missed, and the way she ran from the room as if the air was poisoned. A red-cord missive, indeed—the colour of urgency, not like the yellow cord of hasty demands. Running from a room full of prodding interests certainly would have topped Lira's list of ways to handle the situation, too, whatever the problem was. Then again, running away was the only solution she was left with most of the time.

Goddesses, was she ever tired of it.

This particular group had yet to be the worst she had been around, however, and she'd had her share. Still, she watched them, careful with what she revealed about herself. Studying people, gauging their actions and reactions, was much more than habit: it was a matter of constant self-preservation, mostly so she knew when she needed to escape and hide for safety's sake.

The only one she needed to hide from at the moment was Luinn, who seemed to invoke the judgment of the entire Janate-Roye family with every glance in her direction. She knew that lot well from the modest dinners her family hosted for families they found of use—or, rather, "of interest" her father usually said, the difference entirely too trivial.

Granted, Luinn's family was far from being a problem, if not more trustworthy and open than others. Of the Grand Families along the eastern border of Gailarin, Luinn's was the most influential and not to be underestimated by any means. With their family's primary home in Ilse Roye, they were stationed almost directly between two major seats of power in the republic: Dahena, home to the Dahes, and Oarenhale, home to Tract Steward Kayte Oaren in Alosaa. For decades, the Janate-Royes had used their location to their advantage, securing deals and alliances from most families on either side of the Gailarin-Alosaa border. All in all, they were clever, capable, and well-courted by many families in the country. As individuals, they were manageable— usually, anyway, provided Luinn's eldest son stayed away from Lira's family. There was little love there, though Luinn tried to smooth the ruffled feathers that resulted from any run-ins, presumably to keep Lira's father from cutting ties.

Either way, the politics was something she took no interest in. She showed up for the dinners, smiled when the moment called for it, and moved on afterwards, happy to fall into her books and poetry and take comfort from their soulful perspective.

She needed those books right then, if only to build a wall between her and Luinn. He had never been unkind to her, but the *you're out of place* look was still there, so clearly paired with the *let me count the ways your choices are entirely beneath you* line of thought. There was also the occasional *do your parents know you're here* glimmer, too, as though being twenty-five years old and fully capable of making her own decisions counted for nothing. He already had seven children to parent, and she was not one of them, nor was she looking for a father. Even if she were, he was not it, and the one surrogate she'd had—the one she truly loved—was several months dead, leaving a deep enough hole in her heart that she could have hidden in her books for years, swearing off people for good.

But then there was Aeley... a small hope she clung to for fear of drowning in the loss.

Making a face at the grief that pushed its way through, Lira sipped her mead, tempted to down the rest of it in one and pen some kind of blistering verse about the pitfalls of love. It was there; she felt it coming. Another one to add to the pile.

A delighted cry went up as kitchen staff swept into the room, carrying trays with green glass bowls and goblets filled with a bright orange-red drink.

Interrupted by desert. It could be worse.

Lira gave an easy smile as one of the women set down a bowl and goblet in front of her. "Thank you, and thank your cook for me. It's been a lovely meal."

The woman offered a gentle smile in return, her hazel-green eyes quick to shine. "That's good to hear, and I'll be sure to. Cook's always up for a bit of ego polishing," she said with a wink, flicking her hair back over her shoulder, a tumbling mass of black-brown curls and narrow braids streaked with white.

Haydin chuckled, peering around Vant to Lira, then up to the woman. "That's putting it a bit mildly, isn't it, Arieve?"

Arieve flashed him a brighter smile, one hand on his shoulder as she leaned close to him. "Shh, we're in company. Can't go telling everyone the house secrets," she said, her golden-brown complexion taking on a subdued flush—likely from how hard she seemed to fight laughing. "Have to keep some mystery, right? And you call yourself household steward. Honestly, Haydin."

"Psh. That's only what it says on the contract." Haydin huffed. "It never said I have to inflate anyone's ego, especially one that's practically devouring the kitchen whole."

Arieve kissed the top of his head. "Yeah, she loves you, too, you old sod. Now eat." She set a bowl and goblet before him. "You're only cranky because she refused to let you dive into this earlier. She says she never agreed to cater to your stomach's arrogance and poor timing. She also says if you don't show up for Crowns and Fools later, she'll play you for every coin you've got next time. Apparently you're looking a bit too much like the red-faced Crown, huffy and puffy and bound to sink the castle."

Haydin glared so hard at Arieve, Lira almost choked on her mead. Vant said nothing, too busy chewing between snickers.

"Right. Well—fine," Haydin grumbled, turning to his food. "Carry on."

With another wink at Lira, Arieve moved on from the table, the empty tray by her side as she ushered the other three staff from the room. On her way out, she nearly collided with Mayr on his way in, both of them laughing as he steadied her, said something in her ear, and escorted her into the hallway.

When he returned, the smile on his face kept the earlier tension at bay. Just as Aeley could not hide all of her feelings, Mayr's worry had been palpable, and the look in his eyes still grasped at whatever havoc played in the High Council's message.

"Sorry," Mayr said, sinking into his seat across from Haydin. "Aeley's not feeling very well at the moment." His smile dimmed, apology weighing it down. "Did I miss anything good?" He glanced at his desert. "Ah, I didn't. Fantastic."

As he tucked into his food, Lira picked at hers, only mildly interested in the creamy dollops of lorenut pudding on a savoury minced fruit tart and the biting drink that accompanied it. There was a warm tone at their end of the table, one she rarely felt at home, at least among family; a welcoming camaraderie she could get lost in, much like the friendly rapport among her family's staff—on the good days, anyway.

With a sigh, she faded into the background once more, content to linger as the conversations shifted around her, the familiar language of business filtering through the noise. At the other end of the table, closest to the door, Priestess Kee was engrossed in a conversation with Winiah, who, by the sounds of it, provided the nearby temple with metal wares. Winiah seemed intensely invested in making sure the Temple of the Four was happy with whatever Winiah provided, and Priestess Kee looked pleased with the ongoing discussion, a soft glow at her cheeks and in her dark eyes.

On the other side of them, between their end of the table and Lira's, the magistrates rushed headlong into economic banter, comparing coffers and cursing Nerrik Taldure, Councilman of Commerce and Economy, for every fullpin and acemark he prescribed for taxes. When that seemed almost too small a topic, Dreca tossed the Councilman of Strategy and National Progress into the discussion, lighting the fire of annoyance in the magistrate beside him: Tarne, who had a great many things to say about community strategy and the High Council's nosy interference, particularly where the Bythrane Lolands were concerned. That only inspired Pergill, Tarne's counterpart in the Bythrane Uplands, who sounded truly plagued by whatever the Council was doing about civil affairs and meddling their way into his own plans to handle issues.

Meanwhile, Magistrate Calohe was more interested in roasting the Councilman of Resources and Development over open flame with suet and sweet relish—an assessment all four shared, apparently, where water rights and forestry were concerned. And as excited as Calohe sounded at the prospect, Lira swore his elbow was even worse, occasionally jabbing her in the arm, or nearly so, as his emphatic gestures grew wider, grander.

It was Gavis, though, who had the quietest conversation at the table, yet one Lira recognized without hearing every word. She knew Gavis's business chatter best, having met vem more than once during vir visits to her father. Gavis's shipping company did business with her family, moving their wines and ales across the republic and over the Sese Channel for what she understood was a decent price. Gavis had yet to be cut off from their business, so she supposed that was good news.

Lost in conversation with Vant and Haydin about the legalities of commerce, Gavis played with vir goblet, running vir fingertip rhythmically around the rim to produce a soft ringing tone that cut just under the voices around them. It appeared to be an absentminded habit, as natural as the way Gavis raked vir fingers through vir shoulder-length russet hair, not one bit of the discussion floundering.

Only Mayr was silent, his grey gaze on his empty bowl, but his attention clearly elsewhere. He brushed his lips with one hand as he stewed over something, his other hand stilled around his goblet, arm resting on the table.

When he finally looked up, Lira caught his glance, the profound disquiet in his eyes all too familiar, dragging him into her corner of the world.

Tilting her head to the side, Lira gave him a small smile and gestured with the subtle lift of her hand. "Are you all right?" she mouthed, hoping he caught her meaning.

It took him a moment, but Mayr returned the smile, the offering sad and tired with a hint of surprise. He nodded, gesturing for her to relax as he mouthed, "It's fine. Thanks."

A lie, but a pleasant one at least. Though what did she know? Her involvement in the affairs of a Tract Steward were limited, leaving her privy to a fraction of what they dealt with, and the High Council rarely saw fit to summon Lira for anything. As for the affairs of a Head of the Guard... for better or for worse, she was denied any access to the inner workings of her family's guards. Their Head of the Guard, Bareda, made a concerted effort to avoid Lira for the most part, though his watchful eye usually fell on her when they were in the same room together, and particularly at the few events her parents hosted. All else was dead space in between, with invisible barricades erected all the way around, and the only way through them was to give up everything that mattered.

Even when words failed her, she still had enough courage to fight *that*.

Though had she been given the choice, if the Goddesses granted her one wish, it would have been to have the kind of strength Aeley did. That ability to fight back, tell everyone to screw themselves to the spiny retribution posts in the Realm of the Dead on their own time, and still live to do it all again another day. Aeley had willingly walked into a den of wolves by accepting the Tract Steward position, only to encounter an entirely new beast along the way — which she promptly dispatched of and had seemingly moved on from, returning to that wolfe den every day since. News of Allon's arrest had found its way through all of Gailarin, the story all but nailed to the sign posts and carts in the village squares. What else was there to say except that

Aeley had clearly done the republic a favour, taking her own brother down?

There was more to Aeley, Lira knew that for a fact, but she still admired the effort. It was far more than Lira had achieved, and the Four only knew how much longer it would take before she could leave most of it behind.

But getting to know more about Aeley, *that* had its merits, and being in Aeley's inner circle... that had its advantages.

"Shall I take you home, then?"

Lira startled, Vant's voice pulling her from the depths. "Hmm?"

"When dinner is finished," Vant said, his lips quirked with amusement. "Did you want me to take you home? Or wherever home is tonight, anyway. I can pick you up in the morning."

Ah, right. Dinner was close to finished, likely to be followed by more banter from the slightly inebriated magistrates, though with their host missing, there was little need for Vant to linger. There was certainly little reason for Lira to stay. Even the conversation had started to fade, their end of the table already quiet.

As for home...

"You're sweet, Vant, but I'm fine, promise. I'll walk," Lira said, pushing her bowl away, the remainder of the pudding and tart a lumpy, abandoned mess she was tempted to force down. She gave him a wink. "You need to get home to

Eyle before he goes locking all the doors on you, thinking you've gone off courting another man."

Vant cast her a disapproving scowl.

Dammit. Shut up, mouth.

Lira winced and patted Vant's arm. "I'm sorry," she said softly. "Poor choice of words. But you really should get home and spend some time with him. I think you'll have your hands full with whatever Aeley has for you tomorrow, so get whatever time you can in now before you're both overworked and spending your marriage attached to your desks. Besides, I feel like walking a bit. I've got a room in the tavern, and it's not far from here—perfect for a stroll."

"But—"

"But it's fine. I'll be—"

"Escorted. You'll be escorted," Mayr interjected. The moment Lira opened her mouth to object, his gaze softened, a faint smile chasing away whatever had kept him silent. "I'm already accompanying Priestess Kee back to the temple. You're more than welcome to join us, assuming you're up for the company? We can even grab Stuck to keep it entertaining." His look hardened slightly, more pointed, insistent, as though chiding her for suggesting she go alone. She had seen that same expression on Korre Dahe's face whenever she made a suggestion he deemed unsafe and unacceptable, enough to swear it was an almost perfect replica save for the cool grey to

Mayr's eyes where Korre's had been a warm brown-green.

Lira shut her mouth, words caught behind it — nothing coherent, though. Mostly unformed questions about why he would bother. Usually she traveled alone, unless joined by Vant. Guards were content to stay out of her business, most of them ordered to let her do whatever she did, particularly if she eventually proved her parents right. But this —

"All right. Thank you," she said, the agreement tumbling out before she could stop it. Her cheeks flushed with the realization. What would they talk about? Short walk or no, there was still plenty of silence to deal with.

In any event, the tension in Vant's shoulders subsided. "Good. Very good," he murmured.

Perhaps it was. If she wanted to get closer to Aeley, then being in the good graces of her Head Guard had to count for something... If anything, maybe he could put in a kind word for her, regardless of whatever gossip reached Aeley's ears. Lira had no doubt Luinn would ensure some of it fell into Aeley's lap, no matter how quiet Lira was.

With nine years of disappointment to her name, she needed all the help she could get.

Chapter Three

Steady, unsteady. The ground trembled, shaking loose dread and an anger she had no mind to control. Rage, tempered in this?

No, she would have Allon's head before she gave that up.

"Hastal would approve," Aeley snarled, hiding behind what was left of the crumbling grey-white wall of the estate. Always crumbling here, locked in the constant reminder, screams staking memory to the sticking place. Perpetual in its cruelty; laughable in its inevitability.

Yeah, she knew she was spinning in a nightmare, but not one bit of that mattered. The past lived here, a greedy bastard of repeating time that only gorged on more, slithering through the cracks and pillaging everything in its wake, gnawing through bone to suck on the marrow.

Fighting. She was always fighting him, fighting this, fighting for them—locked in the fight to stop Allon from ruining them all, taking life with him and leaving disaster in its stead. It seemed like she had spent her entire lifetime so far trying not to plunge her knife into his heart just to get him to finally stop. This was the ongoing storm they could not weather for whatever future he left them. Something had to give—

Explosives, blasting, piercing to her left. Crumbling ceiling, shattered glass to her right.

Decisions caught in the middle.

She gritted her teeth against the burning throb in her twisted ankle, sword clutched so tight her knuckles ached, holding for the footsteps, then—

Charging into the hall, she swung out, sending Allon's man back several paces. A cry came her way, a glare. His companion took every offence, lunging at her with a blood-slicked short sword, metal scraping metal as their swords clashed. A drive back, a shove forward, a cry in frustrated rage—she gave it everything she had, damned if she did, damned if she never tried. Over her dead body would Allon take their people and hurt them. She would see their family's home brought to ashes before that sick heap of cock rot won. He wanted the chaos—thrived on it. She was playing right into his greasy, threatening hands, breathing in the stench and practically living off the poison. Locked in the same dance, over and over.

Never again.

A surge forward, a duck down beneath a strike, she rammed her arm against her opponent, gold bracer slammed against her forearm, sending him back. Cries went up around her, and a rush of bodies stormed out from behind, around, taking on the extra fighters that scurried into the hallway, weapons brandished. Explosives went in the distance, vibrating the floor beneath her, threatening to pull her down with the crawling cracks while a barely registered fear crept up the walls alongside them, tearing apart memories. Some other hall, some other fight, but it may as well have been right beside her for all the grief it caused, suppressed beneath the numbness of it all.

The fight. It was all she breathed then, blood and grit and dust clinging to her, tickling every bit of instinct caged beneath the surface, every sense on fire and clambering to keep ahead of the threat.

A shove came her way, a body crashed into hers, knocking her back onto the ground. The flash of sword coming for her head was the cue to roll away, curses lost to the dirty floor. To her right, Stuck slammed one guy against the wall face-first, her hand on the back of his head, making forehead meet wall over and over. The breaking of bone was such a quiet crack lost in the grunts and groans and clashing metal around them.

Stumbling upright, Aeley cried foul at the rage searing through her ankle and dragged herself to the wall before turning and blocking a strike. Sword back on sword, her opponent came up close, heaving heat across her cheek through the long, matted hair that clung to his gritty, sweaty face. Behind him, Mayr and Stick laid a beating down on their own adversaries, fists out and knives catching what little light filtered in from the cracked windows, their armour scraped and filthy. Pellon rambled off obscenities to her left, just up the hall, taking on more fighters than he could handle, blood pouring down the side of his face, a gash above his brow.

"Stuck! Pell," Aeley yelled, her good foot on the guy's stomach in front of her, a scream fighting for release as she shoved him back. She needed space, the bastard.

Stuck was moving, a blur in the background—

Suspended in Stuck's hold around his neck, Aeley's opponent stood frozen, eyes wide as Aeley's sword ran him through, guts falling in around the blade as fabric gave with the tearing, waiting to soak in his blood.

And the blood came, so quick on the withdrawal as Stuck let him fall and ran to Pellon's aid, not a moment's hesitation from one kill to the next.

Crumpled at Aeley's feet, death took over, consuming another life, never looking back. Not like a part of Aeley fought to, a small voice that grew fainter. His death was far from the first she had seen, and it never would count on the list of the worst she had witnessed. Nor was he the first she had killed, his body added to her count of three so far, all of them there, within the walls of an estate she had called a second home since childhood. All of them that day. All of them... hers.

And damn it all, her soul refused to take it without an ounce of satisfaction, the self-righteous ass of a—

A blast rocked the floor, so much closer this time— just one corridor away, shaking down the ceiling, crashing, chunks of rock falling around her, pelting the corpse in the face and sending her ducking, arms covering her head—

She woke with a chill that raced from one side to another and back again, unable to stop trembling beneath the heat and sweat that made her kick the blankets off with a nauseated huff. Her headache bit back, stabbing just as surely as her sword had run the guy through, this time with the blades of a hundred bad ideas, nearly all of them conjured from the bottom of the empty decanters she had left behind before crawling into bed. Because drinking with ghosts was better than drinking alone, and there were so many ghosts, especially where Allon had walked. Where her father had haunted in his waking life.

Aeley groaned and buried her face in the damp pillow, the scent of morning breath making her stomach turn. A bucket. She really should have brought a bucket up. Over. In. *Whatever.*

Flipping over onto her back only made it worse—she was in her father's room again, the worn white and green quilt from her bedroom dangling onto the floor, one corner pinned beneath her hip. A familiar fragment of childhood caught in the thin fabric embroidered by her mother's hand.

Ghosts. How they loved to cling, especially when she was drunk, but even worse when she was sober.

Eyes squeezed shut against the light that peeked through the cracks in the heavy burgundy curtains, Aeley covered her face with both arms. Another groan tumbled out, mostly at how both sets of stained-glass windows taunted her with their gods-awful cheery blues and yellows and oranges. She felt like the ass end of something huge and ugly stuck on the inability to take care of business without a blow to the insides. Almost as if instead of consuming the bottle, the bottle had sucked her in headfirst, with her skull scraping all the way down the bottleneck, ears getting caught in the slide and nearly ripping off. Even worse, she probably smelled like it, too. *Vant's going to love this —*

She froze, eyes forced open to stare at the high ceiling, its intense, dark red hue entirely too easy to focus on as clarity slunk back. Vant. Their meeting.

By the Four, she had really backed herself into that corner with a paintbrush in one hand and rash decisions in the other.

Dammit.

Aeley dragged herself from the bed, shoulder aching from all the knife-throwing after dinner. She had laid into the target with more force than necessary, the image of Allon's face behind every strike. The rage from Oly Valley had yet to simmer fully. Part of her refused to let go of it completely, lest she forget how ultimate betrayal felt. *That self-serving bastard, he's family. He's supposed to be family —*

Family best done without. One less name on the tree. One more face behind prison walls.

And somewhere, her soul was still looking for the bits it had left pinned to the corpses.

"Goddesses, no." Aeley raced from the bed to the water bucket beside the fireplace, stomach contents barely making it in.

She had been taught to fight, defend—take lives if necessary. But expectation and the execution were vastly different things. The sweat streaming down her back under her armour, the weight so much worse in the end when she had stood among the rubble, taking in the damage, her black cloak as tattered as the skin on several of the corpses. And the blasts... those damn explosions, the screams, the blood, the world coming down—

Her stomach went on the assault again, bringing up the stench of everything that just made it worse, flipping in an ongoing cycle of memory out, stomach up. She had gone through three weeks of it already, with Goddesses-knew how many left. How much more could she possibly throw up without completely rotting her stomach out? It already hurt daily, practically being peeled away in layers by whatever ravaged the rest of her slowly, her body and mind taken in chunks.

And here she was, still seeking comfort in what had been her father's deathbed. Life was found only in death as of late—the echoes of it, anyway, no matter which way she turned. And that turning... it never ended, the spin and stumble and sickness all tied together with thickening threads. One face in every direction and *still* she felt as though she was seeing less and less.

She had more than this. She was better than this. And she had no idea what she was doing with any of it, no matter what the "it" actually was at any given time.

Spitting out the foul taste in her mouth, Aeley wiped her lips with the back of her hand, the crumpled, soiled sleeve of her gown catching her attention. *Ugh.* She needed to change. *Something about being appropriate... something something professional.*

Appropriate or not, getting to that point took more effort than she wanted as she slipped out of the room and moved slowly towards hers, one door down on the other side of the hall, between her father's room and Mayr's—or, rather, the room kept for the serving Head of the Guard, located on the same side as her father's room, which was the suite always occupied by the head of the Dahe family. A suite that was fine enough to visit when she felt awful, but not one to live in, no matter how much she was the only Dahe left. Sometimes ghosts were best left confined to their own spaces—or surrendered to.

Voices in the hall quieted, gazes following her as she escaped to her room and closed the door. Guards. Damn guards. Congregating outside of her suite and chatting idly while her head felt like a child's kicking ball stuffed inside an ink well. She even recognized the guards without looking, one of them making her stomach turn all over again. She loved Stuck, but she certainly by all that was sacred did not love her right then.

Water helped, at least, the simple act of washing barely clearing her head but letting her scrub off the sweat and layers of disgust. Goddesses, it felt good to stand there by the round table near the window, gripping onto the washbowl with both hands, just holding on to the lukewarm metal with every intention of letting it go eventually, but not really caring when. Her dark green gown and matching shift lay in a pile on the floor, boots and thin white stockings next to them, the relatively cool temperature of the room a welcome touch on her bare skin. Thankfully the curtains were still shut from the day before, more out of habit than anything else: the layers of deep gold curtains kept the light well away from her, trapping the soft purples and blues of the stained glass behind a blissful barrier.

The grey stone of the walls spoke to her soul much more deeply, the warm tone of the dark red wood panels throughout the rooms stringing life together with reminders, some of them better than others, but necessary.

When you're too busy losing yourself, hold onto anything that works. Washing her face for the third time, Aeley sighed into her hands, water sliding down both arms to her elbow and dripping to the floor. This was not what she had signed up for. Ever since she held a tiny wooden sword as a child, she had dreamed of being a fighter. Holding the line of right between wrongs and telling them to back down.

"Time dares us all, but forever does not yield; as the heart of Kattal beats, so do we" —those were the words of the Dahe family motto, engraved around the gold edges of the red and black quartered shield that hung above the mantel of the fireplace in her bedroom, a match to the shield in her father's suite. At the centre of the shield stood two gold bearcats, facing away from each other, rampant and ready to strike anyone who dared get close to the heart of the nation they protected.

She had recited that motto a thousand times. Gripped every blade with the loyalty they inspired. She had trained with their family guard for years, learning what it meant to defend, and to sacrifice. For a while, just a matter of months, she had thought her place would be by her father's side as Head of the Guard. He was the politician, she the armour. They had spent years pulling each other through the trials of their family, especially when Allon tested every bit of her father's efforts to parent them both on his own.

But when her father had let her down gently, telling her he had a different path in mind for her skills, she reluctantly agreed, never wanting to let him down. He had never asked her to play politician, not until then, and she had thought they would have years left before she took on the role.

Years they never had; years stolen from them by an illness no one could pinpoint, soothe, or even slow down. Sickness had come on fast after the fatigue, weeks that drove him to his sickbed permanently. Everything after that had been a race to the bottom no one could keep up with, and suddenly the scariest thing she could think of had flipped and twisted, changing faces from the fear of losing her life to losing his.

Now, both fears played constantly, brought to life and death all at the same time, dancing over the finest lines of hurt and back again. In the end, she had all that was left of her father: his life, his home, his everything... except for that tender soul she had cuddled up to as a child, clinging to him for dear life when the world tried to take her down. She had lost her mother, and all of her grandparents and uncles had been killed by plague well before that, with even both aunts lost in a fray—but never her father, not until it was real, and her life surreal, and everything falling apart. She had followed through on his ask, taking on the Tract Steward duties, but beyond that...

Aeley grabbed one of the cream-coloured towels folded neatly beside the bowl and sighed into it, wishing the feelings away. She'd had enough of those last night. Right then, she needed clothes because everything else hurt.

After fumbling through the armoires, their rich red wood with black tinge looking so much darker without the light, Aeley drew on a shirt and pants she assumed were decent.

Out. She needed out.

That strange wrenching in her chest was back, straining breath and thought and usefulness. She needed a deep breath, one that sucked her in whole and spat her out anywhere but there.

One hand on the footboard of her bed, she pulled on her boots, cursing as she nearly tripped over. She also succeeded in smashing her toes on the gold-plated corner of the bed frame, the shock jolting the memory of her throbbing ankle, threatening to revive the injury it had taken weeks to recover from.

Done. She was *done*. Considering the furniture in the room was decorated with carvings of wolves, hawks, and bearcats, she was feeling more and more like their prey, tangled up in the ferns and flowers engraved among them that only seemed to grapple at her, keeping her there for the kill.

She hurried from the room, not sparing a moment on the smaller adjoining room to her right where she stored her weapons, books, and other cherished items—too many reminders, not enough space to breathe, her chest restricting tighter at the thought, breaths becoming even more painful.

The hallway was no better, though slamming the door behind her felt good.

Stuck glanced in Aeley's direction. Still talking to three guards just outside of Aeley's father's suite, Stuck's shoulder-length brown hair was tied up in a high tail that swung back and forth as she spoke. Gates, Pillara, and Erune laughed quietly along with her, their own glances at Aeley far from subtle.

Of the four of them, Stuck had served the longest, having been with the Dahe guard for nearly eight years with her best friend, Ralaern, though everyone usually just called him Stick. The two of them were nigh inseparable—only one reason why she was called Stuck. More than that, she was known to stick to just about anyone or anything she believed in, including undying loyalty to Korre, even months after his death. Now she seemed stuck to Aeley like a here-and-there sticky paste that liked to play games but was never far away. Given a holler, Stuck always answered with a bright green-gold gaze and a willingness to tackle the task at hand, often with Stick by her side.

Gates, Pillara, and Erune, however, had almost eleven years of service between them: Gates four years, while Pillara and Erune had three. Still young, still learning, but Aeley liked them enough to keep their hopes up about staying for years more. She loved Gates's ability to turn anything into an unabashed pile of optimism, and the way ne abhorred working anything but busy daytime shifts, thriving off the energy with keen instincts and attention to detail. Pillara was plenty of fun to be around, especially at night, during the quiet shifts when she usually went around the perimeter of the estate with a big stick, ready to ward off anyone who dared enter without her approval. Erune was still working through the various positions of the roster, his fate at Mayr's mercy, assuming Mayr could figure out where he wanted Erune assigned on a permanent basis. Until then, he was an on-off, in-out guard, switching with other guards at multiple posts.

As Aeley headed for the main staircase to her left, she overheard Stuck excuse herself from the conversation. Footfalls were quick to follow after Aeley, while the voices of the other guards drifted down the hallway in the opposite direction.

Gritting her teeth, Aeley tried to ignore the echoes of her nightmare. They were no better than the memories that surfaced whenever she looked at anything in the house, reminded of her father, of Allon, of a life that would never be again, and a future she tried so hard to want, but hated herself more. How could she pull everything together for the entire region of Gailarin when she could barely stand to think about Oly Valley, a single village on the western border? How was she going to manage one of the most influential and integral tracts of the country when she had yet to fully deal with the consequences of Allon's actions, including a house she would likely leave in disrepair because what was the point of fixing it when living in the main estate was difficult enough?

Stuck following ten steps back as Aeley descended the stairs failed to help.

"You know," Aeley drawled, wincing as she stopped and turned around, "you could just catch a ride on my heels instead of following so far back."

The grin Stuck flashed her was typical: bright, paired with that *don't fight me, you'll lose* glint in her eyes. "That subtle, huh?"

"As a rusted, holey bucket of nails and armour on a flagpole in a windy storm."

Stuck snorted and stopped on the stair beside Aeley. "Clearly Stick's fault. I only play in the storm with non-holey buckets."

Aeley opened her mouth to reply but had nothing. Another one of Stuck's damn annoying traits. Instead, she scowled down at Stuck. There was a noticeable height difference between them, with Aeley almost towering over Stuck like most people did, though she was no competition for Stuck's muscular physique, the years of constant training and sparring having their advantage.

"So, breakfast?" Stuck practically sang. Her grin confirmed she did it on purpose, her golden-brown skin taking on a slight flush as she met Aeley's gaze.

"You know, don't you?" Aeley narrowed her eyes, her headache straining to agree that it was a good idea.

"What? That you're still plastered as a wet brick? Or that you're about three words from pushing me down the stairwell?" Before Aeley could answer, Stuck slipped an arm around her shoulders, only to withdraw the moment Aeley jolted. "Come on, then, Steward," Stuck said quietly, frowning at Aeley and stepping back, giving her space. "Let's get you stuffed and toughed. I hear it's going to be gruelling with Vant going solicitor."

There was no use in arguing, not when Stuck was right. Aeley stayed silent as she followed Stuck down the rest of the stairs into the front foyer, then to the right, towards the dining room, all the while trying to ignore how the swirled patterns in the grey and black floor flirted with her nausea. As Aeley entered the dining room, Stuck headed down the corridor towards the kitchen to inform the staff that Aeley had bothered to get out of bed.

Mayr was already at the dining room table, waiting for her with his own breakfast barely touched. A stack of what she suspected were guard reports sat piled next to his arm, one set of papers in his hand. His other hand pressed to his forehead, his lips drawn in a shifting frown as he read. As always, he was dressed in black, with his black leather bracers tied on and a short sword strapped to his waist along with two knives. With his long hair plaited into a loose braid that trailed down his back, his black tattoos were almost fully visible above his collar.

"Morning," Aeley said, lowering into her seat, slow, steady, careful.

"Hey..." Mayr blinked and laid down the papers, a small smile creeping across his lips. "How you feeling?"

Aeley scowled at her empty plate before Mayr handed her a bowl of roasted meat in dark, savoury syrup. "Ten counts of awful."

Mayr released the bowl into her grasp, but not without a look. She knew that look, too—the concerned, *you really need to talk to me* glare.

"Don't start," she muttered, adding food to her plate, followed by spoonfuls of everything on the table. Some kind of fruit salad she would probably pick through. Jelly-filled pastries she would have lived on for the day if she could have been assured they would stay down. Fluffy chunks of heavily seasoned eggs she could have happily thrown at the wall and made pretty pictures with, because it was easier than eating them, or even being near them, their smell nauseating.

Meanwhile, her headache pounded a lively tune on her skull.

She should have stayed in bed.

"Ugh." Aeley held her forehead and stared at the small mound on her plate. Dinner the night before came to mind, or what she could remember of it, anyway. Though considering she barely remembered how she made it to bed to begin with—stumbling in, she was certain—she could only hope she kept track of all the important matters they had discussed. Watery images and snippets of conversations floated through her thoughts, followed by the blur of a corridor. It hurt to think. Why did it have to be only late morning?

"So you disappeared for a while," she said quietly, poking at her food with her fork, tempted just to stab it all.

"Hmm?"

"Last night. After dinner."

"Oh, yeah, right." Mayr sipped his drink before digging back into his breakfast, already a quarter gone since Aeley had sat down. "Priestess Kee—I'd promised I'd walk her back to the temple. After everything that's gone on, there's no way I'm letting anyone do that walk by themselves at night, especially not from here. Can't be too careful, not when Allon's involved. But that cute girl of yours," he added with a mischievous grin, "I had to walk her home, too. And she's staying at the tavern, in case you're interested."

Head still lowered, Aeley flicked a glare at him. "I'm not, and quit that. She's just... just—"

"Just a dinner guest. So you're going to keep saying. And *I'm* going to keep calling you out on that because it's—"

"Time for you to shut up."

Mayr snorted a laugh, then chewed around a spoonful of eggs before adding, "She's nice."

"Mayr—"

"And she thinks Stuck's funny—"

"If you don't shut your mouth right now—"

"—and I'm pretty sure she's very, *very* unmarried or otherwise uninvolved."

"*Dammit, Mayr!*" Aeley threw a piece of fruit at him, satisfied as it hit his shoulder and bounced to the floor.

Mayr looked at the floor, looked at Aeley, then tsked at her and continued eating.

And that damned headache *still* came roaring back with five times more vengeance than he had.

A spoon scraped a glazed brown clay plate, the pitch doing awful things to Aeley's head until she pressed into her temples, her thumb on one side and fingers on the other, spanned across her forehead. A girl's thin body shuffled around the dining room. Colours moved in and out of Aeley's sight, and the muffled tones of Mayr's voice poked through the spinning images in her head, the blurred face of the woman from dinner bleeding through and making her want more than another drink.

"What?" She pulled her hand away to find Mayr leaning forward in his seat.

"Nothing. Just wondering if you should really be in public. Might be contagious."

"Like your really terrible humour?"

"It comes and goes," Mayr countered with a shrug. "At least I can see straight."

"And here I was going to ask if I was wearing pants," Aeley muttered. For a moment, it seemed her words were too quiet for him to hear. *Perfect. He'll have some smart—*

He peered under the table.

"Unless I was drinking whatever you were, I'd say you are." Mayr straightened and grinned. "You've successfully overcome the nice girl image from last night. Now you just look like you'll tear heads off."

I'll start with my own. "Thanks." Aeley toyed with her food. Her gaze strayed to the white cuff of her tunic. Good choice, wearing it instead of one of her bodices. Had she tried, she would still be struggling with the laces. It was a terrible morning.

She peeked into her goblet—empty except for the few drops of water clinging to the metal. *Fine. Now to get something that'll fight this headache.* Without speaking to Hana, the serving girl standing in the corner, Aeley motioned for her to fetch one of the recently filled decanters from the cart along the wall. When the cool metal slipped into her hand, she reminded herself it was the only way to fight the emotions storming through her, threatening to overtake her senses. Tipping the decanter, Aeley waited to see her goblet filled to the brim.

Mayr's hand slid over the goblet, covering the opening.

"Mayr." Aeley threw him a glare, one brow lifted as she drew the decanter back. Why did he look like he wanted to yell at her?

"Maybe not today, yeah? You've been like this since we took down Allon. Maybe it's time we try something different, don't you think?" Mayr waved at Hana and cut Aeley off before she protested. "Bring me jaka root, a sprig of ferras, and an egg. All as raw as you've got."

Hana rushed away, casting a confused glance at Aeley before disappearing from the room.

"What *are* you doing?" Brushing his hand away, Aeley tipped the decanter forward again.

Mayr pulled his hand back, and the goblet with it. He cradled the goblet to his chest. "Giving you another option. Just trust me."

"I don't."

"Again, a terrible liar."

"Why do I even bother?"

"Because I'm smart. Quick. Incredibly sexy. And I have your back—like right now. So put it down."

Aeley lowered the decanter. "I don't know why you're acting like I've done something wrong. I do this all the time."

"I know." Once Hana returned with a bowl, Mayr placed the goblet on the table. "Ah, good, thank you. Don't need that. Got everything else here," he said, taking the items from the bowl. He cracked the egg and emptied it in Aeley's goblet, then drew the orange-brown stalk of ferras between his fingers, loosening the tiny yellow leaves into the yolk. The jaka root came next as he grated it with his knife, flakes of dark violet-grey skin tumbling down and exposing bright yellow flesh. The blade clattered against the goblet as he stirred the mixture. Satisfied, he offered the goblet to Aeley.

"Mayr, that's disgusting," Aeley said slowly. "You expect me to drink it?"

"Yeah, if you value getting around without falling on your face. You have a meeting with Vant. You're going to want to keep a thought for more than a moment if you expect to get anything done. The sooner you drink it, the sooner it's done."

"*You* drink it."

"I don't need it."

"I don't need your jokes. I need you to listen to me."

"I have. Trust me, this is as serious as I'm getting today. Drink it and stop making me into a bad guy."

Aeley eyed the goblet. "You sure it's a good idea?"

Mayr grunted. "My family's used this for generations. Shut up and take it, would you?

Otherwise, I'm pouring this on you and leaving you to deal with it, sober or not."

"Fine. If it gets you to stop harassing me, fine." Aeley snatched the goblet and drank deep. The sticky mass slid down her throat, making her gag.

She pulled the goblet from her lips, ready to spit out the bitter taste. Her throat burned, and sick—she was going to be sick. Throwing the goblet at Mayr, she coughed, expecting to see the little food in her stomach spray across the table. With each cough, her headache flared and her stomach churned. For what was supposed to be a cure, it hurt more than it helped.

"Are you trying to kill me?" She wiped her mouth with the back of her hand. To her surprise, the bile that had been creeping up retreated and her stomach started to settle.

"If I was, you'd know." Mayr turned the rolling goblet upright. "Now finish eating. Can't sit through a solicitor's jabber with an empty stomach. And don't give me that face—I'll only go get Pell so we can dunk your unsuspecting ass into an entire vat of this."

"You're lucky that you're you," Aeley muttered, halfheartedly making another effort to eat. He had a point, however. Vant was a good man, always in control of his faculties, and he understood his role, fulfilling it to his greatest ability. She needed that confidence and the wealth of his knowledge if she was going to get through this.

Mayr held his goblet of water towards her. Accepting it as a peace offering, she tried to focus on the meeting. It was not how she wanted to spend an afternoon, but without it, the High Council could become a problem she did not need. What she needed was to get things back under control. Part of her wondered if that was Mayr's point, and why he had insisted she drink the horrid, scorching mixture.

Maybe he should be Steward. He's got everything under control better than I do.

Did he dream like she did? Even after Allon's betrayal and the fight, he acted as if nothing was different. He was calm, as though a great weight had been lifted. Could she blame him? Allon never had kind things to say about Mayr, and Mayr usually refused to waste time on those who disrespected him.

One reason I need him around, always. He judges people better than I do. Aeley sighed and pushed her emptied plate away. If only she could send Mayr to the High Council instead...

No, she had to do it herself. She could not shirk her responsibilities.

But by the Four, she could damn well imagine it in secret... then pray for all the courage to survive whatever waited on the other side.

The scroll was still there, lying around like any other message, though she had no desire to touch it, not again. She would rather pick up a scalding baking sheet and drop the whole lot of perfectly baked pastries onto a muddy floor than read that damned summons once again.

Standing in her study, Aeley stared at the crumpled Council summons on her desk, the parchment still rolled and tied. Save for her memories, she needed nothing else for her meeting with Vant but that summons. Vant already knew what had happened with Allon: she had told him about it before, after the fight in Oly Valley. An appearance before the High Council was merely a formality to appease them, particularly Cota Dalenvrae, Councilman of Law and Justice, who preferred everything in a nice, neat package of organization and logic. She swore he was happiest when wading up to his eyeballs in paperwork. Still, her official testimony and presence would make things easier for Council to lock Allon up and throw away the key, no other questions asked—and no chance for pardon. Ever.

Stop being so damn ridiculous. Just get it done. Aeley snatched up the summons, dragged herself out of the study, and made her way down the corridor to the meeting room. The door was open slightly, and sunlight poured into the hall through the gap. Vant was early. She took a breath and pushed the door further, ready to greet him.

Aeley stopped cold.

What was *she* doing there?

The woman from dinner sat at the table, parchment stacked in front of her and a brown leather documents case off to the side. She scribbled with a brown quill across one page, but paused as she lifted her head.

Aeley missed taking one breath, then another, her cheeks going warm. Contrary to the common fashion, the woman's white gown covered everything but her throat and wrists. A comb decorated with small, glittering jewels held her dark hair back on one side, and in the daylight, her skin had a faint, pink hue.

But what if she went without the gown? Just how lovely would she be without all that hiding, not to mention why she's even hiding to begin with?

She had so many questions.

Similar thoughts had crossed her mind several times, tucked between memories of dark corridors and slipping into sleep. They had warmed her at the time, leaving her yearning for company, but now they left her blushing. With her luck, her face was as red as it felt.

Aeley cleared her throat and continued forward, finally noting how Vant paced the side of the room with a large book in his hands. "Thank you for coming, Vant. I appreciate you taking the time to help me."

Vant turned towards her, a smile pulling back his taut face as he stilled. "Naturally, my dear. You ask, I obey." He followed her questioning gaze to his companion, almost looking surprised. "Wait, have you two not met?"

"Not officially, no." Aeley hoped that was all he noticed.

"I could swear you had," he mumbled. "This is Lira, your new scribe. She will accompany me from now on."

Lira pushed up from her chair. Even from there, the ink splotching her fingers was noticeable. "Aeley."

If only she could have said Aeley's name again. Sweetness laced the syllables when Lira spoke, a gentle flow and tone that caught Aeley's attention and kept it there, waiting to hear something more.

"Lira," Aeley said quietly. "Scribe. Seems familiar. Almost like..."

She *had* seen her before.

"You've been here before, when my father was..." Aeley cleared her throat. "You used to come with my father's scribe, Klyrin. You carried his things. I saw you when you'd go into their meetings."

Lira nodded and brushed the loose curls of her hair over her shoulder. "He took me in as his apprentice. When Korre—I mean, your father—died, Klyrin decided to retire. He stayed to help your father, but his own health has been failing.

He's allowed me to take his place." She clasped her hands before her. "But I don't have to, if you'd rather not. I can find someone else—"

"No!" Aeley interrupted, a little too quickly. That damned heat raged across her cheeks again. "I mean, no, please, you can stay." She gestured for them to sit before she made it worse.

"So, shall we discuss why we are here?" Vant settled into a chair and laid his book on the table. He pointed at the scroll in Aeley's hand. "We're returning to this, are we?"

Aeley set the scroll on the table and stepped back. "The High Council wants me to attend Allon's hearing. I also need to provide a document about the ordeal, written from my own words. They want to put him away for good, but they want my final argument for it first."

Vant let out a breath and rubbed the back of his neck. "I understand." He thumbed through his book, stopping every few pages to skim over the words. "Are you sure you want Lira here? We can go through this together if you feel uncomfortable with a stranger."

Aeley shook her head. "It's all right. We need to learn how to work together. We might as well start with this." *Besides, looking at her makes me feel better, and—*

"It's odd that you aren't doing it yourself," Lira said.

Did you just…? Blinking at the quiet comment, Aeley had no answer.

Vant's jaw dropped. "Lira."

"Ah, I've done it again, haven't I? Said something only I should hear." Lira pressed her lips together.

"And you were doing so well," Vant muttered. "It is not your place to question."

"Meaning I should apologize." Lira's glance met Aeley's. "I'm sorry for being bold. It tends to happen when something interests me. Apparently, I now owe Vant for losing my end of our deal."

"*Lira!*" Vant warned hoarsely.

"And there it is again. And again, I apologize."

Glimpsing the brief strain around Lira's eyes and lips, Aeley doubted the blunt slips were by accident. Where had they been the night before, and why now? "Apology accepted. What deal?"

Lira hesitated, suddenly shirking back. "Nothing. Just something… silly." She brushed her parchment. "So the document. Where shall we start?"

And now we're back to hiding. Did I say something wrong? Aeley cleared her throat. "I wouldn't mind starting with what you were saying."

"I was only talking."

"So was I. I'm giving you the chance to finish. Or do we have to make a deal, too?"

Lira's lips parted slightly as though she were considering a clever response. Instead, she closed her mouth and nodded. "You ask and I answer.

While I understood why your father couldn't do this sort of thing, can I ask why you're not doing it yourself? Surely it's a sensitive matter, best handled with fewer parties. Not that I'm complaining." She tilted her head, a small smile curving her lips. "I'm just curious. I've always wondered why you helped your father with everything else, but never this. Though you don't have to answer if you don't want to."

Aeley breathed in. *A beautiful girl with questions… when she's willing to voice them. And me…* "No, it's fine. Fact is, I can't write worth a damn, not like this. Simple messages and sign my name, yes, but anything else becomes a jumbled mess of letters and scratches and smeared ink. We decided a long time ago that I was better talking."

"Oh," Lira said, quiet and revealing nothing of what she thought, save for a quick smile. She drew the back of her hand over a blank parchment and readied the quill. "We should get to it, then. Make sure you're ready sooner rather than later."

Lira sounded like Mayr right then, except Aeley cursed how the words just stopped. She wanted Lira to keep talking. Her soft voice broke through the dull pain behind Aeley's eyes and pushed the fog away, that smooth tone calm enough to let Aeley forget about the empty decanters and terrible remedies.

Instead, Vant's voice took over as he read from the book, one finger following along with the words. "I, Aeley Dahe, rightful elected Tract Steward of the lands within the boundaries of the northeast republic region herein known as Gailarin, do so swear to this testimony as full truth under the watchful and just Mothers of—"

"Vant, wait. Hold on." Aeley held out her hands. "Can we pretend, just for today, that I *don't* understand a blessed word of whatever you just said? Like the Goddesses have robbed me of my brains. Can we not get through this by just, I don't know… talking about what I want to say and then work out the legal words after? Or if you think of something good along the way, just write it down and I'll read it."

Vant quirked one brow. "I… suppose."

Lira paused, the quill hovering above the page. "Go on. Tell us what happened, and we'll translate it into what the councilmen expect. You can read it and sign it. No one will know the difference."

"You really don't mind?" Aeley asked.

"Not in the least." Lira offered a smile, her grey eyes bright under her long lashes. "I'm here for you." Her gaze stayed locked to Aeley's for a long moment, in a silence that ignored Vant's presence. A rosy blush spread across her cheeks.

Wait… Was she flirting?

"Fair enough," Aeley murmured. She focused on Vant, dreading every word. "So I was here, attending to my duties after the inauguration. Trying to settle in, make sure things were seen to.

I knew Allon wasn't happy about losing the election, but there wasn't any indication he'd do anything. He disappeared to our other estate, and I didn't expect to hear anything. Well, maybe some threatening letters, but that's nothing new."

Vant nodded as he listened and wrote on a piece of parchment. His white quill scratched the page erratically as Aeley continued.

"The next thing I know, we have one of his staff showing up here, going on about how Allon's planning to take out a village. The guy didn't know when, but he knew it was Oly Valley. He didn't know the exact plan, either, but he knew it was bad. Deaths expected, mostly, though you never know with Allon," Aeley muttered. "He thinks he's clever and expects the world to give him whatever he wants. When he doesn't get it, he takes it out on anyone he can, however he can. And he's got these damned bloody asses who actually *believe* in him, willing to do whatever—"

"You need to refrain from embellishing the story with personal feelings," Vant interrupted. "Your credibility wanes the more personal it gets. Use only facts."

Aeley sighed. "Fine."

"What did you do when the servant told you?" Lira inquired.

"I got a group of my guards together, then went and enlisted republic soldiers from the villages close by—all of them volunteers. The rest stayed here to make sure it wasn't just a distraction. Then we left." Aeley shrugged. "I wanted to beat Allon to the village, but he attacked them before we got there. We ran into a messenger just as we entered the Valley—that's when I found out about Allon taking women and children. That he'd burned some of the place down, the traitor."

"And your response was to what, pursue him? Punish him?" Vant asked.

"Well, no. And yes." Aeley stared at the ceiling. "I don't know. I just wanted to stop him. He's always causing trouble and *I* have to clean it up. I couldn't just let him get away with it this time. He killed people. Innocent people. He kidnapped others who he should've just kept his grubby, little, filthy paws off—"

"You're doing it again," Lira said in a gentle voice.

"Sorry. I just can't—" Aeley crossed her arms. "You don't know what it's like with him. There's nothing nice to say. No defence. He hurts people. He's cruel. That's what he offers the world." She leaned forward and rested her folded arms on the table. "I took my small army of guards, soldiers, and a militia to his estate. We sacked it. Killed his guards before they did any more damage. The militia got the women and children, and I found Allon in the rubble. He had some guys running around trying to blow us to the ever-loving Four." She breathed out, pushing against the memories edging their way to the surface, glimpses of images poking holes in her attempt. *The bodies. So many limp bodies. Lying in the dust, bloody, the boot marks, stones falling, hitting...*

"Most of us got out," Aeley continued softly, "except three of my guards. Mayr and I arrested Allon and dragged him back here, handed him over to the Council when they came around. That's the end of the story."

"Why did you attack? Why couldn't you just go and talk it out with him in a more peaceful manner?" Lira fidgeted in her seat, almost as though she expected the question to start an argument.

"What does it matter? He committed a crime. I stopped him from committing more."

"Well, the Council reserves the right to decide he's been treated unfair—"

"The councilmen do not necessarily accept a crime with another crime," Vant said, cutting Lira off, his tone flat. "If your decision seems—"

"Shh," Aeley interrupted, mostly because the more Lira talked, the more Aeley's headache subsided. Vant's voice only encouraged it to continue. Before she could stop herself, she touched Lira's free hand resting beside the stack of papers, and the idea of those dainty fingers traveling over her, skin on skin... it did nothing helpful, just left a nagging ache. "Carry on."

For a moment, Aeley thought Lira shivered at the touch, and that made everything three times worse.

"Your decision has to be justified," Lira said. "They have to know there was just cause to attack and kill; to put him in that position. I'm not trying to cause you trouble, but they could ask. They may not. It doesn't hurt to disclose that you had reason. And you did, right?"

Aeley pulled her hand back. "Considering he wouldn't respond to anything less than an attack, yes. He prefers violence. Playing nice gets you nowhere, because he likes causing pain. No cost is too high. I knew if we went in without willing to fight, we'd lose and no one would be saved. He doesn't give in. He also knows *I* won't give into *him*."

"So you argue your actions were completely justified on the grounds you felt there was no other viable alternative to saving lives?" Vant asked.

"Yes," Aeley answered. She pointed at his parchment. "Write that down, exactly. I don't want there to be any mistake. I'm not sorry about what I did." *Just sorry that I'm reminded of it every single day.*

Vant's lips moved while he wrote. Once he finished, he slid the parchment towards Lira, who wrote as she read his hastily scribbled notes.

Aeley gazed over Lira as she worked. The neckline of her dress curved gently downwards, decorated with thin, red threads twisted and knotted in an elaborate pattern. Beyond that, the gown was a shield of modesty wrapped around her, so unlike everyone else that moved in and out of Aeley's life, setting her apart, maybe even more than she wanted—at least in Aeley's mind. It did nothing but pique Aeley's curiosity, roused questions that would probably receive no answer. She needed to know more than just a name and an occupation. What was below the surface of propriety, and what else did she have to say?

"Finished."

As Lira broke the silence, all Aeley could do was blink. Already?

Lira slid the thin stack of parchment across the table. Sure enough, the document bore Aeley's words, disguised by formality. As she read it over, a faint, pulsing ache filled Aeley's head every time she saw Allon's name. When she finally signed her name at the bottom of the last page, there was no cure for the darkness it left behind, as if her heart tumbled to her stomach and hit every rib on its way, taking on damage it would never heal from. She hated the testimony—how the truth hurt more than the lies.

Vant rolled the document shut and fastened it with a yellow cord before returning it. Aeley accepted the testimony without words, but her heavy sigh likely said everything.

"If there is nothing else," Vant started, standing as he collected his things, "I have another appointment to attend."

"No, that's fine. I was just going to offer you something to eat. But by all means, go." Aeley stood next to him and rested a hand on his arm. "Thank you, really."

"Never a hesitation. I will see you later." After a kiss to Aeley's cheek, Vant strolled from the room.

"I should go, too," Lira said, slipping her quill into a thin, wooden case. "Before we get into a rant about the justice system being so—" Her fingers paused in midair.

"Hmm…" Aeley caught the grimace on Lira's face, right before annoyance set in. "Did you want to talk about it?"

Lira shook her head. "It's nothing. Ignore me. It's best if you do. I'm less trouble then." She gathered her things and walked around the table. "I have some errands to see to before going home."

Dare I ask what any of that meant?

"I understand. Please." Aeley raised her arm towards the door, but stopped. "Wait. Just one thing before you leave."

"Yes?"

"I have to go to Council in three days. More like two, I guess. I'd hate to go alone, especially since my mouth's bound to run off." Aeley swallowed, her mouth dry. "Since you seem to understand this, would it be too much to ask for you to maybe join me? You don't have to, but I just thought—"

Lira's warm, delighted smile nearly did Aeley in.

Want... she wanted more time, wanted more of a chance, her nerve twisted into a growing mass of tight, shifting knots that had absolutely nothing to do with running away and everything to do with a need to get close, to touch...

"No, it's fine," Lira said. "Of course I will. Can't have you sabotaging the hearing. I know he deserves what he gets."

"Really?" Aeley battled back the sigh of relief that dared to claw its way out. "Great. I'll... see you then?"

"Absolutely. I'll come early. We can make sure you have everything before you leave." Lira dipped her head and hugged her documents case close. "I'll just go for now."

Lira swept out of the room, her white skirt swaying back and forth. Aeley watched her every step until the last bit of her dress's back hem disappeared around the corner.

Well, that's... something. Between the gnawing anxiety of seeing her brother and the pounding headache of the hearing, at least there was finally one good reason to obey the High Council's call.

Chapter Four

The dreams. By the Four, the dreams. Please don't make me babble about them. I can't... we...

Aeley stole a glance at Lira beside her, only to turn away just as quickly, clenching her jaws and cursing herself for all the images that single look slammed against her focus. *Disaster. A complete and utter disaster just waiting to happen.*

They stood at the bottom of the stairs that led up to the front doors to the estate, waiting for the carriage, and it should have been a simple matter, just to stand there and do nothing else. Still, as Lira fussed with her hair, taming the curls into a less chaotic tumble around her shoulders, Aeley's gaze snapped back to her, all to follow Lira's hands wherever they touched. It only worsened as Lira tugged on her shawl to pull it tighter, and Aeley could think of nothing else but wanting to *be* that shawl around her shoulders, clinging, holding on...

Goddesses, it was going to be a long ride to the Council meeting.

Though it was a cool late-summer morning, not all of Aeley's shivers were due to the breeze.

The meeting with Vant and Lira had inspired her dreams to twist around her desires, taking her away from memories that left her wanting less sleep to visions that had her crying out for more. Instead of Allon and her anger and the constant battle to survive, the images revolved around Lira, the softness she brought to life, and a teasing intimacy Aeley could not ignore—one she could only play out on her own body until she was spent and her fingers frustrated, needing someone else to play with.

She kept the dreams to herself, refusing to mention them to anyone, including Mayr. No doubt he would taunt her without any measure of mercy. It was bad enough she had woken up in a sweat more than once—she did *not* need anyone's help in making it worse.

One thing was for certain: she was not going to say a word about it to Lira. Anything else would make the ride awkward, even more so than the last three nights. At the rate her thoughts were taking her, the ride to Vasserey Call was going to end up much longer than usual.

"There it is," Mayr said, pointing to the black gates on the other side of the carriage circle.

Drawn by two grey horses, the small, closed carriage slowed to a stop before them. With a nod at the driver, Mayr opened the door and gestured for them to get in. Lira went without argument, climbing the narrow steps and sliding across the black cushions.

"After you." Mayr's hand slid across Aeley's back with a gentle push towards the steps.

"No, after you. No need to be formal. It's a meeting, not a ball," Aeley argued, digging her boot into the dirt.

"That's fine, but I'm still not getting in."

"What?"

"I'm sitting up front with the driver."

"Why? It's not like she's going to bite—"

Mayr rolled his eyes. "I know that." Turning into her, he lowered his voice. "I'm giving *you* the chance to bite *her*."

Aeley caught herself before doing something she regretted. "*What*?" No. Just no. He could *not* do that to her. Not then, not like that, and not with Lira waiting *right there*. He was more than taunting her: he was being a damned ass, enough that she could have kicked him in the shin for it. It was either that or stare at him like a mortified fool, and she was already halfway to that point.

"*Seriously*, Ae? Are you really—" Mayr let out a frustrated breath and leaned closer. "I've been watching you," he murmured. "Something's going on. Should've seen your face when she walked in on breakfast—you stared at her like the day is long. Nervous, fidgety. Not at all like you. But smitten... I know it well, and you've got it."

"That's not—I'm not—she's just—" Aeley bit her tongue and twisted her heel. *Bastard*. Calling her out, grinding out her bluff. *But if he noticed...* She froze, realization washing over her and leaving a burn all its own, none of it good. *Lira could've noticed it, too. Oh, no. Please, no. This could be a terrible ride if she did.*

"Look, if you like her, you like her. And she seems nice." Mayr smiled softly as he rubbed her shoulder. "*Nice*, Ae, which is what you need right now. We had a lovely chat when I took her down to Orae's the other night, mostly about Vant and your father, but also those damned magistrates at dinner, and we had a few good laughs at their expense." He tapped her nose. "You could use a few laughs, and someone who's got nothing to do with the mess we've been dealing with. Either way, I'm not getting in for the same reason I wouldn't let you bring the gaffa nectar. This is a perfect chance, so don't mess it up." He stepped back. "Now. *Get. In.*"

Biting back half-formed retorts, Aeley gathered her light cloak around her and climbed into the carriage. The moment she took her seat on the cushion across from Lira, Mayr slammed the door closed, confining them in a space usually comfortable for four people, but for Aeley right then, it had all the cramped tension of a locked linen chest.

The carriage rocked before it jolted and rolled forward, the clip-clop of hooves taking on a familiar rhythm. Aeley opened the thick, dark mauve curtains around both windows to study the path and trees as they traveled around the carriage circle and down the avenue to the main road. The bright green leaves of summer had started to change, the faint touches of golds, reds, and oranges a calming sight, almost enough to forgive the bumps in the road—and how her anxiety was nearly crawling up the walls, desperate to escape before they reached Vasserey.

Out of the corner of her eye, she caught the movement of darker colours as Lira shuffled on her seat, flattening the folds of her dusky blue gown and pulling her burgundy shawl tighter around her shoulders. *One of us should say something.* When Lira drew further into the corner, Aeley took a deep breath and let it out slowly, almost counting along to the horses' steps. *Guess it's supposed to be me.*

Aeley leaned forward, her hands clasped on one knee, fingers locked together. "So... thank you for agreeing to come with us."

Lira's gaze softened with her wistful smile. "You're welcome, though I won't lie and say it's not a surprise." She raised her hand, faint blotches of ink still staining her skin. "Not that it's bad—just unexpected."

"It's fine. I get it. This gives us time to get to know each other a little better. We don't know each other at all—"

"Well, you don't know *me*."

"What?" Aeley pulled back, her brow furrowed. "What does *that* mean?"

Lira shrugged. "It doesn't really go both ways. I know some things about you."

"Really?" Aeley's frown deepened. "Let me guess: my father got talking, and you just happened to be there?"

"In some cases, yes, but I've seen you here and there, heard other things in passing. Some things I've figured out on my own." Lira stared at her hands and rubbed her knuckles. "I've seen you in the villages, too. We were in the same village square once, a couple months ago."

"You're joking," Aeley muttered, then squinted at Lira, trying to grab at some sort of memory. "I don't remember seeing you."

"No, no joke. You were with the magistrate, giving a speech and riling the crowd." Lira smiled, but the sadness in it... "I tend to be good at being invisible."

Invisible? Hardly, Aeley wanted to argue, but instead, all that came out was, "As good as you are at speaking your mind, apparently."

Because yes, self, that's helpful. Now piss off, would you?

Thankfully, Lira smirked. "Sometimes. Sometimes not good enough."

"Maybe we should talk about some of the other things you're good at."

"Or not. I'd hate to bore you before the meeting. What? You don't want to talk about yourself?"

"Don't you?"

102

Lira leaned into the corner, her tightened fists pulled under her shawl. "Ask me what I know about you. You'd be surprised."

"You're evading the question," Aeley said softly.

"And so are you. I asked you first, meaning you should answer. I hear it's the polite thing to do." Past Lira's sweet smile was a hint of sarcasm, her grey gaze clouded with what appeared to be regret, maybe even nervousness. "You wouldn't want to break with etiquette now, not when we're so close to the Council meeting. You need to be in proper form—and it'll make Allon look that much worse. Not that he needs help, I'm sure. But aren't you the least bit curious about how much I know of you?"

Aeley watched Lira carefully. There would be no winning the argument, not while Lira pushed her away, for whatever her reasons were. Had Aeley done something wrong? Offended her somehow? Or was it a matter of testing a new employer, gauging the waters of trust? She could understand both, if Lira would just give her a chance and tell her what the problem was, or at least offer a hint, especially if an apology was in order. Aeley could do apologies. She had made so many of them as of late, what was one more?

Either way, don't push it. If she wanted to know more about Lira, she had to wait. "So, what do you know about me, then?" Aeley asked, settling back against the cushion, her hands in her lap.

Lira looked much too satisfied as she played with the corner of her shawl. "Well, I know your father adored you and couldn't stop saying how proud he was. And I know he'd be incredibly happy the people chose you for their next leader, not because it keeps the title in the family, but because you're the right person. We can put our trust in you." Her lips twisted, eyes glimmering with amusement, yet laced with a touch of darkness. "I also know you're tougher than he was, not likely to withstand the issues like he did—and certainly not when it comes to your brother breaking the law. Korre was quiet, but you're not. He preferred to avoid confrontation, but you never have."

Confrontation. Aeley almost laughed. That was putting it mildly, and in that polite, annoying way people had when talking about her. She would have preferred people said what they really meant: that she had been in too many fights growing up, leaving behind broken noses and bruised pride, and that she *still* did so, because she was never going to *'grow out of it,'* or whatever it was they expected of her. She could count the number of times on her fingers and toes twice over when it came to how many *concerns* people had shared with her father over her choices.

Maybe it was because her mother died when Aeley was three years old, stealing away the model of ladylike demeanor she was expected to idolize and imitate. Maybe it was because she preferred a fighter's life to playing the dainty wife for some Grand Family's heir, proving loyalty at the tip of a sword instead of idle chatter. Or maybe it was because her destiny was to keep Allon from destroying their family with his poor choice in friends and bad decisions.

If he'd not been able to run around doing whatever he wanted all these years, taking things that didn't belong to him and lying, maybe things would've been settled by now. If only Father had punished him. If only he'd had the courage... Aeley scowled and folded her arms across her chest. *No, that's unfair. He did the best he could. He just wasn't like me.*

"You could say the same about Allon," Aeley mumbled.

"True," Lira said. "You share a boldness and restlessness. More like your mother, your father always said. But you're not one in the same. Allon is chaos; you are order. If you weren't, we wouldn't be going to see the High Council. Not like this."

Aeley stared at Lira. Her tone was harsher than expected, but the words...

"What? Surprised someone noticed?" Lira smirked, that satisfied look returning.

Aeley blinked away what few responses came to mind. "A little." *A lot, coming from you.* "I've just been so caught up in cleaning his messes, there's no thinking about it. That's part of the reason why

I started training to begin with: someone needed to keep him in his place. Dead would be better."

She stopped and curled her tongue behind her teeth. *Why* had she said that? *Sure, I meant it, but now? With her? So much for being charming.*

"Let's just pretend I didn't say that. Ignore me," Aeley muttered.

"What? I don't deserve the honesty?"

Aeley shrank back. "What? No. That's not—"

"Relax. I'm just joking. Sometimes I do that, often at the worst times." Lira drew a hand through her hair and coiled curls around one finger as she frowned. "You wanted to know more about me, so you should probably know that one little thing. Though if you prefer your scribe to be serious, I could try—"

"Goddesses, no." Aeley held up her hand. "It's… refreshing."

"'*Refreshing*'?" Lira snorted quietly. "I've never been referred to as that." One of her brows arched. "Are you trying to flatter me?"

"Hey, I'm just being honest," Aeley said, her tone soft and not as confused as her thoughts. Did Lira not get compliments that often? That was another question to add to her list. "And no, I don't need more seriousness, especially not all the time. Truth is, everyone's been trying to keep everything like it used to be, saying the same things they always said to my father and treating me the same way they always have. But it's nice to have something different." She sighed.

"Sometimes I think things have been the same for too long. Maybe it's why other things have fallen through the cracks. We need to have change. I can't keep doing the same thing, over and over again. I need more than this," she whispered.

"Hmm. As Tract Steward, or as a woman?"

Aeley choked on air then, unable to stop the fit of coughs that followed. "Damn, you really cut straight through things, don't you?"

Lira pulled away from the corner and slid towards Aeley until their knees touched. "There's no point dancing around something if there's truth to be discovered in the answer." She tilted her head, her lips pursed. "That and I'm curious about why your confidence is shaken. When I saw you in the village square, you were strong. People hung onto every word and talked about it for days. Your vigour, tenacity, and inner strength—none of it escaped anyone. Seems a bit lacking now. So is it the position or is it personal?"

"Everything," Aeley mumbled, surprised at how easily it came out—and how truthful it was, even if she should have kept quiet. She leaned back and gazed out the window, not sure how to feel about her sudden candid honesty with Lira, who knew more than her silence let on. Usually Aeley reserved the most personal talks with Mayr and Pellon, but Lira… something in her wanted to keep talking, even if she regretted it later.

Focused on the grey and white houses along the road, Aeley considered her next words. "I want to find my own way," she said finally. "It can't always go back to my father. He's gone, and I'm not him. I need to redefine myself, or find that part of me I know is in there and put it into whatever I do. It's for the rest of my life, if I want it. Right now, it just seems like forever. I'm buried under the same old issues that my father dealt with."

Aeley snorted and drew her heel along the floor. "The most alive I've felt was when we were taking out Allon. I hated it, but it made me realize I need more. Signing papers, being nice, and always turning in circles to make people happy isn't how I want to spend my life. There's got to be more."

"I imagine it's not easy doing it alone, either."

The question sounded so pointed, Aeley paused. "No," she admitted, staring at Lira, not sure where the conversation was headed. Except hope—she had that, and if Lira's next words were to—

"I'm surprised you don't just marry your Head of the Guard." Lira pointed to the carriage wall behind Aeley. "You seem to have something there worth pursuing."

Wait—what?

Again, Aeley choked, this time with a quicker recovery. "*Mayr?*"

"Well, wasn't he kissing you before we left?"

"No!" Aeley made a face. "We're friends—family, really. Always have been. Never lovers."

"Oh…"

"Besides, we'd end up killing each other if we ever tried. And me, I don't even like sleeping with—" *Nope, don't go there. That's a whole discussion I don't want to have. Not right now. Not like this.* "Actually, never mind."

"Wait, you can finish—"

Aeley tapped the window, gesturing to the lush, green ferns lining the red dirt road. "We're almost to the Hall. Is there anything we need to talk about before we go in? You know all the councilmen, right?"

Lira's disapproving scowl came her way, and it stuck around longer than Aeley had hoped. "Yes, I know them. No, there's nothing to talk about—legally or politically, that is."

Not questioning what that choice of words meant, Aeley nodded and gazed out the window, content to sit in silence for the rest of the journey, not that there was much more to it. The dirt road had already changed into a smooth path of flat grey stones, and the carriage wheels clattered along its surface. They had officially entered Vasserey Call, the grand expanse of city as welcoming as it always was. Long runs of buildings, public squares, marketplaces, and parks sprawled throughout, sectioned into multiple districts, many of them arranged into smaller communities around the primary assemblies and guilds: commerce, law, artistry, medicine and welfare, scholarly pursuits, and the intertwined assembles of military, political, and civil affairs. Vasserey Call was the largest city in Gailarin and in competition for the title of largest city in all of Kattal, rivaled by only three others: Maiden Mist in the south, not far past the Gailarin-Eruelme border; Nirah Bell, the largest city in the Riaes tract, close to the republic's southwest borders; and Grace-upon-Alatayle, the massive port city in Alosaa. All of them were large enough to boast populations in the thousands, various establishments of all types for every level of means, and even hospitals, theatres, arenas, and elaborate public gardens—completely unlike Dahena, which had always been small and modest.

Of the four major cities, however, Vasserey Call was the most significant in terms of governance, being the only city to host the highest seats of power in Kattal: High Council, which was centralized in High Council Hall; the Sacred Assembly, where priests from across the republic congregated; and the governing assemblies, where the fate of industry, order, and social matters were debated and decided under the watchful guidance of the councilmen.

High Council Hall stood at the end of the long stretch of winding main road, a lavish building of bright white and grey marble complemented by exquisite stained-glass mosaics of every colour.

There were also several courtyards with little ponds and ornate bench swings, and all through the building and across the grounds, there was the splendour of an artist's eye through the perspective of landscapes, seascapes, statues, and metalwork, among other valuable pieces, much of which preceded the Hall itself. Adorned with creeping vines and extravagant red and yellow flowers throughout, the Hall was a sample of the beauty of Kattal collected into one place, matched only by the Temples of the Four. Aeley had always marveled at the sight, comforted by its openness.

Hold onto that; discard everything else, she told herself as the carriage slowed to a stop. *Allon can't take this from me, too. This ends today. Anything else is a waste of time.*

If she stared at the twelve councilmen, or even the white walls enclosing them in the Council Chambers, she could contain her anger. She could not—*would not*—allow her gaze to slip to the corner to her left, filled by the dark form of her brother with his greasy, blond hair hanging in tangles and his dust-caked skin. The rattle of chains filled the room, and every time Allon whined for more slack or attention to his needs, Aeley clenched her fists.

Mayr tapped her arm, a reminder that he was there. Behind him, Lira stood with her hands clasped. The High Council and their respective agents, all of whom stood off to the side of the room, remained silent as the scroll with Aeley's testimony passed from one councilman to another.

If only she could have beat Allon's head against one of the massive gold shields on the walls, particularly the one that represented Gailarin—a fitting tribute and end all at the same time.

Biting back a frustrated sigh, Aeley clasped her hands behind her back and twisted her heel into the white marble floor, her gaze focused on the shields on the back wall, far behind the long, black table in the centre of the room where the councilmen sat. There were five shields in total, each dedicated to one tract in the republic, three of them hanging on the back wall and the other two on the side walls, all taller than her and wide like the doorway into the stables at home. The Gailarin shield kept her attention the longest, its familiarity caught in the warmth of the light hitting it from the large circular window in the centre of the ceiling. No other windows were present to compete with it or its shine, just the gleaming gold, white, and the varied colours of the long coats the councilmen wore.

Someone coughed—one of the council agents—while Allon grumbled and snorted, goading the guards that kept him in place, and Aeley focused harder on the shield. The stark black bar of the fess ordinary design cut across the centre of the shield, the image of a bearcat in statant guardant position outlined in black above the bar, all four feet on the ground, face outwards, while below the bar, the black outline of a heaven's horse was displayed guardant, wings outstretched. Within the bar itself, a gold long bow lay horizontally between two gold anchors, representing both the battle and nautical aspects of the tract. As a whole, the shield signified strength, stamina, and vigilance with a courageous ferocity to preserve liberty and the future, with dreams and hopes never forgotten.

Everything Allon had pissed over with his antics.

She really needed him gone. Now.

Aeley peered at the Council, impatience taking over. She squeezed her hand behind her back and dug her nails in, just enough to temper her frustration. Nine councilmen sat at the black table, arranged in a line and facing the main entrance behind her, each taking their turn with her testimony. *In the interest of full disclosure*, Councilman Cota had said, even though the final decision over Allon's charges and sentencing was down to him and Councilman Severn. Lower had a say in it, too, given his duties as Councilman of Tract Stewards and Republic Leadership.

Whatever Cota's reasons, she really wanted to *disclose* how much she hated them all right then.

Then there was how annoying she found the sympathetic, hazel gaze of Laece, the Councilman of Arts, Crafts, and Guilds. Their visible need to rush over and hug Aeley was almost as infuriating as the unadulterated pity in the eyes of Madlen Giltree, the councilman who oversaw all of the healers and welfare and medical practices in Kattal.

If there was anything Aeley needed, it was *not* pity. Sympathy and hugs, fine; Laece was one of the nicest ones of the bunch. But pity? No. What she *needed* was Allon locked up before he said another word, preferably before she snapped and stormed out, a rather harsh and resounding *"Forget you,"* shouted in the process.

The looks on a couple other faces, though… they kept her there, giving her some kind of hope. Padremet, the chief minister of civil affairs and social welfare, looked fit to tie Allon up hirself and drag him off for forced penance—however creative it might be, considering Padremet's limitless imagination and fresh perspective on solving problems. Beside hir sat Nerrik Taldure, controller of Kattal's commerce and economy, whose green eyes had darkened to storm-level degree. His gaze stayed on Allon as though he was imagining all the ways to make Allon pay for the damages inflicted, even it required selling body parts to pay the debt due.

For the other five at the table, their expressions floated between the two extremes, most of them flicking glances between Aeley and Allon, no words spoken as they waited, a couple of them fidgeting while another fussed over the stack of parchment beside them. Like all of their Council counterparts, they each wore a chain of office around their neck, the elaborate design crafted from silver and emeralds. They also wore long coats, the colours of their individual coats denoting their position. Yet each coat bore the same bearcat shield of the High Council on the back, accompanied by vines that spiraled around the shield and carried forward along the arms to the cuffs.

The final three councilmen stood before Aeley in coats that appeared barely worn, with Cota in charcoal grey and its silver emblems, marking him as the one in charge of law and justice. Severn stood beside him, her dark red coat and black emblems that of the Councilman of Public Protection, while Lower stood to her other side in his sky-blue and silver-black emblems. Their backs remained turned to Aeley and Allon as they focused on the other Council members, waiting.

When the scroll finally passed over the table and returned to Cota, he looked at Aeley, his pale green gaze hard, determined. She took a deep breath, praying he ended the torment. His compassion usually reached that far, even if it took a while to get there.

"You swear to this, full and true?" Cota asked, holding up the scroll, the light-coloured parchment a sharp contrast to the warm tones of his umber-brown skin.

Aeley flicked a glance at the puckered scar on the left side of his face, not lingering on it for long. As usual, the long, jagged scar from temple to jaw was visible to the full, his dark brown hair kept short and parted around it. She still had no idea where the scar had come from, save for a fight that was one of the best-kept secrets in the republic, and something about his youth being tested—or was it his integrity, maybe his skill, and whatever the occasional rumour suggested? Her father had taken the truth with him to the Realm of the Dead. Still, that single scar reinforced how serious Cota was, making him the perfect choice to rule over Allon's hearing. She needed to keep faith in him.

"It is," Aeley answered, straightening her back. "All of it's the truth."

"Liar!" Allon yelled. He rattled the chains before laughing. "Just a filthy liar."

"You have *nothing* to add?" Lower asked. His blue eyes widened, and he rolled his wrist as though prompting her to embellish her story, his narrow silver bracelets clinking together.

Tempting, she wanted to tell him, but relented. In the back of her mind, Lira's comments reminded her not to make it more personal than necessary. Even if Lower thought it was a good idea, she lacked trust in his little time on the Council. Slightly younger than her, he liked the chatter, but the more experienced members of the High Council did not necessarily welcome his constant thoughts, at least not the verbalized kind. He could be easy to get along with, if not completely suffered through by those preferring quiet, though he meant well, and he had a way with knowledge, given his experiences as a scholar.

Severn was one who preferred silence, however, standing in her dark red coat over black tunic, pants, and thigh-high boots with black leather straps crisscrossed up her thighs, carrying a collection of small knives up to her hips. Long black hair and a dark, prodding gaze only added to her *fight me* look, though the loudest additions to her tone that day were the thick bronze knuckles on both hands—usually reserved for when she was at a trial, mostly to ward off the offenders if they came for her.

Given all she knew about Severn, Aeley had no doubt Severn frightened most people, including Lower. As the councilman in control of everything that fell under public security and protection of the republic, including its military, navy, and bounty hunters, her unyielding attitude served the role. In the grand scheme of Kattal, few people were more powerful than her, if any.

Returning to Lower's question, Aeley shook her head. What more could she say? She was tired of talking about the issue as it was, and there was no way she would talk about her personal problems. Not in front of any of them, and *never* in front of Allon. The darkness inside her mind... that was hers alone.

"Somebody's a little pet," Allon sang.

Aeley gritted her teeth. Could they not silence him, or shove a wet rag into his mouth and let him choke?

Annoyance flashed across Cota's face. "Allon, as prisoner, you can say something," Cota said, his voice huskier than usual.

"Not that we're going to listen," Mayr whispered into Aeley's ear.

She slapped his chest with the back of her hand.

"You mean *I* get to talk and *you* get to listen? Well, now!" Allon chortled and rattled the chains. "I mean, what an honour, being listened to—"

"Answer the question," Severn interrupted, never raising her smooth, low voice.

"Or what? You'll *punish* me?"

"Ah, clever." Severn chuckled and stepped towards Allon, her hands clasped before her. "If the questions don't interest you, we'll assume you have nothing to say, throw out whatever rights you still have, and conveniently misplace you." She smiled slyly, her wide eyes crinkling with a hint of laughter. "Perhaps where you'll never see the light of day. We'll, oops, lose the keys. Maybe forget your name altogether?" She tapped her head, then shrugged. "It's funny how memory can slip every now and again."

"Oh, oh. Scary lady. I'd say I'm frightened, but I shouldn't lie, right?" Allon went silent before clearing his throat. "Dearest Council, as much as I'd *love* to go back to working in your mines, I find it's just not as comfortable as the lifestyle to which I am accustomed. I really *must* suggest doing something about that terrible rock and—"

"This is going nowhere," Lower said, spinning on his heel. He rolled his eyes, reminding Aeley of their previous discussions about Allon.

"If all you are going to do is make a mockery of this hearing, we have no choice but to get straight to the sentencing," Cota announced. He held up Aeley's scroll. "Based on this testimony—"

"Boo!" Allon shouted.

Cota ignored Allon and continued. "*And* the testimonies from women and children taken to your estate—"

"They liked it!"

"—*and* the testimonies from the rest of the citizens of Oly Valley, including one of our own soldiers—"

"Kill that backstabbing mercenary and his stupid girlfriend!"

"*You are hereby charged with crimes against the people!*" Lower yelled and rushed towards Allon.

For a moment, Aeley hoped his temper would guide his fist into Allon's face.

The look of disapproval from Cota spoke volumes, however, his glare at Lower even louder than Lower's outburst.

Lower backed away, regaining composure as he muttered, "Sorry," his hands clasped behind his back, head lowered as he shifted back against the table.

Cota's scowl followed him before turning onto Allon. "You are hereby charged with crimes against Kattal and her people," he said calmly. "Your actions carry the weight of a life sentence, to be served at Footshred prison and its quarry unless we deem it fit to move you elsewhere." He nodded to the guards beside Allon. "Take him."

The guards seized Allon and dragged him towards the closed metal door in the wall to Aeley's left. The two additional guards standing on either side of the doorway were wary as they removed the heavy barricade and unbolted the door.

"Hey, *she* attacked *me*! Why don't you punish her?" Allon shouted, struggling to escape. "Make her haul rocks and break her back." The guards pulled harder, letting go as he fell. He scrambled from the floor and jeered at the guards.

The moment he turned towards her, Aeley froze.

His smile twisted his face, ugly and cruel, and all she could do was shudder. He enjoyed the game, taunting her as the guards yanked him up. The door guards were quick to join in and help haul him away. All of them slipped through the doorway and disappeared, returning Allon to the prison carriage parked just outside.

The room fell silent—*too* silent, given the looks the councilmen exchanged with one another before staring at Aeley. They hesitated for far too long, at least to her liking.

"Maybe you should have a seat," Lower suggested. Clearing his throat, he gestured to the chairs behind Aeley. When she refused to sit, he returned to his empty seat at the Council table and gripped the low back of the cushioned wooden chair. "I know it's been trying being here with us, but we all expected it. I'd love to say you're dismissed, but we have some further business."

"What?" Aeley frowned as Severn and Cota took their seats, neither of them saying a word.

"I'd also suggest your companions wait outside." Lower gestured to the closed door of the chamber. "They're free to stroll around, wander the Hall at their leisure. We just want to talk to you. Won't take long, I promise." He waved his hands. "Go on. She'll be fine."

Mayr turned Aeley around, her back to the Council. "Leave? Don't leave? What do you want us to do?"

Aeley peered over her shoulder at Lower. His foot tapped the floor impatiently, though it seemed more like a nervous habit than anything else if the worried look on his face could be believed. "Go on. He doesn't lie. Must be Steward business. It's fine."

Mayr nodded, but said nothing else as he escorted Lira from the room and closed the door behind them. Still hearing Allon's voice in her head, Aeley faced the Council, her skin prickling as her own concerns pushed to the surface. She had the awful sense the day was about to get worse.

Lower shuffled his feet, hands shoved into his coat pockets. "As you know, my role as Councilman of Tract Stewards and Republic Leadership includes receiving and executing the last wishes of our leaders, including your father. He left me with a testament to his wishes for the estate, his children, and possessions. You are heir to his estate and such were his wishes."

"Yes, I know. He showed me the document, too." Aeley glanced at each councilman. Only Lower's face took on a flush as he watched her. "I don't understand what the problem is, though. When I was inaugurated, everything came to me. Those are completed requests."

"Well…" Lower drew a hand through his dark red hair, the curled ends brushing his shoulders. "When did he show you this document?"

"Two years ago."

"Right, about that... There was another one, more recent. He gave it to me just days before he died, during my visit. Told me not to say a word."

What? Aeley scowled. "Impossible. He would've told me."

"No, no, he wouldn't have. Not at that point. He didn't want you to worry more than you did. Said you were running yourself ragged and it could wait. Said if he died, he wanted you taken care of."

"What do you mean *'taken care of'*?" As Aeley narrowed her eyes, Lower shifted his weight from one foot to the other. "Where's this going, exactly?"

"A marriage."

Life screeched to a stop right then.

No.

No, no, no.

Never. Over her very dead, very decomposing body.

"A *what*?" Aeley almost yelled, whatever composure she had left threatening to scamper off. "*Are you joking?*"

Lower held up his hands. "This happens more than you think. Your father and I discussed it at great lengths. He said he conversed with the family for some time, and they told me the same when I asked. Korre wanted to make sure you had everything you needed, no matter who got the position. It took him a couple years to pull it together, so I'm told, and the family is fully willing—"

"I'm not!" Aeley thrust out her hand. "Give me the testament. I know you've got it there. Give it over."

"See, I knew you'd take it like this." Lower picked up the thick scroll with its frayed edges and walked it to her. "That's why I brought it. See? It's in your father's hand."

Aeley snatched the scroll, wanting to tear it open. Instead, she unrolled the parchment carefully and read it through—more like bounced from word to word, her sight blurred and pissing off on her as much as her patience had. She stumbled on the words about marriage, taking them one moment at a time just to make sure she understood them.

Lower was right: her father wanted her to marry into the Grand Family of Derossa, a family about which she knew little, except for the questionable parts.

They had two sons, if she recalled the lineage correctly. Maybe even more children, the very thought niggling at her. She had never seen any of them, let alone spent any time in their presence, having only her father's stories to go off. Their former patriarch, Mather, had once been Tract Steward, but his son, Asha, lost the title to Korre after an election Asha had not played fairly, or with kindness. Rumours said their family had never recovered, explaining why they never attended the regional dinners or galas. From all she understood, they exiled themselves from the society they felt betrayed them.

And now, her father wanted her to marry one.

"This can't be happening." Aeley squeezed her eyes shut, wanting to scream at her father with so much rage she shook. He had brought the issue to her before, and they discussed it, but he *never* said he had made a plan. What a fool she was, convinced he had let the matter go.

"I know it's a surprise," Lower started, "but your father believed in it, and so do we. You're young, with plenty to do. Usually Tract Stewards have families to help them through the tough times and stay focused. Your father had your mother—a marriage arranged by *her* father. Korre was happy and thought you could be, too. It could be helpful, considering what Allon's done to tarnish the family name."

"So *what?*" Aeley spat out. "I don't have any way out of this?"

"We would strongly advise against that." Lower touched her shoulder, then frowned as she recoiled. "Give it a try. At least *talk* to them. They're nice guys. I've met them myself. And it wouldn't be bad for the two families to be brought together. Their grandfather was an excellent Tract Steward, and your father carried on the excellence. Might as well keep it all in the family, yeah?"

It took everything she had not to attack him where he stood.

Chapter Five

"I could kill him!" Aeley yelled.

"Which one?" Mayr threw his knife at the target on the study wall. "You're going to have to be a *bit* more specific."

"*Who do you think?*"

"Hey, it was your father who made the deal."

"Well, fine, I could kill him, too!" Aeley released the knife in her hand with a forceful throw. The blade rammed into the target, though it was nowhere near good enough. Completely off centre.

"Kind of difficult, considering he was burned and all."

"So I'll just throw some dirt in a bowl and yell at it until I'm ready to dump it in some filthy hole."

"Now you just sound like you've completely lost it." Mayr threw another knife, the blade taking the centre circle without issue while mocking her poor attempts. "Are you sure you should be seeing anyone today, let alone these two suitors? Someone should tell them to run for their lives."

Aeley chewed on her lip. Four days had passed since the meeting with the High Council. The first night, she had gotten drunk and raved about the ridiculousness of the situation. The second night, a letter had come from the Derossa family, requesting an audience, both of which launched her into drinking away the backstabbing misery of betrayal. The third night... she remembered little of it, waking up the next morning confused, but calm.

Yet the anger was back again, not to be dismissed for a fourth time. To make matters worse, every drop of gaffa nectar, ale, wine, and anything else worth drinking had disappeared from the estate. Gone, in the middle of the third night while she slept off her drunkenness. Yes, she had consumed enough to deserve the headache and fractured memories, but she had not drunk *everything*.

All of her suspicions focused on Mayr, regardless of how he insisted he knew nothing, even saying it with a straight face, as sincerely as he could manage. *And he says* I'm *a bad liar?*

She held back the urge to yell at him. "How could he do this to me?"

"I know. You've been asking that since you left the meeting. Doesn't matter how many times you put it out there, no one's ever going to have the answer."

Aeley stomped towards the wall and yanked the knives from the target. "After everything, he went and did this without telling me."

"But *you* agreed to give these people a chance, regardless of what your father did. *You* went and listened to that cute little scribe when she said you should meet with them. You could've just refused it all, but no, you went and invited them in."

"I know," Aeley muttered. Lira *had* persuaded her on their ride home from the Council meeting, that much was true. *Remember our discussion before the meeting, she said. Remember what it was you wanted, she said. She sounds exactly like Lower. How is any of this going to be good?*

Mayr leaned against the desk, playing with the feathery end of a black quill. "You should just tell them no. Tell the Council to mind their own relationships and stay out of yours." He arched one brow. "I loved Korre—still do—but your father's wishes aren't law, even if Lower acts like they are. I mean, what's to lose? It's not like they'll punish you with prison."

"Don't you think I've thought of that already? That I've already asked myself the exact same thing?" Aeley waved one hand at the door, her grasp tight around the knives when all she wanted to do was throw them down and scream. "I almost did. Almost wrote two letters that day, one telling the Derossas to find someone else and another telling the Council to leave me alone."

"Funny how you say 'almost.'" Mayr snorted and pulled his hair over his shoulder to examine the ends. "Can't imagine what stopped you. The old Aeley wouldn't have backed off."

"The old Aeley wasn't in charge of an entire region, nor was she the sole, and free, member of the Dahe family," Aeley countered through clenched teeth. She slammed the four knives to her desk. A pile of scrolls collapsed and rolled across the desk, dragging on her annoyance that much more. "Sure, there aren't laws that say I *have* to enact whatever my father said, but there's more to it. In case you didn't notice, the family's reputation has been pissed all over. What Allon did reflects on me, too, and I have to pull everything together before anyone else gets any ideas. I have enemies; I know that, and I can't afford to sink our family's name before I've really begun as Steward. I'm not off to a great start."

She moved to the window and stared out, the red earth and green trees distorted in the coloured pane. "Father made a deal. Despite not talking to me, he talked them up. They made agreements. If I don't follow through—or at least *try*—that gives the other Grands reason to lose respect. Even fight for a reelection, knowing some of them. Though if the Derossa family feels slighted, who knows what they'll do." Aeley cast a look over her shoulder, back at Mayr. "Asha Derossa didn't make Father's life easy. He took losing the stewardship badly and wanted to destroy my father's reputation. He even tried to use my mother in his games, until she exposed his lies in public. I don't think he would've forgotten." She snorted. "And don't even get me started on his wife, Etalynn—she *hated* losing it all. It's probably why they agreed to this marriage between families. At last, they get something back."

Mayr scowled at her. "So you're being used is what you're saying."

"No, I'm saying there are advantages. I suppose I'd be using them."

"To make nice."

"To keep my head above water." Aeley folded her arms and leaned against the windowsill. "Being Steward is as political as it is caretaker or defender. As much as I hate it, going through with this could mean the difference between protection and losing everything." She rested her head against the windowpane with a sigh. "Father prided himself on integrity and dignity. That's what people liked about him, and it made being Steward worthwhile. Breaking deals was never acceptable. I can't start destroying everything he built up—everything *I* helped him with. And if keeping a deal means keeping the peace, it might be worth it."

"While giving yourself up?"

"That's the job, Mayr," Aeley said softly. "If there was anything Father taught me, it's that we don't live for ourselves."

"And we know how well *that* worked out." Mayr sighed and tilted his head back. "Sorry. Just..." He crossed the room to join her and gripped her shoulders. "Don't kill everything about the old Aeley. She's got to stay in there somewhere. As much as I loved your father, there was something lacking. Don't settle for being exactly like him." He nodded towards the door. "You should probably get to it."

Aeley raised her arm. "Escort a lady?"

"I suppose, if you manage to find a lady," Mayr said with a sigh. When she slapped his chest, he wrapped his arm around hers and pulled her from the room. "What? Don't you think this'll make them jealous?"

"Hardly."

On their way to the meeting room, she kept the rest of her worries to herself. After what she said to Mayr, she was back to questioning everything again. It was a decision not made lightly, if she could make it at all. *Someone give me the strength. Maybe even the brain I seem to be lacking these days.*

They entered the room quietly, and Mayr drifted off to the side, several steps away from Aeley. Two men conversed at the window, well-dressed in black leather long coats and pants with elegant, embroidered tunics. The taller, muscular man wore his brown hair long, tied back with black cord, and a tunic of deep blue trimmed with sleek black and silver ribbons. Beside him, the shorter, heavier man wore his hair short, though the colour was the same dark shade, almost as dark as his green-black tunic.

The soft noise of a third person stole her attention. Snapping her gaze to the right, her heart raced faster than her thoughts could spin themselves dry.

Nothing made sense anymore.

"Lira?" Aeley glanced at the men by the window. They turned, waiting for her to address them, but her focus was already back on Lira and her pale purple gown, a simple, modest version of the newest fashion. Two layers of purple cuffs fell over her forearms with a single layer of white lace in between, all of their lightness contrasted by the rich purple ribbons tied in a crisscrossed pattern around her waist and elbows. Two white combs held her hair back, their teal crystals catching the light.

Lovely as Lira was, Aeley was too confused to fully appreciate it right then. Was Lira there to help her keep the meeting moving forward? Not that Aeley had any reason for a scribe at the meeting: they were there to talk, and Aeley usually handled talk a little too well. Had someone put Lira up to it, then—Lower, perhaps? Was it an underhanded way to ensure Aeley was *actually* following through?

No, no, and no. Please no.

She prayed Lira was there for something else. Playing spy for Council was *not* reassuring.

Aeley cleared her throat. "Why are you here?" *Say work. Please say work.*

With a hesitant smile, Lira neared Aeley, the hem of her gown sweeping over the toes of her brown boots. "Aeley, I'd like you to meet Emon and Ryler Derossa—my brothers."

"Wait... what? *Brothers?*" Aeley's heart pounded to a halt. Words—she had none. What could she *possibly* say to *that*? Her gaze alternated between the men and Lira. "That makes you—"

"Lira Derossa, yes."

And in just three words, everything went from awful to a godsforsaken mess.

"So, hold on, you knew and—"

Lira leaned into Aeley, their faces almost touching. "We can get into this later," Lira whispered, her breath playing warmth over Aeley's cheek. Her words were strained, almost forced—pleading. "But for right now, you should just talk to them. Only them. They're the ones being considered. As far as you should be concerned, I don't exist. I can't."

It was easier said than done, and with absolutely no answers, only more questions.

Aeley hated how she was still unable to move past stunned. She wanted to enjoy Lira being so close, not get caught up in trying to understand the game being played with her as the fool in the middle. Still, the look on Lira's face, the urgency in her tone... "All right, fine. We'll talk after."

Aeley straightened as Lira pulled away. "Emon. Ryler."

The taller of the two men approached her first, his smile and blue eyes appearing sincere as he reached for her hand. His lips pressed to her knuckles, the warmth not so much a comfort as it was a sharp kick to her realization that she had gone cold.

Once he released her fingers, he held his hand to his chest. "Pleased to meet you in person, Aeley Dahe. We've heard plenty about you, but it's nice to be in the same space for once. It's so difficult to trust the words of insipid fools who waste their time on fanciful notions and rumours." His smile twisted into a smirk. "I have to admit we're honoured. It feels like it's been entirely too long since a Dahe took it upon themselves to show us the grace of a meeting, what with your father's death and all, and with kind words, no less, without a band of guards. Here we expected to be talking to you from behind a closed door."

Before Aeley could respond, he stepped back and bowed his head. "I'm Emon, the eldest and heir to our father's vast fortune. Though when I say vast, I'm certain you're not aware of just what all that implies. You are, after all, a politician's daughter, and one best suited to warfare, as I understand it, not one for commerce." He raked a lukewarm glance over her. "I wouldn't expect you to know all of what that entails, other than the coins that are traded in your particular part of the region. I'd be happy to explain it to you. Small words, of course, to keep it simple and not waste your time."

Oh, she expected he would—and every part of her wanted to return his offer with a kick in the balls.

Great, just what I needed: another man who thinks he's a gift to the rest of us, as if seeing one locked up wasn't enough.

Ryler coughed, but it sounded forced. Aeley could swear he said, "Pompous," at the same time. He pushed past his brother to take her hand. "Ryler; middle child, but the smarter one, or so I've been told. At this point, I'd wager I'm already looking better than my competition. Emon's the one who runs his mouth, and I'm the one who has to clean up the mess, though I'm sure you understand how it goes." With a weak hand, he gestured to Lira. "And apparently you've already met this one. Not much you need to know about her." He tilted his head and pursed his lips, his storm-grey eyes similar to Lira's but a shade lighter. "Actually, we're not all too sure why she's here. She doesn't get anything out of any of this or the estate. I'm sure she's good for something, just less... influential."

"Less everything," Emon muttered, almost too quiet to hear as he turned his face away slightly. He cleared his throat and offered Aeley what resembled a strained smile—one with all the chill of a grimace and a hint of side-eye, enough to have Mayr stepping closer to Lira with a warning glare at Aeley. "Don't worry about her: her inclusion is a formality, not a suggestion. Certainly *I'm* the one you'll want to get to know intimately, given the control I'll have over everything once Father's gone. If you want to be Steward for your entire life and want for nothing, I can make it happen. You want the support? I can make it so no one ever challenges the Dahes again." Emon clasped his hands behind him, though Aeley caught his slight point towards Ryler. "Second-born has some merits worth pursuing, but he still has to go through me."

"We can fix that," Ryler murmured behind his hand as he wiped his lips, then straightened and clapped Emon's shoulder. "What he means to say is that he steals from the wealthy and pools it all in some underground tunnel while I make an honest living and stow it under my mattress, even if it's a mere pittance in comparison." He winked. "Then again, keeping it small keeps me from being so delusional. And dead. Did I mention I like being alive? I'm terribly fond of breathing, though it always feels like someone's trying to kill me. Ever feel that way, Aeley? Er, Steward Dahe. Whatever we call you? Paranoia: yes? No?"

The glare Emon threw his brother was about two notches short of murderous. What would happen if Aeley left the room and locked them in together?

Emon recovered quickly, standing to his full height. "Please excuse Ryler. When he's excited, he tends to say things most people wouldn't. Ever. It's been a hard lesson for him, learning when to stay quiet. It seems that wisdom was one of the few things passed along to our sister. I suppose it's what makes her such a good servant." Emon tilted his head. "Sorry, I meant *scribe*."

And now comes Lira with one of her clever retorts. Make him look even more like the ass he clearly is.

Lira remained silent. Humiliation flashed across her face, a flicker of regret. She stared at the floor, her chin lowering slightly.

For all her opinions, she had nothing to say.

What are you doing? Aeley gawked at her. Even in her silence, Lira said more than her brothers, not all of it good. There was beauty in how she denied her pride, setting her apart from the rest of the Grand Families. There was also an ugliness, a cruel fall as ego crushed strength into passivity. *If only…*

Aeley cleared her throat, the muscles in her back as tense as the contempt crawling across Mayr's face. With a hand on one of the knives on his belt, he stepped in front of Lira, shielding her, casting Aeley a second wary glance as he shook his head. He was one warning away from shouting Emon and Ryler down, though maybe not before he punched them in the face.

Not the best start to this mess, especially since I'd be tempted to let him deal that damage. How do they think any of this is right? Insulting me is one thing, but shaming her is another. She fought a scowl, her fingers itching to do something. *Yet I still have to be nice, still have to let them in. Otherwise I'll have them and whoever they've got supporting them breathing down my neck and destroying what little we've got left. One battle at a time, at least in theory.*

"Pleasure to meet you," Aeley said, her mouth dry as she forced the lies out, "though perhaps you're right: it's best if we leave Lira out of the discussion from now on. For all intents and purposes, address her as my scribe and nothing more, preferably with all of the respect accorded to her station relative to me." She glanced at Lira with a wince and a pathetic smile in apology. Neither were good enough, even if Lira returned them with a weak smile and a shrug, and the words... they sat foully on her tongue, worse than licking a bucket of sawdust laced with a poison that refused to act, just festered. Diplomacy needed to piss right off.

"We should just get to this, then," Aeley continued, dragging her attention back to Emon. "We all know why we're here, so we may as well skip to the contract. You mentioned the marriage agreement in your letter. I'm curious to know how much you know about it, seeing as I just learned of it."

Emon did not hesitate, his hands clasped behind his back as he spoke. "Everything, actually. We discussed it at length with your father after he brought it to *our* father. Nearly made every one of us fall over. But we talked it over, drank perhaps a little too much, swapped stories about how great things were before your mother destroyed our father's life. Then we decided it was the best course of action for the republic. The four of us worked out the details of the arrangement."

"Which are?" Aeley asked, aware of what the contract stated but needing them to say it, dreading it for all it meant, what it suggested. There was no denying the feelings that whispered she was being sold, and by one of the only people she truly trusted... or *had* trusted, though her father had taken that to his death, too.

"You can choose," Ryler answered. "Whichever one of us you prefer, we will honour that choice. And the date of that marriage is your choice, too, within a year's time from when you officially pick one of us as your spouse—all of which has to be announced publicly after half a year's courtship by both of us." He leaned forward, his voice quieted but no less matter-of-fact. "Something about making sure we're all kept to our word. We'd hate to have one of us skipping out of a deal. People tend to get a little angry when their leaders turn out to be liars. Then they call for inquiries and make demands and just talk so much nonsense. We'd *hate* to put you in that position."

"And it needs to be clarified that *we* are marrying into *your* family, not the other way around," Emon added.

"Meaning?" Aeley took a breath and held it.

"Meaning you remain Tract Steward in your own right," Emon answered. "*We* offer you a portion of our wealth in exchange for bearing the Dahe name, recognizing our children have rights to the future candidate positions. We also offer our connections, resources, all estates and lands inherited when our father passes—which may be soon."

"In return, you agree to protect our family and extend certain rights to the surviving members," Ryler added, glancing at Emon before meeting Aeley's gaze. "You know, to keep us from starving or having our throats slit. The usual. Guts hanging out, brains smashed in, eyes rolling across the road. It'd be like these horrible dreams I keep having where I wake up and the whole family's hanging from the ceiling of the latrine by their right ankle." He shrugged and slipped his hands into his pockets. "Suppose that means something, but I'm pretty sure it's a call for protection, don't you? We don't all have grunts with swords easily at our disposal. Considering how much wealth Emon keeps saying we're sitting on, I'm sure we can use the help. I'm not thrilled with the idea that I could be eating metal for having too many coins."

"I see," Aeley muttered. *This is too rushed. Too everything. One acts like he's the only one in the world worth knowing; the other sounds like he's missing a piece of whatever should be saving him from absurdity. Help me*, she wanted to say when she glimpsed Lira, her grey eyes still downcast.

The disappointment on Lira's face threw her, and for all the problems she had, Aeley's only question right then was *Why?*

Ryler shuffled his feet, the curious silence shattered. "I know you're not pleased about this, but it won't be bad. Not really. We're committed to this. We'll give you everything if you're willing to give us a try. No tricks," he said, holding up his hands.

"We have nearly eight months to get to know each other. You don't need to make the final decision today," Emon told her, his voice low. He touched her elbow, a light tap she wanted to swat away. "We need to spend some time. Maybe we can just agree to that today and we'll go?"

I have to make an effort, Aeley reminded herself. *Just need to keep the Grands off my back long enough to figure out how to maneuver through this disaster, then figure out a way to survive it afterwards.*

Despite Emon's arrogance, there would always be someone worse than him in the world. Goddesses knew Allon was ten times Emon's superior in that regard, and Allon was far from unique. At least Emon appeared older than her, almost in his mid-thirties, and sounded like he was used to leading the family charge. If they could focus on that, and if he could leave the insults aside, maybe they could find some sort of ground in the middle.

As for Ryler... If she overlooked his tendency to say too much, there was a chance he could be bearable, at least enough to learn something valuable about him to keep him in line.

"I suppose," Aeley said. "Yes. Fine. I'll send for you... to spend time."

Emon and Ryler each took one of her hands, said their thanks, and bowed their head before striding from the room. Mayr followed close on their heels, silent as he cast Aeley an unimpressed look.

Yeah, she knew, and she would never hear the end of it.

"That went well," Lira said, her quiet voice breaking the silence.

"I guess, considering they walked out with their heads still attached." Aeley turned sharply to face Lira. "Why didn't you tell me? There you were, going on about how I should just meet with them, but you knew the entire time. I spent that whole damn carriage ride going on and on and you said nothing."

Lira watched the doorway, her gaze not meeting Aeley's. "I just didn't, that's all you need to know." She drew her arms around herself, but dropped them just as quickly. "Call it minding my own."

"No, that's not good enough." Aeley pointed to the door. "And why didn't you say anything during *any* of that? They were insulting you, and you said *nothing*."

"You didn't, either, at least not anything they'll listen to or respect." Lira stepped around Aeley, headed for the door. "I have to go. Vant needs me—"

Aeley grabbed her arm. "Why can't you be honest with me?" she whispered, loosening her grip as Lira turned back. "I can think of something to say to them—"

"No. Don't. Don't make this harder than it already is."

"But—"

"*But* the door is still open. *But* I can't get into this." Lira moved away.

Aeley rushed to the door and slammed it shut.

"It's closed now," Aeley said, leaning back against the wood, "and Vant can wait. The only one stopping you right now is *you*. And I'm asking. It's polite to answer the question, Lira *Derossa*, or so you once reminded me."

"Of course that's what you'd remember from that conversation," Lira mumbled.

"I remember plenty of things you've said, and the things you haven't said. Why didn't you tell me?"

"It wasn't my place. I'm not supposed to say anything." Lira bit her lip, her gaze falling to the floor. "The Council didn't wake up the morning of

Allon's trial and suddenly realize what they had. Emon and Ryler went to them days before. They told me to keep my mouth shut. They also pointed out that if I spoiled the contract and talked you out of it, they'd make me rethink my place in our family and your employment. I was lucky that they let me come today to begin with."

So coercion. Threats. The same games I'm sure they play with everyone else. The same games Asha played with the people around my father—ones they're trying to play with me. "Why? Why is there hostility at all? Is it because you're the baby of the family and they don't want you involved?" Aeley grimaced. She could have kicked herself for that last question.

Lira tilted her head, her unhappy smile all but kicking Aeley for her. "They don't necessarily like to share what's theirs, whether it's attention or the wealth Emon keeps prattling on about. Though they're right: I don't get anything from the family's estate. I'm not worth the same as them. They also don't approve of certain choices I've made. Not that I approve of any of their choices, either. Mine just tend to be more shaming. Or so they keep telling me."

"Choices?"

"Being a scribe isn't considered a place of honour in our family," Lira replied softly. "To be honest, it's almost as bad as being labeled a traitor of the republic. Pride is almost above all else in our family, just below loyalty. I chose to do something I loved. They see it as burning away everything the family's built up, worthy of exile, among other things they don't agree with. Other choices I can't take back. Choices I'm not ever going to be sorry for making." Lira raised her chin and straightened her shoulders. "But this isn't about me. None of this was. I was just here to observe. This is about *you*. Now you've seen them for yourself, what do you think?"

"About what? Them?"

"Yes. I gave you your answer. Now I'm asking you, in all honesty, what do you think? You didn't turn them away. You didn't tell them no. You agreed. Obviously that means you're still going along with it."

Aeley stepped back. How could she think the honesty would last longer than a few moments? There was no use in pushing further—today.

"I'm not any happier about it," Aeley said, crossing her arms. "I don't see how it'd work. I'll probably end up locking them away just to get peace of mind. But they're who Father chose. They're who the Council thinks will keep things together." She sighed. "I can tell you I can't stand them and I wish I didn't have to do anything. But all things considered, it could be worse. I *know* worse. And maybe it's better to keep them close, to watch what they do. Maybe marriage would keep at least one of them out of trouble. But honestly, that's all I've got. I don't know how to fix this."

Lira's lashes fluttered as she gazed at the floor. "I know you're in a delicate position, but your father would've known what he was doing. He'd want to keep your place secure, safe. They offer that. If you can find a way to play along with them, it won't be that hard. Just make reasons to see them, involve them. Have more meetings. Do things. Have a ball and invite them." She touched Aeley's arm, the gentle weight prompting Aeley to take a breath. "Yes, it's a perfect idea. You're a new Steward. You need to get involved with the other families, better introduce yourself. You can learn about my family at the same time."

"What about you? Would you come if I did?"

The gleam in Lira's eyes was obvious, but confusing. "Absolutely. Now, I really have to get to Vant. I'll watch for the invitation."

As Lira left the room, Aeley wondered if she had missed something.

Chapter Six

Vant had left without her, heaping even more grief onto her humiliation.

Sniffling back tears as they threatened to spill, Lira clutched Vant's message in one hand, still standing in the front foyer of the Dahe estate, unable to move. The plan had been simple: attend the meeting with Aeley and her brothers, keep her head down and her mouth out of trouble, then meet Vant in the foyer so they could go to his home and work on several documents, followed by a lovely dinner with him and his husband and a quiet sneak back into her parents' house later in the evening, hopefully while no one but the guards were looking. So simple. So bloody simple.

Which in no way explained why she was standing alone in an empty foyer with everything hurting and nothing going right.

The meeting had been a disaster—she never should have bothered. She knew her brothers, knew their cruelty. What had *ever* made her think it could have gone any differently? How could she have duped herself into such an awful idea?

For all the time she had spent with Aeley up until then, all those moments shared, she had done her best to be honest and forthcoming and *tried*, just simply *tried* to connect, to make a thread of *something* happen that could resemble some sort of relationship other than knowing each other's names and nothing else. She was tired of hiding, of blending into the shadows and pretending her existence was for nothing. *This one thing.* She had wanted *this one single thing.*

But now…

She had been absolutely humiliated, not just in front of Aeley, but in front of someone Aeley trusted and loved dearly, and all without Lira standing up to say a damned bloody word in her own defence. A meeting so terrible, Aeley called her out afterwards just to chide and scold and dig into business that could only make things worse.

Goddesses knew what Aeley thought of her past the pathetic display. Certainly not as a marriage prospect. No, that was still reserved for Emon and Ryler, thanks to Korre's meddling.

Why? Why had Korre approached *them*? Of all the people he could have gone to, of all the families he could have tied to the Dahes, he chose *hers*? The same Korre who had given her a chance to be happy; who had seen her struggling to find her place and gave her a chance to find it without judgment, without shaming, without a lick of anything her parents considered appropriate for the circumstances. All of those years of being so smart, so careful, and he saddled Aeley with *this*? It was a foolish mess Lira would have strongly advised him against had he asked her... had he cared enough to at least *tell her*.

Instead, this was it, his legacy, and Lira was being shoved into the shadows again, her fighting words buried where the rest of her apparently belonged.

Even Vant had left her there, unable to wait just long enough for her to run from the meeting as quickly as she could. At least he had been kind enough to leave a message explaining his absence.

> *Gone to Vasserey Call with Solicitor Jaiel—something's come up and the Council wants to see us immediately, without delay. So terribly sorry we could not wait for you. Will be back first thing in the morning. Meet me at the tavern at noon and we'll spend the day, dinner and all. I owe you. Again, my apologies.*

Apologies. Everywhere she turned there was something to be sorry for, usually on her end. Was it sad that for once, the relief was there that someone was apologizing to *her*?

"Quit it," Lira muttered, wiping her eyes dry. "Quit this mess right now. Head up, back straight, decisions made. Everything else is done. Forward now." There was only ever forward; going back would never be an option worth taking. However small the steps, no matter how much it hurt, she had to keep moving onwards. And if that meant doing it all alone... well, fine, then.

She slipped Vant's message into her documents case, keeping it safe among the blank parchment, the hard, flat case containing her white-spotted brown quill, and the small vial of ink she always kept on hand. Haydin had been kind enough to hold onto her case while she attended the meeting, ensuring that nothing went missing—or was outright stolen by her brothers, which would not have been the first time. After the meeting, Haydin had returned the case and given her the message from Vant before heading off with two household staff to help solve some sort of catastrophe in the kitchen.

Only the guards in the halls remained. Two of them walked the long stretch of hallway to her left, a third paced behind her in the corridors by the kitchen, and a fourth peeked around the corner at the top of the stairs. Their gazes caught hers briefly before they glanced away, their expressions unreadable.

They could keep their opinions. She just needed her wits.

With the documents case under her arm, she let herself out of the estate and stopped on the staircase leading down to the carriage path. If she could just find a quiet space to—

Oh, Goddesses, no.

Now things were bypassing humiliating and aiming for intentionally cruel.

At the bottom of the stairs sat a lavish black and sky-blue closed carriage she was all too familiar with, drawn by a pair of tawny beige horses. The driver looked bored, his attention suddenly swinging in the opposite direction, likely falling on the flock of small, orange-crested brown birds congregated on the well-kept lawn encircled by the carriage path. Inside the carriage, Emon perched on the edge of one seat, annoyed as usual, his long legs stretched out and crossed at the ankles in the open doorway. All he needed was a silver cane to resemble their father almost exactly, save for their father's grey hair, though the shared impatience more than made up for it. Ryler leaned against the carriage on the outside, arms folded over his chest, looking ready to start a brawl with five angry drunks and a barrel of hammers.

"Hello, sis."

She could have slapped that self-righteous smirk off Ryler's face with every book she had.

"Ryler," Lira said through gritted teeth, ensuring the door was closed tight behind her. "Emon." She clutched her case and willed herself to breathe deeply for several counts. She *would not* give them any satisfaction whatsoever, not any more than they'd already had.

"Finished dallying?" Emon's gaze met hers, the blue of his eyes lost to the shadows playing in the carriage. "Get in and let's go. I've got better things to do."

Like the deepest, rankest pits of the Realm of the Dead would she step foot into that cursed carriage.

"Dammit, Lira! Just get your ass in and shut up with the attitude." Ryler banged the carriage door open further. The door slammed against the side of the carriage, birds scattering and crying foul into the sky.

Lira jolted back, her shoulder hitting the doorframe behind her. No. Not like this. Not again. "I never asked you to wait," she said coolly, tempted to storm back into the house as if she owned it; to take comfort in its walls and maybe even holler for help. Would the guards come if she shouted loud enough? "Why don't *you* run along, play the good children since you're so obsessed with yourselves you think it actually works."

Emon's eyes flashed as he leaned forward into the sunlight, almost crawling out of the carriage. "Found that bite again, have you?" He jerked his head to the side, jaws clenched, one fist in his lap, the other gripping the carriage. "*Get. In.* I won't say it again. You're expected."

Ha! She bet she was. Her mother would want every detail, every piece of gossip she could wring out of their scrawny little throats— anything to dig her way out of the hole Lira's father had put them in.

Lira raised her chin and straightened. "I really don't care. I'll walk."

"I swear, Lira—" Ryler growled as he stepped forward, one foot, two, his hands flexing, threatening like claws. "I'll come up there and you'll damn well get in—"

"Or you'll damn well worry about your own sorry ass and leave," a deeper voice interrupted, the gruff tone getting harder with every word. "*Now.*"

All attention snapped towards the overflowing flower gardens to Lira's right. On the crude stone path that cut through the gardens and under the arbours, Mayr leaned against one of the black spiraled lantern posts only feet away, his arms crossed over his chest. "And if you manage to do it all by yourself, I may just forget about this," he added dryly, his glance still pinned on Emon and Ryler.

Lira froze, her grip tight on her case. Matters were quickly devolving into a nightmare, half mortifying and half disaster in the making. She was never going to live it down, not from the indignant look on Emon's face, and certainly not from Mayr's unwavering glare.

Ryler snorted. "Forget this." He pushed Emon back into the carriage before casting Lira a look over his shoulder. "You can walk. Walk to your heart's damned spoiled content, for all I care. Don't get lost," he sneered, then climbed into the carriage and slammed the door shut. An audible thump set the carriage moving, the driver barely sparing Lira a glance as the horses took them around the carriage circle and out the gates, down towards the road.

A breath of relief came out before she could stop it, the muscles in her back aching as she relaxed, her shoulders dropping along with the tension. It took her a moment to realize she was gripping the twisted metal banister of the staircase, leaning into it. It took her another moment to notice Mayr was at the bottom of the stairs.

"Better?" he asked, his voice quiet, the harsh tone gone. He held out his hand, offering to help her down.

If not for the shame gnawing on her courage, she would have accepted.

"Yes, thank you." She descended the stairs on her own, one hand on the railing to keep her focused, the other clutching her documents case for fear of losing what little comfort it provided. Once she stood beside Mayr, she smoothed her skirt, tugged her sleeves to resettle the cuffs over her wrists, and nudged her hair combs back to tighten their hold. She forced a small smile to counter Mayr's worried frown. "It's fine. *I'm* fine."

"Yeah, but are you all right?"

"I'm fi—"

"—Fine. So I heard." Distance crept between them as Mayr peered at the open gates, then back to her, unvoiced thoughts playing in his gaze, sombre as they were pensive. "How are you getting home?"

I'm not.

She had no mind to, even if she'd had the means. There was no dealing with Emon and Ryler when they were being brutish and controlling... which was most of the time, unless their father clipped them up the head and told them to back off. That rarely happened, though, and certainly not in a situation like this where everything was at stake. The fate of their family's survival was in question, and there would be no quarter given her way, even if her mother had all but fawned over her before Lira left for the meeting.

Where did that leave her, exactly?

Going home was right out: it was a long walk to Deros Glengale, one that would take the rest of the day and the night, right on into late morning, if not the afternoon. She could have attempted to walk to Vant's, which was closer and may have only taken the afternoon and evening, but then she would put Eyle out, and she had no intention of doing that.

The rest of the Grand Families were nowhere on the list of possibility, given her status as an outcast from most circles, not that she wanted to spend time with them as it was. And the tavern… while it was usually her first option, she did not doubt Emon and Ryler would crash the place and drag her home, particularly if her parents demanded it. She barely had enough coins to rent a room for the night and get a meal, anyway, the thin pouch scrunched into her boot mocking her with its lack of weight, a handful of coins pressed against her ankle. What else remained of her wages from Vant was tucked away at home, hidden somewhere no one knew about, most of it set aside to go towards a small place of her own— a little cottage in a secluded space.

For a moment—just a moment—she glanced at the Dahe's estate, a whisper of a thought twined around the spare bit of hope she kept locked away. If she just went back in, maybe…

Lira looked back at the garden, the rich, vibrant hues of the various late-summer flowers taking all her focus. No, staying at the estate felt too much like crawling back and begging for leniency when she had done nothing wrong. Besides, if she went in and Aeley found her, Aeley would want to talk about it—the last thing Lira wanted right then. Talk was more often than not how she found herself digging one foot in a grave and the other into the land of castaways.

She had no idea where she was going, but she would not stay there.

"I'm fine," she said softly, almost patting Mayr's arm before pulling back to keep her hand balled at her side. "I'll stay in the village tonight. Thank you for sending them away. I'll... see you again soon."

Before she swept past, she caught his scowl, and the furrow to his brow deepened as she put distance between them. No fight followed as she walked through the carriage circle to the gates, the silence a welcome companion. When she turned back, stopped just on the other side of the towering black gates with their tree-shaped lanterns and bearcat statues, Mayr was gone.

Left to fight her own battles again, she carried on down the tree-lined avenue to the dusty red road that led into the village. Her thoughts spun as she walked along the roadside, taking solace in the rustle of leaves with the occasional shrill birdsong that poked through, a gentle breeze cooling her cheeks.

A *ball*. Had she seriously suggested Aeley throw a ball to get to know Emon and Ryler?

By the blessed patience of the Four, she was a bloody disaster sometimes.

And *her*? Attending that ball? At Aeley's request?

Every part of her had screamed *yes* back there in that room, the consequences be damned. Agreement had come so easily, without thought, without worry, just the drop of a chance she could maybe—*maybe*—get Aeley's attention in the way she wanted. She had spent months hiding behind Korre and Vant, watching, waiting for an opportunity without so much as a word. And now...

Showing up at the ball would throw her right back into the world she wanted to escape. The focus would end up on Emon and Ryler, who lived to be stared at and talked about and fondled by anyone with affluence, while Aeley courted whatever asinine plan they had concocted with their father. In the clatter that would ensue between egos and schemes, Lira would fade into the background and find a book big enough to hide in.

If only she could have made her brothers disappear as easily as she did. Humiliate them for once and take their parents down in the process. If High Council could ever find it in their books to care, she would have happily worked to gather whatever proof they wanted, all to see her brothers locked away, their hands gripping prison bars or a pickaxe instead of her wrist. Or her elbow. Or her hair. Anything to get them to just *stop*.

But her family had never liked the word *stop*, not unless they were the ones using it, then everyone was expected to listen and hop to whatever commands were given next.

She would give anything to be able to say it and have the world fall in place around her. Just once. Just long enough to grab everything and run far away from them. Permanently. Without looking back. Without peering over her shoulder. Without worrying they would track her down and haul her back, kicking and screaming and terrified to be locked up in their cagey, self-absorbed world.

She wanted the misery to stop. Shift face. Find something else to do and leave her to what actually made her happy.

And what she would give just to tell Aeley to stop and look at her long enough to see someone worth keeping around.

Tears crept into her eyes, and she swore faint footsteps followed her on the side of the road, occasionally catching on the rocks. She had no idea where she was going, or how she was going to get there. She had been humiliated in front of the one person she really, truly liked in ways she had never expected to, especially after years of being told she ought to be ashamed for what went on in her head.

Could there have been a moment there, any moment, where Aeley had taken an interest in her? She had no idea what to think, and now she was being followed without having much of anything useful to hit out with if the person turned out to be another problem to fight. She was so damned tired of defending herself. Even when she had someone's help in doing so, they always left her—and damn Korre for that, too, for making her think she could do this.

Blinking away the tears, wiping them with the back of her hand, Lira dared to glance behind her. Someone in dark clothes, several paces back.

She focused on the road ahead, a horse and cart in the distance on their way towards her. The come and go she could deal with, but that—

Again, she peered behind her. Frowned. Stopped and turned to get a proper look.

"Stuck?"

A sheepish grin greeted her as Stuck drew closer, her face red as though she had been out in the sun for too long—or she had been rushing. "Ah, damn, you heard me." She winked and shrugged. "He said follow; never said a word about covert. Not loud enough for me to hear, anyway."

Lira shook her head, trying to clear the cobwebs playing sticky games with her questions. "What? Who said?"

"Ehhh..." Stuck scratched at the back of her neck, giving the tail of her brown hair a bit of sway before she settled her hand on her waist, next to one of the knives on her belt. Her other hand rested on the hilt of her short sword, its narrow red and gold bands peeking out from beneath her fingers. "Mayr was a bit concerned. Something about bastards needing a balling. Or maybe he was just talking about our new recruits—still haven't figured out which." She gave another wink, another shrug, and Lira laughed softly but quickly contained it. "So, where we going?" Stuck asked, more singing the words.

Lira's gaze fell to her feet as she circled one heel in the dirt. "I told him I'm fine."

"As the rain we're not getting, I'm sure." Stuck quirked a brow. "Temple or tavern? Which one is it?"

"What?"

"Your safe place for the night. Temple or tavern? Unless you've gone split down the middle and taken to drinking with the priests."

All right, *that* time the laughter could not be helped, and it felt good, even with the image stuck in Lira's head. "I can't… with the tavern, not tonight. I just don't know if—"

"The temple will like you? Bah, they like everyone. Come on, then. Let's go raid their pantries." Before Lira could argue, Stuck carried on ahead, whistling as she kept one ear turned in Lira's direction.

It took ten paces before Lira rushed after her, not wanting to be left behind.

"Ah, good, we're here during quiet time."

Lira threw Stuck a questioning glance, not wanting to disturb the villagers and priests gathered by the altar. While visiting the Temple was not a habit of hers, she was reasonably certain there was an abundance of quiet at any time in any temple, this one included. Was that not one of the reasons people visited—for the peace, calm, and quiet contemplation?

It seemed the unspoken thought made its way through to Stuck, who grinned in reply. "Well, relatively speaking," Stuck murmured. "Nap time, maybe?"

And there Lira went again, chuckling at Stuck's jokes. It was strange, all the laughter, though it greatly improved her mood, even if she was still mortified about seeing Aeley again... still afraid to go home.

Fussing with her hair combs, Lira turned towards the altar, trying not to stare at anyone or anything too long. The temple was just on the edge of Dahena, a fair walk from the Dahe estate and well past the village proper. Like all of the Temples of the Four in Kattal, it was a spacious place of grandeur and beauty wrapped in pure white marble and flowers and the heavy, woodsy-berry scent of incense. Tall, spiraled pillars of the same white marble stood at the edge of the rounded worship space, separating it from the corridor that led further into the temple where all of the rooms were, apparent from the priests that came and went from the front of the temple.

The altar in the centre, however, was of black stone, no less striking than the large circular window in the ceiling directly above it, the glass in the centre a vivid blood-red that cast a tinge on everything nearby. Though the edge of the red light crept towards the four marble goddess statues that guarded the temple entrance behind Lira and Stuck, it never touched the finely chiseled artistry, leaving the images of the Goddesses bathed in the unimpeded sunlight streaming in from the wide-open doors. Save for the occasional hushed voice and the faint tinkle of wind chimes, there was little noise, just... blissful quiet.

"I'll be right back," Stuck whispered, leaning closer to Lira. "Make your peace, get comfortable—whatever you'd like. Just don't head off, all right?" She gave Lira a serious-unserious pointed look before sauntering away, her footfalls silent.

With a sigh, Lira turned back to the altar, frowned, and glanced at her documents case. Offerings had been left on the altar by those seeking favour and giving thanks, including pieces of parchment, bundles of flowers, food and drink kept in four large bowls and glass goblets, and even two small dolls sewn from what looked like white and green linens and pillow stuffing, a tiny lock of baby-fine blond hair attached to each with a red ribbon.

She had never laid down an offering. Then again, she rarely spent time in the temples, preferring to ensconce herself in a library, curled up in a chair with a blanket, warm cider, and notes in the margins... most of them her doing, much to everyone's annoyance. Her family had generally kept to themselves since before she was born, and tromping off to temple had never been their way, not with her father paranoid about a past that was long gone and her mother as bitter as the day was long. Ryler was more likely to vandalize the outside columns than be caught anywhere inside, and Emon—he would use the altar as his own personal table, feet up on the corner as he saw to trimming both his nails and his accounts.

Still, if she was going to ask to stay for the night...

Lira drifted towards the wall and sat down, legs crossed beneath her as she opened her case onto her lap and pulled out her quill, ink vial, and a blank piece of parchment. After scribbling down a bit of the poem she had been playing with for weeks—or more specifically, the only verse she could pin down with certainty while the others fought her for every syllable—she put everything away as the ink dried. Once everything was back in its place, she folded the parchment into a small packet, keeping the edges clean and neat, and gathered everything up before going to the altar.

Standing there, aware of the couple kneeling several feet behind her alongside a priestess in full red robes and veil, their heads bowed, palms held open and outwards, Lira took a breath, not even sure of what she was doing. *Making it up, really.* She stared at the candles in the middle of the altar, each one large and white with four wicks, all of them lit. Around the base of each candle lay a fresh crown of bright orange, blue, and red flowers tied with trailing strands of dark green, purple, and white ribbons. One candle per goddess, with the offerings spread out around them meant to be shared, bringing the four goddesses together.

Lira rubbed her thumb along one edge of the squared parchment in her hand, then set it down close to the second candle from the right, beside a rolled parchment tied shut with pale blue ribbon. In all of the paintings and tapestries and sketches she had seen, Laytia, the Goddess of Wisdom, was always the second from the right, and that was who she needed help from now, because she was feeling far from wise and one step from falling down the hole of nothing and getting lost at the bottom.

Though the others... She could use their help, too, given how complicated everything was. How tangled. Certainly love was at stake, and a problem onto itself, giving her multiple reasons to appeal to Emeraliss. As for Hastal's protection and Navara's justice—she would have begged at their feet to secure either of those, even just the one, instead of fighting on her own and getting nowhere. Maybe staying the night would offer a hint of inspiration, something she could take with her to keep hope kindled. For now, this was as good as she could offer, the best that she could ask, and she prayed Laytia liked poetry as much as everyone said She did.

"Good, you're still here."

Lira jolted back at the whisper, then glanced at Stuck, who had somehow crept up to her side without warning.

"Come on." Stuck tugged at Lira's sleeve, pulling her across the room to the corridor, nearly knocking into a priest as he carried a silver bowl towards the altar. The vibrant red robe laced closed over his chest, loose white tunic, and dark pants marked him as one of the middle-ranking priests.

"Sorry!" Lira stopped to steady him as Stuck rolled her eyes.

"No harm done," the priest said softly. "See?" As he turned over the empty bowl, a bracer the colour of his light tan skin peeked out from beneath his sleeve. He offered her an assuring smile, bright blue eyes glimmering with a hint of laughter. "I believe I had it coming, though, bringing nothing else with me. Empty bowls make Hastal a bit... tetchy."

Stuck snorted. "Then She starts threatening to filch off Navara and, well, we all know how *that* goes."

"Mm, indeed. Holy battles over a fishbone and a cork." The priest grinned, bowed his head, and continued towards the altar. The long ends of the black ribbon in his wavy brown hair swayed back and forth, hanging down his back in tight coils.

"More like a fishbone and half a biscuit," Stuck muttered before leading Lira the rest of the way by her cuff.

When they neared one of the spiral pillars, Lira stopped short, her cheeks warm as she came face to face with Priestess Kee. All of the memories from the dinner with Aeley and the others came flooding back. How Aeley had stumbled by Lira's chair, so close and yet so far. And then that single touch... that bit of sudden connection...

"Oh, hello again." Lira hugged her case close to her chest, her glance alternating between Stuck and Kee. "I'm sorry, Priestess, she dragged you out and—"

Kee chuckled, one hand raised. "I'm afraid it's not all that much of an imposition, at least not the kind that needs an apology, not when it's laundry day." She smiled and shook her head. Her floor-length veil moved across her broad shoulders with lightness and ease, the white and gold flecks in the fabric shimmering in the light, bright against her long black hair. "Now, Surie tells me you're in need of refuge?"

Surie? Lira glanced at Stuck, who grimaced in return. Stuck drew her flattened fingers back in forth in front of her throat and shook her head, mouthing *No.*

"Just for the night," Lira said, her attention back on Kee. "I... can't go home right now." *Really, really can't.* "Things are... complicated. I don't have anywhere else to go," she struggled to add, her gaze falling to the floor.

"I understand." Without hesitation, Kee rubbed Lira's shoulder. Her tone was as gentle as her touch, the softness of her red robes sweeping over Lira's hand like a soothing caress. "Come, we'll find you a room. Surie, you're with us, yes?"

"Until the morning, Overseer," Stuck said, cutting off Lira's protest with a raised hand. "I leave when she leaves."

Lira dared to protest a second time, only to be silenced by Stuck's pull on her sleeve. They followed Kee through the long, quiet corridor, past closed doors and open rooms and too many priests to count.

She wanted to escape her brothers, but this was too much—too much attention after being used to so little, and too much protection by people she barely knew after she had done nothing to earn it. She had half a mind to march up to Mayr and tell him to quit it; that she did not need the pity or the protection or the prodding into her personal affairs.

But then she considered the alternative, remembered the bitter reality, and deep down... part of her wanted to get used to it, to hold it close and call it hers when so little was.

Another part of her wished her brothers would shrivel up and go away forever.

The marriage contract had been beyond her knowledge until Allon's trial, and she had begged her way into the recent meeting with Aeley, going so far as to pay Emon and Ryler a portion of her earnings just to be allowed to attend, even though their father had encouraged Lira's presence anyway. And their mother... She had been *oh* so ready to help Lira prepare for the meeting, including offering to get Lira a better dress, do her hair, and help her present like a worthy marriage prospect.

It was a farce, all of it tripping over the threads of reputation. Her mother saw power in putting Lira out where she could be seen, but all her brothers saw was uselessness and, if she were extra lucky, competition. Despite the wording of the contract, Lira had never been intended as an option, a fact she had confirmed with her father, who blamed Korre for the confusion as though it were a grievous error that Asha would begrudge given the circumstances. Emon and Ryler had been the only heirs under consideration during the contract's signing, so for her to come forth now...

How sweet it would be if the final blow could be hers. One act of revenge that could gut them completely, reputation and all. She'd had her own plans before the contract came to light, and none of them included a single thing about her family.

In essence, they had sped up the process in some ways while interrupting it in others.

Still, she was stubborn, a survivor, even if it ended up hurting worse than anything else had. She would have to go home sometime, but in a day, maybe two. Perhaps things would simmer down before then and she could walk back into the flames without feeling the full heat—or maybe they would be willing to ignore her on her return, especially if, by special chance, an invitation came from Aeley to attend some sort of event.

Today she would lick her wounds in private, but tomorrow... tomorrow was back to business, with every chance of losing everything.

Chapter Seven

The ball was in two days, and Goddesses alive, she was never going to get through it without throwing something. The urge was there already, Aeley's fingers itching every time she picked up a knife. The target in her office had already been assaulted fifty ways from the highest point of patience, so what was one more? Even the black box of quills on her desk looked like a good option, though smashing the blue glass bowl of candied fruit she kept in the top drawer of her desk would make a far more satisfying sound—a smash, crash, then the skittering of tiny little shards of edible relief lost to the dirt and the dust.

A hundred invitations had been sent out, and several replies were still trickling in—all for the first ball of her hosting, with no one but Haydin, Cook, and Mayr to oversee the details and advise her when she needed to lay off the sarcasm and teeth-grinding. Yet only one of them was truly helpful in that case, because Cook's dark humour was a terrible influence and Mayr... there was no hope for any of them at this rate.

It was terrifying. She had invited the key members from the three dozen Grand Families in Gailarin and all twelve members of High Council. Thankfully, less than half of the councilmen were able to attend, including Lower, who she wanted there if only to show him that *yes*, she *was* upholding her end of the deal, lest he nag her about it till the end of days. For all of his scholarly experience, he was prone to poking sleeping bears when he ought to run away, and *someone* needed to save him from himself before his new post became his last.

The only saving grace was Lira's reply to the invitation, the only one Aeley cared about right then: a yes, which was *still* a surprise, considering how the meeting with the Derossas had gone.

Aeley sighed. She needed more than a week and a half to ease the memory of the meeting and her talk with Lira afterwards. Mayr had been in a foul mood since, or at least whenever the names of Lira's brothers were invoked, or the meeting, or the ball, or the contract, or anything, big or small, that tied to them in any way. Save for Lira.

Surprisingly, or maybe not so surprisingly, Mayr was fine with Lira. He went so far as to offer her playful winks, jokes, and the occasional arm during the few times she had come by the estate with Vant to work on stacks of legal notices and contracts. Dealing with the documents was far more bearable with Lira's presence and the cute way she always wore her work well after the ink dried. Aeley would have gladly pushed over every stack of parchment and sent them fluttering and scattering across the floor just to see Lira lay among them, hair unbound and fanned out over the words, ink-stained fingers free of any burden.

She could still dream.

Though she could not fathom why any councilman was being ushered into her study just after noon, and being escorted by Stuck, no less, who shared a look with Cota before closing the door and leaving him alone with Aeley. The Councilman of Law and Justice did not make a habit of house visits, and certainly not as impromptu as this one when he had already indicated he would be at the ball, usually meaning business could wait until then.

Either she had more work to do or she had messed up by massive proportions already... ending in more work no matter how she twisted the angles.

"Councilman Cota," Aeley started as she pushed up from her desk, her voice cracking on his name. With a wince, she cleared her throat and tried again. "Welcome. It's nice to see you again."

Cota offered her a kind, easy smile and waved just the once, motioning for her to sit. "It's not," he said, his laugh as soft as his deep voice, "but thank you for trying. May I?"

One brow quirked, Aeley gestured to the chair on the other side of her desk. "Yes, of course, please do. The standing makes me nervous." She paused midway in taking her seat, her face warm as she gripped the chair arms tight enough to hurt. "And I did *not* just say that," she muttered, lowering slowly the rest of the way. Lira was rubbing off on her, and it made her fantasies worse, their taunts difficult to ignore.

Cota chuckling at her, though, that was one step away from frightening. "You did, and it looks good on you. Let loose a little. Be comfortable in your own skin. Everyone always looks like I'm about to thrust the uncivil disobedience acts upon them, none of which are particularly sociable." His smile slid from amused to mischievous, the glint in his pale green eyes playing it further. "Though if I truly wanted to punish someone, I'd read them the entire general law omnibus, appendices and all, right down to the very last stop, then act it out with stocking puppets and pink paste."

Aeley choked out a laugh, only to slap her hand over her mouth, her eyes rolled to the ceiling to keep her from making it worse.

"See? That's better already."

Before Cota could continue, a knock on the door stole their attention. After Aeley's holler to enter, Haydin crept into the room with a tray, carrying goblets and a pitcher that he left on Aeley's desk. Without a word, just a small, tired smile, he left the room and shut the door behind him.

"So to what do I owe the honour?" Aeley resisted making a face as she poured them both drinks, the bittersweet berry juice a reminder that her usual libations were still missing, except for whatever Cook kept locked away in the cellar for the ball—and anywhere else she was stocking it without Aeley's knowing. As far as she could tell, the entire staff was in on the scheme.

Cota accepted the drink all the same and sat back in his chair, one leg crossed over the other, never looking more comfortable. Usually he was staunch and serious when it came to Council matters, at least on Council grounds. His relaxed, cheerful side was not one she knew well, though it was a welcome change from the rigid rules and expectations she dealt with. She could see why her father liked spending time with him—they seemed similar enough to have gotten on well, just with individual variations on the same approach: business first and kindness always.

"I thought I'd check on you," he said before sipping his drink. "See how you were finding the matters of being Tract Steward. Perhaps even find out where your head is at with the marriage contract, considering it's not something to be taken lightly."

Aeley snorted. That was putting it too mildly. "Really? I'm surprised you'd be interested in it. It's more Councilman Lower's purview, and maybe even Councilman Nerrik's, since it's looking more and more like a business transaction. I don't doubt he's already worked out the commerce side to all of this—what it'll mean for trade."

"Maybe so, though it does overlap with my jurisdiction—it *is* a contract, after all." Again, Cota offered that soft smile. "A legal document and binding agreement, both of which tend to get my attention, whether anyone wants them to or not."

Nodding, Aeley downed her drink and poured another before leaning back. She ran one finger along the edge of her desk, carefully weighing how little she should say. How much could she trust him? Her father had spoken highly of Cota, though that was a relationship formed over years of work together. She was a young pup who had been told to roll over and fetch and was already doing a miserable job at it.

"It's a trial, I'll be honest," she said finally, staring at the empty space past her desk. "I've met the brothers, and Lira, and it's…"

"Bothersome?" Cota finished as she struggled to.

Aeley flicked a look up. There was no judgment in his gaze, only honesty. "That's one way to put it. I can't just wake up one morning and say 'this is the answer' and move on." She sighed and rubbed her forehead as she shut her eyes against another headache. "If I'd just seen this coming… if Father had just talked to me about it. It's like being put in the corner and being forgotten about, but with no way out, either. And it's not even being done in private—it's out there for everyone to see, to hear about. One wrong step and I'm done." She glared at the drawers of her desk, her grip tight around her goblet. "I'm still furious at him, too. I couldn't *be* any angrier with him, and I really don't understand how he could even *think* I'd be all right with this."

She finished off her drink to shut herself up, acutely aware that Cota watched her. Goddesses knew what he thought of the mess. Had he *met* the family—really, truly getting to know them—or was he as smitten with them as Lower was? At what point was one of those damned politicians going to be in her corner without making her jump over the flaming fences of doom first?

Cota withdrew a brown leather case from inside his charcoal-grey long coat, the thin, flat case no bigger than his hand. He pulled out a folded package of parchment and offered it over the desk. "This might help. I was asked to give it to you after you'd met them."

Curiously curious.

Aeley took the note, opened it—and nearly threw it across the room seeing her father's handwriting.

"Go on, read it," Cota said. "I'll wait."

Aeley scowled at the letter. Betrayal. She already had enough of that to deal with, and if this made it worse...

She read slowly, taking in every word with underlying dread, part of her practically climbing up the wall and scratching the target board to shreds.

Aeley…

I know that face, and dearest, I know I deserve it. I'm sorry. None of this has gone the way I'd hoped, and absolutely not how you'd planned. The fault is mine. If anything, know that. And don't hold back on wishing I could pay for the mistakes made: I'm taking the guilt with me, packed in my other case. I have some explaining to do to Navara when I get there, and I'm not looking forward to the interrogation. Say what you will about the Goddesses: She drives the hardest and pushes the furthest, and I'm pretty sure She'll have your side on this.

But for now, this isn't what you think it is, but it is what it looks like. And if there's anyone who understands what I mean by that, it's Cota. If any part of this doesn't make sense, ask him. He's the one witnessing every word of this and keeping my hand steady—

Aeley glanced at Cota. Their gazes met briefly, his look back at her all too knowing, so silent in its remembrance. *Overlaps with his jurisdiction, my ass.* Brow furrowed, she continued reading.

> *Safety, dearest. That's what this contract is about. It won't look like it now, but I'm hoping it'll give you the foundation you need. Steady the ship. Make sure you're taken care of. I don't want you drowning, because being Steward—and I know you will be—it's a dangerous sea to sail, particularly if part of the crew is plotting a mutiny. I worry you'll be stumbling around without anyone to have your back on your level. And bless Mayr and Pellon... they'll take care of you, I'll never doubt that, but they're not players in the political arena. You need someone who is to help weather that storm.*
>
> *But then there's Allon, and that's a torment in itself, I know. My fault, again. Always my fault where he's concerned, for never doing what I should've. I don't know what tricks he'll get up to after I'm gone, but the onus falls on you to keep him under control, something I never could manage well enough without the threat of losing him completely. I never wanted to push either of you away. But I'm hoping that*

a solid partnership — a family to fall back on — might grant you safety from Allon's choices. Maybe even get him to fall in line. If the partnership is solid enough, it could make you that much harder for Allon to take down. Because he'll try, little girl. We both know he'll try his damnedest, and you'll be left fighting this, hopefully with someone who can fight back.

None of this will be easy. I thought we'd have another fifteen, twenty years left, long enough to bring you into the position slowly; for me to step down. But death is being a cruel bastard, and I'm scrambling just to pull everything together in time.

This marriage... it's not anything more than a way to protect you. There's a storm coming, one that's just touching the horizon, but I can't explain it. I feel it, though, and you need to be strong. In a place of power. You need people on your side, a united tract. They won't survive if the tract is fractured — if they aren't working together, under strong leadership.

That's why this particular union, as counterintuitive as it seems. It won't help if the Families are breathing down your neck or taking advantage of your political inexperience. You excel at being a soldier, and I couldn't be prouder (Cota's laughing at my cocky grin right now, in fact). But my darling girl, you can't skewer everyone who stabs you in the back. Even if they're lining up to try, you'll need to let them live and shut them down within the game, not insert-pointy-end-here. Cota terribly disapproves of the bloodshed first, questions second, maybe third, approach.

Aeley snorted a laugh. The glance she stole at Cota was met with a quirked brow and an approving nod.

"If you are where I think you are, I really do," he said, though his smirk suggested there was more to it, a small comfort in itself.

"But I don't like questions," Aeley muttered, returning to the letter.

I'm sorry if this sounds like a devaluing; that I'm making you into a commodity. You're not, and I don't want you to forget that. Maybe I really am being a complete bastard here as much as I'm playing politician and being a father. It's not going to be easy for you. It'll be downright awful. You're going to want to quit, or at least set fire to everything. Allon will test every thread of patience you have, and everyone else will snap the rest. But hold on, find some peace. If not in a spouse, then in something else—something good. Someone good. There'll be those who'll try to take that goodness, and not always at the tip of a sword. There are individuals far more devious, more cunning, and I still haven't found a way to deal with them that won't end up in bloodshed.

Yet maybe that's the point in the difference between you and me. You're the leader they need now, especially if things come to pass as I fear they might. You need to have a strong footing. Comrades in arms are one thing, but support from all sides is necessary now. I'm counting on your fight because nothing's what it seems. Enemies wear the faces of friends and vice versa. It may take all the fight you have to figure out which is which... But by all means, fight them, darling girl, and if they're an enemy... court justice.

I'm sorry for locking you in. It doesn't excuse what I did, and it doesn't make it right. I've rethought signing the contract, but I can't fix it now, not *without causing more trouble for you. I doubt my ability to protect you, even now. I can't help but think I've run you into a wall you can't avoid… If I have, I'm sorry, dearest. I have every faith you'll figure this out.*

Being Tract Steward is lonely business. Doing it alone is even worse. This marriage is meant to give you someone to turn to. I've arranged it, but you can do whatever you so please within it. I didn't take another spouse or a lover, but that doesn't dictate what you can do. Whatever you and your marriage prospect work out, that's what counts.

Though if you see it in your heart to, find some way to help Lira out of the mess she's in? This is where I admit that I've secretly been hoping you can use the marriage to convince her parents to finally stop twisting the poor girl into the ground. Find her a good place, protection. I regret I couldn't do more for her, even though I offered. Maybe you'll have more luck.

All my love —

Aeley dropped the letter, staring at it as it settled on her desk, the pages skewed. She had never wanted to burn something so badly but rescue it from the flames all at the same time, risking life and limb just to clutch it close and hold it until she died, even if it ate her hand away completely.

The apologies she could deal with, but his reasons... the responsibility he threw at her...

And *Lira.* Just what was she supposed to do about *that*? Especially when her thoughts kept straying and straggling and wanting...

"Why didn't he tell me any of this? Why now?" she whispered, unable to glance up from the scratches of black ink, noting the smudges, the way some words were barely finished, and the numerous times he had crossed out mistakes. By the end, it looked as though someone else had finished the sentences, or at least ensured they made the words legible.

"He knew you wouldn't have agreed," Cota replied quietly. "You would've fought him every step of the way, and rightfully so—your father never denied that. But he wanted to avoid the fight, especially since he didn't have any fight left. His illness had done him in. He didn't think you could afford that battle, either, one of many, so he negotiated what he could, convinced it was the best chance for you going forward." Leaning forward on the edge of his seat, elbows on his knees, Cota clasped his hands and kept his gaze on hers. "Korre couldn't bear the thought of running you off with it, making you hate him right up to death and beyond. He wanted to enjoy what little time he had with you, so he stayed silent. He'll have to make his peace with Navara and Emeraliss where that matter's concerned, but he was adamant about bearing the burden, no matter my advice."

"But why you to begin with? Fine, he didn't want me to see it before he died, but why you, and why now?"

"He didn't trust anyone or anything at that point." Cota shook his head, a distant look in his eyes. "This was written just after he'd signed the contract, just before he was confined to his sickbed permanently. He visited me, wrote this in my office, and left it with me before he gave the contract to Lower. He couldn't trust doing it here, and he wanted me to be witness, so I helped him the best I could." He shrugged. "It was too personal to give to someone he didn't know, and as it pertains to you…" A small smile crept across his lips. "He knew I'd do right by the law—by you. He also knew I'd never let Allon get his hands on it."

Cota sat back, hands clasped on one knee. "I don't blame you for wanting to get out of it. I respect that decision, and I argued on your behalf when he refused to tell you. I'll *still* argue on your behalf. But you're faced with a difficult decision, one that can't be made lightly either way. I won't presume to tell you what to do, just offer my counsel should you want it."

Aeley cursed under her breath and pushed back from the desk, settling deeper in her chair. How could such a mess descend into an even worse disaster? It was easier when she'd had no idea why her father had done it—when she could blame him because the reasons had failed to matter. "It's not like I have many options. The contract is binding. I can't go ripping it up and tossing it around, especially with the Grand Families already spreading the rumours. I've had several congratulate me and ask about the wedding. Then they've gone off to refine those same bloody rumours."

Yeah, she could take a good guess at just who was spreading those rumours, locking her into the contract with padlocks and chains. She had plenty of options where the Grand Families were concerned, but Lira's family topped the list. Etalynn Derossa came to mind every time, as obvious as a pool of red ink bleeding through the page.

"You can choose to disregard the contract. Given the circumstances—that this wasn't your idea or your doing—there's still precedent for you to get out of it, even if Lower's convinced you're obligated to follow through. And if *I* say there's a way out—"

"There's a way out."

Cota smiled and nodded. "The benefits of being a stickler for the law. As much as your father's responsible for this, he did leave you a means to get out of it: not only did he *not* include you at their meetings and have you sign the contract, he chose me as witness to his confession. My word over those who negotiated the contract; my defence of an affected party that was never appropriately consulted. I can overrule whatever Lower says or does. He's young, stubborn at times and over his head at others, but he can be reasoned with." His smile deepened. "He still respects me as a senior member of Council, which I can certainly use to your advantage."

Aeley let out a sigh. "But?" It was there; she heard it in his tone, even with that mischievous glance.

"But tearing up the contract or otherwise ignoring it has its downfalls. If the Grand Families are aware of what's happening, that leaves you open to attack from all sides." Cota raised his hand. "Make no mistake: my family will take no offence, and I know several others who'd be just as happy to let you run with whatever decision you make. We'd go so far as defending you. As a Dalenvrae, I have pull with others."

Again, that *but* was in his voice.

"But you can't influence them all," Aeley murmured, finishing it for him.

"Unfortunately, no. You're new to governance, a fact that hasn't escaped anyone, especially those with influence. While I'd never side with those who'd want to oust you for breaking the contract, I can't stop their every move, either. There are dangers everywhere, and you need to be careful where you step—*how* you step. Especially with what your father cautioned in his letter; about the difficult things coming that you don't know about. Other things that'll require you to fight." He offered a sad smile, almost apologetic. "I can protect you in some ways, Severn and Lower in others, but you'd have to weather the foul circumstances mostly on your own."

"Doomed going in, doomed going out?"

Another sad smile, this time tired with a hint of regret. "The choice is yours, Steward. I'll support you either way, but the choice remains yours, as do the repercussions."

Of course they do. Dammit.

"I'll think about it. Weigh my options, now that I have them." Aeley stood as Cota pushed up from his chair. She grasped his forearm in parting. "Thank you."

"You're welcome." Cota gestured to the door. "I'll let myself out."

As he did, Aeley sat on the corner of her desk, watching the door close behind him.

Well, that certainly puts everything into perspective, doesn't it?

Fingers tapping the desk, Aeley stared at the door, the dark red wood and gold handle fading into the background as her thoughts reeled over the letter, then what Cota had said. She was still going to rage at her father's ghost, even if it was a matter of principle, but at least there was a reason for the circumstances. As much as she hated to admit it, she understood the why, not that it did any good with the *how*.

And Cota... just what was he warning her against? The pointed words, the cautioning tone—Cota and her father knew more than they let on, she just had no idea what to do with it. Cota had gone so far as to mention Severn, whose interests centred on crime, law enforcement, and keeping the peace. If she got pulled into the situation, it would be an understatement to say things had gone poorly.

Aeley glanced behind her to the letter. There was still a ball to attend. Still a contract to deal with. Still the expectations to be managed. Her father had apologized profusely, which was a start, but even more telling was how he had not spent one word on extolling the virtues of Emon or Ryler, just a request to take care of Lira.

She snorted, a smile finding its way to her lips. Maybe he *had* seen more than he let on, placing her in the position to get them under control, too—not just Allon. Knowingly or unknowingly, he had granted her the means to make adjustments to how things went where they were concerned, perhaps even put them in their place a few rungs down the ladder.

Though Lira was still the odd card in the hand, one she had no idea how to play. Her head said one thing, her curiosity another—and neither one mattered if Lira felt nothing back.

For now...

Aeley snatched up the letter, content to sit on the desk, clutching a fresh piece of her father's memory. She would still host the ball and play nice, but she would keep both eyes wide open. Friends were good and enemies a headache, but the neither-nors in between were sneaky, and they needed a good watching.

If only she could be that certain about everything else.

Chapter Eight

She hated dancing. As Emon's arm curled around her waist again, Aeley wanted to push him away. When his gloved hand took hers, she almost blurted out how much she despised the mundane steps and turns. Though after a glance at the other dancers—how everyone seemed to watch her every move, waiting for her to trip, to fall, to leave—she allowed Emon to pull her into the crowd, spinning and moving in small steps to avoid the other couples. She needed to remain composed, the perfect host.

Or the perfect bride.

Sarcasm dripped from every image *that* struck up. *We met two weeks ago, and now we're here, in public, acting like we know each other.* Forcing a smile at Emon as they parted, she mirrored his hand movements and circled around another couple. *You should consider yourself lucky*, she wanted to tell him. It was thanks to her father's insistence that she knew what she was doing. Had she never relented and learned, she would have made a disgrace of herself, embarrassing Emon in the process.

And I've already got an idea about how he handles embarrassment. His confidence never wavered, overshadowed only by his pride. *Guess I can't blame him. He's the eldest, like I am. There's a bit of arrogance that comes with that. Except I have no idea how this would work—we'd spend most of our marriage butting heads and mistrusting each other.*

His brother was no less a concern. Aeley gazed across the room to Ryler, immersed in conversation with Luinn by one of the tables along the wall. While he walked the finer edges away from being a bore, Ryler was still just as stubborn as Emon—a family trait they all shared. Ryler vied for her attention just as much as his brother, sending her gifts of fine jewels and imported goods from countries about which she knew little. They had even presented her with two daggers before the ball began, each encrusted with various polished gems and elaborate designs on the blades, lying in separate wooden boxes lined with fur.

The daggers were a simple, obvious play on their part, but she had accepted the gifts nevertheless, with the same kindness in which they were presented. They could have just as easily ignored her fondness for weapons. For a moment, she had wondered if the gifts were a peace offering, not that she believed it, though hoped... maybe only a little, to a measure no bigger than a speck of ground herbs.

Still, the daggers were not the only move played that night with the intention to turn her head: judging by Ryler's golden long coat, *someone* had informed him about her preference for the colour. Emon, however, wore a green long coat that looked new, soft to the touch with gold buttons and trim. Both matched her flowing gold gown and thick black bodice laced with gold ribbon.

And yet, as flattered as she should have been, the attention to detail was trivial. None of it was about her, it was about them. They would play to what they figured she found attractive until they exhausted their ideas and moved onto other options.

Ha. That's a set of circles they'll have to keep spinning in. Me, attracted to either of them? Never going to happen. Not even vaguely enough to make it easier to pretend like I want this. Between the obvious jabs at my family and the disrespect dripping from every other word, not to mention the rubbish hiding in between, I can't decide if they're purposely trying to run me off or if it's really just a test to see what I'll put up with. She held back a frown. *Unless one or both of them want out of the contract just as much as I do. This could be them pushing me to break it first so they don't have to. Not. Bloody. Likely. Not if that's the game.*

Aeley peered over Emon's shoulder at the other guests. Compared to the sea of brightly coloured attire and multitude of late-summer flowers, the grey stone walls looked dull, despite the silver gilding reflecting the torchlight. Red and black banners with the Dahe crest hung on the walls, a variety of wreaths between them, decorated with a rainbow's worth of ribbons, pearls, and even more flowers—all of which sent up a wave of nausea as she forced herself through the steps. She was going to toss her stomach if she had to spend the rest of the night in Emon's hold, constantly staring at the walls just to avoid his face.

Thankfully, Mayr and Pellon were in attendance, their faces a welcome reminder that no matter what came of the contract, she would never be alone. Neither of them agreed with Korre's choice, even after his letter. In fact, the explanation only put them more on edge, both increasingly on guard whenever Emon and Ryler were around, especially right then, while Emon's hands were on her. Mayr lingered in the crowd, not far from the tables, ready to intervene, while Pellon stayed further back, making his way around the ballroom to check on the other guards. Even Stick and Stuck were there, stationed along the wall, with Stuck looking more than ready to run both Emon and Ryler on a spit.

Aeley had told them all to stand down, at least enough to let her try and sort the situation on her own with what diplomacy she could scrounge up. As bad as the marriage could be, the repercussions of breaking a social contract could devastate what little success she had achieved.

Although, if Emon and Ryler so much as laid a hand on Lira, Mayr, Pellon, and the rest of the guard had permission to handle the situation however they saw fit, just short of gutting them.

"Am I exhausting you yet?"

Aeley caught Emon's grin before he spun them around and swayed gently. He almost seemed as charming as the young women in the room thought he was, their wistful gazes leaving her somewhere between laughter and wishing for the strongest drink possible. "Would you like the answer you want or should I say something else?"

Emon chuckled and winked. "Glad to see you have a sense of humour. I'd abhor marrying a woman who doesn't. I'd either have to chase her out or marry her off to our stable hand. The old fool's got no taste at all, and doesn't mind taking what's left over." He gestured in Ryler's direction. "Might want to watch his humour, though. Sarcastic, mostly, when he's not just completely insulting."

I have no doubt. "Not subtle like yours?" Aeley asked, focusing her own sarcasm into her smile.

"Goddesses, no, but thanks for noticing." He leaned down to whisper in her ear, the rush of his breath across her skin even more sickening than the obnoxiousness of the flower arrangements she wanted to kick to shreds. "Mostly we just wonder what he keeps ingesting that makes him such a liability. I'm concerned about it, really. Maybe you can help me put him away somewhere quiet, somewhere where he's not likely to hurt himself or others with his foolish notions. My parents worry he'll become like Lira and lose us what respect we've managed to hang onto. It hasn't been easy, you know."

Aeley nearly pulled him to a stop. "What hasn't been easy?"

"Living in the shadows. Keeping our heads high. Making deals and saying all the right things to buy back good opinions. You've been a lucky girl," he continued, pressing his cheek to hers, his voice low. "So protected. So safe. Doing whatever you want and getting away with it. Funny how you've never once asked me how it's been growing up. If it was hard to constantly hear my father called a liar and my mother called his accomplice, as if she were a common criminal."

"Now hold on—" She pushed him away.

Emon drew her close, his hold tight around her waist as they moved slowly. "I'm going to say this just the once: you might think we're not worth your time, but you don't know anything about what we've been through to get here. Ryler tries not to show it," he murmured, "but it's taken a toll on him, and that worries me. I'm the eldest. I'm responsible for keeping our family in good standing. I could use the help, even if you don't know what you're doing or if you know full well what you're about and just don't care."

"What about your sister? Can't bear to spare one kind word about her?"

"For good reason: she can't be helped." Emon snorted and tossed his head, stepping back to put space between them. "She's made it clear she doesn't care about the family. I've got to protect those who do. She works for you, so I understand why you need to say something, but your loyalty's misplaced. One day, you'll see just how fickle she can be," he said quietly. "She'll betray you like she has us, and if you aren't careful, she'll take whatever you give and rip it out from right under you. She's clever, calculated, and very much on her own side. But I'm me: constant, smart, always in control. Take me as your husband and the Derossas won't be any trouble ever again, I'll make sure of it. Take Ryler and you'll be cleaning up his mistakes until you die."

Caught between gagging and snorting, Aeley gritted her teeth. *Don't get me started. Here you are asking for my help and insulting me all at the same time. Maybe Ryler really is the smarter of you two. At this rate, I'd rather marry Mayr.* She kept moving, trying not to meet the gazes of the onlookers. Was this how marriage with Emon would be?

No matter how much she wanted to tear into him, she had to keep control. *Can't do anything I'll regret. Just pretend I care. Let him show me who he really is. Wouldn't want him causing trouble.*

Yet that rubbish about Lira…

Lies. Nothing but lies.

"So what comes after this?"

Aeley blinked at Emon's question. His expression was lax, his touch gentle, as if he had said nothing before then. "After what?" *If you say anything about a bed, I will kick you in the—*

"After this ball. It's certainly a successful event, and worthy of our first public outing, but where does it go after this? Riding, perhaps? Or maybe something closer to home—sparring?"

She almost laughed. "You? Spar? And here I thought you were a man of commerce, not at all interested in anything more dangerous than a quill."

"Flattering as *that* is," Emon replied with a smirk, "I *do* know the pointed end from the blunt. Father ensured we both knew how to, even though I was the one who excelled. I was taught by the best swordsmen he could hire, no expense spared. I can duel with the best of them—and live."

"I don't know if you could keep up." *Considering my teachers included a couple of the highest-ranking officers in the army and not fancy dancing men.* "Maybe we'll put it to the test one day."

"Tomorrow?"

I'm damn well hiding tomorrow. "Sadly, no... I have responsibilities to attend to. I'll give it some thought and send for you. Maybe we can make a day of it, with something else other than waving weapons at one another. Can't have you ruining perfectly lovely clothing," she said, fingering the sleeve of his coat.

"You have a point there. I go through enough as is."

"Yes, well..." Aeley stopped, stuck on what to say next.

The moment the music stopped, she knew her next move.

"I'd love to keep dancing, but I have to get some air." Aeley pushed Emon away with a gentle hand.

Emon gave her a once-over, his eyes narrowed. "You're not running away, are you? You said you'd give us a fair chance tonight."

"I know I did. And I'm not running. I just need to take a break."

"Then you owe Ryler a dance, don't you?"

"Yes," Aeley said, unable to fight the sigh that slipped out. "I've only danced with him three times. You, five. I owe him as much time. But you'll see me again later." *Unless someone knocks me out or puts you out of my misery.*

She walked through the ballroom, trying hard not to rush or look desperate to escape upstairs and slam a few doors. Once she squeezed through the crowd and onto the balcony, a breath of relief took over, the suffocating sensation of being stuck in a glass box without anywhere to hide slowly fading into the darkness. Vines climbed up the wall of the house and down the balcony steps, the thick ends wound around the bronze statues of the four Goddesses at the bottom of the stairs. Beyond them, the garden slept under long shadows, save for where moonlight touched the earth. Even in the dark, she noticed the muted shades of the blood-red and bright orange tree leaves, while the white and blue flowers withered. When the night air rushed over her with a faint bite, she rubbed her bare arms and willed herself to stop shivering.

"Tired of them yet?"

Aeley jumped before spinning around to face Lira.

She may as well have hit the floor with all the breath she lost in that single glimpse.

Gone was Lira's modest appearance, replaced by a fine black gown with a neckline that sat just above her breasts, much of what she normally hid on display. Thick black ribbons were tied around her waist, similar to the narrow black ribbons around her elbows where the three tiers of delicate, gauzy black cuffs started. Even her hair was up and fastened with thin strands of white metal, barely hiding her neck, despite the few curls that escaped and brushed her naked shoulders.

Too many responses rolled through Aeley's mind, most of them inappropriate. Certainly the fantasies that accompanied them were best kept to herself. Holding her waist and willing herself to breathe, Aeley leaned against the balcony rail. "How do you put up with them?"

"I avoid them," Lira replied, moving to stand beside Aeley. She leaned forward, with her elbows on the railing. "Being a scribe helps. It gives me a reason to get away from them. Vant gets me what work he can, and I stay in the villages sometimes when it becomes too much." She shook her head, another curl slipping from the metal strands. "Our family is all deals, trade, and politics. It wasn't always like this, though. My grandfather would kill my father for what he's done." She looked at Aeley, the dark paint around her eyes making them all the sadder. "It's why I loved your father. He gave me the chance to do what *I* wanted, despite the Derossa name. Despite how much my father wanted revenge. I don't want to rely on my family's wealth and power, so Klyrin and Korre agreed I could train as scribe."

"And now you're here."

"Yes."

"And that makes you happy?"

"You have no idea," Lira whispered, wringing her fingers. "I wanted this. I like you."

Aeley blinked, trying to think of something to say. *Anything*. On one hand, it sounded like a friend to another friend. On the other hand…

Before she could respond, Lira cleared her throat. "Are you regretting your decision yet?"

"What?"

"Agreeing to consider this whole marriage thing. Do you think it's worth putting up with them?"

Forget them—I'm still stuck on the other thing. "I don't know," Aeley said.

"I'm still a little surprised that you agreed."

"I guarantee you that I'm even more surprised."

"So, why?"

Aeley laughed, all the while battling the temptation to brush away the rogue curls playing around Lira's shoulders, and maybe do some of her own brushing along her skin, just to see... "You sound like Mayr. He's still asking me that. Though I guess it's the price."

"For what?"

"For not wanting to lose everything. For not wanting to be alone." Clearing her throat, Aeley tore her gaze from Lira's softly lit face and stared at the bushes below. "Being Steward is lonely. We live to serve, and we have to make some tough decisions, always reminded that the people put us here and they could petition to take us out if we fail them."

Memories took over Aeley's thoughts. "I watched my father my whole life, and while I thought he was the strongest man I knew, he did everything alone. He never took another wife after my mother died, though there have been times where I think he should've. I don't want that life. I don't want to be alone forever, even if it means putting up with a husband I can't stand."

"Even when they're in love with themselves?" Lira asked, leaning close to Aeley. A waft of her sweet perfume caught Aeley's focus, fruity and fragrant like an orchard in the height of summer. Aeley could have rolled around in it and died happy so long as Lira was there, tumbling around with her.

Aeley cleared her throat and shifted her feet, her damned bodice annoying her to no end. "If my father hadn't already made a deal with your family, I wouldn't have approached them. But he did and now I have to see it through. It doesn't mean I get to be happy. Duty's always been more important. Besides, if it weren't them, it'd be someone else who was important. It doesn't make it any easier."

Lira nodded. "I doubt they'll make anyone truly happy. Out of all the choices and it had to be them," she muttered.

"It could be any one of the available men and I still wouldn't be happy about it." The words tumbled from Aeley's lips before she could stop herself. "It isn't just your brothers being themselves, it's the whole concept of giving myself over to a guy, especially one I don't care for. I have no interest in sleeping with them, or procreating. And it isn't because I don't know how—I know *how*. I've slept with guys before; I just don't care for it." She snorted. "Goddesses know I snuck out that first time anyway, then every time after, nearly getting caught and hating how disenchanted I was come morning. I didn't enjoy it in the least, not with any of the few encounters I've tried. I told myself it'd get better even though it only ever got worse. I know Father wanted me to find someone nice, but his idea of nice isn't the same as mine."

"Is it the same reason why you and Mayr aren't together?"

"Mostly," Aeley replied. "That and he's my best friend. We never wanted to ruin it." She tilted her head back to stare at the stars and let out a sigh. "If only it weren't your brothers. If only it was y—"

She could not have closed her mouth any faster.

Oh, no. No, no. Bad idea. Very bad idea.

She had said too much already, but damn it all, it never failed to keep happening whenever they were together. Rarely did she tell anyone her most private thoughts, and when she did, she trusted only Mayr and Pellon. Even then, she preferred to keep her deepest thoughts to herself, protecting them as if they were precious, easily shattered and stomped all over. Why did she keep exposing those secrets when she was with Lira? It would only lead to humiliation and heartbreak and—

"What were you saying?" Lira asked softly, her eyes searching Aeley's. Curious. Interested.

Dangerous. So dangerous.

"Nothing. Never mind. I was rambling."

"Or telling the truth."

When Aeley turned towards her, Lira stepped closer—much closer, enough to touch, to feel, to want much more than standing on a balcony together, surrounded by people she never wanted to see. Just Lira and her, in the quiet, with no one else around and nothing more to do than just breathe, her heart thumping itself gleefully out of her chest.

As Lira leaned in, their chests pressed together. Beneath the simple gold pendant around Lira's neck, her chest rose and fell gently, the sight doing nothing to tame Aeley's hopes.

"Imagine you could tell me everything, without worrying about what I'd think," Lira murmured, the heat of her breath playing over Aeley's lips. "Maybe this is exactly the change you wanted. Maybe you just need more time to put everything together. Or maybe you just need all the pieces."

Before Aeley could speak, Lira's lips touched hers, coaxing a soft kiss from her with a tender push and tug. Slow, drawn out, without a care in the world.

Thoughts... she had them... somewhere, reeling.

But this—

Aeley raised her hand to the balcony to keep steady, barely registering that her fingers only made it halfway before stopping in the air. And the silence… was it in her head or had the music stopped?

By the time Aeley realized what was happening, Lira's lips left hers.

They parted with such a bittersweet chill, Aeley's hopes whimpered at the loss. She had just started to kiss Lira back, intending to take it deeper, in the search for more, and now —

"Something for you to think about," Lira whispered. Without waiting for a reply, she headed for the ballroom.

She paused in the doorway and looked back, the light from the room casting a lovely pale glow over her. Her lips showed the hint of a smile, but the gleam in her eyes said everything.

Then, Lira turned and escaped into the crowd.

Sucking in a breath, Aeley backed against the railing. For being just a kiss, she felt weak, wrung out and hanging from a line, blowing in the wind. Drawing her fingers across her lips, she savoured the memory of their touch. There was an invitation in it, a challenge. Another option.

Chapter Nine

Aeley stared at the door of the study, her stomach flipping. Lira's message said they would meet at midday, but it was well past that. Where was she?

Two days later and here I am, practically jumping out of my skin. Keep it together.

Except keeping it together was a complete waste in the quiet moments. Being alone was one thing she abhorred. Since the ball, sleeping was even more difficult, taunted by the memory of Lira kissing her. Ten years had passed since Aeley had last been kissed, the difference being that this time she wanted everything else that could come with it. There were too many things she wanted to be true; too many hopes ignited, not just by Lira's lips, but in how she drew honest answers from Aeley, and in how she listened, taking it all in.

What she told Lira about not wanting to be alone had been the truth. It was also the first time she had said it out loud, always worried she would lose something if she admitted it—that her strength would be ripped away, leaving her with only weakness. She had spent her life acting strong, as though she had everything under control, even when she was sinking in her choices.

Lira inspired her to break through the illusion Aeley had enforced. Did Lira realize that? Did she have any idea of the effect she had? Could she even begin to understand what a difference she made?

There was so much to say, so much to do. Aeley had indicated nothing of what she wanted in her message to Lira, but there was no point. *She's smart. She knows. She'd be expecting it.*

Unable to focus, Aeley threw her black quill across the study, aiming for the door. It stopped short and hit the floor, no doubt staining it with loose drops of ink. She tapped her desk rhythmically, then her feet, and glanced around the room.

There was no use in waiting alone anymore, especially if her father's portrait was only going to taunt her worse than her own nerves did.

Aeley pushed aside the parchment in front of her, the page destroyed with nonsense images she had scribbled, and left the room to wander the corridors, smiling at the staff as they bustled along with their chores. For a moment, she considered searching for Mayr, but his teasing at breakfast was enough for one day.

When she stepped into the hall that led to the main staircase, a door opening and closing sounded from down the hall, followed by Haydin's voice and a woman's light laugh.

Finally.

Aeley rushed to the end of the corridor, past the guards on duty in the hallway, but slowed as she neared the foyer. As she crossed the threshold, her gaze found Lira without hesitation. And there her heart went, tripping all over itself again.

Lira dipped her head and removed her thin white cloak. Her face was flushed as though she had run, and her tousled hair was unbound, no combs to be seen. "Sorry. I was caught up in things."

With a nod, Haydin left them in the entrance hall and disappeared up the stairs. Given his emotionless expression, Aeley suspected he knew nothing of what was going on between them. Maybe. Hopefully. Or maybe he knew and was simply allowing her to keep a secret to herself.

Now what? Aeley turned her attention back to Lira. She had thought the letter through and chosen her words carefully, but nothing else. Whatever she might have wanted to say was gone, her mind blank. Staring at Lira, she waited for the words to come.

"That bad?" Lira grinned and stepped into the hallway Aeley had just come through, her cloak draped over her arms. The skirt of her pale green dress swept back and forth, its hem just touching the floor, bright purple ribbons trailing down the back from where they were tied around her waist in a bow. Pretty as it was, nothing could do away with the shock of Lira in her black gown.

"Yeah," Aeley replied, her mouth dry. She followed Lira back into the hallway, daring to walk next to her, close enough for their arms to brush every few steps.

"Questions?"

Aeley hesitated before answering. "Many." It took all the restraint she had to keep from asking them all at once.

"Ask one and let's go from there."

Easier said than done. "You were serious, right?" Aeley asked, expecting Lira to laugh.

"I was. I am," Lira murmured. "I just figured it would get the message across better than rambling."

"Well, it definitely worked."

Lira stopped. She pressed the back of her hand to Aeley's black leather bodice, just beneath where it started under Aeley's chest, over her white tunic. "I shouldn't have, should I? I should've just... I thought I noticed you noticing me." A faint blush spread across her cheeks. "I thought maybe when you said you weren't interested in them, you were indicating something else. But I made a mess of it, didn't I?"

"No. I mean yes. Wait, no." Aeley cast a look to the ceiling and sighed out her frustration. "*Yes*, I noticed you. *No*, you didn't make a mess of it. I'm just surprised. How long—"

"Long enough." Lira fussed with her hair, brushing it back and tucking unruly strands behind her ear. "With your father constantly going on about you, and then seeing you… it just sort of happened. I didn't think I should say anything. Then there was the Council meeting and it changed everything. But when we talked the other night, you said you didn't enjoy men as much and, well, I figured my chance was then." She bit her lip and looked away. "I'm used to doing what I have to do right away, no waiting. Whenever I wait, I lose. I've never been good at competing, not against my brothers."

I don't doubt it. They'll fight to win.

"So if I didn't scare you off, what happens now?" Lira asked quietly.

Aeley glanced at the narrow corridor to their left. The hallway was partially shrouded in darkness, ending in stairs that led to the lower floor. It was a perfect hiding spot, rarely accessed except in times of detaining a lawbreaker or pulling food from the cellars in the winter.

No point in dragging this out when it's obvious.

Ignoring Lira's confusion, she grabbed Lira's hand and led her into the darkness, stopping before they reached the stairs.

"What are you—"

"This." Aeley backed Lira against the wall and leaned in, one flattened palm pressed to the cool stone above Lira's shoulder as she held onto Lira's waist with the other hand, Lira's arms and cloak pinned between them. Another small step forward, the slip of her knee between both of Lira's, and she was close, so close, enough to kiss the lips that had teased hers and left her pining for more. Close enough to taste the sweetness that lingered on Lira's neck, in her hair, with that quiet call to a calm summer's day when everything was at peace, at the ready for exploration, all warmth, light, and anticipation.

They traded heated breaths in the shadows, Lira's lips haunting hers in an almost-kiss but never touching. Just that constant play of time, waiting, daring Aeley to make the next move...

Fast, hard, she pressed her lips to Lira's, every intention stripped down, bared, not willing to play cute any longer.

Lira sighed into the kiss, taking it deeper, one of her knees shifting to guide Aeley's leg closer and bring their hips together. Aeley went with it, not in any mind to argue or turn back, not as lust tossed around images in her mind, ones she ached to make real. The thought of Lira naked on top of her, riding her thigh, wet and ready and coming...

"We should finish what you started," Aeley murmured before gently biting at Lira's bottom lip, tugging, teasing. She had a perfectly good bed waiting and not a lick of care for duty, not unless the commands came from Lira—then she would serve to the very ends of her ability, on both knees.

Forget business. She was taking the day off.

As she kissed Lira again, her fingers glided down Lira's spine, all to settle in the small of her back, circling once, twice—

Lira moaned and pressed harder against Aeley, grinding into Aeley's touch. Fingertips crept up Aeley's waist, then slid over the belt with her knife, down the thick fabric of her pants, and slipped just beneath her bodice, the tender touch making its way upward over Aeley's stomach.

"Off," Lira muttered against her lips. "This needs... off."

Laughing softly, Aeley kissed her a third time, her tongue playing over Lira's. With her fingers still in the small of Lira's back, she drew out another moan, a deeper grind. The rub of Lira against her thigh, her chest, her waist... and heat, such a perfect heat between them, their breaths shallow, shared, needing much more than a coarse wall in a public corridor. Her dreams had never felt this good, no matter how blissful they were.

"Upstairs," she whispered. Drawing her hand through Lira's hair, she tugged lightly on the loose curls, loving the softness to the thick strands wrapped around her fingers.

Lira's sharp breath answered, accompanied by the tilt back of her head against the wall. Holding Lira's head in her hands, guiding the tilt further and caressing the back of Lira's neck, Aeley trailed kisses down her throat, over her collarbone, and along the neckline of Lira's dress, the thin fabric teasing her lips. The slow crawl of Lira's touch moved up Aeley's chest, over one hardened nipple, her fingertips playing lightly, unrelenting as Aeley moaned quietly and shivered.

Yeah, bed. They needed a bed—

"Aeley! *Aeley!*"

Aeley stopped, her lips still on Lira's. She sucked in a breath and waited. Boots pounded the floor in the hallway.

Haydin was on the hunt for her.

Please don't yell for me again. Please don't—

"Aeley! Where are you?" Haydin called.

Aeley grunted and rested both hands against the wall on either side of Lira, then leaned into her, their foreheads pressed together.

"Go on," Lira whispered. "It sounds urgent. We can do this later."

"Fine," Aeley grumbled. She rocked on her heel before kissing Lira again, just for a moment longer, needing to sink deeper into her...

"Aeley!" Haydin sounded further away.

"*By the Four,*" Aeley bit out. She rushed into the hallway. "I'm here."

Haydin appeared from around the corner at the end of the hall. He ambled back up the hallway towards her, panic splashed across his face, one hand pressed to his back as he drew close with a faint limp. "Thank the Goddesses—

you're needed!" He pointed towards the entrance hall.

"I'm here now. We'll go together." Aeley ushered him ahead, wary of his hobble. As Lira stepped out of the dark corridor, Aeley mouthed her apology and rushed after Haydin.

The messenger, a young man no older than sixteen, stood in the foyer, rolling his wide-brimmed hat between his hands. He gaped as Aeley approached him, then bowed and straightened awkwardly.

"Go on," Aeley said.

"There's been a problem between our village and the next, Steward," he said, hesitating as though trying to decide how much to say. "An attack on the road, with casualties. Dreca sent me to fetch you. He needs to talk to you about it right away, but he can't leave."

"All right."

"He says as Tract Steward, you *have* to be there," he insisted.

"I know, and I said I would. I just need a few moments to get the guards together." Aeley drew one hand across her belt to the hilt of her knife. "We'll take horses to get there faster. You go and we'll follow."

He pulled on his cap and nodded, then ran out the door and down the stairs to the horse waiting in the carriage circle. One of the Dahe guards was already there, standing beside the horse with the reins in one hand and their other hand on the horse's mane.

Of course. Just when something good happens, it all goes again.

Spinning on her heel, Aeley peered past Haydin. Several steps behind him, Lira waited in the middle of the hall. She intended to tell Lira to stay, so they could continue their conversation afterwards...

And yet, "Coming?" was all that came out of her mouth.

She did not have to ask twice.

Blood dried around the wound in the man's head, his face turned towards the long stretch of red dirt road.

Aeley pressed her fingers to his neck and stared at the overturned cart not far from where she crouched. The cart's contents had been destroyed, left scattered around it in clumps and shreds, as lost and ragged as the boy standing on the side of the road, his traveling clothes torn under a layer of dust. When his gaze caught hers, she turned away. There was no point in telling him his father was dead. He already knew.

Drawing away from the corpse, she flicked a hand at two of the six guards with her. "Take him to the estate and fetch one of the healers. They'll see to it everything is handled."

As the guards carried the body to the wagon they had brought, Aeley returned to the ditch where Dreca and Lira waited with the boy: Hano, only twelve years old. He was also from the Alosaa tract, making him her responsibility and hers alone.

If only she could look him in the eye for longer than a moment.

The grief he displayed openly reminded her of losing her father, of watching him slip away to something she could not scare off or fight. Hano had witnessed his father's death, and those images would haunt him for the rest of his life. Nothing she could say would take that away or resurrect the dead. She could not fix it. The best she could do for Hano was keep him safe and find the people responsible. In some ways, she felt as powerless as he did.

Aeley stopped before Hano and hunched forward, hands on her knees, her eyes leveled with his. "Hano, I know you've told Dreca what happened, but now I need you to tell me. I know it's not easy. I know it hurts to talk about it. But it's important that I know everything just as you saw it. We only want to help you." She gave him a small smile as Dreca squeezed Hano's shoulder in encouragement.

Hano hesitated, twisting a worn cap in his hands. "We were riding through, going home," he mumbled. "Da thought cutting through here would be faster. Safer." He looked to the ground, his hands still. "We've done it before. Nothing ever happened, not ever."

Lira wrapped her arm around his shoulders and leaned into him, whispering in his ear.

Hano nodded and wiped his face with the back of his hand. "We were just talking and laughing and then he saw the empty cart in middle of the road and we stopped. We couldn't go around it—it took up the whole thing. There was no one in it and the horse had run off. It wouldn't move itself, so Da got out to do something about it. Told me to stay where I was."

He raised his head, his widened eyes darkened with fear. "That's when they jumped out at him. Hiding in the cart under blankets. Hiding behind the trees. They weren't there and then suddenly, they were."

"Who? How many?" Aeley asked.

"I don't know. Just… people. Men, I guess, all in dark clothes, black cloaks. Maybe five. Six. I don't know. I couldn't see their faces and it was too fast to count," Hano muttered, lowering his head again. "I couldn't really see anything at all. I was too…"

And there it is: the guilt. The burden that shouldn't be his to bear. Aeley hugged him close. "We understand. Your father would understand. It isn't your fault." She eased him back and squeezed his other shoulder. "We'll focus on something else. What did these people do? They ambushed your father, then what?"

"They called him names. Made fun of him. Then they hit him." Hano sniffled and continued. "But I don't know what else. They started coming for me, and then the next thing I know, the horse was unhitched and our cart was tipping. They were laughing. I jumped out and ran. I thought they'd follow me, but they didn't. They just yelled and laughed, and I heard my father yell at me to just keep running. He didn't want me to stop," he murmured, wiping his face.

Dreca moved closer to Hano. "And then you found me, and we came out here together." He glanced angrily at Aeley, as if she was the one responsible for dealing Hano the hurt he was trying so hard to fight. "And then I sent for you. Now we have to do something about it—and that's *your* job."

I can't do much without knowing more, Aeley wanted to argue, *and I can't get what I need without talking to him. Stop looking at me like I'm doing something wrong.*

"Hano, think very carefully," Aeley said. "Did you hear anything, like a name? Or notice if any of these people had something particular about them, like a funny voice, a certain kind of movement, anything?" When Hano shook his head, Aeley held back a sigh and considered her options. There was not much to work with, but for his sake, she could not tell him that. She had only flimsy thoughts scrambling over each other to work themselves into a theory she could stop poking holes in.

Aeley motioned to Dreca and led him to the overturned cart, well away from other ears, both of them glancing at Hano as they spoke.

"I'll do what I can, but there isn't much here." Aeley flicked her wrist towards the road. "He can't think of anything specific. He didn't see their faces. The other cart's gone. Horse is gone. There's *nothing* that says who did this. All we know is some group thought it was fun to attack an innocent man and his son."

"And they killed him."

"Yes, and for all we know, his death could've been an accident. They could've been aiming to injure but not murder. Something struck his head, but we don't know what or why. It could've just as easily been a robbery gone wrong—"

"Hano swears everything's still here, just smashed up," Dreca corrected. "Can't be a robbery if they left with nothing."

"True," Aeley muttered, "but we still don't have enough particulars to run with. It's not the first time this sort of thing has happened—you know it comes and goes just as easily as the highwaymen do. And Goddesses know the Shardenn and the lesser gangs love random and unusual. It wouldn't surprise me if it was them, considering how quiet they've all been since before Father died. They could've finally gotten bored enough to start acting up again."

She paused, her gaze on Hano as Lira hugged him while he cried on her shoulder. His tears would flow for a while yet, though she wished she could tear into the past and get him the answer as to why, or at least who, had brought that heartbreak onto him. "We'll put the gangs on the suspect list, and I'm not ruling out unaffiliated highwaymen," she continued, "but it could be something else altogether, someone not organized under any specific banner, just a group hitting out because they've got nothing better to do. But no matter who did this, we need more to go on. *I* need more to go on. I'll happily arrest them, but we have to find them first."

Aeley sighed, her attention back on Dreca. "I'll make sure Hano gets to where he's supposed to be—he can't stay here, not like this, and certainly not anywhere *near* this. I'll take him back to his mother and explain everything to her. While I'm there, I'll apologize to Steward Oaren and make sure he knows we'll do something about it." She picked at the cart, giving a frown at the worn wood. "In the meantime, see if you can't find something we can use. Maybe you'll have more luck, being magistrate. Perhaps one of the other magistrates knows something. I wouldn't mind better news."

As she walked away, she caught the snark in how Dreca uttered her father's name, followed by a rant of underhanded grumbling too incoherent to make out.

Coherent or not, she still imagined the rest of the complaint, finishing it in silence. Part of her wanted to spin him around and dare him to say it to her face; the other part told her to keep walking. Her father could have done no better. No comparison would change the fact that a man was dead, a family was ruined, and she was the one who had to make sense of it. If she had to keep proving herself, she would.

Chapter Ten

She'd had it with politicians. Every last one.

Aeley stared Kayte Oaren down, as unwavering as the glare his emerald-green eyes pinned on her. Hano had finally been reunited with his mother, Vilde, both of them lost to grief as Kayte's wife, Rosayra, led them to a private sitting room to find some measure of comfort. Meanwhile, household staff prepared them a bedroom for the evening in the Oaren estate. Both Kayte and Rosayra had insisted Hano and Vilde stay with them rather than returning home several towns over, delaying the shock of stepping into a house now frighteningly full of memory neither could confront yet. To everyone's relief, Vilde had agreed, her arms tight around her son as though she were a moment's breath from losing him, too.

For their sakes, Aeley prayed Hano and Vilde could get at least a bit of dinner down and some version of rest, even though the newly fallen night brought its own challenges. It had taken a day and a half to ride from Dahena to Oarenhale, with a brief stop at the Gailarin-Alosaa border for rest and a warm meal. Hano slept for most of the trip, exhausted and curled up under several layers of blankets in the closed carriage they had brought just for him. Stuck and Aeley had sat with him, keeping a watchful eye from inside the carriage while Mayr and Stick had sat on the driver's box, guiding the four-horse team.

The rest of their entourage consisted of four other armed guards on horseback, which seemed to have given Hano the confidence to close his eyes and trust they would keep him safe. The fact he had kept eyeing their weapons had not escaped Aeley, though nothing came from it. Just that constant stare, that clouded expression— blank, tearstained, searching.

Kayte, however, was not searching, not with the look on his stern face. *He* was more interested in using weapons as they were meant to be used. Right then, though, he was dragging Aeley through the proverbial fire with just as much efficiency.

"So you have nothing at all," he reiterated for the third time, his words drawn out, deep and annoyed.

Aeley's few months of being in charge of Gailarin paled miserably in comparison to Kayte's ten years as Tract Steward of Alosaa. Standing before him without anyone but Mayr did nothing to ease the tension, not without her father there to speak on the same level of experience. Korre and Kayte had understood each other perfectly, their propensity for governance and policy well matched, even with Korre old enough to be Kayte's father. Korre's softer, pensive manner had balanced Kayte's harder, highly intelligent approach, their methods and strategies blended to benefit both tracts.

Aeley and Kayte understood each other in a different way: as fighters, quick to defend, likely to offend. Two fires from different sides of a thin line never meant to be crossed without armour, a cool head, and a tub of ice for the loser to recover in. Both had been raised to respect a blade and use it wisely, but Kayte's experience had no patience for Aeley's lack. Not yet. Not with something as serious as innocents being killed on the road, apparently for no reason at all.

Which apparently was her fault, according to Kayte's look.

"We have the testimony of a child, that's it," Aeley said, straightening her back to relieve the tightness in her shoulders. "Though I have people working on getting more. It's anybody's guess, honestly."

Kayte snorted and brushed back the thick braids of his black-blond hair, the beaded ends hanging to his chest, bringing a touch of muted colour to his charcoal-grey tunic. He moved away from the furthest black-framed window, one of many in the spacious meeting room that gave a dark, distant view of the lights and ships on the

Sese Channel. "I'll give you three guesses, and the first two are the only ones that count."

He crossed the room, his footfalls almost silent on the rich teal floor, and scowled as he sat on the edge of the long, heavy table not far from Aeley. "I told your father to do something about those damn gangs," Kayte muttered, scratching at his finely trimmed beard, his dark brown skin almost black in the flickering dance between candlelight and shadows. "Told him to get his bloody damn gumption together and chase them off, even if it meant shucking his pride and coming to me. He could've even begged Severn to spare a good chunk of military instead of just mucking through with a few measly agents." Kayte cast Aeley another glare. "Apparently he hid behind another one of his damned bloody walls of *not listening*. Like father, like daughter, hmm?"

Aeley gritted her teeth, her fists clenched at her hips. "No, just haven't gotten around to it yet. And if he didn't see the need, I trust that."

"Open your damned eyes, Dahe!" Kayte thrust his hand towards the windows, green eyes flashing as he shouted. "That's trust out there, dying on the road, leaving kids without parents. Let's try 'haven't gotten around to it yet' on that kid, yeah? See how well it goes down. Guaranteed to hurt as much as seeing his mother curling into a ball night after night, weeping the time away. Or are you going to save that for when their funds are dwindling—maybe midwinter when they're at their lowest point?"

"Hey, Oaren, not fair," Mayr said, stepping closer to Aeley, slightly in front of her, his body angled towards Kayte. "Calm it. She's just being honest."

Kayte raised his hand to silence Mayr. Thick gold bracelets slid down his forearm, clinking against each other, their simple design echoed by a dozen gold hoops and glossy pearls in his ears. "Not doubting her honesty, just her commitment. She might be new to this, but she's not *that* new. She knows this. She's sat in on the meetings before. She knows the score, don't you, Dahe? And that's what makes this all so sad—that for a trained fighter, you sure as the day is long are sitting on your ass, hiding behind your father. If you aren't out there taming the brutes, what good's all that training that's wasting away?"

Before Aeley could answer, trying hard to keep her tongue without biting it off, Kayte stormed towards her, his extra height, muscle, and strength all reminders that she had nothing to scare him with. Not a single thing. He kept a clean record with honesty and sincerity, played by the rules even when he was trying to change them, and his people loved him. She had... throwing Allon in prison.

"If your next words aren't *I'm going home and hunting them down like the bastards they are*, I don't want to hear it," Kayte snarled, a foot of distance between them. A waft of musk and spice played by Aeley's face as he raised a pointed finger to her. "Your problems become our problems. Same goes with the other tracts. None of us are in isolation, so fix your problems before we have to step in and handle them ourselves."

Kayte stepped back, his gaze traveling over her. "You're not a kid, Dahe. No one's coddling you. No one's stopping you, either, so don't go running the excuses." His finger returned to her face, his fingertip a breath away. "Get it sorted. Stop pretending you're something you're not and get it done. Otherwise what's the bloody point? Or is your brother going to be your only legacy? Finally cleaning up the rubbish but only so far as your own front door? Protecting that sheltered life, too afraid to get your hands dirty."

A hot flush seared across Aeley's face. "You think intimidation's going to drag up details suddenly? That treating me like a child is going to get results? Because I'll tell you right now, that's not how it works." She tightened her grip on the hilt of the sword strapped to her waist. "I can't reach into that kid's head and grab whatever I damn well want, Oaren, and you bloody well know it. As for the gangs—I didn't have time to sort that mess when I was too busy chasing after what I was told to do. I *still* haven't had the time, not with sorting the mess I was left. And yeah, that includes a brother I'd see in prison for life, *starting with my own front door*. Can't clean up anyone else's messes when I can't get my own straightened out."

She stepped up to Kayte, closing the space between them. "If the Shar-denn's responsible for this—if *any* of the gangs are responsible for it—I'll see to it they're punished. But I'm not running headlong into their filthy holes without some kind of plan. Proof. Protection. None of it will help Hano if they didn't do a damn thing to his father."

"You're still not getting it." Kayte snorted and backed away, shaking his head. "You can't just focus on one case at a time, kid. You can't close your eyes to the bigger picture. Change the life of one, fine, you'll feel good about it. Change the life of many and you'll be able to keep your tract under control. You don't have time to dawdle— for Goddesses' sake, Dahe, they attacked close enough to practically throw stones at your damn windows! What else are they willing to try, and even closer to home? Gang or not, that's someone about to get comfortable, and it's a real good start to something insidious. I've seen it before—fix it now before it gets worse, and don't hide behind pity. It won't help anyone."

Kayte was out the door before Aeley could think of a worthy retort.

"Bastard," Aeley seethed, biting down hard.

She needed to hit something. Repeatedly.

"He's testing you, Ae." Mayr clasped her arm and pulled her close. "He's pushing to get results, and he's hurting for that kid. You know it, he knows it—we all know it. He's lost people, too. Just keep it together, yeah?"

"So you agree with him, then?" Aeley snapped.

Mayr scowled. "I didn't say that, and don't go biting my fingers off. I'm just trying to keep you from doing something that'll get you kicked out. *Permanently.*"

Oh, she had no intention of getting kicked out, not yet. But finding something to beat the stuffing out of sounded like the perfect medicine.

Once to the left, two to the right—or so the last guard had said after Aeley asked about the closest training room.

She followed the instructions, walking down the centre of the brightly lit hallways. The walls were dark beige in the torchlight, their soft earthy tone joined by charcoal-grey stone, all of it contrasted with a cream-coloured floor broken up by slivers of reds, golds, teals, and greens arranged in various shapes: flowers, ships, webs, and designs without a discernable form. Like in the rest of the Oaren estate, the corridors were wide, allowing for plenty of space to move without feeling closed in.

Though unlike at the Dahe estate where the training rooms were underground, the room she had been directed to was on the main level, and when she stepped inside, she was met with the same spaciousness as other rooms. A long run of large windows on the opposite wall gave a beautiful view of lantern-lit gardens and one of the exquisite full-glass warm houses where plants were kept in the colder months. The dark waters of the Channel stayed quiet along the horizon, the closest lighthouse a bright white tower in the night, its fire casting a warm glow on the port and the dozen ships moored to the expansive docks. All of the windows were open, allowing the cool touch of the late-summer to enter, filling the room with a beckoning breath and the rustle of trees. The jingle of several wind chimes trickled through, joined by faint, airy whistles from the garden.

Breathing in the scent of sea and coming autumn, Aeley crossed the room to one of the weapons racks. There were several racks and options, not that she expected less: the Oaren family had been soldiers for countless generations. While Kayte was known for his prowess with weapons and strategy, the skill displayed by both of his sisters was nothing to discount. Aeley had watched the three of them compete the year before Kayte became Tract Steward, her focus clinging to the way they moved with confidence and proficiency, the memory still weighted with all the awe she could muster at sixteen. Their ability had inspired her, forcing her to work harder, train better.

Now... Aeley caressed one staff, taking comfort in the familiarity of the hard wood and coarse grain. She needed to work hard now, but not to train—to dispel the anger, its clawing grip threatening to take more of her down with it, fast and with relentless fury.

Taking the staff in hand, Aeley backed away to the colourful training circles in the centre of the room and twisted her arm this way and that, the heavy staff following the motion. She needed its consistency, its predictability. Its lack of judgment.

Judgment. She was surrounded by it. Every turn, every corner, every gaze. It followed her like an unforgiving shadow, cold in how lightly it touched without leaving a visible stain but crushing her under its enormous weight.

Aeley spun the staff in both hands, irritation whirling with it.

Kayte had all but accused her of not caring—as if she saw the loss of life and innocence as something not worth doing anything about. As if she were cold and unfeeling, with nothing to worry about.

And damn him for that, because he couldn't be any more wrong.

She *did* care. She had all the sympathy and empathy in the world for Hano, and she felt damn sorry for his mother, because Vilde was the one left to shoulder the familial responsibilities. While Aeley had lost her mother as a young child, she knew how hard it was for Korre as a widow and single parent. Then, after losing him...

She felt for them, deeply, the sorrow as fresh for them as it was for her when her father had taken his last breath, that awful rattle still stuck in her thoughts.

And then—*then*—for Mayr to go and defend Kayte. To *agree*—

"Ha!" Aeley thrust the staff downwards, fists tight around the shaft.

No one thought she could do the job.

Not even her best friend.

Turning on her heel, Aeley surged through strike after controlled strike, throwing her shoulder and back into the movements, working every muscle that screamed foul at the tension keeping them in a constant ache.

It was all colliding into a perfect storm: the judgment, the doubt, the lack of faith. Her shoulders were breaking from the strain, her thoughts rambling on chaos, pressed between thick sheets of criticism and condescension.

People honestly thought she did not care. That she would fail to fix it if she could. That she had avoided thinking about what she could do to find the people responsible for killing Hano's father. Did Kayte truly think she was so cold she had *not* run through all of the crime numbers, gang-related incidents, and every bit of news she remembered in the last few months?

"I can't do anything with information I don't have," Aeley spat out, jamming the end of the staff to the floor, satisfied with the loud *crack*. "I can't just wave my hand and make things appear. I can't read his mind. *Magic. Isn't. Real.* You bloody infuriating bastard from the pits of *I don't really give a filthy rotten damn!*"

The punching bag by the window took all of her rage. The staff struck as hard as she hit out with it, the bag swaying from the beating.

Pounding. Just pounding, clobbering away, all the force she had driving harder and taking her scream with it.

"*No one. Believes. I can do this,*" she shouted, assaulting the brown leather bag with every word. The bag swung faster, its chain rattling. The staff thudded and vibrated and scraped her hands with the thrashing, rubbing skin raw, rage biting back.

She was done. Between Dreca's comments and the Council and her father's devious wishes and now Kayte—

She. Was. Done.

Enough that beating the life out of a punching bag would only resolve her anger for the night. Tomorrow it would be right back to it, everything piling on and adding up.

So much rage. Not enough release. No balance whatsoever—

"*Hey! Dahe!*"

Aeley spun around, the husky voice just another one to shout back at.

Rosayra, Kayte's wife and Head of the Oaren Guard, stood by a table by the furthest wall, peeling off her blue leather long coat marked with the Oaren family crest, the hue almost a match to the rich blue of her pants. "You want a real challenge, challenge me." Rosayra pulled a cord from inside one of her brown knee-high boots and tied back her long red hair, the white tips sweeping across her neck. "Or you just that angry that a real person isn't worth the effort?"

Aeley snorted and eyed Rosayra up. She was short like Stuck, but with light blue-grey eyes ringed with thick amber and white skin almost pale enough to match her tight, long-sleeved shirt. Granted, she was said to be a nightmare with a blade, able to keep up with Kayte, or so Aeley had heard. Perhaps she should put it to the test.

"If you've got nothing better to do," Aeley said coolly.

"Oh, I've got plenty *better*." Rosayra drew her sword, its sheath on her belt next to a jeweled knife, the golden hilt encrusted with emeralds and white stones—diamonds, Aeley supposed, given Kayte's love of pretty, shiny things. "But you're ready to kill, so let's make it good." Standing in the middle of the training circle, she beckoned to Aeley with one hand then flicked her fingers, dragging the offer into insult.

Aeley threw down the staff and grabbed her sword. She rushed at Rosayra, dealing the first strike—

Rosayra stepped into the movement, blocking with her blade and pushing. Instead of striking back, Rosayra ducked low under Aeley's raised arm and grabbed her leg just beneath the knee, giving a strong jerk that took Aeley down to the floor and sent her sword skittering away.

"Dammit!" Aeley scrambled to get up and retrieve her sword. *So she likes it dirty. Fine by me.*

"Oh, yeah. Bring it to me, honey." Rosayra laughed, a low, wicked sound that made Aeley's skin crawl with annoyance. "Make it hurt, yeah?"

Sword in hand, Aeley stepped back into the ring, this time tamping her anger down. Ever since her official inauguration as Tract Steward, she had spent less and less time sparring and training. The last time she had actually fought— really, truly put her skills to the test—had been in Oly Valley, against Allon and his men. Sparring fell to the wayside after that, the thought of picking up a sword and putting someone at the other end of it more than mildly disturbing. Nightmares only encouraged reluctance.

But the fight... going through the motions...

Aeley struck again, low, then again with a quick high near Rosayra's shoulder, opting for restrained assault rather than a wild, desperate attempt like the last time. Something in it felt like ordering the chaos; a fight against rogue elements, insisting they fall in line. Rosayra matched the strength, thrust for thrust. The blades clanged in a varied rhythm, with a quickened pace as they moved across the floor, pushing forward, driving back, and grabbing at each other's arms, wrists, a surprise hook around the ankle with one foot—anything that spoiled a perfectly polite fight.

She was done with being polite. She wanted to play dirty, more than once tempted to toss the sword aside and punch out, just to see what Rosayra would do. Judging from the slight crookedness in Rosayra's nose, someone had already done that at least once.

"Honey, don't even think about it." Rosayra rolled her wrist, sword turning and twisting with it, her other hand up as she stepped around the training circle. "I've got my fight face on, but it doesn't mean your fist needs to be in it." She snorted a laugh. "Put me into black and blue territory and Kayte'll make sure you hear about it for months."

"What's he going to do, tell on me? Yell at me with very strong words?"

Rosayra laughed, a little too delightful as she doubled over and slapped her knee. "Precious, no. Worse: he'll sign you up for all sorts of task forces without telling you and send you all the work and representatives just to make your life a special type of political torture. Then he'll put your name on it for Council to see, just to make it extra fun." Rosayra smirked. "Trust me, take the sword fight—unless you *want* to be rolling on a massive management pyre. He really can't keep his committees to himself. He likes to share the headache."

Aeley cursed a long string of unfinished expletives, not willing to call Rosayra's bluff. Kayte was a proven mix of politician and fighter, given to act on both sides when it suited him best. The last thing she needed was to be permanently tied up in tasks and committees and having the High Council breathe down her neck for results.

To make it worse, laughter came from the doorway.

Aeley snapped her attention to the interruption. "Stuck," she muttered. "What? You want to get in on this?"

Stuck laughed and pushed back her dark hair. Leaning against the doorframe, she clutched a partially eaten, orange gosa fruit in one hand. "No, no," she said, waving it off, "you're doing just fine. Keep going." Stuck took a bite of the gosa and pointed at Rosayra. "Watch for her left side, when she wiggles her fingers—she feigns after that," she offered, chewing around her words. "And don't kill your right flank."

"Thanks," Aeley said dryly.

Rosayra launched the next attack before Aeley could say anything more, thrusting out towards

Aeley's middle before spinning away and dealing a strike to Aeley's side.

Aeley thwarted both attempts to catch her off guard, followed by a series of rapid strikes and a shove at Rosayra's shoulder.

After that, they fell into another rhythm, the intensity not as forceful. If anything, it was a cooling down, the movements closer to rote than rage.

When Aeley backed away, sword lowered, her hand up, palm out, Rosayra quirked a brow. "We done, then?"

"For now." Aeley sheathed her sword and offered her empty palm. "Let's call a draw."

Rosayra clasped Aeley's forearm. "Deal." Her grip tightened. "And this is where you tell me what the problem is."

Aeley peered at Stuck, who nodded and slipped into the hallway. Still eating while she leaned against the wall opposite the doorway, Stuck's glance may have not been on Aeley, but it was still very much there.

"It's your husband," Aeley mumbled. "We're not... seeing eye to eye right now. Not about the mess with Hano, or anything else, really. Apparently I'm five, he's bitter, and there's not much to be done about it."

"Ah." Rosayra slid her sword into its sheath and tugged Aeley over to the windows by the cuff. "Explains why he looked fit to throw one."

She leaned back against the wall between windows, one elbow on the window ledge.

Aeley snorted. "Yeah, fit to throw *me*—out into the Channel, probably. Let me wash up on some random shore somewhere." She sighed. "I'm not Steward enough, not by his standards. He thinks I don't care about fixing things, that I'm weak. He thinks I'm like my father, avoiding confrontation where it matters most. Going by him, my training is rubbish and I'm useless."

Rosayra's lips twisted in an odd smile. "Can I give you some advice?"

"If you want."

"Kayte…" Rosayra sighed. "You know he was in the same position as you, yeah? Lost his mother in that accident, then he was elected in and had to live up to her legacy as Steward. But he also lost Dollie and Parnes before that, and that's never settled with him. It never settled with his mother, either, and she wasn't one for emotional displays, just constant worry."

Aeley nodded. She remembered attending all three funerals. His mother, Calles, died from complications after slipping on a lengthy set of stairs and tumbling down all the way to the bottom, damaging her neck in the process. Dolante—Dollie—had been the eldest son and the decorated captain of the *Stalwart Fortitude*, one of the fastest ships in Kattal, but the sea had claimed him for its own. He had gone down with his ship and crew in a violent storm that overturned almost everything on the Alatayle Sea that night. His body had been recovered on the rocky shore of Garsy Isle with less than a dozen sailors and parts of the wreckage.

Parnes, however, was killed by the Shar-denn in a highway robbery gone poorly. While Parnes had fought back, he had been no match for a mob of angry gang members and their knives. Since then, it had been Kayte, his younger brother, and their two sisters left to carry on with the family name, their aging father mostly withdrawn from the public eye.

"It's not been easy for him, either," Rosayra continued, her voice soft, "especially in the beginning. The never-ending expectations—following in Calles's very successful steps—it's been a fight, some days more than others, even with him having the training. But it's been worth the clawing and the scratching; that fight to grow and do good and prove it's all going to work out. The fight'll be worth it for you, too, if you're up to it. You just need to find your way—forget the rage parties, put down your pity purse, and you'll figure it out." She gave a sad smile and rubbed Aeley's shoulder. "And if it's any consolation, Kayte doesn't hate you—he just runs hot on the attitude, which isn't any different than you. You're always going to run the risk of bashing heads. Kayte's got his own problems to deal with, and we're weathering it the best we can, but he's not going around planning your demise."

"It'll just always feel like it."

"Honey, it won't, and you know better. Pity purse, remember? Chuck the bitch at the door and leave it there." Rosayra crossed her arms, that sad smile in her pale blue-grey eyes, bright hair spilling over her shoulder. "You've known Kayte long enough to know it blows over. But if you *really* want to know him, you need to count a few things. Mostly that he feels deeply. He's one of the most empathetic people I know, but it also makes him vulnerable, and sometimes he hurts others while taking care of things because he's being so raw, so honest." She gazed out the windows, scratching distractedly at her arm before returning to Aeley. "He takes death personally, *especially* when they're on his watch. When he can't step in and save someone from harm, it guts him. It's in his blood—most of the Oarens are like that, to varying degrees, and he's not even the worst. It's just his way."

"So I should just... what? Ignore him?" Aeley scowled at the window, a flicker of light catching her eye from on the horizon. "Just roll over and play good girl? Keep my mouth shut around him?"

"No, that's not what I'm saying." Rosayra poked Aeley's arm. "I'm saying take time to cool off and approach things again later with some patience. You need to learn *patience* with each other. It's all personal. Accept that and move on. And it's not even just the gangs or the crimes, it's the losing family. It'll always be about losing family. You're just as prickly about it as he is, so give a little, get a little."

Rosayra turned Aeley to face her, both hands on Aeley's shoulders. "He feels for you, baby Tract Steward. He isn't getting all cuddly about it, but it's there. He's also grieving over your father. Kayte liked him, he really did, no matter the criticisms. But he doesn't want you to fall apart. He also doesn't want you messing everything up, not after your father busted his balls to do good. It's hard work, and Kayte... he takes the work seriously." She swept Aeley's hair over her shoulder. "You need to find your own way and keep going. Kayte'll respect that most."

Aeley said nothing, letting the words sink in to sort out the doubts that still clung, reluctant to let them go completely.

"He'll always test your patience," Rosayra said quietly. "Emeraliss knows he tests mine. But I still love him, and I'll protect him right on through my dying breath. You just need to give him some space to feel and sort things out. And if he pushes you, then push back—but in the right way, where it counts most: in Steward matters. Hit the governance hard and don't be afraid to defend yourself when he goes off." She stepped back and shook her head. "He'll be fine after he pisses around for a bit, grumbling to the merfolk. You'll see. Just... when he *does* give his apology—and it'll be quiet, but it'll be there—just rub it in a little. Only a little. Put yourself on equal footing with him. He'll respect that, even if he doesn't show it." Rosayra chuckled, a hand at her lips as she peered out the window. "Korre knew how to do it. Half the Council does it—Cota, Severn, and Nerrik do it all the time. You can learn, too. It certainly worked for me."

Rosayra raised her left hand, then pointed at it with the other, showing off the marriage ring on her middle finger, a collection of tiny emeralds and teal stones embedded in the white gold band.

She gave Aeley a wink. "It'll come. It just needs a bit of time and a lot of fight. But I see you, honey, and so does he. We've also been hearing some strange whispers about your other predicament—marriage, *really*? To *that* lot?" Rosayra whistled low as she shook her head. "You need to explain that to me, because we're... concerned. If they pulled anything around us, I'd make them pay through every orifice. But dinner. This is what dinner's for. Come on," she said, tugging Aeley by the elbow, "let's go get you fed and watered."

Aeley followed, unwilling to protest. She needed the friend, and Rosayra felt like one, or something like it. Maybe she was simply an ally, a mediator when it came to Aeley and Kayte's clash of similarities. Either way, she was grateful for that touch of kindness. With everything threatening to completely fall apart, she needed more than tough love.

Chapter Eleven

"How much should I bet that Dreca has nothing?"

Aeley made a face at Mayr and shifted in her saddle. As she flicked her gaze to the road, past Stick and Stuck riding ahead of them, she was all too relieved to focus on the silhouette of the village looming ahead in the mid-morning light. Behind her, the other four guards followed on horseback, their low voices and soft laughs mixed with the noisy wheels of the empty carriage—all of them reminders of a long trip she had no interest in repeating, not unless it was to share better news. Though after four days away from home, she wanted nothing more than to curl up in bed and see no one, save Lira.

"That's not even a worthy bet," she said. "If you're going to be smart, you need to come up with something that isn't so ridiculous."

Mayr snorted and loosened the reins around his gloved hands. "And here we go again. You've been a pleasure to deal with this entire trip. What? Left your girlfriend at home and you're taking it out on me?"

"No." *Though she would've made it more bearable.* "I just hate doing these things. I feel bad for Hano and his mother, but I don't *do* the crying, weepy stuff. Couldn't get out of there fast enough," Aeley muttered. "And Kayte, by the Goddesses, Kayte. He wanted to skewer me like the boar on the table."

"I'll give you that much. He was looking to sharpen a few weapons on your knees." Mayr drew his black stallion closer to hers. "Good apology, though, yours. He might just allow you back into his region. Maybe even under his roof."

"Oh, the excitement."

"Could be worse—your father could've set you up with someone just like him."

Aeley slouched. *That.* After everything, she could have damn well done without *another* reminder.

"Great. You *had* to ruin my morning, didn't you? Just couldn't keep it to yourself." Aeley scowled. "I'd say you owe me a drink, but you still won't confess and tell me where you hid the stuff to begin with."

Mayr held up one hand. "I told you: it wasn't me."

She would have believed him more if he looked her in the eye. "Have it your way."

"And you're welcome."

"What?"

"In answer to the gratitude you're so kindly not expressing out loud. You're welcome for the time I've taken to escort you and the meetings I've sat in, including hugging one very distraught woman and carrying an exhausted kid to bed. Oh, and you're welcome for talking Kayte down when he was yelling. You know, I could've been relaxing with the other guards and—"

"Thank you, Mayr, really. Especially since I've been sleeping *so* well and *love* dealing with dead people and laws. Because it makes being a Steward so *easy*."

"And since when have you ever opted for easy?" Mayr smirked. "You knew this came with it. Told me you were prepared. Even when I tried talking you out of it, you went ahead anyway, just like you always do." He tapped her arm. "Don't tell me you're ready to run. Don't tell me you're a liar. I'd hate to think I don't know you. And if you're going to waste everything because it's not *easy*, I can't be held responsible for what I may do." His eyes darkened, echoing the wickedness in his grin. "You, me, stuck in a locked room for days and I won't shut up. Or I'll sing. Loudly. After drinking until I giggle. Then bang on some pots and pans. Nothing says 'get back to work' like a finely tuned headache."

Aeley laughed softly and stared at her fists. She could see the image in her mind, even more absurd than he made it sound. It was almost as ridiculous as taking things out on him that were none of his doing. His words were as effective as a slap, forcing her into clarity. How was it she could lose herself and he always found her? "I don't know how you do it."

"What? Devise really terrible torture techniques?"

"No. Put up with me."

"Oh. That." He tilted his head to the side. "Because I'm talented. Or maybe it's just because I'm too perfect for my own good."

"Mayr," Aeley scolded gently.

"Ah, we were being serious. Here, let me try again." Mayr gave a small smile, his gaze softening. "I get it, Ae, I do. I've known you longer than we've really known ourselves, shared more than just training and reckless decisions. I've seen you at your worst, and I'd love to see you at your best, which isn't now, but it'll come. You gave me a second glance when others wouldn't have bothered. You didn't let status and politics tell you how it should be." He shrugged. "So you're having a rough time. So you need to get angry. It's better to be blunt with me than say the wrong things to someone who could make being Steward that much harder."

"I could make it easier, though." Aeley let out an aggravated breath. "I don't thank you half as much as I should, and that's on me, like so many other things. I'm getting so caught up in trying to do the right thing, everything else suffers." She looked pointedly at Mayr. "And I'm sorry for that. You're getting stuck in the middle."

"And I suspect that's where I should be. I've never had any delusions about what being Head of the Guard meant, just like I've never had any delusions about what a Steward really is. Just don't forget I'm on your side. And don't listen to me when I try to be smart: half of it's just my lips moving with one foot in my mouth. The rest is trying to remind you not everything's as bad as it seems."

Always the optimist in the secret. "Thanks," she murmured.

Mayr shifted his weight and leaned away as she patted his arm. "You're welcome, but can we find something else to talk about now? I've used up all the seriousness I've got left after putting up with Kayte. Next to him, you're almost as sweet as that girl you're wishing you were laying flat on her back and—"

"*How does it always come back to this?*" Aeley glared at Mayr, her cheeks going warm. From the gleam in Mayr's eyes and his throaty laugh, she could guess at how red her face was. Since the ball, he had poked around, trying to find out what happened between her and Lira—secrets she was *not* about to tell him, no matter how close they were. "We're not talking about this again!"

Mayr's laughter continued, but he said nothing more as they neared the village. Home was on the other side, close and far all at the same time. *We'll just ride through. No stopping.*

Aeley laughed softly, fully expecting a warm reception and plenty of relief to go around, what with Pellon in charge of the guards while Mayr was away and Haydin in charge of the estate. Pellon and Haydin usually made a good team, both of them set in their task to keep things under control and in good order, but with the cancellation of their annual celebration for the Feast of Eleia, the official first day of autumn, there was bound to be a couple patience-testing thorns of chaos thrown into the quiet they both preferred.

Even worse, she was coming back the day before the Feast, which would no doubt put Haydin into a spin over the fact they could have gone ahead with the party instead of obeying Aeley's brisk instructions to call it off before she had left for Alosaa.

"What?" Mayr cast her a glance, one brow arched. "Something on my face again?"

"No, just thinking of how much Haydin's going to hate me." Aeley flashed him a grin. "You know how much he loves getting everyone together, but this—"

The rest of her words failed as she sniffed the air.

Smoke. Burning wood. The scents drifted on the breeze, but nowhere near as lightly as they should have. Thick. They were much too thick to be normal, no less worrisome than the grey hue to the sky above the village, joined by a slow-moving cloud of what could only amount to trouble.

Dread dropped hard in Aeley, a massive weight in her guts that refused to let up as she passed through the outskirts of the village. She shared more than one look with Mayr, who scowled and stayed silent, his hardened gaze shifting from one direction to the next, all humour and complaint lost to alertness.

When they entered the village core, tired and soot-smattered faces stared back at them, gazes following them with fear and anger and a heavy, gnawing dread of their own.

"*Dammit*," Mayr spat out and drew closer, his leg nearly touching Aeley's. With a whistle, he caught Stick and Stuck's attention, then motioned for them to slow down and pull in closer. Just as quickly, he glanced behind him and gestured for the rest of the guards to hurry along and close the gaps around Aeley.

Aeley guided her horse deeper into the village as fast as Stick's wary lead would let her, his ice-blue eyes narrowed every time he peered in her direction. He said nothing, but the stern looks he shared with Stuck said everything. The fact he kept turning one ear towards Aeley did nothing to ease the tension, nor did the way he continued to slip his hand through his short white-blond hair as though trying to keep calm.

They stopped in the centre of the village, off to one side of the village square. Aeley slid from the saddle and spun around slowly. Villagers passed by, some gaping at her but saying nothing, as if she should have already known what happened. Others rushed past, carrying buckets filled with water. Her gaze followed until they disappeared into a dark alley across the square. Without a word, she hurried after them, leaving Mayr behind and the guards shouting after her.

She stopped at the end of the alley, an even stronger waft of smoke catching her by surprise. What had been the village meeting hall lay in a heap of cracked and burned beams with a portion of one wall still erect. Villagers poured water on the wreckage while others tossed down dirt and stomped around in the mud to put out the last flickers of flame. What remained of the tables, benches, and tapestries peeked out of the destruction in an array of charred corners and soggy edges, though from the looks of it, everything had gone up in flames, likely from the inside out.

"Aeley!"

Dreca's broad form jostled towards her, his light brown cheeks streaked with soot.

"What's happened?" she demanded softly as he stopped.

"Went up well before dawn," he answered between gasps for air. "We got as many hands to help as we could. Pellon sent down some of yours, too. Finally got it put out for good." He wiped his mouth and pointed towards the other end of the village. "No different than that falling barn a couple days back. Finally got the support beams back in place."

"Wait—*what*?" Aeley clasped Dreca's shoulders. "*What's going on?*"

Dreca's thick lips drew into a tight line. "You left and we've had problems. Another attack the night you went. The butcher, Naret. Minding his own business, and on the way home from the tavern in the middle of the night, someone grabbed him and knocked him out. Dumped him in his own well. Left him for his brother to find the next day—lucky that he did. No one would've known.

"That night, the barn we use to store the harvest overflow went," he continued, pausing to cough. "Someone took out a few beams and part of it came down. Woke a few people up. The rest of us set to fixing it. Then today, we wake up to this."

"This is..." Aeley stopped, most of her words wrapped around a growing rage that wanted to hit out at someone—ghosts, at that point, ones that played and mocked and left everyone hurting. "Let me guess: you don't have any idea of who's doing it."

"We've got nothing, except for the same as that kid," Dreca told her, his voice hardening. "Just some shadowy figures no one can get a hold of. By the time we find out what they've done, they're gone. Naret said they attacked him. One of the villagers said they saw a couple shadows run past their house earlier, but didn't think of it until the fire was dying down."

Aeley snarled and kicked at the ground, sending a rock into the rubble. "Those damned bloody bastards. There's nothing, no problems, and then suddenly—"

"Aeley!" a woman hollered from behind, her voice echoing in the alley.

Aeley spun on her heel, caught between relief and bitter confusion. "Lira!"

"I came to the village to check on some things and see if you'd come home yet. Mayr sent me down here." Lira stopped at Aeley's side and pulled her dark mauve shawl taut around her shoulders. Behind her, Stick and Stuck lingered in the alley, watchful of them both, each keeping their hands near the knives at their waist. "What's going on?"

Dreca grunted, his face scrunched with his irritation. Just how many times had he told the story to the villagers *and* the guards *and* the Kattal soldiers that called Dahena home, several of whom were examining the wreckage and casting scowls Aeley's way? Going over it again and again would only remind him of how much worse it could have been. How bad it already *had* been.

"I'll tell you when I get home," Aeley murmured. "It's not good news."

"I hate to say it, but this isn't something your usual highwaymen go around doing," Dreca said, exhaustion creeping through his anger, "and maybe it's the gangs, but it's also something your brother would do. Something he *has* done. You're sure he's stuck where they want him to be?"

"Absolutely," Aeley answered. "This can't be him. They wouldn't let him out of their sight. No one will."

"Then maybe it's someone he calls friend. Or someone feeling inspired." Dreca rubbed his eyes, then seemed to remember his hands were dirty. Frowning at his fingers, he closed them into fists, steadying how badly they trembled, and crossed his arms. "We need answers. This is your business, even more than mine. I don't think these people are even from here. Probably from some other village, thinking they can harass us into whatever they want."

"So they haven't made any demands, just tearing things apart?"

"By the looks of it."

Aeley sighed and stared at the sky in a feeble attempt to make sense from the chaos. It was destruction wrapped around a puzzle—and she hated puzzles. Someone who made demands or staked a claim and called her out was easier to deal with. Even one of the gang bosses would have been preferable to the disaster they were in. At least then, she would have had a verified name and a better chance at coming up with a solid plan of attack instead of only guessing at the whos and whats and whys. But playing ghost... how was she supposed to target *that* with any sort of accuracy?

And if it's Allon...

No, Dreca was wrong. There was no way Allon could have arranged what was happening, not from prison.

And yet...

It was a name she had, one with a face and a mouth still very much attached.

"We can't keep doing this, Aeley. Attacking a stranger on the road was one thing, but now they're coming into our villages." Dreca thrust his hand towards the crowd gathered around the rubble. "What if they start coming into our homes? Who knows what they'll do. They've already hurt people. What stops them from hurting anyone else?" He jabbed a finger at her. "You need to do something. *Anything*."

"I know. I'm just as worried," Aeley said quietly. "I hate that this happened, and I certainly won't stand for where it's going. I'll put a stop to it, I promise." She raked her fingers through her hair, the greasy, blonde tangles needing a wash — just one more thing that would have to wait until she made sense of the fire and the danger it signaled. *I need to go home, think about this.*

Her glance drifted to Lira, who stared at the destroyed hall in silence and pulled her shawl tight around her shoulders. A cloud of emotions shifted across Lira's face, though surprise was missing, and for good reason: Aeley should have seen the escalation coming.

My fault, not leaving a proper protection detail behind for the village. But maybe she'll have some good ideas as to where to start with all of this. She knows things I don't.

"I'll work on it, Dreca. I'll set this right," Aeley murmured.

When Dreca gave her a skeptical glare, she held up her hands. "I *will*. Honestly. I'll just... I'll think of something useful. For now, tell people I'm going to figure this out and to stay safe. Stay inside and don't stay alone. And don't be out at night. I'll send teams of my guards down and get Mayr to round up the soldiers to stand watch, too. Eyes at night and patrols might deter whoever's doing this. Either way, we'll catch them."

"Is that a promise?" Dreca asked.

"I put Allon where he deserved. I'll do the same here." Aeley squeezed his arm. "We'll get this figured out, and when we do, they'll pay for every moment."

Aeley fell into her chair with a sigh, familiarity taking over. The back of her chair pressed into her neck, detracting from the tension around her spine, though what she would give for a pair of boiling hot cloths laid over her shoulder blades. As she hung her legs over the edge of her desk, she closed her eyes and pushed away the echoes of Dreca's voice in her mind. Even Kayte's harsh voice and Vilde's wails disappeared into the darkness seeping in between her thoughts. Silence was a blessing. For the first time in days, she relaxed.

"Should I leave you and your chair alone?"

Opening one eye, Aeley peered at Lira, curled up in the chair beside the window. If it were anyone else, she would have closed her eye and pretended to snore her way out of a reply. "Why? Are you jealous?"

Lira smiled tiredly, dark circles around her eyes. "Only if you're doing things you should be doing to me."

Aeley choked. Sputtering as she jerked forward, she stomped the floor and coughed, trying not to laugh and make it worse. There was no mistaking the invitation in Lira's words this time.

A knock on the door only added to the noise in her head. "Come in," Aeley hollered, her voice hoarse, cracking on the words. When the door opened, she tried not to laugh at Lira's low chuckle, or the way Lira bit her bottom lip, teasing Aeley for every moment of distraction she could get.

Mayr entered the study, followed by Haydin.

"What now?" Aeley groaned and eyed the parchment in Haydin's hands.

"You might want to read them." Mayr nodded, the look on his face feeding the stomach-twisting suspicion that she was missing something.

Haydin laid the notes on the desk. "They came while you were gone. One yesterday and one this morning—"

"*After* the fire," Mayr clarified.

Aeley perched on the edge of her chair. "What? Haydin, who delivered them?"

"A young man," Haydin answered with a shrug.

"Did you know him? Do *we* know him?"

Haydin shook his head. "Nor was he a talkative fellow. I took the letters and he went off."

Well, isn't that just fantastic. Aeley ripped open the letters and laid them side by side, then focused on the letter to the right:

> *If you're enjoying what's happening now, you'll love what comes next, so make your decisions good ones—there won't be any second chances.*
> *— . C .*

Biting the inside of her cheek, Aeley glanced at the letter to the left:

This is only the beginning, and we can do so much worse—buck it up and play nice with what we've left you or suffer till the end.
— . C .

Aeley glared at the sliver of worn desk between the letters, the blurred black ink of both messages haunting the peripheral of her vision. It appeared the same person had penned them, at least at first glance. The effect was lost once she read them over a second time, noting the slight differences in strokes and weights, a skill she was quickly honing with Lira's help. Even so, they sounded like something Allon would compose. He always had communicated most effectively with threats and violence. Was he even allowed to send letters from prison or had he goaded someone into doing it for him?

Though the initial at the end... that was something new, and certainly not his. He had never shied away from scratching his name into every foul thing he did, particularly when it would draw blood twenty ways from the nearest fall into the pits of soul-sticking guilt and lifelong despair.

But friends, acquaintances, servants, suckers, and fools... the bastard did have those.

Or had, anyway—whoever's left after Oly Valley... Aeley sighed and tugged a hand through her hair, fingers dragging to a stop partway. *Maybe Dreca's right. Maybe Allon's people are doing this. He's never been one to let go of a grudge—neither of us has. And with all the ways he loves punishing people for pushing back against him... He's not the only fool in the world who'd go along with this.*

Still... the signatures bothered her. Not quite a name, but an entity nonetheless.

One step closer and yet so far.

"So?" Mayr asked. "Do I get to crack heads?" When Aeley failed to answer, he leaned against her desk and tried to read the letters upside down. "They're signed."

"They're also not very encouraging." She crumpled the letters, her next step clear. "I'm going to the quarry. I need to see Allon."

Mayr fell back, his jaw dropping. "You're joking. Or you're that far gone. Probably a bit of both. We're done with him, remember?"

"I thought I was. I *want* to be." Aeley threw the balled parchment at the wall. "Except these are all wrong. I can't be sure of what they are until I find out what he knows. If he's involved..." She cleared her throat and stood. "You can either approve or not. Either way, I'm going."

"Fine, you're taking Pell and whoever else I damn well feel like throwing at you," Mayr countered, his eyes narrowed. "You want me working with the guards and soldiers and drawing them up assignments, and that's just fine with me, but you're *not* traipsing off on your own. Eight-guard contingent, whether you like it or not."

Lira cleared her throat, one fingertip against her lips.

Aeley took the hint. "Fine, you do that. I won't be going by myself, anyway."

"By carriage or horse?" Haydin asked.

From the corner of her eye, Aeley caught Lira's slide forward in her chair and the wave of her hand. As she flicked her glance to Lira, Lira mouthed the word, "Carriage," and all Aeley could do was agree.

Aeley returned her attention to Haydin. "The carriage will be fine," Aeley said with a faint, tired smile, "but tell the driver we don't have all day. I don't want to be there any longer than we need to be."

Especially if she was about to waste her time—the very summary of her entire relationship with Allon, from first to last and every damned step in between.

Chapter Twelve

Every bump and hole the carriage wheels encountered brought them closer, encouraging Aeley's teeth to graze Lira's skin more than once. Normally the long ride to Footshred was tedious, but lost in Lira's scent and the sweet taste of her lips, Aeley failed to notice, reminded only as she glimpsed through the window.

"Wait," Lira whispered. She shuffled down the seat, head sliding further down into the corner while the waist of her disheveled gown pulled higher. Her hair tumbled over the edge of the cushion, the ends dusting the floor near her jeweled comb, discarded soon after the carriage had left the estate. The moment she settled, she tugged on Aeley's belt.

Aeley grinned and shifted her knee, pinning Lira's skirt. With the ball of her other foot rammed into the corner of the door behind her, she pushed against the frame and leaned over Lira to kiss her again, ignoring the creaking protests of the wood as their lips played and fingers traveled.

The carriage jostled over another dip in the road, a deeper drop, and Aeley slapped the wall with one hand to keep steady.

Dammit. In some ways, the small space did nothing to encourage intimacy, at least not the comfortable kind. Her foot was numb, and there was a notable lack of adequate space to lie properly, even though Lira's raised knee knocking her hip only fed Aeley's fantasies as to all of the positions they could explore.

Lira drew her head back to glance out the window, exposing her neck. It was an enticing target, one Aeley refused to pass up, her lips taking to Lira's throat with small kisses and the briefest licks.

"We should be getting there soon," Lira murmured.

Aeley nipped at Lira's throat. How long would it take for bruises to form? At least Lira had her shawl, lying in a heap on the floor. She could hide any marks from curious guards.

"We should talk about how this is going to happen," Lira continued. One elbow digging into the cushion, she propped herself up.

Lira's chin almost hit Aeley's face. Grunting, Aeley pulled away and wiped her lips on the back of her hand. "If you wanted me to stop, you could've just asked. No need to bring *him* into it."

"Who said I wanted you to stop? I just said we needed a plan." Lira pushed up and tugged her skirt out from under Aeley's knee. As she leaned into the corner, she tried to straighten the rumpled gown, tugging it back into place before jamming her comb into her hair. "We didn't really talk before we left. It would help to know what you're after."

Aeley crossed the divide to sit on the other cushion, annoyed at the interruption. She tossed the shawl onto Lira's seat, careful to bite back any words that could get her into trouble. Sunlight illuminated the faint marks Aeley had left on Lira's skin—a reminder of the satisfying end she intended to achieve for them both one day, assuming they could just *get* there instead of constantly being separated by one issue or another.

There was still hope, however: Lira had never told her to stop, her moans a driving force to continue, and her touch was just as full of intention to rid Aeley of whatever barriers were in their way. Even with everything covered, her modesty seemed to be slipping away, and Aeley was allowed to enjoy it for all it was worth.

Lira continued to stare at her, waiting for an answer. "I want him to be sorry," Aeley mumbled, peering out the window.

"You're never going to get that." Lira draped the mauve shawl over her lap and wound the frayed ends around her fingers. "He doesn't think he's wrong."

Aeley snapped her head towards Lira and raised one brow. "So you've met him, then?"

"No."

"Sounds like you have."

Lira shrugged and gazed at the carriage floor. "I know enough men like him to know exactly how he is. His actions say everything."

Do you realize that raises more questions than answers? Aeley shifted in her seat, unable to get comfortable. Should she bother asking to hear more? *She probably won't answer anyway. She'll deflect the conversation like she always does.*

"How do you want me to handle him?"

Aeley blinked at the question. "What?"

"How do you want me to play this? Silent or mouthy? You brought me along, so I'm going to assume you want me in there with you. If he starts to talk to me, what do you want me to do?"

What, other than let me punch him in the face?

"Ignore him. He likes attention," Aeley answered. She could imagine how Allon would take any other reaction. It was bad enough he would think she brought Lira to him as a gift or as a means to taunt him. Why had she not considered how he would see it before agreeing to Lira's company? "Actually, maybe you should just stay out of the room when I'm with him."

"What? Why?"

"He'll be a complete ass if he sees you."

"You don't think I can handle him? He's in a prison with guards, all of whom probably want to break his neck. And you've met my brothers. His pride can say no worse."

"And here I thought maybe I should teach you something about defending yourself." Aeley started to laugh, but caught herself. No, not so funny, and certainly not as funny as it sounded in her head. "But I thought you wanted to join me for the ride—to do what we *were* doing. Why are you suddenly obsessed with him?"

"I'm not obsessed, I'm curious. There's a difference," Lira argued with a scowl. "You don't want to talk about him. So, naturally, it's exactly what I want to hear. You believe he'd be better off dead. It can't be easy to keep all that anger locked up." She leaned forward, her pinched expression relaxing as she laid her hand on Aeley's knee. "Besides, do you want a relationship or just someone to sleep with? Talking is the difference between the two."

"So you *want* to hear how much I hate him?"

"If it helps." Lira pressed against the side of the carriage. "But not right now. We're here."

Aeley breathed in, dread rousing the ghosts of *bad* and *worse* in the pit of her stomach. *This isn't any different than the Council meeting. Get in, do what I came to do, get out. It really doesn't need to be any more complicated.*

The carriage stopped, its wheels grinding the fragile, black stones covering the ground. Without waiting for the driver or for Pellon, Aeley opened the door and jumped down, her boots crushing the stones into shards with high-pitched snaps as though they were glass. They were almost as sharp, giving Footshred prison its name. Behind her, the black stones stretched out and around the quarry pits like a moat, a deterrent to prisoners who thought they could escape in thin soles or none at all.

Cupping her hand over her eyes, Aeley stared into the distance. Trees were sparse and the land was mostly barren, a red landscape spotted with small yellow and green plants, unlike the ferns found in the rest of the republic. Even the sunlight felt worse there in the open, accompanied by the heat rising up from the black stones, colliding together in an uncomfortable middle. Was it any coincidence the strongest stones and the most coveted jewels came from here?

The carriage rocked as Lira hopped down. "Absolutely miserable," she muttered, fanning herself. Lira draped her shawl over her arm and glanced at the barracks. Around them, Pellon had climbed down from the carriage driver's box and joined the rest of the seven guards dismounted from their horses, none of them getting close enough to interrupt.

"Exactly." Aeley slammed the door closed. She gazed past the barracks to the metal and wood fences. On the other side, the earth dipped low, disappearing into a void. Guards wearing thin breastplates and bracers over simple, dusty tunics walked the perimeter, each with a sword on their back. A few of the men carried spears, their gazes directed downwards. Among them, a young man weaved in and out with a bucket, offering what she suspected was water. The way he skipped along suggested he was pleased with his work. *All the prisoners must be below—he wouldn't be so happy if they were close.*

"Are you ready?" Lira asked.

With a tug on Lira's sleeve, Aeley started towards the long, grey building between them and the barracks. Two guards in leather armour greeted them as they walked through the arched entrance and iron gates, followed by Pellon and three other Dahe guards who stayed close behind.

They stopped in the receiving hall, the space not much bigger than the dining room at the Dahe estate. Before them stood four bronze statues with crowns of small, yellow leaves and green stones for irises, staring at the door as if judging whomever walked in: likenesses of the four Goddesses, each of them unique and just as much trouble as the next—all of whom Aeley had endeavoured to avoid for as long as possible.

On one end stood the statue of Emeraliss, their Goddess of Love, displayed in a flimsy gown that looked as if the wind had torn wet clothes off the line and whipped the fabric around Her, with haphazard strands of jewels and beads thrown in for an impulsive touch of grace. Her hair was just as untamed, unbound in a long mass of waves and braids. As always, her statue stood proud with a scepter in one hand and a massive bronze bird perched on her other wrist, its wings slightly unfurled and its elaborate tail finely painted with gold and flecks of silver to give a hint of sparkle. Emeraliss was a picture of that which was wild, with a bird that spoke only of peace—a strange blend of contradictions that always walked a fine line.

At the other end, the statue for Laytia, Goddess of Wisdom, stood with a similar scepter, but no bird, just six stones in the palm of her outstretched hand—something about time and doom, though Aeley had never delved too far into those stories, afraid to peer into an abyss that might have peered back a little too deeply. Aeley *did* appreciate how Laytia had all the fond welcome of stepping into a modest, lived-in home filled with the passion of a healthy fire, good food, a soft tune, and a lust for life. Compared to Emeraliss, Laytia always seemed more secretive and with good reason, though never without that glance that refused to reveal why. The appearance of this statue was homely, in a gown with tiers of skirts and sashes, chains and belts draped over her hips to her feet. Far more orderly than Emeraliss, Laytia's hair was bound in four separate handfuls of knee-length twists and tied into sheaves, almost as if someone had mistaken the strands for grass.

The two statues in the centre, however, were nothing like their counterparts, and both appeared at home in the prison. The Goddesses themselves could have walked the corridors and blended in, save for the wagging tongues that would have chased after them for fear of being left behind… or for fear of being taken to whatever flavour of justice awaited them. Both statues held staves crossed between them, but in their free hands, one held a balanced set of scales while the other held a shield.

Navara and Hastal, Goddesses of Justice and Protection.

Aeley eyed Navara's scales, never wanting to know what those plates would say about her once her time was up and breathing was a luxury long gone and ripped away. Justice could be a fickle mistress, and Navara was its very embodiment, the complicated game of souls at Navara's fingertips like a set of discs played by her everlasting rules. Under her influence, the blessing of mortality was a fair-weather wisp of maybes and possiblys threaded through the larger, delicate fabric of disaster and calm. Navara walked between the worlds, never to see the line that separated them — She *was* the line, as full of life as She was death. A frightening vision of chainmail and silk, She was adorned with scale and sinew, and a patchy circlet peeked through the tight curls at her forehead, as short as the rest of her hair.

A breath away from leaving the room completely, Aeley glanced at the statue of Hastal and sighed at the comfort in the familiar: fire and fray, teeth and claws, and a call to Aeley's own inner nature. Hastal held fast, strong, never to bend, never to yield to a choice without conviction. Always at the ready to defend, always with the will to try. She was the soulful voice of the forest, the piercing cry of battle, and the whisper of every primal urge to survive. Armoured plates revealed bits of her short battle dress and its layers of sheared, tooth-trimmed strips, as heavy and brutal as the four antlers of her headdress and the bones that dangled around her shoulders. The shield in her grasp had no equal, an indestructible legend that had all the heft of an anvil and every resilience against the heat of adversity.

If Aeley were ever forced to take a knee to anyone, Hastal would be her choice... and she would go cursing all the while, but sinking to the ground nevertheless, ready to take down the bastard who forced her to kneel in the first place. Somehow, she suspected Hastal would have approved.

Unable to bear the stern look of the statues any longer, Aeley gazed at the low ceiling just beyond them. They had always unnerved her, all four of them, no matter what version of statue they were, though she never understood why. *Maybe it's because their statues are everywhere, always staring at us, as if we need to be sorry for something.*

Or maybe it was because it was already difficult enough dealing with people and she needed an out, with the Goddesses the easiest to leave in a ditch somewhere and far less likely to get her thrown in prison.

Aeley eyed the empty corridor to her left, several of the open doors letting light into the hallway. Torch cradles hung on the walls, but there was little else to see, save for the tiny shards of black stone glinting on the floor. To the right was more of the same. It was not a place to entertain visitors, and there were no appearances to keep.

"Well, now, it's nice to have company," a woman's husky voice called from the corridor to Aeley's right, "especially when we don't have to add you to our pens. A real, honest visit from a law-abider. Come on in, get comfortable. We don't bite. Usually."

Aeley forced a smile for the broad-shouldered warden. "Rea."

Rea stopped at Aeley's side and thrust out her hand. "Nice to see you, Steward." The men following Rea gathered around her, all three taller than Rea by at least a foot, with muscular bodies under leather armour. She nodded at the guards. "Don't mind them. They follow me *everywhere*. Comes with the job, not that I mind," she said, winking and leaning forward, her voice lowered. "Makes being warden a little more fun. So much better-looking than what we've got working in the hole out there, and a hundred times nicer to talk to."

"I can imagine," Aeley murmured. She clasped Rea's forearm, her jaws clenched as Rea squeezed her arm tight. *Stop being a child, me. She* was *a guard here once. Can't be dainty and weak in a place like this. Just smile like you want to be here.* With a glimpse at Lira, she took a breath and relaxed. Not doing it alone made a difference, more than she wanted to admit. "Thank you for receiving us personally."

"Always. Can't ever say I'm a poor mistress," Rea said with playful smile, almost as warm as the dark, even tan to her golden-brown skin. "Well, then, Aeley Dahe, visiting *me*. We should consider ourselves lucky, boys: she's the well-behaved one. Shouldn't give us a goddess's pinch of trouble. And I'm terribly sorry about your father. Nice guy. Did good things. Earned respect honestly. It's a real shame he's left us."

"Thanks," Aeley muttered. Could she just get to Allon and move on?

Rea tousled her short red hair, the shade almost as vibrant as Pellon's. "What can I offer you? I'd say come on into my office and we'll have a meal, trade some stories. But nine guesses says this isn't a social call, and the tenth is hoping for a drink because I'm bored today. Can't sit still, even if the Council paid me better." Her gaze shifted to Lira. "Or maybe this *is* a social call, except you're dressed too pretty to be here.

Maybe we should get you changed into something ugly filthy so the men keep their tongues in their heads."

Lira opened her mouth to respond, but Aeley stopped her, raising one hand to her chest. "We're here for an interrogation," Aeley replied.

"Oh?" Rea pouted, though the corners of her eyes crinkled. Her lips slid into a grin. "Shame it's all business. Luckily, we love interrogations, too. And I'm sure I don't even have to guess at who it is. Some snide little coward of a man you just happen to be related to, you poor, poor girl. I'm right, aren't I?"

"If he's still alive, then yes."

"Ah, good. Gives us some reason to heckle him some more. He knows how to test everyone's patience. Don't know how you managed him." Rea motioned to her guards. "Bring Allon up. And don't bother making him look nice. She doesn't care."

The men were down the hall and around a corner before Rea spoke again. "Come on. Follow me," she instructed, leading them down the same corridor she had come up. When she stopped and raised her arm through an open doorway, Aeley obeyed, pulling Lira into the small room lit by a single torch. Pellon slipped in behind them but stayed at the door, his arms crossed tightly over his chest, no different than usual when Allon was around. Silent as Pellon was, the contempt in his blue-green eyes burned with every word he bit back. Silence, where he was concerned, only led to worry, and whenever Allon was involved, that same silence usually meant Pellon was one punch away from sending Allon straight to the floor, never to wake again.

Rea pointed to the table in the middle of the room: simple, accompanied by three chairs. "Have a seat. He'll be along shortly, assuming he doesn't have to be subdued. Sometimes he needs the extra encouragement."

Rattling filled the hallway, followed by clanging metal and loud voices.

"Just stay here where it's safe. I'll be back. And I'll bring something tasty. We'll toast to your father," Rea said before rushing out of the room.

"I can't believe you volunteered to join me here," Aeley muttered to Lira and dragged her heel across the stone floor. Four prison guards hustled past the room, but only one acknowledged them, his dark expression almost a scowl.

Lira sat in one of the chairs and stretched her legs. "It's a long ride."

Yelling filled the hall, the words hard to understand. Allon, perhaps? *Some of that encouragement she mentioned?*

A dirt-covered man in dark, torn clothing entered the room, the chain shackled to his ankles dragging along the stone. He held his head low, his hands bandaged and unchained. Two guards guided him from behind, pushing him towards the single chair on the other side of the table. They barked and swatted his head as he hesitated.

Behind them, the noise in the hall continued. For a moment, Aeley wondered if they had the wrong prisoner.

"Nice to see you, Aeley, or at least your feet. Still dressing like a man, are we? Maybe even raided my clothing, seeing as all of it's apparently yours, or so I'm told."

"Allon," Aeley greeted through clenched teeth. When he raised his head, she saw him clearly, even with dirt caked all over him. His complexion was darker, but not just from the sun: he was bruised, with his nose disjointed and his grin missing a tooth. "I'm glad to see someone pummeled you."

"Ha, funny. Always so funny." Allon grunted. "I'm not going to run away, you mindless idiots. Give a man a chair!" He ducked as one of the guards raised a fist. The other guard kicked over the chair, but Allon snickered and pulled the chair upright before falling into it. "Have to do everything myself."

Aeley stood behind her empty chair, gripping the bar across its back instead of her knife. Lira shifted in her seat and pushed away from the table.

The movement caught Allon's attention. "What's this? An offering? A bribe? It's been so long since I had one of you." He reached for Lira.

One of the guards slammed Allon's hand down, pinning his wrist to the table.

"I wasn't going to touch her, grunt!" Allon tugged back, struggling to get free. As he yanked harder, the guard let go and laughed. Allon teetered in the chair, almost falling over. "Would you quit it? The Council said to make me work off my punishment, not dismember me."

"Same thing," one guard said to the other, both of them laughing harder.

"Please tell me you brought her to make this meeting easier on me." Allon stared at Lira. "You were even at my hearing. I remember you now, hiding behind my sister." He looked up at Aeley, a smile creeping across his lips. "Is there something you'd like to tell me? Have you finally found someone who can stand your uppity sense of justice? Maybe someone to tickle the part of you that you just don't use? You know, the part of you guys would pay a fortune to see since you keep it locked away and rusting. The part that makes you such a—"

Both guards slapped the back of Allon's head. He jolted forward, his forehead almost hitting the table. "And apparently this is less of a family reunion and more of a beating." Allon drew his hands into his lap, his expression confused between sneer and scowl. "What do you *want*?"

"I want to know what you've been up to." Aeley lifted her chin. "Have you been abiding by the laws around your punishment?"

"If by 'punishment,' you mean lifelong torture without pay or rights while wasting away, and by 'abiding,' you mean breaking some bones and making other people wealthy, then yeah, guess I have." Allon raised his hands, palms up. The bandages were soiled with dirt and blood. "Would you like to peek at the holes in my hands? I think I saved you some pus—" He ducked, anticipating a slap.

When the guards remained still, instead, disappointment flashed across his face.

As Allon's green eyes flicked towards Lira, he brightened. "Maybe you'd like to take a look? You seem nice. Quiet. Not likely to beat a man to death. Tell me if I should be getting a second opinion about these."

Aeley dug her heel into the floor while Lira restrained herself, the muscles in her neck tense, her chin still raised. Pellon stepped closer to them, but stopped as Aeley raised her hand, motioning for him to stay back.

"We don't care," Aeley said. "What we *do* care about is if you've had any contact with anyone. Been doing anything."

"Why?" Allon asked. "Has someone been having a party without me?"

"Someone's been causing trouble, doing things you would do. Doing things you've *done*. Except you're here." Aeley crossed her arms. "What *I* want to know is if you've had friends come by and ask for ideas?"

Allon huffed and pursed his lips, mocking her as he pretended to think. "Now, I'm not too sure—head's been knocked around a little too much, you know—but I remember a few people gracing me with their presence before I got locked in here permanently. But wouldn't you know: I just can't seem to remember any names. Funny, isn't it? Throw a man away and his memory just goes." He whistled and waved his hand towards the open door.

"Allon, quit it. Names!" Aeley demanded and slapped the table.

"I'd love to, Ae, really, but they wouldn't help." Allon smacked his lips and leaned to the side, staring at Lira. "They weren't here for plans. They were offering condolences and trying to get me out. A few thought they'd buy my way out, but you know, I just couldn't let them. I convinced them to save their wealth for what was more important. Nice folks, though. People I'm happy to call friends. They understand the value of loyalty."

Had she not known better, she would have thought he was speaking directly to Lira, as though they knew each other.

"So you're saying you don't know anyone who'd be attacking villages?" Aeley passed a glance over him, her eyes narrowed. "That no one's decided to take on where you left off—maybe as revenge?"

Allon straightened, his expression blank. "I'm saying I have no idea what you're talking about. I haven't done a thing other than haul rocks and bust ribs. I don't have time to think about what's going on in your perfect little world when I need to focus on surviving. In case you didn't notice, people don't like me. So when I've got a couple dozen guys who'd love to kill me, it's kind of difficult to coordinate measly attacks on villages that aren't worth my piss."

"So, it isn't you?"

"It isn't me. Whatever's going on, you're wasting time. What would Father say?"

Sucking in a sharp breath as she rocked on her heel, Aeley bit her tongue.

"You know what he'd say?" Allon continued. "He'd tell you you're in over your head. He'd say you need help from someone who knows what to do."

"You don't know *what* he'd say. You never paid attention," Aeley spat out.

"So *you* say. I paid attention to the important things, to the important people. If you weren't so concerned with me, you'd have done the same by now." Allon snorted and flipped back his hair. "But it's not like you don't have *any* other ideas, now is it?" Lips pursed, he stared her down. "Because let's be honest: this is a fishing trip. There's no way you spent all that time being Father's perfect little heir without picking up *some* names. I hate your guts, but you're a *bit* better at this than you're playing."

Aeley eased back, eyeing him in the brief silence. That come-and-go perception of his was annoying, but it had its uses. "Yeah, you think?"

"Yeah, I think, and here's your problem—" Allon leaned forward, his hands settling on the table in front of him, the chain of his leg shackles jangling along the floor. "While you're up in here, catching nothing on a limp line, you've got enough viable options playing their games back home." He smirked. "Or have the gangs bought you out? Looking the other way, are we, and getting stabbed in the back? Or was that win reserved just for me?" He raised one hand. "No, wait, let me guess: *you* think that with Father dearest dead, they just—" Allon whistled a bird's song, his hand fluttering away. "—ran off, business all packed up? Because that's pretty damn shallow, even for you."

"Guess that means we loosened up a few things in your empty head."

"Ah, and we've just gone back to fishing, hmm? I prove how smart I am, you steal the ideas. Excellent precedent, Steward."

Aeley clenched her jaws. "Is this going somewhere or are we pissing circles all day?"

"I've got nothing *but* circles to piss in, thanks to this bloody fine establishment." Allon leaned back and settled into his chair on an angle, the chain rattling. "But since this is fantastically more entertaining than the yard with foul beasts almighty, let's just say this: Cigils, Shar-denn, Glim Takers. Bark up their trees for a bit, flush out the bastards. They love when the catastrophe's ripe for the taking, and a change in leadership—well," he said, smiling, "there's so much chaos, they really won't be able to help themselves. With things so muddled, going from experienced to a child in an adult's opinions, they'll be dying to mess around with you."

"The chaos," Lira muttered.

"Smart *and* easy... on the eyes." Allon chuckled, rubbing at his lips with one hand. "Though answer me this, easy one: anyone sent in the spies yet? Any of Severn's bastard hunters after those gallant sackers of villages?"

Clasping Lira's shoulder, Aeley stepped forward before Lira could reply—if she even intended to. Allon was much too comfortable with Lira. Too familiar, that tone suggesting things Aeley could barely stomach. "Maybe I have, maybe I haven't. What's it to you?"

"Nothing, just wondering how far you've thought any of this through." Allon sighed, eyes rolled towards to the ceiling. "I'll make this simple: you'd be better doing the sniffing around on your own to keep from spooking the gangs— they tend to get an extra sense about these things when you send in the usuals. Do it and they'll run, keep sacking things. You know the rest. As for the gangs themselves, I'd concentrate on two of them: Cigils and Glim. And before you give me that look," he said, raising his hand, "yeah, I know the instinct is to run with the Shar-denn, but with circumstances as they are, the bigger they are, the less likely they're behind it."

Aeley snorted. "That doesn't make any sense."

"Actually," Allon drawled, looking bored, "it does, if you've been following the score. One—" he circled his bandaged hand in the air "—the Tract Steward is dead, comfort be the Tract Steward; a switch from old to new with questionable space in between and the unrest that comes with it. And two—" his hand circled again "—high-profile criminal case right here, if you haven't noticed. If they're doing things I'd do, and so soon, that sounds like someone riding someone else's bright idea. In fact, that'll be all this is: riding the chaos, taking advantage of the confusion." Allon lowered his hand. "They're testing you, and likely pushing territory boundaries while they're at it—none of which the Shar-denn will have an interest in. They've got much more devious ways of doing that, and they don't have to be so damn blatant about it. Then again, strength in numbers and in prowess. They don't have anything to prove right now. With Father out, that's one barb hacked off with several more left—and you aren't one of them."

"But the other ones—"

"Have been at war with the Shar-denn for *years*. They're small, ambitious. Any opportunity is an opportunity worth exploiting. So now, with you in power? They're stretching their muscles, seeing what you'll do. Seeing what they can get away with." Allon shrugged. "Wouldn't surprise me if this was all part of the larger turf war—you *do* know about that, right? How Cig and Glim have been fighting the Shar over territory? They've been pushing that bloody mess for years." Disgust flashed across his face. "Distasteful. It's one of the only things I agree with Father about. I told him to hit them back hard if they acted up, but of course he didn't."

A wry smile crept over his lips as he continued. "But see, that means you've inherited the problem, and you can thank him for being spineless. With him gone, expect Cig and Glim to get worse—they're going to fight for more power while you're getting settled. They'll be looking to destabilize things further, especially the longer *you* take to set things straight. And the Shar's just going to stand back and watch it all fall apart—they'll be looking at how you handle it. Then when you're done with the other two, *that's* when they'll strike." He shrugged one shoulder. "Or maybe they'll consider you rubbish for the loss and let you rot. I've heard about them doing both. Either way, it's the little fish you're after. If you can get through them, you'll be ready for the bigger one."

They stared each other down, neither one moving in the silence. As much as Aeley hated to admit it, Allon had a point. Several points, which made her hate him more. Did she believe him? Did she *not* believe him? Could she afford to do the latter? Ignoring him sounded like a better plan, but if she was wrong only to find out he was right...

It did nothing to help the matter of what she could do about it and how. Gangs took time. Resources. People. And if sending in the hunters and spies made them scatter or enticed them to hit harder, what was she left with? She could take the issue to Severn... but then Severn would turn around and accuse Aeley of being useless, then likely take over the issue and bump Aeley to the lowest rung of control over her own tract.

No, going to Severn was not an option, not yet. If she was going to prove herself, she needed to do it on her own. By her own choices. Her own team.

If she could just figure out what any of that looked like—who she could trust or at least rely on.

"*But,*" Allon said, the disdain in his tone souring her thoughts further, "it could just as well not be any of them. Either way, you've got a fight on your hands, and if you're taking on the gangs... well, you'd better do it soon. They'll only get unrulier, and that'll be on *your* head, no matter what Father did or didn't do. You sure you got the stones to do this? Or did you drop them at the Valley and they got crushed? Because you're lost if you're coming to me." He smiled, his eyes gleaming. "Thanks for proving my point—that I'm better at this than you are. You really have *no idea* what you're doing, do you?"

Aeley gritted her teeth, calling on all the patience she had right then. That was enough of him for one day.

"We're done here," she said, tapping Lira's shoulder.

As Lira followed Aeley to the door with Pellon right behind them, Allon shouted, "You're an absolute idiot if you don't think about it. Your face says you're in trouble. The fact you're here says you don't know what you're doing."

Aeley stepped over the threshold and slid a hand across Lira's back, guiding her into the hall.

"Maybe you should go ask your potential husbands for help," Allon suggested.

Aeley stopped cold.

No.

Aeley turned back, carefully controlling her breath. "How do you know about it?"

Allon grimaced as he fidgeted in his chair. "People talk. Councilmen when they're waiting for a hearing to start. Noble families coming to see loved ones—at least, the ones they think are being saved by the justice system." He looked at the ceiling. "Our father—our sweet, loving, caring father who doted on you and indulged everything you ever wanted—has made you consider marriage to a family you know nothing about. Good thing for you I know something. Like the fact they've never stopped thinking like Stewards."

He pointed at Aeley but stretched his body as if trying to see Lira standing in the hall. "If you're stuck, why don't you run to them? More resources, more people, more of everything. Considering you're probably thinking you didn't get anything of much value from me, you should take it. Might go a long way for your marriage." He smirked. "And you'll have to forgive me, but I'll miss whatever dismal wedding your adoring little sycophants plan for you. Send me a note, though, and I'll try and remember to send you a gift. Probably something covered in my own blood, just for luck."

Allon laughed, his voice echoing off the walls.

With nothing left to say, Aeley spun on her heel and left him there.

Chapter Thirteen

"So that was a lovely reunion."

Aeley opened one eye to peer at Lira, still lying on the seat across from her—a worthy distraction from the never-ending cycle of questionable thoughts in her head. She pulled herself out of the corner of the carriage and leaned towards Lira. "Wasn't it, though? Almost went as expected."

"Almost?" Lira sat up and tapped Aeley's knee, the light touch enough to leave Aeley flinching. "Expecting a confession, weren't you?"

"No. The fact he knows about the marriage contract is interesting, though. I'm also surprised he'd even suggest something so helpful."

"Maybe punishment's been good for him."

"Or not. I don't see the quarry making him any wiser, just stronger."

And no less correct.

The bastard.

Aeley fell back against the seat, arms crossed over her chest as she glanced out the window, one foot up on the seat across from her, her boot close to Lira's gown but not touching—just threatening to jam the sole of her foot through the wood while she sorted through the mess her mind was in. Night had descended around them, casting the woods on either side of the road into a deep darkness almost as bleak as the void she tried to make sense of. Except the carriage driver had lit his lantern, offering a soft light by the door, where her thoughts offered nothing but gnawing frustration at someone she could do nothing more about.

Damn Allon, and double damn his answers.

Meanwhile, people had been talking about her personal business behind her back, and talked about it around Allon, if not directly *to* him, robbing her of privacy where he was concerned. Though what he said...

Scowling at the night, Aeley seethed over Allon's points about the gangs—how they rang truer the more she considered them. There was no stopping the barrage of memories that slammed down around his words, forcing everything she knew about the gangs to the fore, scraps of conversation and assumptions mixed together in a tangle of confusion and anger, more than a little of it hurled in her father's direction. For years he had kept her on the periphery of the issue, refusing to include her in whatever plans he concocted with Severn and Gavert, Severn's predecessor on the High Council and the one who had groomed Severn to take over his position. Korre had insisted he handle the matter himself with agents of his choice rather than let Aeley handle it, despite her training and willingness to intervene.

A lack of trust—that was what had kept her firmly situated on the *not helpful* side of the line he had drawn. A lack of trust in her; a lack of trust in the gangs to not make things worse. Somewhere between the two, Aeley had been pushed to the side and told to wait, her training squandered on governance matters that had nothing to do with the fight. Meanwhile, the arrests and confrontations were left to members of Kattal's military, bounty hunters, and officers of the law that answered directly to Korre outside of their family's guard.

Protection, Korre had said every time she asked him why he refused to put her to the test. His tone had varied with each reply, sometimes annoyed, sometimes fond, but the answer was always the same, which infuriated her more. He had seen her trained, ensured she had the best tutors, from Lensen, the Head of the Guard before Mayr, all the way through the ranks to high-ranking generals in the military who had owed Korre several favours. Yet, when all of that could have been put to use, he balked and hid behind being a father, purposely keeping the information out of her hands. Partially because he feared Aeley's version of handling the matter would attract more trouble, and partially because he suspected the gangs would have found a way to gut her for stepping into their business.

"And considering you're the only one I can trust to handle our *business,"* Korre had said the last time, his wince hard to forget as he collapsed in his chair, looking too exhausted to even spit the words out, *"I need to keep you alive. You're the named heir, dearest, and the most likely candidate to follow on my heels. You're the only one who can..."*

He had never finished that thought, the words lost to a round of coughs that ended in blood spattered in his hand. A handkerchief had accompanied him to his bed, with Aeley escorting him every step of the way and three guards closed in around them, as protective of Korre as he was of her. They had left that discussion there, never to be addressed again, only seared into Aeley's recollections.

On the other hand, he had also instructed Mayr, Pellon, and the rest of the guards to stay well out of the matter, and that provided a small comfort, knowing she was not the only one denied a chance at settling the scores. By no means were any of them to approach the gangs, or so Korre had instructed, mostly in an attempt to keep their focus on the protection of their family and the Dahe household rather than seeing them dead on his doorstep. The broader scope was for him to worry about, not them, and he went to his death with that commitment still in his grasp.

But death had not stopped this, and the days of playing obedient heir were over. This was on Aeley's watch now, with whatever resources she had, no different than any of the other Tract Stewards. She could approach Severn for assistance or not, but either way, the choice was Aeley's, not someone else's.

Even so, she could still loathe her father's insistence and curse his protectiveness. Her experience with the gangs was limited, more than even Allon's, who no doubt had gone drinking with the lot of them and perhaps even known it, but never cared. There was every possibility that he did, in fact, know more about them than Aeley—and damn him to every cursed mountainside in the Realm of the Dead for that.

Even worse was how Allon was right: she *was* in over her head, and she abhorred how accurate he could be when he wanted to hit every one of her nerves.

Aeley stole a glance at Lira, loving how her grey gaze never strayed from Aeley's face, but more in love with the gentle tilt of Lira's head to the side, how her dark hair tumbled in a mass of mussed curls over one shoulder, her ice-blue dress a soft cream-yellow in the faint touch of candlelight.

"Did you want to talk about it?" Lira asked quietly, curled up in the corner beneath her shawl, legs drawn up on the seat next to her. Every bit of calm worth lying next to, if only the carriage would allow for it without leaving Aeley aching in all ways.

Tempted as she was to let Lira in on her thoughts, however, she let the chance wander off, denying it with the shake of her head. There would be a time to talk, but not then, and not about the gangs. It was hard enough to admit how little she knew, let alone involve Lira in it— not that she anticipated Lira knew much more than her, though even if she did, that would only make it worse.

"No, but thanks." Aeley offered a smile and tapped her foot against Lira's, earning a light laugh that drifted away too quickly, lost to the wheels, creaks, and the muffled tones of Pellon's voice and the driver's. They would be home soon enough. The familiar feel of returning to Dahena settled in as the foot path to the temple entered her sight, her gaze following the dimming light of the lanterns the priests kept at the gates to the path.

If only the path to the answers she needed could be as welcoming.

With a sigh, Aeley stared at the floor, picking out thoughts one at a time. Allon had mentioned all three known gangs in Kattal, each one as likely as the next to mob and steal and even kill their way through their intentions. Well, almost as likely: the Shar-denn were always the first to opt for death when everything else got in their way, including the general displeasure that arose when someone was left breathing. They valued silence over most things, immortalized by their motto, "*The only way out is dead.*"

The Cigils and the Glim Takers, on the other hand, were no strangers to the concept, though they left less of a trail of dead bodies to follow, either in hesitation, strategy, or they were far more discreet with it than the Shar-denn, who had no qualms with leaving the corpses to rot in the open.

And yet, that was one of the biggest differences among them: the Shar-denn thrived on the attention and fear-mongering, their mission revolving around the coldness of life with goals that included heavy-handed taunts and making a mockery of compassion. The Cigils and Glim Takers tended to be quieter, preferring to do business in closer quarters, the doors more firmly closed around their crimes. Where the Shar-denn would set fire to a city and let it burn while they sat at the centre of it, feasting on stolen goods and victims for trafficking, the Cigils and Glim Takers would have crawled into the darkness and sold the city out from under its ruins, well out of sight but never far from the profit.

None of it helped the current issue, only confounded it. While the attack on the road against Hano and his father sounded like the Shar-denn's love of opportunity, it lacked a certain flourish often attributed to them. There was almost a sloppiness, particularly in leaving

Hano behind—a child they could have easily taken to sell however they saw fit and turned a few coins, at least from what little she knew of the matter. It was one of the most profitable parts of their enterprise, so vile it had disgusted Korre enough to request military support of heightening degrees as the years had gone on, no matter his preference for peaceful resolve—one of the rare times the ends had matched the means Severn could provide, and Korre had accepted it with few other options on the table.

The fires in the village were quiet, however, the work of shadows, and while that would never disqualify the Shar-denn, who lived with the shadows as if they were replacements for a soul, it failed to single them out.

All of which circled back to Allon.

Aeley glared at the doorframe, wishing the driver would snuff the lantern to let her stew in utter darkness, or at least relieve some of the headache pushing against her eyes. Spiteful as he was, Allon made a valid point: Korre had never struck back at the Cigils and Glim Takers as hard as he had the Shar-denn, though rightfully so, given how large the Shar-denn was rumoured to be. Theories put the Shar-denn's numbers in the low thousands across Kattal, with the highest rates of activity concentrated in pockets and focused on the cities. Having been around for generations, the length of their reach was well past debate, only action. Too large to control quickly and too well organized to accurately pin down and flush out, the Shar-denn continued to proliferate. It was almost enough to justify the creation of a specialized militia to handle them, and them alone, though Severn had yet to reach that point, at least to Aeley's knowledge.

By comparison, the Cigils and the Glim Takers were in their toddling stages. According to Korre, they had come up together for the better part of fifty years, even surviving the plague that killed thousands of citizens nearly ten years after the first recorded appearances of the gangs in public record. That plague had taken mostly the older generations, including what remained of Aeley's grandparents and both of her father's siblings, leaving Korre the sole surviving member of the Dahe line. Her mother's family had fared just as poorly.

Yet the gangs had continued forward, whatever their numbers, which never seemed to rival the Shar-denn's. Nor had their crimes reached the same terrifying depths as the Shar-denn's, not that they were any less dangerous, just less widespread. For the most part, their activity was confined to ill-defined spots throughout Kattal, mostly outside of the cities, around smaller communities, and further inside the borders than where the Shar-denn tended to haunt.

And again, it all comes around to what he said.

Boundaries. Territory. A turf war. Destabilization.

While none of the gangs had dared attack Dahena before, there was every possibility they were using the village as a means to settle scores with her father while making a point to each other. Their politics were another beast altogether, one she had yet to understand, but she could grasp enough to see Allon's point, even agree with it. Gailarin was vulnerable with her at the helm, and any of the gangs could use that to their advantage. Since Korre's death they had lain low, though their patience seemed to have worn thin.

Or maybe that was the entire point.

"They're testing you, and likely pushing territory boundaries while they're at it."

Maybe, just maybe, that had been the message all along and she had been too ignorant to see it.

A glance out the window did nothing to assuage the misery that took up permanent residence in Aeley's gut. They were in Dahena, passing through the centre of town, though the life the village usually displayed with vigour choked on a fearful silence. Windows were boarded up, but there was little else anyone could do to keep safe from vandalism. If there was nuisance to be had, whoever was responsible would find a way, and they were most likely not the Shar-denn. *Nuisance* was not what the Shar-denn aimed for, not when *attention-seeking disaster* spoke more to their level of commitment and expertise, and they liked leaving a bit of signature behind to tease the rage of the authorities.

No, this was the work of the other gangs, so much so they should have just signed their names in the ashes. The last thing she needed was a game. If they wanted her attention, they had it, but if they wanted something else from her, they would have to make their identity known. She needed more than initialed threats.

On the other hand, perhaps initials were all she needed, with the Cigils taking the top spot in her consideration. If they were tired of playing in the corners with the Glim Takers, their ambitions set on higher aspirations that edged them closer to competing with the Shar-denn, the letters in her study were all the evidence she needed to start an investigation into them... assuming she could secure the means to do so without getting someone killed in the process.

As the carriage rolled along the avenue to the gates of the estate, Aeley welcomed the distraction. She offered Lira a smile as she stretched out and leaned forward, close enough to rest her hand over Lira's. "Sorry," she said, caressing Lira's knuckles with the back of her hand for a second time. "I'm not usually this bad a travel companion."

Lira snorted softly, her fingers turning over beneath Aeley's to brush her palm. "I think, under the circumstances, you're more than allowed to keep silence closer." Her small smile back was the barest hint of comfort. "He's entirely too trying."

"More than you know," Aeley muttered, drawing Lira in for a kiss as the carriage made its way around the carriage circle.

The moment the carriage stopped, Aeley pushed open the door. Out. She needed out. "Hopefully Mayr's found something." She jumped down and stared up the stairs to the door of the estate, the sight alone offering much-needed warmth. After a trip that had felt twice as long as the ride out to the quarry, she was ready to call the day finished and hide under the blankets, with every hope that Lira would be willing to join her... Goddesses help her luck there.

Lira stepped down from the carriage. "If he hasn't found anything?"

"We'll have to rethink our plan of attack." They had to, anyway, though that was a discussion for later. Hand in hand with Lira, Aeley pulled her up the stairs as Pellon disbanded the guards and headed for the Guard House. The front doors opened as they reached the last few steps, with Haydin waiting just beyond them in the foyer, his familiar face easing Aeley's irritation.

"How did it go?" Haydin ushered them inside before closing the doors. "Was he any help?"

"He says he has nothing to do with it." Aeley peered up the main staircase and around the corners. "Is Mayr here? Do we know if he's discovered anything?"

Haydin shook his head, his gaze falling to the floor.

"Well." Aeley sighed. "Thanks, Haydin," she said with a weak smile, allowing him to wander off to see about dinner. She could wait to hear Mayr's report, in addition to giving him her own just to see what he made of it. *Enough of people. I just want to do nothing right now. Well, almost nothing.* With Lira, there was more than one way to spend the time before dinner. Staring down the corridor, Aeley let her thoughts wander to where they had left off before the assault on the road...

Aeley tensed, her back strained as she straightened and flexed her free hand.

The assault.

The village had been attacked, which was bad enough, but with Lira's regular visits to Dahena...

Without definitive answers, the situation remained dangerous. Allon claimed he knew nothing, but his candid replies only stressed how vigilant they all needed to be. If she ignored the possibility of him being right about everything, she put Gailarin at risk, especially those in Dahena, including her own household and Lira, who had no means to defend herself if a mob attacked. The escalation of organized violence in a village no gang had previously bothered with rightfully unsettled them all, but if it was part of a gang war with Aeley played between them like a toy everyone wanted to share but no one wanted to forfeit, anyone associated with her could be in danger. *Everyone* was at risk.

Still, there was something—a fragment of uncertainty that niggled at her thoughts. Allon had lied about *something*. He knew more than he let on, she just had no idea what he held back or why.

Then there was Lira.

Allon had been much too pleased with Lira, his suggestive glances tempting Aeley to jam his eyeballs further into his skull and roll them backwards.

He looked at her like he'd jump on her. Like he wanted his filthy hands all over her. It's bad enough I can't figure out which part he's lying about, but now that he's seen her...

She tugged Lira into the corridor.

Lira followed without protest. "Where are we going?"

"No one's here to bother us. Perfect time to teach you a few things about defending yourself."

"Defending myself? Why?"

Aeley stopped in the middle of the corridor. "Because Allon can't be trusted. And whoever's responsible for the attacks are too damn unpredictable." She turned to the darkened hallway behind Lira, already imagining the route to the armoury. "You need to know how to do something in case they come after you. Using a quill won't do any good."

"I'd say I can take care of myself, but is there any point in arguing?"

"No. Especially since I've seen how you are with your brothers."

"That's a low strike," Lira grumbled.

"Not from what I've seen."

Lira sucked in a breath, then nudged Aeley. "Go on, then. I'll let you have your way."

Aeley almost refuted that, her mouth opening to counter the comment, but she changed her mind and pulled Lira towards the downwards staircase. The hall below was dimly lit, but Aeley could maneuver the hall with her eyes closed. *Father always said I spent too much time down here.*

They turned another corner and stopped in the first open doorway. Metal blades in the large, windowless room reflected the light from the hall. Chains and ropes hung on the walls, looped around pegs. Wooden racks held up swords and axes, and in between, shields stood upright in thick, slotted blocks. Quivers filled with arrows leaned against the corners with bows on the wall above them. Standing before the wall on the other side of the room were tall, wooden targets, painted with black circles and marred with deep marks.

She led Lira towards the middle of the room, her gaze going to the knives on a long table cluttered with dismantled arrow shafts and polishing rags. *Perfect. We'll start with those.*

"Why don't you stand right there?" Aeley pointed to the other side of the table. As Lira took her suggestion, Aeley snatched up three of the six knives and weighed them in her hand. They were worn and nicked from frequent use, requiring cleaning and sharpening, but their blades were heavy and strong. *As long as they end up in the target and not in me, they'll suffice.*

Walking around the table, she stopped at Lira's side and pointed at one target. "Ready to throw something?"

"You're going to give me a sharp weapon?" Lira eyed the blades. "Are you sure you don't want armour—breastplate, maybe? Something to keep your eyes in your head?"

"It won't be that bad." Aeley raised one knife. "This goes into your hand and then goes that way. Couldn't be simpler."

"You didn't see what happened the last time my father made me hold a sword. A complete disaster."

"Someone lost an arm?"

"No, but close."

"A toe?"

Lira tilted her head. "Let's just say I'm not allowed to touch anything sharper than a dining knife."

"And that's probably because you're supervised." Aeley snorted a laugh, only to cover her mouth with the back of her hand. It would have been easier to quit laughing if Lira's cynical expression could have stopped making the whole thing more amusing. "This won't be anything like that, I promise. I learned when I was five years old. It's the first weapon I ever learned to use, and you can do it, too. It's simple. It's small. Anyone can carry a knife, especially one good enough to throw from a bit of distance, just to buy time so you can run away." She shrugged. "And if we can at least get you to stand right here, maybe I'll teach you some other things."

She raised the knife higher. Lira flinched.

"You really are afraid of it, aren't you?" Aeley lowered the knife.

"A little. I just don't want to hurt you. I tell you: I'm not good at this."

"Nothing will happen. It's safe."

"Don't say I didn't give you fair warning. And don't laugh every time I miss, either," Lira whispered.

"Of course I won't," Aeley said softly, leaning in to kiss Lira. "Have some faith. I'll help you through it. Here, I'll show you exactly the way I learned. Watch where everything goes." Turning to face the target, Aeley moved her left leg forward and leaned back on the other. She chose one of the dark circles and raised her left arm, holding it on an even line with her chest. With a slow breath and a firm grip on the knife in her right hand, she drew her arm back. In one smooth, coordinated movement, she shifted her weight over her outstretched leg and jerked her arm forward, releasing the knife. It cut through the air and embedded in the target, exactly where she had wanted it to go. A perfect throw.

Aeley held up another knife. "Your turn."

Lira hesitated, but finally accepted the knife. "How do I hold it? Do I just—"

"Hold it out with your thumb on top, like you're going to hit something with it. It's not a dining knife and it's not your quill. Yes, just like that. Don't grip too—no—yes, there." Aeley pointed to the target. "Now, face it."

With a shaky breath, Lira faced the target. "Here goes," she murmured, mimicking Aeley's stance.

"Left leg forward, since you write with your right hand," Aeley instructed as Lira fidgeted, "and keep them bent, but not too much. Don't lean forward until you throw and get that other foot—here, I'll help." She stepped into Lira, her hips a light touch against Lira's.

The moment Lira leaned back and pressed against Aeley's chest, Aeley clenched Lira's fist around the knife, resisting the urge to call off the lesson. She breathed in deeply once, twice, and counted down from five.

They were so close, in the same small space. Just them, alone, with Lira's scent right there, her hair soft on Aeley's skin, and the chance to touch... to hold... to bed down and forget everything else, just for a short while.

Until something else comes calling.

No. She needed to focus. Whatever her happier thoughts, the lesson had to happen, no excuses.

But after…

Aeley fought back the exasperated sigh of frustration working its way up and tapped Lira's lagging leg. "Point this just a little that way. Now stay back, just as you are, and bring up your arm," Aeley said, trying not to slide her hand up Lira's body but almost failing. She lifted Lira's tensed wrist towards the target, holding her arm even. One glance at Lira's face caught exactly what Lira felt, the strain around her mouth and eyes a gentle punch to Aeley's gut.

"It's all right," Aeley said softly, squeezing Lira's wrist. "You're doing fine. Relax everything." When Lira's shoulders dropped, Aeley continued, her voice hushed. "Since you're new to this, you need a guide. Use your non-throwing arm to tell you when to release. Now, pull your knife hand back." Stepping around Lira, Aeley stopped Lira's hand from drawing too far. "Hold it around here, at your ear. Any further back and you'll overdo it. When you're ready, throw the knife in one move. As your arm comes down, lean forward to give it strength, and let go at the level of your other arm. And don't stop. Just let go and keep bringing your hand down." She gestured to the target. "Go for it. Even if it fails, there's nothing to lose."

"But—"

"No," Aeley argued. "Keep it pointed at the target and you won't kill anyone. This thing won't bounce that far."

"I still think this is a bad idea," Lira muttered. She took a breath, then another, the muscles in her hand flexing. On her third breath, she threw the knife.

The blade struck the target higher than the mark before clattering to the floor. Lira straightened, followed quickly by the sag of her shoulders, echoing the relief on her face.

"Good." Aeley smiled as she clasped Lira's shoulder in a light squeeze... and held on longer than necessary. "Though I'm thinking we need to work on releasing at the right time. Maybe your wrist, too." Aeley handed Lira the last knife. "Let's try again." Once Lira assumed the stance again, Aeley stepped in behind her.

She hated the distance between them. They were *that* close and still much too far apart with everything in the way, whether it was duty or fabric or etiquette or any number of restrictions Aeley loathed right then—all of them reasons why she buried her face in the tangles of Lira's hair and breathed in, content to stay with the warmth it brought and the idea of calm. Quiet. A call to linger, like purposely getting lost on a sunny summer's day and telling the rest of the world to disappear and play without them until they were ready to get back to business.

Still, business never did itself... except she was damned tired of *doing* herself, and having Lira right there, a weapon between them, Lira trusting Aeley enough to try...

"Keep this up here," Aeley murmured, sliding her arm under Lira's and lifting it. She wrapped her other hand around Lira's fist. "And draw back very, very slowly."

The blade neared her face, but she remained still, giving trust of her own. As tense as Lira was, as tight as she held onto the blade, Lira followed Aeley's guidance—slow, but willing. Trusting Aeley's judgment. Putting some measure of faith into herself, enough to not give up after the first go, assured they could make it through together, no matter the failure.

Was it wrong to want more, to see where it could lead? To see it for all of its hopeful intimacy and run with the whispers of sensuality in trusting and being trusted? There had been so little trust as of late, so much of it shattered and left in shards, offering new wounds before the old ones could heal.

But this—she could get used to this.

Aeley cleared her throat. "This time, you're going to bend your wrist a little, like this," she instructed as she moved Lira's arm, "and release here." She stopped, holding Lira's wrist at chest height. "And carry on. That part was good. Actually, all of it was good. You're already better at it than you thought."

"It didn't stick, though," Lira said, turning her head. "And isn't that the whole point?"

"You hit it, and it's a better start than missing it completely." Aeley rested her chin on Lira's shoulder, her lips just shy of grazing Lira's cheek. "You should be kinder to yourself," she said quietly, "and less tense. Relax and it'll come." Leaning back, she let Lira take her stance, the blade catching the torchlight. "Wait."

Lira stopped, frozen in position. "What?"

"Just let me—" Aeley brushed Lira's hair over her non-throwing shoulder, her fingers taking a slow path over Lira's arm, reluctant to draw away. "To keep it from getting caught," she murmured before finally moving aside. If only being close meant something other than opening herself for getting stepped on, hit, or making Lira miss the target—she would have loved to press against Lira and guide each throw, to learn about her through touch and lesson, and, maybe even more than that, see that a smile made it to Lira's face by the end of it, her misgivings overcome and put aside.

Still, there was no contending with circumstances, not if she wanted Lira to succeed. "Go on," Aeley said.

Giving a nod and an arched brow to echo the amusement in her smirk, Lira returned her focus to the target. After a deep, controlled breath, she leaned forward and released the knife. This time, the blade sank into the target enough to keep from falling.

Lira inhaled sharply. "Well… all right, then," she said, her head tilting to the side. "Either that's luck or I'm really not that bad." Without moving out of her stance, she peered over her shoulder. "Just to make sure I have this right, show me again without the knife?"

Goddesses, help me. This isn't getting any easier. Just one look and I'm undone, completely gone—

"If you want." Aeley stepped into Lira again, cursing silently at the touch of body on body, chest to back, Lira's waist there for the holding. "Here." Her hand followed Lira's arm back, her fist near Aeley's face. Warm and loosely clenched inside Aeley's grasp, Lira's tender fingers were a perfect fit in Aeley's. Of all the things she could think of those fingers to do—of all the places where she wanted them—all she could focus on was keeping Lira posed like that for as long as she could. "From here. You'll get used to it."

A turn of head brought Lira's parted lips close to hers, the space between them barely there as the heat of Lira's breath played over Aeley's lips. Fist still poised above her shoulder, curled inside Aeley's, Lira said nothing, only watched. Her soft grey gaze stayed locked onto Aeley's in the quiet search for something while offering something hopeful in return, almost as though she was weighing options and liked what they brought to mind.

If only Aeley could have tapped into those thoughts, wandered through them to find out what Lira wanted. Needed. She would have settled for knowing what Lira searched for, and if Aeley could ever satisfy that quest. If only Lira would just talk to her. Let her in. Let them be. Let it go...

"Thank you," Lira whispered. Arching back into Aeley, she closed the distance between them with lips, body, and plenty of intention—a hard kiss, a gentle rub of back along chest, the hold of her fingers as they left Aeley's grasp and wrapped around Aeley's fist. She took over, stealing breath and chasing thoughts from Aeley's mind, spinning them off into a dark oblivion of nothing.

Aeley kissed her back just as hard, the lesson forgotten, duty as over as it would ever be.

Fist unfurled from Lira's, Aeley caressed Lira's jaw, fingertips gliding over the curves all to cup Lira's cheek and pull her closer. She hummed into the kiss as Lira turned into her, the press of Lira's hip against her stomach enough to send her deeper into their kiss, her focus lost all over again.

Lira's hand on her shoulder did nothing to restore clarity, not when that tender touch traveled down Aeley's arm, across her chest, and down her waist, never once pausing, simply moving with agonizing slowness as it roamed towards her thigh. Only then did that touch rest, Lira's fingers on the buckle of Aeley's belt, playing with it, her thumb dipping downwards, cautiously close to where it could do all the right things.

Aeley growled softly. She needed those fingers to journey lower, to slip inside her over and over again. Slow. Fast. Commanding with every trick in between. She wanted Lira in her, stroking through the wet warmth between her legs and easing the growing ache, taking Aeley for all she had—for all that Lira inspired, desire practically begging to be fondled and used and run ragged.

Here. Now.

All else forgotten, all else denied.

As if reading her mind, Lira took them that much closer, her leg slipping between both of Aeley's before she guided Aeley back, both hands clasped around Aeley's arms. Aeley stumbled into the table, her lower back meeting the edge with a quick, sharp pain as Lira pinned her there.

When fingertips drew over one of her breasts, teasing her hardened nipple, Aeley moaned and broke the kiss, desperate for a breath, shallow as it was. Lira's touch continued to play, circling the nipple before pinching hard, only to rub the sting away as Aeley arched against the table, gripping the edge—clawing at it as she rode Lira's thigh, her clit all but screaming for up-close attention, away from the scrape of fabric as it slipped and dragged, daring her to come.

Lira's mouth only worsened matters as she took to Aeley's neck with a nip and a lick and a low, playful chuckle that drove Aeley further into torment. Moistened lips roved over Aeley's throat, and the tip of Lira's tongue circled on Aeley's skin, calling forward a shiver, then two, another moan tumbling from Aeley before she could stop it. Slow, careful, Lira trailed wet kisses down Aeley's chest, working over the neckline of her tunic.

Damn her clothes, and damn the way Lira looked at her right then; how she nipped and tugged at the beige fabric with her gaze coming up from under lowered lashes, throwing Aeley all the agreement she needed.

Forget it all. I'm done playing.

Aeley spun them around and pushed Lira against the table. Lira's gasp of surprise and the look to match were worth every bit of satisfaction coursing through Aeley, taking pleasure along for the ride. Both hands resting on the table on either side of Lira, Aeley kissed her way across Lira's cheek, down her throat, tasting and teasing before she took a path up to Lira's jaw.

Between them, shallow breaths kept the silence at bay, moans coming and going just as quickly, lost to calls for more. Lira grabbed, tugged, and dug into Aeley with both hands— running through her hair, clawing across her shoulder blades, slipping around the back of her neck to keep her close. Encouraged by Lira's soft groan, Aeley bit Lira's neck and sucked lightly until Lira urged Aeley's head back, her tender grip squeezing Aeley's jaw.

"Wait," Lira whispered. "The table. Let me—"

Before she could finish, Aeley hoisted her onto the table, hands staying on Lira's hips in wait for another instruction.

"That works." Lira drew her close, both hands fisted in Aeley's tunic, demanding another deep kiss, hard enough to hurt.

Lost in the motions, Aeley surrendered as Lira's knowing hands wrapped around the curve of her breasts, just long enough to cup their weight and play before Lira's touch scaled over Aeley's ribs to her stomach.

The moment Lira's fingers slid under Aeley's belt and into her pants, Aeley held her breath. The smooth, warm touch of skin on skin, of Lira's deft fingers so close to her, *on* her, nothing between them but heat... A shiver raced through Aeley, almost chasing after Lira's fingers as they journeyed deeper into the tangle of curls between her legs. Towards that slick, wet crevice where her clit needed relief, a touch to come—

Aeley groaned and pulled away. "Is that where this is going?" she asked, her voice husky, quiet.

She wanted Lira to say it. She *needed* Lira to say it—to give Aeley all the reason in the world to ignore the last of her inhibitions and take Lira with her. To say *forget you* to everything else and get lost in the fall. Because this *was* falling, far and fast and fiercely, and it was terrifying. If she hit the ground without any way out...

"Considering we've been working our way to it," Lira said softly. "Unless..."

She pulled on her skirt, a slow crawl of thin, ice-blue fabric that crept up her legs and kept going. The more she exposed of herself, the more the knot in Aeley's gut twisted and burned, feeding her needy ache for release.

If she just waited... if she watched the show Lira was willing to put on, so beautiful, brazen, and bawdy... if she allowed Lira to take over completely and come undone before her, sweeping Aeley along with the seduction...

Goddesses, no.

There was no waiting, not as the skirt passed over Lira's knees, the pace quicker as the hem graced Lira's naked thighs, just at the edge of her short, dark blue underskirt.

She knew what she was doing—and Aeley refused to disappoint.

Kissing Lira again, she reached behind Lira to untie the laces of her gown, fingers fumbling until the ties dangled freely in her grasp. At her waist, Lira appeared to have a much easier time of things: she unbuckled Aeley's belt and tossed it away—more threw it over Aeley's shoulder, the metal clanking on the ground somewhere nearby, her knife abandoned with it.

With small yanks on Lira's dress, Aeley tugged the laces from the top grommets, stopping only to let Lira pull Aeley's tunic off. Cool air hit her skin, leaving her shuddering under Lira's caress as the heat of her palms slid up Aeley's chest, claiming another shiver while small bumps rose along Aeley's arms. Tender as she touched, Lira cupped Aeley's breasts and brushed her thumbs over Aeley's nipples before dragging her fingertips down Aeley's ribs.

Aeley fought the ongoing trembles that tripped one over another as Lira explored, her own focus even more set on getting the damned dress out of her way, as difficult as it was to concentrate. She worked harder on the laces, jerked quicker until the dress loosened. Not to waste a moment more, Aeley guided the sleeves down Lira's arms, holding her breath as the dress pooled around Lira's hips, so much more of her bared in the torchlight. Daring to touch, she stroked along Lira's sides, slow to work her way upwards. She followed the curves of Lira's body with her fingertips, up her waist, and between her breasts, up to her throat, all to travel back down and around. Happy to carry forward, she held Lira's breasts in her hands, the sight all too stunning to do nothing with.

Without warning, she drew one hardened nipple past her lips and sucked gently, teeth grazing, biting down as Lira groaned and clutched Aeley close, her legs closing around

Aeley's waist, pulling her in. Unable to keep back her quiet laugh, Aeley licked at Lira's breast with long strokes and lashed at the nipple with the tip of her tongue, darting over it, never letting up even as Lira clawed at Aeley's naked back, nails tearing into her. Lira moaned for more, gripping Aeley's hair and tugging hard enough to interrupt Aeley's focus.

The hint taken, Aeley traced a wet, messy path across Lira's chest with her tongue, lapping up the sweat beaded on Lira's skin, sweet like the pink berries used in Lira's perfume.

When she turned and nipped at Lira's dry nipple, digging in harder with her teeth, Lira cried out her surprise, nails scraping down Aeley's shoulders.

Aeley did nothing but smile up at her. She had her own plans, most of which ended in Lira crying her name and losing control. If that was one way to make it happen, she had no qualms about where she put her mouth and when, and no apologies, not if it kept Lira's lust-laden glare on her like it was right then.

"Just for that—" Lira whispered, fumbling with the drawstring at Aeley's waist. Aeley's pants came undone after a single tug on the string, and Lira pushed them down her hips.

Just as quickly, Lira slipped her hand between Aeley's legs and raked over her clit without any mercy whatsoever.

Aeley gasped, whimpered, her knees threatening to give.

Cruel. So blissfully cruel.

Lira moved with ease through Aeley's slickness, fingers gliding between her folds without hesitation, blazing a determined path of their own. One fingertip stroked her clit, followed by a second, only to alternate and work in tandem, switching between light and fast to hard and slow.

It was enough to leave Aeley crying out half-formed expletives, her nerves nearly climbing up the wall—or at least scratching the table out of its very existence.

If this was punishment for playing dirty…

I'm not sorry. Not even a little. Not—

Lira hummed, low and quiet, both fingers pressed to Aeley's clit, massaging, then circling around it. She teased, toyed, and stroked incessantly, drawing it out longer with every sound that tumbled out of Aeley in reply.

It may as well have been lightning that surged from Aeley's groin to her heart—there was no stopping her from trembling and groaning between shaky breaths.

Aeley slammed her hand on the table, trying to fight her shivers and buckling knees as one fingertip crept into her. Lira's moistened palm cupped Aeley as she worked her fingers, twisting and turning, pushing into Aeley before she rubbed the edges of her opening with a second finger.

"*Yes, there,*" Aeley cried, slapping the table again. She lowered herself on Lira's hand before pulling upwards, needing so much more—as much as Lira was willing to give. To share.

Lira gave a slow smile and drew her finger out to the tip before pushing in once more, slipping further into Aeley. Just as soon as her touch almost settled, she repeated it all again, each draw back and thrust in quicker than the last.

But it was Lira's two fingers working her at the same time that had Aeley wanting to scream. The stretch... the burn... the *everything* Lira brought to it.

Too good. Too fast. They needed to even it out. Aeley refused to be the only one getting something, and not this quick, not if she was going to come before she wanted. After the day she'd had, this was one thing she wanted to do slowly. And right. And well.

Aeley pulled Lira's hand away and groaned inwardly at how Lira's fingers glistened in the light, bathed in Aeley from the palm down. "Hold on. Just let me do something first."

She rushed to undress, fighting with one stubborn boot then the other before throwing them down with her pants in a careless heap beside the table. Her focus was on Lira the next moment, everything else forgotten but Lira's gaze as it crept over her, accompanied by a smirk that quickly shifted into a bite of Lira's bottom lip.

Kissing at that lip, favouring it for herself before kissing Lira fully, Aeley slid her hands up Lira's thighs, urging her gown and silky blue underskirt up her hips. With the gathered fabric clutched in both hands, she pulled it all over Lira's head and tossed it aside, a crumpled mess that landed close to one of the racks of blades, followed by the rest of Lira's clothes.

Lira shuffled up the table and leaned back on her elbows, one knee bent slightly upwards, looking entirely too comfortable surrounded by knives, arrows, and filthy rags that should have been nowhere near her and yet... she was naked. On display. Open for the adoration. And not seeming to care a whit about being caught among the disarray. Other than the bruises on her neck from where Aeley had bitten her, the only mark on Lira's body was a dark patch of skin on her thigh. All else was pale skin and dark hair, including the curls between her legs.

If ever there was a sight more beautiful, Aeley never wanted to know about it.

But a painting...

She would have given her titles, lands, and her dignity just to immortalize the scene before her.

"Like what you see?" Lira asked, the amused delight in her soft voice echoed in her smile. She hooked one ankle over Aeley's shoulder, baring herself to Aeley, guiding her closer.

Familiarity struck Aeley—hard, fast, unbidden as memories took over with names, images, touches of the few men she had lain with so many years before. This—and whatever *this* became—was nothing like those times. She had felt nothing for them, faking her way through and running away afterwards, never wanting to stick around for the explanations that came with it. She had never wanted to stay, and certainly she had never wanted *them* to stay, preferring to forget them altogether. They were shadow-cast figures in the background, confined to the pits of her mind; mistakes she'd had to make to finally get the hint that she would never be any man's lover—and that she was happier not to be, content to let them look but never touch.

Yet with Lira, she was freer, able to feel, to laugh, to *want*, almost as if she *had* to know what it felt like to touch Lira, surrendering to whatever could come of it or otherwise lose her mind. Part of it was exploring the unknown, of knowing what it could be to give herself over to another woman, to relinquish control just for a little while with someone she wanted close, but the rest... It was as though she could understand more and be understood better. Men had come and gone, leaving her with little to hold on to, but Lira... Aeley wanted to know every part of her. With one look, Lira could take her down, lead her into the deepest, darkest depths of intimacy and pleasure, and have her any way she wanted—spread, screaming, and deliriously sated.

And with Lira posed, ready to play...

"All right," Lira said quietly, breaking the silence, "if we're going to play it this way, let me start."

Aeley jerked her gaze up to Lira's, thoughts skittering away as she tried to understand what Lira meant.

One stroke later, she understood *completely*, the heat of a flush rushing across her cheeks.

She had stared too long without doing anything, but now she was reduced to watching Lira stroke herself, caressing her clit, flicking the tip, sinking deep—doing everything Aeley wanted to do herself. There was no ignoring the shift of Lira's hips as she rose into the touch, or her low moans as fingers slipped into her, past one knuckle, then another...

Leaning down into her, Aeley kissed Lira's stomach and gave a playful nip before she worked her way downwards. The trail of kisses took her close to where Lira's fingers moved inside her, Lira's hips lifting as the tip of Aeley's tongue swirled the moist curls and danced on the warm skin beneath, every breath she took in accompanied by Lira's heady scent.

When Lira started to pull her hand away, Aeley caught her fingers with her mouth, drawing them in with her tongue and lips to lick at the salty wetness. Tasting, teasing, she sucked on Lira's fingertips and raked her tongue over the sharp nails, almost chuckling as Lira groaned, her other hand fisted in Aeley's hair while the table rocked beneath her.

Just as quickly as she had taken to Lira's fingers, Aeley released them and dipped her head further, close enough to blow a slow, hot breath over Lira's clit.

Lira gasped and shuddered, her body tensing, but it was nothing compared to the whimper that followed, or the way she clutched Aeley's shoulder, nails digging in.

With a gentle grip on Lira's thighs, Aeley urged Lira to open up to her completely, to let her in, rather than push her away with words or keep her at a distance when it came to personal truths and secrets. If this was how she had to work her way into getting to know Lira deeply, and to *maybe* be considered worthy enough of discovering more about Lira inside and out, Aeley would do her damnedest to give Lira whatever she wanted, however she desired it.

Aeley drew her tongue over Lira's swollen folds, a lengthy stroke that left Lira shivering and shifting to keep close to Aeley's mouth. Brushing her fingers along the slick lips, Aeley eased them open and lapped at Lira's clit once, twice, then again, even faster and flicking the tip, all for Lira to groan and cry out her approval. Another tremble raced through Lira, her fist in Aeley's hair tight as she tugged, needing more.

Not to leave Lira wanting, Aeley slipped her tongue between the soaked folds, seeking depth in the heat. When Lira cried out her name, she drove deeper, her finger sliding into Lira's opening as she worked her tongue over the soft edges, teasing its way into her, even if just the tip. Aeley nudged the tightness, her finger easing in and out with long, careful strokes before adding a second finger. Lira whimpered between hitched breaths, the muscles of her stomach and legs strained as her climax surged closer.

A climax Aeley was determined to make happen as she clenched Lira's swollen clit between her teeth and sucked in a breath.

Lira cried out even louder, her hips lifting off the table completely. The table moved with her, protesting with creaks. She gripped her thighs tight enough to bruise. "*By the Four—*" She clawed at the table with one hand, her other hand sinking into Aeley's hair, but not without raking her nails up Aeley's neck. "If you want to keep biting," she said hoarsely, "maybe you should come up here so I can do something about it."

"Fine with me." Aeley wiped her mouth with the back of her hand, intent on finishing the rest of that particular quest later. Perhaps when they were on a bed—anything that took her off of her feet. *I can barely stand right now...*

Lira shuffled across the table, knocking the rags, knives, and all but one of the arrows to the floor, the lot of shafts rolling away well beyond the scattered blades. Not sparing them more than a glance, Aeley climbed onto the table and crawled towards Lira, thankful for the thick wood and strong build, even if the table gave a groan of its own.

The last arrow, however—it stayed in Lira's hands, somehow looking all the more dangerous as she toyed with the black-feathered end and waited for Aeley to settle between her legs.

"Just what do you expect to do with that?" Aeley kneeled, then sat back on her legs, knees parted, pressed to Lira's thighs as Lira closed her legs around Aeley. Gliding one hand along Lira's inner thigh and up to her hip, she loved how Lira trembled at almost every touch, still needing release.

In silent reply, Lira brushed the feathered end along Aeley's neck before drawing it downwards. Sleek and cold, the wooden shaft trailed over her, the black feather leaving shivers in its wake. Lira led it down further, teasing Aeley's nipple with the tip.

Aeley groaned, her lip caught painfully between her teeth as she bit down and fidgeted. Moving in and out of the feather-light touch, she craved and cursed it all at once. Even worse was how the torment continued, tracing a path between Aeley's breasts, down to her stomach, and coming to a stop so close between her legs, she could only stare as the feather teased the inside of her thigh, barely touching her wetness but threatening to venture through it. The thin rod rested prone between them, waiting, drawing on the wrenching anticipation that gnawed at her curiosity as much as it lusted to come in a rush of relief.

But then, Lira was always one to inspire curiosity, with her secrets, and her smarts, and her—

Aeley cried out, almost toppling over Lira as the arrow shaft slipped between her legs, sliding back and forth between her slick folds, rubbing ever deeper, the shock of its cold lost to her warmth.

"Lira." Aeley whimpered, struggling to stay upright, fumbling to get a hold on Lira's hips, to stay in place... She *needed* to stay right there, to let the arrow glide and move and take her closer to the end, but by the sheer wicked graces of the Goddesses did she *ever* want to rip the damned arrow out of Lira's hand and finish her off with a few hard strokes.

And then—*then*—as the feather brushed across her swollen clit, all those tiny wisps on her tip...

She whined and writhed and nearly screamed for it to stop, needing a breath, needing more, needing the foul thing to erupt in flames and just consume her with it. How could she have ever thought Lira was leagues away from being trouble? Modesty... it counted for so little then, as forgotten as everything else discarded on the dirty floor.

Lira's throaty laugh drove the aggravation deeper. "Mmm, mixing pleasure with pleasure. Weapons and sex—sounds exactly like you."

In a blink, the feather was gone from Aeley's clit, followed by Lira tossing the arrow over her shoulder, abandoning it to whatever fate awaited as it hit a fully stocked rack of weapons and clattered down the blades to the floor.

Before Aeley could react, Lira grasped Aeley's throat, just enough to stop Aeley's breath. Their gazes met, their parted lips close but not touching.

It was over in an instant, broken by Lira's lips as they crushed Aeley's, tongue delving deep, claiming hard and hurting for it. Sinking down onto Lira, Aeley rested one leg between both of Lira's, her thigh soaked as she ground into Lira's wetness. Lira's grip journeyed across her back, pulling them closer together, keeping them joined. When Lira slipped a hand between Aeley's legs, Aeley returned the gesture, bucking as Lira's fingers slid into her.

She gave a low growl and drove two fingers inside Lira, jerking back before pushing in again, Lira's loud cries urging her faster, rougher, sharper. However difficult it was to focus as Lira's fingers did the same to her, she fully intended to make Lira scream, her own moans and cries joining Lira's in an aching chorus.

Aeley stole a sloppy kiss between panted breaths, whimpering as Lira slipped a third finger inside her, the burn an excruciating pleasure she wanted to ride for several moments yet.

"Yes," she whispered against Lira's lips and stroked inside Lira with the fierce need to race to the end, all the while never wanting Lira's moans and shivers to be over. Passion raged through her like wildfire, capturing her, keeping her there, fighting to stay in control while every other part of her screamed to let go—to let everything fall into Lira's hands and leave the unspoken words between them to unravel as they would. Each time Lira's fingers flitted across her throbbing clit, Aeley nearly screamed and clawed at the table, her emotions tangled among fractured thoughts. The end… she hated the end. The inevitable stop that would mess with her feelings and leave her cold… desperate… yearning for Lira's warmth. Her tenderness. That quiet way she had of making sense from everything else that failed to.

The table rocked with their rhythm, its creaks and groans adding to the clamour. Lira tensed around Aeley's fingers, almost pushing them out as she raked her nails across Aeley's back, digging in, scraping, her legs wrapped around Aeley's waist.

With the barest push in, Lira's scream came just as quickly, her body strained to a stop before shaking. The milky rush of her release coated

Aeley's hand as Aeley worked her through it, teasing it to the full with a flick at Lira's clit.

Before Aeley could move away, Lira slipped her fingers into Aeley again, still trembling as she stroked. Aeley rode her touch, knees locked, jammed into the table, muscles pulling taut in her back. The end was coming, like a ball of energy spinning out of control and taking her with it. And teeth—it had teeth that tore at her insides, wrenching every nerve, leaving her a mess of jolts and whines and instinct.

But the thumb on her clit, pressing, circling, raking—

She crashed right there, release slamming through her.

"*Yes*," Aeley hissed, clutching Lira's shoulders and burying her face in Lira's hair. She rocked as she came, her strength gone with it. Lira's touch kept at her, tenderly rubbing, and she bit down to keep from screaming loud enough to bring *all* the guards to attention.

The surge peaked and ebbed slowly, her mind foggy in the fading glow of release. In the crawl of the calm that took over, it took her more than few moments to realize Lira rocked her gently, her embrace a soothing comfort.

"So..." Lira murmured against Aeley's temple. "What do you think? There's hitting the target and then there's hitting the target. Which one do you think I'm better at?"

Blinking, Aeley could do nothing but laugh and pray the table stayed together beneath them.

Chapter Fourteen

They burst into the study, still laughing at the ridiculousness of it all.

Lira ran for the desk, more than ready to repeat what they had done in the armoury, but she made every effort to try patience first rather than mess with the parchment on Aeley's desk. Behind her, Aeley slammed the door shut, her triumphant "Ha!" all but drowned out by the bang. If they had timed it right, Haydin would search for them shortly to let them know dinner was ready.

Though with the way Aeley leaned back, biting her bottom lip as Lira faced her, dinner was the last thing on her mind—likely because the shoulder of Lira's gown was busy slipping downwards, revealing skin and taking over with its own plans.

"I don't think I tied it right," Aeley said before she crossed the room, arms outstretched.

"I thought something felt off." Not that Lira minded in the least—it offered the perfect excuse for more attention, an unexpected wave of tender affection she welcomed, so rare in how softly it touched her harsher expectations. Lira turned into the desk and pulled her tangled hair over her shoulder. When Aeley jerked on the laces, she chuckled. "Too much in a hurry to get things cleaned up."

"We were in a… questionable position." Aeley tugged out the laces. "The guards would harass me for days if they knew," she said before finding the missed holes and threading the laces through.

Lira counted every one, listening to Aeley mutter under her breath and loving every moment of it. *Only three. Not a bad count.*

Aeley yanked on the laces, drawing Lira against her. "We were lucky as is with the door wide open. It would've been a perfect time to get caught."

"Wouldn't have been the first time," Lira murmured.

"What?"

Damn.

"I wouldn't have cared, I said."

After a final pull, Aeley tied the laces and rested her chin on Lira's shoulder. "I heard what you said," she whispered, "I just wanted clarification." She paused, her lips pressed to Lira's shoulder before she continued. "The fact is, I don't know as much about you as you apparently do me. I try, but you keep pushing me away. Except for once, when I cornered you, and I hated doing it. While I'm in for whatever this is, I'm just curious why we don't talk about you."

Because I stand to lose everything when I do.

Lira swallowed back the bitterness and bile that came with every answer she could give but never wanted to share. Nothing good would come of talking about herself, her truths, and she hated the idea of ruining their time together, the only real enjoyment she had other than the precious moments she could escape into her books and close the door on everyone else.

"There's not much to talk about," she said, turning away, her chin up, back straight.

When Aeley pulled her back by the laces, Lira struggled to give in without a complete fight. "And that's a lie. What happened to all that honesty you wanted from me? That only goes one way?" An arm slipped around Lira's waist, its comfort more of a relief than she wanted to admit. Aeley pressed her mouth to Lira's ear, the warmth of her breath playing across Lira's skin, threatening to entice her with a fight that matched Lira's. "Or maybe I should ask if you want a relationship or just someone to sleep with."

"And that's playing dirty," Lira mumbled. "Nice to know you were listening to me."

"Fair question."

"With a not-so-fair answer."

"All the more reason to talk about it. You can't just say one thing and give another. Or give nothing. Sometimes that's how it feels. Every time, you evade. Every secret, you keep, which seems to be everything about you. Give me something," Aeley said softly. "Anything. Let me know you without always having to guess. I want to know you as *you*, not whatever my head makes up, or anyone else for that matter."

And just like that, the sweetness in her words was gone, dragged down by the painful reality.

There was always someone talking, always someone watching Lira behind her back, controlling the circumstances, trying to shepherd her in the direction of their choosing—the last thing she wanted to bring to Aeley's life, especially when Aeley had her own problems to contend with.

As Lira pulled away again, Aeley let her go, though Lira swore the heat of Aeley's gaze followed her to the stained-glass window.

"You're about as favourable to your family as I am Allon," Aeley continued, her tone quiet but edged with annoyance—or was it something else altogether? "I'm curious as to why. And I know you've already told me some of it, but there's more. Every time you change the subject, I know there are things you don't want to tell me. Maybe you're scared, maybe you think it's worthless, but I want to hear them. Considering I'm supposed to marry into your family, I'm interested to know everything about what I'm getting into."

Snorting, Lira fell into the chair in the corner. Elbows at rest on the chair arms, she kept her hands in her lap, limp, lacking fight as she eyed

Aeley's crossed arms. There was no stop to the sarcasm that surged up. "Run, that's all I have to say."

"From who? You? Or them?"

Goddesses, was *that* ever the question of the day.

"Your choice," Lira muttered. "Depends on who you think is more trouble."

With a sigh that seemed to draw fatigue from every exhausted nerve, Lira tilted her head back, her gaze cast to the shadows dancing with the firelight on the ceiling. To her left, in the hearth on the other side of the room, the fire blazed with a warmth she was quickly losing a grasp on as a cruel chill skittered through her. On its heels, an icy set of memories took hold of what should have been beloved nostalgia, seizing time and freezing it in place—a stark reminder of how she had ended up there to begin with. So many moments lost to that cold counsel, so much time tied to a place she never wanted to revisit but was forced to relive often enough, never to forget. Never to stray, not without consequence.

She was damned tired of it.

Every word, every glance, every expectation— she would have set fire to them all if someone had just given her fresh kindling. The match was there somewhere, tied to the last remaining leg of her will to fight, though both had been reduced to a feeble crawl the longer she lingered in the dark.

But the dark provided safety of a sort, isolating as it was, and the promise of being able to curl up in a corner and disappear was as natural a draw as taking breath.

And yet…

She hated the corners as much as she hated sharp edges. She loathed the isolation as much as she feared standing in the open. Never left alone, but always standing alone. Never free, but always in a free fall. Forever pulled to one end and the other, with a choice demanded but always slapped down as wrong the moment she made it, no matter which side of the line the decision ended up on.

That was why she never spoke about herself, why she never volunteered details: she always betrayed the very mess she feared to admit she was, a push and pull that no one else needed to get in the middle of lest they be torn away. She already excelled at pushing people from her life— she did *not* need help making it worse.

Except that look on Aeley's face, the gentle aggravation in her tone…

There was no point in disputing Aeley's argument: she had every right to want something in return for what she gave, all at the cost of revealing shreds of her own vulnerability, as much as she tried not to show it. Still, she offered Lira glimpses of what ate at her most, and that drew Lira closer, filling her head with questions she was too afraid to find answers for.

It was not so different than Aeley's worry that she had nothing to hold onto where Lira was concerned; no clear details where she needed to see the larger portrait. Though the fact she wanted to understand any part of Lira at all and would fight for it, no matter how dirty she had to play, that made a difference. For all the fight Lira was losing, Aeley seemed to have more than enough to spare.

If she reached out, would her hand come back with nothing? If she offered her touch, would she come back burned? Or was hope there somewhere, woven through the threads of Aeley's intentions?

Tired. She was so very tired of falling, of wandering the journey alone, lost in the middle and running to the ends of nowhere.

Lira sighed again, a lighter breath with the flimsiest grasp on her courage. "I've been here before," she said, her glance flicking to Aeley, "and I got caught, except it wasn't funny, not like tonight would've been if the guards had seen us downstairs. More of a fight, really."

The desk creaked as Aeley leaned against it, her arms still crossed. "Meaning?"

"Meaning my mother found me and a servant, both of us sixteen and curious, messing around in bed. We'd known each other since we were girls—her mother worked for my mother. We thought we'd get to know each other even better. She said I was cute," Lira said and gazed out the window with a smile—a hopeful memory, even then. Nara's touch had felt like bliss slipping over her body, hesitant in one moment but so full of life the next, testing all the right places as Lira returned the touch, the taste of Nara in her, on her, and not one regret to be had. It had been nothing like she imagined and so much more, her skin on fire beneath shaky hands that sought to learn everything. No boy alive had inspired that in her, and Nara had been the only one she needed and wanted, easily taking Lira to be hers.

Lira would have given herself to Nara for an adolescent's count of forever, maybe even beyond. *She always was too irresistible to be away from…*

The memories passed with the mockery of silence, and she faced Aeley again, her smile gone. "My mother didn't think it was so sweet. She sent all of our female servants away and brought in men. That was after she kicked me screaming from bed and threw Nara into the hall with her clothes and called her a tramp. Said if I wanted the pleasure, the servants' hands were too filthy. I should save it for a woman of a Grand Family or a councilman. And then—*then*—she kept trying to correct it."

"Correct it?"

Goddesses, she wanted to be sick.

"She forced me to meet with boys my age and insisted I play nice to make friends," Lira replied, the well-used target on the wall taking all of her focus right then. "And when I say play nice, I mean it in *every* sense of the word. *Be willing*, she said. Show them my worth." Lira fisted her fingers tight enough to dig her nails into her palms. "I can't remember the number of times I'd walk into a gala hosted by her where the guests were mostly men. She'd dress me up in the best dresses we could afford, just to make sure they saw me, baring what parts of me were socially acceptable. Practically threw me at them when I didn't want to be there. I never wanted those parties and I never wanted *them*," she whispered.

She dared to steal a glance at Aeley, only mildly relieved by the darkness settling in Aeley's eyes. The clouded look of anger did nothing to strip away the disgust gnawing at Lira's guts.

"I guess it's an understatement to say that you didn't get along," Aeley said, her tone almost as dry as it was bitter.

"We still don't." Lira stared at the floor, more than one shouted insult flittering through her thoughts. "We fought all the time, even more than now. I almost ran away a couple times, but I was persuaded to stay—by my father, mostly, though Emon and Ryler had their moments. Then, when I was nineteen, Mother thought she'd play harder to make me listen. She had me meet with a younger son in one of the more prominent Grands." Eyes closed, she tried to will away the sickness threatening its way up. His damned hand on her knee… the path his fingers traveled... "We had a nice time until he tried to get under my skirt. I told him to tuck in his privates before I battered them until he barely recognized them, and that I'd spread the word, including a letter posted in public, a trip to the Tract Steward—your father—*and* I'd tell the girl he liked. He couldn't run fast enough."

And run he had—straight into the Riaes tract for three whole years, not one word in her direction, at least not directly. There still was no accounting for the source of the fresh wave of rumours that came after that, though whether that was his doing or his family's, she had no proof. The damage had been done, however, and the Derossas paid for it handsomely, not one family wanting to come within a foot of her reputation, citing that she was too *difficult*.

Meanwhile, her mother *still* threw *difficult* in her face, even six years later, and she never even needed to utter a word. The glares alone were more than sufficient to remind Lira of her failure to comply, but the silence... sometimes it stabbed so much more deeply than her mother's wretched screaming.

"But I don't get why." Aeley waved her hand, her face flushed with whatever she was feeling. "Not the guy. I get that. Allon would've told him to go through with it. But your mother—why? You're allowed to be with whomever you want, and it's certainly not something that needs fixing."

She huffed, her arms crossed over her chest as she scowled. "It's not against our laws or any rules—"

"Except when they're family rules," Lira interrupted. "My parents saw value in me being a daughter, mostly because they want me to bear heirs to salvage the family line." By the Four, did she *ever* spit that out—the most ill-mannered, rotted, rank-tasting tripe to ever be forced down her throat. They may as well have branded her and sold her at market for all the good it did to her self-respect. "They wanted to keep me open for marriages—*all* marriages, not some smaller number based on what I'm comfortable with. What I want doesn't make a bloody difference. My father never got over losing what he always expected to be his. He planned his life around the assumption he'd be Steward. My mother, too. They thought if they could pawn all of us off to wealthy, influential families, we might be able to reclaim some of what was lost."

"But—"

"*But* the number of sons and fathers willing to marry me grossly outnumbers the daughters, and they're the ones who'll all so happily see me a mother before the first year of marriage is out," Lira finished, the thought itself more like a shudder that refused to stop clinging to her fears. "And if that wasn't enough, I'm supposed to keep my hands clean. The other families don't want a scribe as a daughter. They want a pretty face with a pretty mouth that'll do whatever they want. Or a girl who can lie as easily as she draws breath and make everyone think she's perfect, even while she's secretly dying inside."

"And there's no room for someone like you," Aeley murmured.

"You know how it is." Lira leaned forward, her hands clasped tightly between her knees, nails daring to draw blood. "Family is *everything*. For the Grands, reputation and status are just as important. We put all of that *first*. You know it. You live it. You talk about duty. You talk about your father and everything he's done. You talk about recovering after Allon's disgrace. You are *exactly* what's expected of you." She dropped her gaze to the floor, her words almost a whisper. "But when someone breaks the rules and ignores expectations by choosing individual happiness over that of family loyalty, that's when they're trouble. I don't act like I'm supposed to. I don't do what I'm supposed to. I'm not dragging the family name around like I should, or playing nice enough for anyone else, and they certainly don't like that I hate the rules to begin with. And while I'm just being me, it's still a choice."

"You shouldn't have to choose. It's not fair." Aeley snorted and crossed the room as Lira curled into the chair, desperate to hide from the hurt inside but having nowhere else to go.

The story of my life.

"Since when has anything in our lives been about being fair?" Lira stared Aeley in the eye.

"Here you are, a contract stuffed down your throat simply because you're the beloved child of your father. You and I both know that daughter or not, he *still* would have signed you off to someone, probably even our family for all I know about Emon and Ryler's bedspread companions. But that's not fair, either." Shaking her head, Lira bit back what ill comments she had towards Korre as far as the contract went. Of all the darkness he sought to chase away, the contract was *not* one of the brighter stars in his choices. "I'm not interested in some empty relationship just for sake of feeding my parents' selfishness, especially if I'm forced into something I'll never want or can't even *stand*. But I'm not as good a daughter as you. I'm not willing to trade that for some duty I inherited merely because I exist. I'm selfish. I choose me."

"That's not selfish," Aeley argued softly, crouching down in front of Lira.

"As sweet as you are, it doesn't change what it is." Lira drew a strained breath, her hands unfurled on the chair arms, their colour once more a pale tan than the ghostly white of rage. "They've deemed me too much of a threat. I've put up too much of a fight. They don't want to show me off anymore. They're afraid if someone proposes to me, I'll shame the prospective spouse and chase them off. And that's definitely true since I started apprenticing under Vant—it's an insult my mother still can't overcome. She hasn't talked to me since. Well, not more than a few pages worth of rants and demands and 'our family needs this, you ungrateful wretch, so hop to it,' if any of that counts as *talking*." She sighed and glanced out the window, her chin propped on one fist. "Not that it doesn't have its uses."

Aeley's breath in kept the inevitable awkward silence at bay. "That's why you spend so much time in the villages and at Vant's and not at home."

"Home isn't home when neither of your parents want you around and your brothers act like they barely know you, just to save face. And the reason why I don't fight them when they belittle me?" Lira gave Aeley a sad smile, the truth bleeding out faster than she could rein it in. "I've fought so hard that all my fighting words are gone. Some days, existing is all I have left." Hands clasped in her lap, Lira twisted her fingers one over the other as she avoided Aeley's gaze. "And that's why we don't talk about me—why it's never about me. There's not much to talk about. My worth is in what I let people see, even you. *Especially* you," Lira murmured.

"Me?"

The heat of a blush spread across Lira's cheeks as she smiled—shyly, and with a slight wobble in its execution, but a genuine smile, nevertheless. "Like I said: I like you. More than like, actually. I didn't want to complicate things with problems that aren't yours. I certainly don't care for being reminded of how much I don't have when all I want is to forget. And I like to do that with you — forget. And be myself, with someone who appreciates it. Someone who doesn't think I'm selfish."

"Oh." Aeley hung her head, almost as though searching for something to say. "*Dammit,*" she muttered. "I'm sorry. I shouldn't have pushed it."

Lira held up her hand, only to draw back with how her fingers shook. "No, you're right. It should go both ways between us, and you deserve to know who you're dealing with. No matter who you choose — "

"Who I *choose*?" Aeley gaped at Lira.

"What?" It was a legitimate issue, one that needed to be addressed eventually. Lira fidgeted and fussed with her skirt. Was Aeley ever going to blink, or was she simply going to keep staring with her mouth open? "I'm assuming Emon and Ryler are still — "

"*Not being considered.* There's only one suitor I'm looking at, and it's never going to be them." Aeley's forehead crinkled with her scowl. "I thought I was making that perfectly clear."

Lira caught her breath, whatever argument she had left choked back by the concern in Aeley's eyes.

Oh.

Aeley's frown continued to call out Lira's poor assumption as Aeley stood and leaned over, gripping the chair and pinning Lira between her arms. Her lips grazed Lira's in the barest touch, a tease that revived the spark of Lira's interest. "Would it help if I said I think you're cute?"

"Maybe," Lira murmured before kissing Aeley, content to let pain surrender to the softness. She pulled back a long moment later, followed by the slow draw of her thumb across Aeley's moistened lips. "And maybe you should be telling them."

Aeley straightened. "Maybe not quite yet. They might have one or two uses before I go breaking their very shallow, entirely self-absorbed hearts."

"Like what?"

"Like lending me some help." Aeley sighed, hard and heavy, ending in a grumble. "Allon *might* be right. *Might*. We need information, and we need more eyes. We need more of everything, especially since I don't necessarily trust Allon, but I don't trust *not* trusting him on this." She pinched the bridge of her nose, eyes closed tight. "Father always said I shouldn't be too proud to ask for help, and usually I am. I think we need it, as much as I hate to admit it. There's already too many people involved, and even more I *really* don't need mucking about, making this harder."

"So you want to ask my brothers? *Really*? How does that not—" Lira eyed Aeley warily. Were they truly having this discussion? Just when they had made so much progress... "You *do* realize making things harder is what they excel at?"

"No, I know, but just go with me here, just for the moment. Do you think they'd be completely useless?"

"Well..." Lira pushed up from the chair and moved to the window, arms crossed as she leaned against the window frame. *Useless* was a far-ranging interpretation, dependent on what Aeley wanted from them. They knew things, yes, and they had easy access to funds to use as they saw fit, all of which put them on a list of potential resources.

Whether or not they *cared* was a separate question Lira already knew the answer to, one that never ended in doing the right thing for the right reason.

Aeley leaned against the frame beside her. "It's a dubious idea," she said quietly, "and I'm still working on the particulars of how to make it that much more... interesting, but putting all the terrible things aside, do you think they'd help if I gave them the right incentive? If I asked them for ideas and to provide some extra protection, would they do it, assuming I could give them something in return?"

"Maybe, if you convince them they'll get something worthy from it." Lira twisted her lips and poked at the stained-glass pane, tracing circles over the blue glass. "A chance to help the Steward and practically be considered Steward by association might be worth the question. If you can stroke their egos and let them in on the position of authority, that might do it. For all I know, my father would push them into it—even provide you with his own version of help. Of course..."

"They'd be doing it for their own good. Yeah, I know—I'm counting on it." Aeley smirked, a playful glimmer in her eyes. "That would be the point, drawing them in to see what I can do. As I said, they have their uses, and I wouldn't mind pulling those strings for a while," she said, slipping her arm around Lira's waist to bring her close, "especially when your mother uses *you*, no matter how dangerously it flirts with the wrong side of the law."

As Aeley's lips pressed to her temple in a gentle, roving kiss, Lira closed her eyes, wishing that just *once* her family could have had nothing to do with it—with *them*. Just her, Aeley—that was all she wanted. Peace, quiet, and the chance to simply be without looking over her shoulder before she ran away completely, hidden where no one could find her.

"Have to say I'm not terribly fond of your mother, not when that's the game she plays," Aeley murmured, a drawn-out kiss warming the centre of Lira's forehead. "Wouldn't mind sharing the loathing. Perhaps we'll just keep it all in the family for now. See if I can't bring your brothers to heel." More kisses trailed a path down Lira's cheek, and both of Aeley's arms were around her, holding her tight. "Use their egos to help someone else for once. They just need a bit of guidance."

Eyes still closed, Lira snorted softly. *Guidance* was one way to put it.

When Aeley cupped her cheeks and tilted her face upwards, Lira opened her eyes. The depth of concern in Aeley's gaze was enough to set her heart beating that little bit faster.

"If you think it'll completely fail, I'll let it be." Aeley stroked Lira's cheeks with her thumbs, each swipe a reminder of better moments. "I'm looking for some guidance of my own here, hoping I can put this mess to rest, maybe even deal some damage of my own in the process. I need the resources, even if it comes with attitude. I can deal with that—I just need the help. And at this point, I can only be so choosy. We still haven't heard anything from Mayr, good or bad, and that could change everything."

Lira sighed, her forehead gently meeting Aeley's as they both leaned forward. What had to be done needed doing, and if that meant playing her brothers for all they were worth to make it happen... "So do it, then, if there's not much else to work with. Just remember they need to be kept in line from time to time."

"Mm," Aeley agreed, though her gaze wandered away. Her thoughts appeared to be elsewhere even as she caressed Lira's neck.

"What?"

"Nothing. Just considering. I think I have a message for you to write."

"Oh? To?"

"Oly Valley."

Lira frowned as she pulled away. *Oly Valley?* "Wasn't that where Allon—"

"Sacked the village? Yes, it was. I met a mercenary there, and assuming he's *still* there, I have a job for him."

"Doing what?"

"Gathering information. Finding out if Allon really has nothing to do with this. I can't ask Mayr, because he's busy handling everything here and in the village. Besides, he's not trained for it. He's skilled at the much less discreet. Meant to be seen and heard. He likes it that way. But Gren... not necessarily."

Lira smiled at the hint of amusement in Aeley's tone, the anger and bitterness from earlier fading away. "You like him, don't you?"

"Admire. I *admire* him." Aeley shrugged and grasped Lira's hand to examine her ink-stained fingers, playing and teasing more than committing to serious scrutiny. "He goes in and just does things, and it works."

"And you think he'll be helpful?"

"Actually, yeah, I do. It can't be any worse than where we are right now. He knows people I don't. People that Allon calls friends."

"Well, then." Lira breathed out. She was all for the distraction—even though someone was suddenly knocking on the door and mentioning dinner. They could work and eat at the same time, and then maybe, if they were still awake, they could catch a breath afterwards, alone. Together. After chasing a scream or two behind closed doors. "What are we waiting for? Slap a quill in my hand and let's get it done."

Chapter Fifteen

"I don't trust them."

Aeley tried not to laugh at Mayr's scowl, or the impatient shift of his feet, or the multitude of grumbles that kept coming her way with the hint of a growl tucked behind them. He tended to judge people quickly and never kept quiet when he found someone he disliked, though the way he eyed Emon and Ryler from across the meeting room was enough reason to keep them away from Mayr's flexing hands. His sour mood did nothing to help the situation: the more the unrest carried on, the more likely he was to start a fight. While she wanted to avoid a brawl, especially one that would sabotage her plans, she knew that feeling all too well—had felt it for too long—and it took every bit of patience she could spare to keep from punching Emon's nose into his skull... or from sending his mother a strongly worded letter with *Get out of my tract* scrawled over it in red ink and a set of shackles to make the point.

The lack of sleep might have something to do with it.

In the four days since their return from Alosaa, both Aeley and Mayr had suffered from the same lack of rest combined with two more attacks and two nights worth of scouring Korre's records about the Cigils and the Glim Takers. Most of their research led to more unsettling truths, confirmed the turf war was real, and more than illustrated neither gang was above wreaking havoc of the recent sort as a means to rattle a new Tract Steward. They had also found initialed threats similar to the ones she received, all related to the Cigils. If anything, the evidence offered enough reason to finally put boots on the ground to find out where the Cigils were operating from and who was responsible.

Between being buried by more bad news and the lack of a single name to throw their fight at, sleep was being as unkind as it could get. They both sported dark circles under their eyes and a quick-to-burn exasperation, except Aeley's came with the benefit of Lira, a warm companion in an otherwise empty bed.

Though the private celebration for the Feast of Eleia had been a nice touch three nights ago—a step out from the strict and serious tones of life, where even Lira relaxed enough to laugh and converse, keeping to Aeley's side for most of it. By all accounts, Haydin had been beside himself, cancelling their family's grand observance as Aeley and Mayr had left for Alosaa, only to arrange a smaller, more intimate affair for the household and villagers from Dahena.

Even so, Aeley swore Haydin loved it in secret, and she had loved seeing Lira let go of what troubled her, whether it was just for the night or forever. Somehow, it had ended in Lira dancing with several of the guards, including an oddly charming go at it with Stuck, who had, as usual, endeavoured to make fools of them all and succeeded in guiding the off-duty guards through their hangovers the next morning with a pail in one hand and a ladle to smack it with in the other.

All the while, Lira had come alive, a glint in her eye, liveliness to her steps, and not as many cares in the world to get tangled around — everything Aeley would have sacrificed time for again and again just to keep seeing, sleep or no.

This meeting, though... It was about to take all of the joy Lira had shown and stuff it right back down into the dankest infested cellar the Derossas owned.

Politics, kiss my ass.

Aeley smirked at Mayr, tempted to pull him to the wall she leaned against just to keep him from pacing. "And what about Gren? Don't trust him, either?" she asked, gesturing to the furthest end of the table in the centre of the room.

Gren, as gruff as usual, sat at the table in a dark brown long coat over even darker, well-worn attire, tapping the wood with a double-edged serrated dagger that he twisted in his hand. He looked bored already, partially reclining in his seat with his arm draped casually over the back of the chair while his glance wandered the room. Had she not known better, she would have thought Gren was Mayr's father, with their similar height and tan skin wrapped around a muscular build. They even shared the same dark hair, despite the blond and grey strands in Gren's hair and how he kept it trimmed to his shoulders, so much shorter than Mayr's.

Even more telling was how Gren's sharp grey gaze never strayed long from where Emon and Ryler stood by the window, conversing quietly, their own glances far from inconspicuous.

All anyone needed to do was drop a single explosive word and they would descend upon each other like rabid predators dying for the taste of blood.

"No, I trust him. It's the other two." Mayr gestured to Emon and Ryler with his chin. "I've heard more than enough of them to last me a lifetime, plus the next dozen after. If you marry either one of them, I'm not going to promise good things. I told you we could handle this on our own."

"Before or after you exhaust yourself to the point where you're useless?"

"Would never happen," Mayr muttered, "and completely irrelevant. Don't change the subject."

"I didn't—you said—" Aeley bit back the rest of her argument, switching focus onto Emon and

Ryler instead, wishing she could read their lips as they mumbled before casting her another skeptical glance. The meeting needed to be short and straight to the point, otherwise someone was going to get skewered and she would end up trapped in the middle, holding the bloody pin.

The flash of a burgundy dress in the doorway caught her eye.

Lira.

Aeley rushed to the door, taking an easier breath. "Good, you're here," she whispered. A glance into the corridor caught Pellon as he slunk back into the hallway and stood against the wall, his every move silent. Along with him, stationed close by, she expected to find another four guards, all quiet in wait.

Slipping one hand up Lira's back, Aeley escorted her to a chair at the table, closest to the door. "We'll start, now that we're all here."

The heated expression on Emon's face while he watched Lira would have been easy to miss had Aeley not expected it—surprise, mixed with annoyance and a touch of disdain. He recovered quickly, drawing a hand through his hair. Clean-shaven and dressed in the finery of a heavily embroidered teal blue shirt, black pants laced up the sides, heavy brown boots with jewel-studded gold buckles at the knees, and a black long coat that looked barely worn, he appeared as immaculate as ever, ready and willing to be adored to his haughty standards. *No doubt to throw his brother's face in the mud and run with the spoils.*

Ryler looked all the more peeved, his hands settled in the deep pockets of his ash-grey long coat, and the glint of the small knife on his belt caught Aeley's attention. He was dressed to travel, wearing a simple white tunic, dark brown pants, and shin-high black boots with dusty, worn red soles. Save for the irritated blinking he seemed unable to stop as he stared at Lira, he appeared almost approachable, if not mildly stodgy.

"We're interested to know why we're here, though we weren't expecting an audience," Emon stated, his gaze on Aeley. There was no waver to his voice, just an insipid calm. "We were hoping it was to get to know us better, like you *promised.* Maybe even that sparring you and I talked about. You remember, don't you? You sounded eager for me to prove myself, show you what a *real* man can do." He flicked his glance to Mayr, blatant as could be.

Aeley gripped the back of Lira's chair and willed herself to remain still, aware Gren watched her but said nothing. The blade in his hand stopped moving, hanging above the table as though he contemplated doing something else with it.

She forced a polite smile with all the joy of stabbing her face with a blunt nail. "There's still plenty of time for that. In a way, it's why you're here. We have need of your skills."

Emon's blue eyes widened, his brow rising. "Really?"

"Yes, we need your help." Aeley cleared her throat. "Rather, *I* need your help."

"Absolutely," Ryler replied. He leaned into the table, fingers splayed across the surface. "Anything—"

"Ryler," Emon warned, slapping a hand to Ryler's chest. "You should wait for her to pose the request before you agree."

"Why? We never get requests from the Dahes—I mean, a Steward. Same thing. This goes a long way in proving they don't hate us like everyone says they do. Or, wait, I think I have it backwards again. It's us who apparently do the hating, isn't it?" Ryler laughed and winked at Aeley. "But that's just talk, right? Who could possibly hate a charming girl like you?"

Mayr growled quietly behind Aeley and moved closer. Holding one hand back, she flicked her wrist and held out two fingers, gesturing for him to stop. As foolish as they seemed to think she was, she still controlled the meeting. Given how quickly Ryler's willingness was already on the table without more than a simple ask, however, the meeting was off to a promising start. Where Ryler went, surely Emon could be enticed to follow, if only to ensure his brother stayed on the path that restored their family's previous glory—a likelihood Lira agreed with, even if Aeley had to tease it out of her.

"Thank you, Ryler, for being eager to help. I appreciate it, truly. It's important to know who's willing to step up to business." Aeley looked at Emon. "I also appreciate your propriety and caution, as well as your patience. Perhaps we can all work together on this, possibly towards a result which pleases all of us?"

"We're listening." Emon crossed his arms, almost daring her to say something he could deny.

Aeley took a breath and counted to three, her pride tamped down by the painful memories of why they were there. Fresh images took over but failed to drown out the old. "We've had a few problems lately. I suspect you've probably heard about the attacks on our villages?"

Ryler quirked a brow at his brother, but said nothing as Emon nodded. "Rumblings have made it our way," Emon said quietly. "And I'll admit we have our concerns. None of this is good for Gailarin, and our parents are increasingly worried that vandalism and assaults will become the new norm. There's a lot of damage that could be done, and it could take this tract down with it. Needless to say, we're not looking forward to where this is going."

"Neither am I," Aeley muttered. Her fingers flirted with the knife on her belt, searching for a distraction before she cleared her throat.

"Unfortunately, there were another two just yesterday. One was in a village near here—an elderly couple was nearly killed after a group of masked thieves decided to sack their home before the sun was up. There was an altercation, things got out of hand, and the couple was left unconscious on their porch. They're currently under the supervision of local healers until their injuries heal, and the village has been placed under constant surveillance.

"The second incident, however, was not far from your estate." Aeley winced, the details of the case too difficult to swallow without thinking of the possible implications. "A young woman was assaulted and left in the middle of the common road."

A young woman who looked far too similar to Lira for Aeley's liking, and it twisted her guts until there was nothing left but bile. She had seen the bruised and battered body with her own eyes—an image that refused to get out of her head no matter what she did, even when she held onto Lira, assured that Lira was safe and nowhere near that road.

"Yes, we heard about it this morning," Emon replied. "Father informed us when we woke. A shame, really, for her to die in such awful circumstances. I've heard there's a witness and something about a mob being responsible—a common problem we're now sharing with your district, it seems." His lips straightened into a tense line, and he glanced at Ryler. When Ryler failed to react, Emon slapped his arm. "Say something."

Ryler shook his head, jolted out of his daze. "Yes, it's terrible. Terrible. Uncouth. Uncivilized." His shaky smile lasted for a moment, replaced by curiosity. "Sorry, where do we come into this?"

Aeley glanced down at Lira, fighting the urge to draw her fingers through the softness of Lira's hair and take comfort from the touch alone. "These attacks aren't slowing down, only increasing. We've also had a hard time finding those responsible, though someone managed to catch one. By luck, as the soldier tells it, just as the thieves were running from the home they ransacked. We hoped he'd talk and tell us who was in charge. We have our suspicions, but we wanted him to confirm it, or deny, whichever came first."

"Has he?" Ryler folded his arms as he scowled. "I mean, it's important to find out what he knows. Terrible things require a name, right?"

"Absolutely, but it would've helped if he hadn't poisoned himself before we had something to work with." With a tired sigh, Aeley rested her hand on Lira's back and subtly twisted one of her curls. "But they're down a man. I suppose that's better than nothing."

"Oh, well." Ryler teetered and gave a soft snort. "That's a real shame, isn't it?"

Emon was tense, his expression hard to read. He stared at Aeley's arm, her hand still on Lira's back. For a moment, he looked concerned. "That still doesn't answer Ryler's question, however. So what is it you want from us?" he asked. "Or are you suggesting we should know something about it?"

"Why? Do you?" Mayr asked, taking another step towards Aeley.

Emon raised his chin. "Nothing of the sort, and you can stop being paranoid. It's hardly worthy of a Tract Steward's right hand." He glanced at Aeley. "So again, what do you want from us? We're not married yet, meaning I can't give you everything that belongs to our family, no matter how pretty or desperate you are."

And there it was: the reminder that even when it seemed they could be civil for more than a few moments, he was ever the bitter bastard.

"I'm not asking for everything," Aeley answered, clenching her teeth. "I'm asking for your help in solving this, especially since they've brought their trouble close enough to practically be standing on your doorstep, and likely because you're *supposed* to be aligning your family with mine. As far as anyone knows, it's a done alliance, meaning my problems, your problems—it's all the same right now." She raised her hands. "We've already got a lead on who's behind it all. This is gang related, with the Cigils marked all over it. No one's accusing you, just looking for your suggestions on what we could do to trap them or at least track them to a single source. You know people I don't, and that might get answers faster than me doing this all on my own. I'm not looking for trouble, just getting this sorted as quickly as we can without making the gangs scatter."

Aeley frowned. "Not to mention we could use the extra protection, at least until we figure out a solution. Or, more hopefully, an end where the gang members are in our keeping, waiting to be tried and punished by the High Council. To that end—" Goddesses, she hated this next part "—you're welcome to spend more time here and in the nearby villages to help. If we combine what we know and our efforts, with this as our central point of operation, we don't have to waste time. Consider it part of stepping back into glory: you help make the problem go away, and I'll let everyone know about it. It'll go a long way to showing your family's ready to step back into leadership. Restore your good name."

"Wait, you want us to stay *here*, with you?" Ryler blinked. "That's hardly an invitation I can—"

"Done," Emon interrupted, "though I offer a counterproposal. Something given, something returned."

The way Lira stiffened was not lost on Aeley. She gripped Lira's shoulder and squeezed. "Make your offer."

"That you make the concerted effort to see both of us during this alliance. We are not your guards to be commanded or your errand boys. We expect nothing less than a full partnership in the effort and full access to the estate. We won't be caged." As Emon's gaze fell to Aeley's hold on Lira's shoulder, the corners of his lips pulled and his nostrils flared, a slight flush creeping up his neck to his cheeks. "In essence, everything we would have once the marriage contract is fulfilled."

Thank you for making this so easy.

Though how much he wanted to rage over her touch on Lira... she may have loved that more.

"Fine. It's a deal." She held out her hand and waited, patient as he hesitated before clasping her arm in agreement.

And just to return the kindness you've shown Mayr today...

Aeley released Emon to lean over Lira's shoulder and slip her hand down Lira's back—without subtlety, and certainly without remorse. "They won't get anywhere, I promise," she whispered against Lira's ear.

A quick glance up found Emon's glare on them both, the disgust in his restrained sneer as obvious as the deepening red hue that took over his face. Compared to him, Ryler appeared merely surprised, his expression shifting among various degrees of confusion before he leaned into Emon and whispered.

"This meeting's finished, yes?" Emon's tone was as cool as it was sharp. "You got everything you wanted?" Not a moment after Aeley nodded, he started for the door. "Good. We're going to our estate and will return this evening with our things."

"Do you want an escort?" Aeley asked.

"Keep thinking like a Tract Steward. Save the protection for the people," Emon called back as he hurried from the room with Ryler behind him.

Aeley took a deep breath and let it out slowly, not quite relaxing completely but surrendering just enough to be relieved.

"Well, aren't you just a risky little gambler?"

Gren's voice was quiet, but jolted Aeley nonetheless. And that smirk—she *knew* that smirk on his face. Goddesses knew she gave it enough.

He wagged his dagger at her. "Don't think I didn't notice what you were doing. Then again, that was the plan, wasn't it?" Gren stood before she answered and jammed the dagger into the sheath strapped to his thigh. "Stewards and games—can't separate the two. Or is it because you're a real people person?"

"Very funny," Aeley said, a roll of her eyes included for good measure, but mostly because she needed to roll her eyes at *someone* for the mess they were in. "Have you used that one on Tracel? I'm sure she'd find it as amusing as I do."

"She thinks I'm hilarious. You're the sarcastic one." Gren gestured to Mayr. "Almost as good as this young pup. Should have my fist in his bloody face for half of what he's spewed since I got here. One full day and he's already itching for a beating."

Mayr snorted. "I'd dare you to try, but I already know you'd be good for it."

"At least you're honest. Better than those fools." Gren pointed at the door. "I'd tell you don't trust them, especially since you're paying me this time, but you know that already, don't you? Both of you," he added with a glance at Lira. "You're just about as pleased with them as the rest of us."

"You have no idea," Lira mumbled, pressing her forehead to the table.

Aeley twirled strands of Lira's hair in one hand, her other hand rubbing Lira's arm to offer some sort of reassurance. "So we're good, then? You'll ask around, poke your nose into things?"

"Already started doing it. Early morning is great for getting into other people's business." Gren grinned. "I should have something by late tonight. Depends on how fast messages travel. In the meantime, I'd worry about those fools who are supposed to be coming back."

"Which ones?" Mayr grumbled.

Gren grunted and feigned hitting Mayr. "Don't be an ass. You know I mean both. Criminals terrifying villages, brothers trying to get something they're never going to deserve— practically the same thing. Either way, watch your backs. And you," he said, jabbing his finger into Mayr's chest, "keep your eyes on *her*. I don't like bureaucrats; never have. This one gets by, though, so make sure she stays alive. Tracel would kill me if I didn't tell you to do your job, so get to it. I've got work to do."

Without another word, he left the room.

"Well, he's charming, about as much as you, Mayr," Lira said, a smile accompanying her light laugh. As she pushed her chair back and stood, however, she looked exhausted, even more than she had when she first entered the room.

"Thanks for noticing." Mayr grinned, the mischief in his gaze not hidden in the least. "Now, if you'll excuse me, *I* have work to do. You should go play nice," he ordered and poked Aeley's nose before walking away. "Play house. Play master and servant. Play anything you want. Just be ready for when they get back." He stopped in the doorway. "And dressed, preferably. Anything less could be controversial."

Mayr disappeared around the corner. "You'd better be returning the alcohol tonight," Aeley yelled.

His response came as a whistled tune, off-key and lively and nowhere near as lewd as the song usually went. She tried not to laugh, but it slipped out anyway.

Lira smirked. "So, what's your plan now... servant?"

Without waiting for Aeley, Lira hurried to the door. As she turned back, she held onto the doorframe, her own playful grin entirely too promising to ignore. "Think of five things to do without clothes. Now think of one you want to do really, really well. Catch me and I might just let you."

When Lira turned and ran through the hall, Aeley was not far behind.

Chapter Sixteen

After sharing the same house with them for a whole week, how was she still sober, especially with that damned funny feeling the worst was yet to come?

Taken by how calm Ryler was while they walked the estate, Aeley allowed him to ramble about how charming he found the house and the grounds. How much of the flattery she should believe was still in question, but it was better than accusations or the confrontations she expected. Both Emon and Ryler had come prepared to work, their knowledge of the gangs nearly equal with her father's.

"The consequence of doing business," Emon had said the first day. *"Exporting goods attracts all manners of hazard, including theft, and we've had our fair share. But our family's business is to make money, not lose it, so we adapted. Either we learn how the thieves work—and who they're working for—and work around them, or we learn to suffer continual loss, none of which is in our blood."*

She had left that matter there, content to accept what knowledge he was willing to offer and even the sparring session they took to the one afternoon, working out their frustrations with a surprising ease.

If anything, the reports and information from the Derossa family only supported what she read in her father's records, as well as giving credence to Allon's comments. The more they dug, the more it confirmed their suspicions that the Cigils were responsible, and they had sent out a hand's count of spies to investigate. Along with them, Emon had contacted several of the Derossa family's associates and requested they make their own discreet inquiries. With luck, one of them would infiltrate the Cigils and bring back something worthy, or at least catch one of their members in a confession.

Though it would have been even more helpful if the gang had done something new—something someone could catch them in the middle of. Since the death of the young woman on the road, nothing more had gone on, and none of the spies reported anything worth knowing, saying it was too early to tell what was happening. Even Gren was still working on digging up solid evidence they could use or a trail of bodies they could follow.

Had the Cigils achieved what they wanted or had they found out there were spies on the hunt and called a stop for the time being? Had someone found something without realizing it, prompting the Cigils to pull back? Or were they laughing at the entire situation, happy to take Aeley for a fool and see how she reacted, only to plan an even harder pushback?

Between worries about the next attack and courting Lira, Aeley tried to entertain Emon and Ryler without revealing her deepest thoughts and burying their attempts to make peace long enough to sort the issue. The possibility of too much honesty getting in the way of dealing with their families was another fire she had no interest in setting.

Ryler pulled her to a stop. "You're thinking again."

"What?" Aeley asked, blinking at his blank stare. Was he scolding her or merely voicing an observation? It was hard to tell with him sometimes, unlike Emon, who was an easier read with the way his emotions often splashed across his face with little effort to hide them. Even so, Ryler was the more tolerable of the two. Manageable, even when they were alone—or as alone as they could be with the guards in the halls, watching them carefully, just short of following right behind them and stepping on their heels. Goddesses knew that was what Mayr wanted, and she knew who else would want to trip Ryler straight through the floor.

"You get this face when you're worried," Ryler said. "Want to share?"

Not really.

"It's about the attacks again, isn't it?"

Maybe. Aeley crossed her arms and shuffled her feet.

Ryler's odd smile matched his shifting expressions. "You can't help yourself, can you? You're one of *those*, paranoid that the whole world's going to fall apart and disappointed when it doesn't."

"No, I'm not. I just hate sitting around doing nothing." Aeley scowled at Ryler's grin. He took too much pleasure in her annoyance. *Maybe I should tell you 'no' now and rip that grin right off your face. If only you weren't useful.* "Honestly, doesn't it bother you that for several days—almost one right after another—there are attacks, but then suddenly nothing? It's just too quiet. I mean, nothing in a week—"

"It's been more than that."

"Fine, *more than a week.* Still the same problem."

"Well, instead of worrying, maybe you should try saying thank you."

"What?"

"Well, *obviously* us being here is helping you." Ryler tilted his head, his faint smirk nudging Aeley's nerves. "The way I see it, things started to quiet down once we stuck our necks out and got people to stick their noses into this business, trying to stir up trouble." Ryler shrugged. "I'd say we started asking the right people the right questions and running the trouble off. People don't like being cornered any more than they like being caught. And considering we've opened up our valuable resources to your use, putting out people we still have to do business with after this whole mess, I'm pretty sure *thank you* is the least you could offer." He arched one of his brows. "Or is this just a use us, abuse us, and hopefully lose us sort of thing? Can't quite bring yourself to tell us to shove it and kill the contract, so degrade us to the status of mangy puppet dog and just basically leave things there to rot?"

It took everything Aeley had not to grind her teeth and kick his shins.

Goddesses, where's Lira when I need her? Aeley let out her frustrations in a slow breath. *Off with Vant, doing her job, naturally. And Mayr's still down in the village checking on their progress.* She frowned at Ryler's all-to-knowing smile. *Why did I listen to Ryler's suggestion to send him, anyway? I should've just gone myself. At this rate, I'll be lucky if we make it to dinner to hear what Mayr has to say about any of it.*

"You just can't bring yourself to say it, can you?" Ryler said quietly. "Even after all the work we've done together, and how friendly we've all been the last few days. Even the voices in my head are more grateful than you." Ryler strolled down the hall with his hands shoved into his pants pockets. When he started whistling a tune she barely recognized, Aeley wondered what else he wanted to say—and if it included pulling what support they had pledged.

Damn you, politics, and triple damn your bloody rubbish sense of ass-wiping diplomacy.

Her father was lucky he was dead. She *never* would have let him hear the end of it. Not even once.

"Ryler, wait." Aeley hurried after him. "It's not that. It's just that—"

Emon rushed into the hall, cutting them off, an odd sight emerging from the shadowy corridor that led to the cells below.

Aeley stopped behind Ryler, almost failing to catch herself as he stepped back and nearly bumped into her.

"Emon." Aeley gave him a once-over. Had he been to the armoury? Or the training room? Unless he had been waiting for them to pass by, though to what end, she had no idea. "It's a bit of a surprise seeing you here. Were you searching for something? Anything I can do?"

Emon's gaze shifted to Ryler's before returning to Aeley. Hands clasped behind him, he offered a tense smile, as forced as usual. "Aeley. *Ryler*. No, nothing. Thank you for the offer, however. I was just checking on things—the cells and weapons and so forth, making sure they were in good standing. You never know when they'll be required, especially if the spies come back with someone worth interrogating." He gave a curt nod. "Everything looks to be in order. If the Cigils have the gall to finally attack again, we'll be ready. It shouldn't be long now, not with how quiet they've been. If they're anything like the others, they're likely setting up for a harder hit or a specific target."

Aeley nearly slapped Ryler's shoulder before gesturing to Emon. "See? He gets it. That's what I'm talking about."

"What?" Emon asked, his smile faltering.

Ryler sighed. "You don't want to know." He jutted his thumb back behind him. "And I'll save you—run, now, before she starts sharing her problems with you."

"Thanks," Emon said. With a stiff bow, he excused himself and walked away.

"Yes, *thanks*," Aeley echoed. "A girl loves being treated like she's ridiculous, especially in front of other people."

Ryler's shoulders sank as he relaxed, his hands in his pockets again. "Suppose I should say that I'm sorry," Ryler murmured, "but since you won't say thank you, we'll just say we're even."

Aeley fought to keep her mouth from running with all the ways he could piss right off a cliff. *Keep it together... Calm. So very calm. Don't be any worse about this.*

Before she could do any further damage, Ryler reached for her. "We should get something to eat," he said, casting a look up the hall.

Just as soon as he touched her, he retracted and hid his hands behind his back.

"What?" Aeley asked. She turned to find Gren walking towards them, his sword strapped to his back and more than two knives on his belt, ready to start a fight. His irritated expression told her nothing, but from the cloak in his hand, he was on his way out again.

He stopped several paces away and crooked a finger, beckoning Aeley to him without glancing at Ryler.

Aeley went without debate, happy for the distraction and not about to argue with why Gren always put distance between him and the Derossa brothers. They were never close to each other in the same room, and getting them to talk without tension chortling its way through the discussion was nigh impossible. The rare dinner where Gren made an appearance and shared the meal with Emon and Ryler at the same table had all the agony of yanking fingers off with a barbed nutcracker.

"I'm taking a trip," Gren announced the moment she was a foot away from him. He pulled her closer by the wrist, positioning her in front of him as if trying to hide from Ryler. "Going up to the Footshred quarries."

"You were there already. What could you possibly get from Allon that's any different?"

Gren snorted. "Not wasting my time on him. Saw him once and that's enough. They're lucky I left him intact. They appreciated the broken face, though." He waved his hand and peered over his shoulder, almost like he expected someone. "Not him. Just a couple guys I know. Maybe even Rea, assuming she's feeling giving. I asked them to keep track of who's been visiting. Names, if they could. Appearances at the least. Origins. Family crests. Anything useful."

"So you still agree with me?"

"I'm willing to bet there's more to it than just someone getting up one morning and deciding to wreak havoc. And I certainly wouldn't trust anyone who says they're friends of his."

"And he says I'm paranoid," Aeley muttered.

"What?"

Aeley waved the question away. "Nothing."

Gren looked her over, eyes narrowed with suspicion. "I'll be back when I'm back. Stay out of trouble," he said, poking her forehead. He turned away and raised his hand, shouting as he sauntered back towards the front foyer, "And a little paranoia's healthy. It'll keep you alive longer than being an ass."

As Aeley glanced at Ryler, she caught his disgust, the disdain in his gaze following after Gren. Once she headed back to him, however, he relaxed, his glance flickering through the hallway before settling back on Aeley.

"So I was thinking..." Ryler started. With an arm around her shoulders, he pulled her into a slow walk. "We should go for a ride in the carriage." Before she could ask why, he placed a finger on her lips. "The sun's up and it's a day worth enjoying. We can go see for ourselves that things are all right, at least for now. Sometimes you need to accept things are peaceful, good, especially when it's quiet and nothing's wrong. Fine, the Cigils might attack tomorrow or the day after or whatever, but what's the point of staying cooped up in here and hiding when there's plenty to enjoy out there? If it takes showing you that you need to take some time away from work, then let's go. You and Emon can fret about things later—together, for all I care."

Aeley pursed her lips. The offer *was* appealing, much to her frustration. She was sick of staring at desks and parchment and battling the temptation to go charging into a fight. "Only thing is we've got dinner to worry about—the magistrates, and Mayr's due back shortly—"

"Yeah, I know, but we'll be back before Dreca and the other magistrates arrive. We'll want to hear their reports. And Mayr's a good boy, trained well. He'll do what he does." Ryler tugged on her hand. "It'll clear what ails you. Maybe even make you smile. Just a little, though. I don't know if the world's ready for a full one yet."

Right then, he was as charming as he said he wanted to be, and that alone left Aeley laughing for the first time since that morning, before Lira had gone off with Vant. Ryler made a good case, bastard that he could be, and a carriage ride was far from a serious commitment. Of all the things she could have been doing, it made more sense than several of the alternatives, especially if it improved morale and kept things peaceful between them.

"Fine, a ride it is. I'll grab a few guards and we'll go."

When Ryler tugged on her hand again, she followed along. Assuming they kept their attitudes and verbal jabs under control, the trip could be what exactly she needed.

Two villages checked, four more left. And no one's falling apart.

Aeley slid across the seat at the back of the carriage and settled in the middle, sparing a glance out the window at the closest guard on horseback and the golden-orange leaves in the woodland beyond them. With Mayr off on business and Pellon remaining at the estate should anyone attack while she was gone, Aeley had chosen a team of four guards to join the ride, not that she expected much to come of it. She only hoped Lira had as quiet of a trip back and forth from Vant's home. Though with Stick and Stuck as her companions for the day, Lira was likely getting an earful of stories about the guards no one should ever tell in polite company.

Chuckling at the possibilities her imagination threw up, Aeley let her head fall back on the cushioned seat as she waited for Ryler to finish talking to the driver and get into the carriage.

There was only one thing wrong with the trip, and it had everything to do with the fact that Lira was nowhere nearby. Aeley had been spoiled for nearly two weeks, having Lira at the estate and enjoying it too much to ever want to see it end. Except with Emon and Ryler there, too, sharing the same house had almost been the most Aeley and Lira could manage... save the few times they had stolen away while Emon and Ryler were off handling their business... or the two nights Lira had crept through the hall to Aeley's room, barely making a sound after Aeley had taught her where all of the weak spots and creaking floorboards were. Or the other two nights Aeley had snuck into Lira's room by way of the back stairs and adamantly refused to go back to her room the next morning until Lira threatened to shove her out into the hall, naked, laughing all the while.

If that was what a possible future together looked like, Aeley was ready to take it on.

The carriage rocked as Ryler climbed in and closed the door before thumping his hand on the roof. As they rolled forward, the carriage bounced back and forth over the uneven ground until finally sinking into the tracks running up the length of the dirt road.

"I told you it wouldn't be so bad." Ryler gazed out the window towards the woodland, his legs crossed, hands clasped at his hip. "You look better than when we left. Guess my terrible, horrible, unthinkable plan is working?"

"It wasn't terrible," Aeley argued, "just unexpected."

Ryler snorted. "Still not used to us, are you? You're still trying to accept what this is. Still uncertain." He snapped his glance back to her. "We're not fools, no matter what you think. We see it. Among other things."

Without warning, he was across the carriage, sitting beside her.

Aeley drew close to the side of the carriage, her grip tight on the edge of the seat as his leg pressed to hers, every instinct on fire and itching to slap him.

Ryler brushed the back of his finger down her cheek, a tender touch that left a bitter chill in its wake. His hand glided over her jaw, her neck, then her back, all to pull her hair over her shoulder as he leaned into her.

She drew her fingertips over her knife, sinking into a painfully familiar mindset. *Don't kill him. I can't kill him. He's playing a game, trying to win me over. Keep control.*

When his lips grazed her ear in a gentle kiss, she pulled the knife from its sheath slowly, ready to go for his ribcage. Lira was allowed to be intimate with her howsoever she liked, but the list of people stopped there. If he wanted more than that kiss, he would lose something of his to pay for it. Game or no, she had not agreed to anything more than a civilized relationship before marriage with a firm set of lines established around what she wanted after it.

A throaty hum sounded against her ear. "How long have you been toying with our sister?" he whispered. His hand snaked under the arm she had bent back, sliding along her waist to grab the wrist of her knife hand.

Aeley tugged back. Her elbow smacked against the wall of the carriage, Ryler's tightening hold still on her arm.

He chuckled, his lips on her cheek as he dug hard into her wrist, forcing her to release the knife. "When were you expecting to make that little announcement, hmm?"

Aeley rammed her knuckles into his throat until he wheezed. "When I was done with this, you ass."

Ryler pulled back, her knife going with him. He tossed it behind him and rubbed his throat. "Kind of you to finally admit it. But that didn't need to be so hard. By the Four, you play rough. I think we need to—"

The carriage slammed to a stop, throwing them back. They tumbled against each other, sharp voices raised around them. Horses snorted loudly, and the carriage rolled back before swerving and stopping again. More voices filled the air, yelling back and forth, the clang of metal both close and distant, grunts and protests mixed into the chaos. The driver shouted for someone to stop, his holler giving way to a scream as the carriage rattled, rocking back and forth. Something pounded the roof, threatening to get in.

Aeley drew one of the small knives she kept in her boots and flicked her glance to the door, the roof, and back to the door again. *Yeah, come on, then, let's go—*

The moment the door opened, Ryler launched himself in front of Aeley, shoving her into the furthest corner, the knife knocked from her hand.

"*Dammit, Ryler!*" Aeley yelled as the knife slid across the floor. She struggled to get Ryler out of her way, not interested in his protection. She just needed to get—

A masked assailant climbed into the carriage, gloved hands reaching for her.

Ryler pushed Aeley back again, hard, pinning her in the corner. He twisted and kicked at the assailant, shouting for them to leave.

"Get off!" She tried to pull him aside. "I can fight—"

Ryler cried out. Jerked back, he was yanked from the carriage, legs-first onto the road. One assailant jumped on him, then a second, both of them pummeling him in a vicious beating. Ryler's arms flung up and out, trying to bat them away.

Another assailant in dark clothes climbed into the carriage with little effort and leapt at Aeley, hands aimed at her face, grabbing her hair. She kicked at his kneecap and rammed her knee up into his waist. He grunted but refused to recoil.

With swift, hard yanks on her hair, he pulled her forward. They tumbled to the floor together, Aeley barely able to get her bearings before being tugged into the doorway, her knees burning as they scraped across the carriage floor.

Fighting for air, Aeley slammed her palm into his face.

He yelped and released her. She scrambled to sit up, her head smashing against the metal doorframe as he came at her again. There was no escape—just a mass of body as he wrapped around her and pulled back.

She fell to the ground, landing on her assailant, flattened beneath her. Aeley pushed back and slammed her elbow into his chest. "That's for attacking me!" she yelled and stumbled back while he struggled to breath.

Hoarse shouts to stand down stole her attention. Bodies—so many bodies moving, taking up the road around the carriage. All four of her guards still stood, one of them limping their way through the fight, most of their horses headed off down the road. The guards struck out against the mob that pushed back on them, swords and knives in the mix, a clash of at least a dozen against four.

Not far from her, Ryler stood with his fists raised, jabbing at one of his attackers before he dodged another blow. His nose bled and his shirt was torn, but he was holding his own in the fight. Behind him, the carriage driver lay on the ground, arms twisted behind his back and his face in the dirt. Blood trickled down his cheek, the wound in his head glistening in the sunlight. Beside him lay his hat and a rock smeared with what she assumed was his blood.

Aeley went for the last of her knives, pulling it from her boot—

She lost it just as quickly as someone kicked her from behind and sent her crashing into the side of the carriage, head smacking into the wood.

Crying out, she pushed off the carriage, her gaze blurred. As she backed away to look for her attacker, another two masked assailants in dark clothes jumped in front of the door.

"I don't think so," one said before pushing his companion towards her.

Aeley shuffled back and glimpsed Ryler lying on the ground. Unmoving.

Damn.

She was on her own, at least until the guards could get to her—assuming they were still standing.

There was no time for assumptions. Fists raised, Aeley dug her feet into the ground. If the Cigils wanted her, they would take a beating first. As her opponent rushed towards her with his fists up, she waited for the right moment. *Aim for the throat or just step aside? I could—*

The world shifted, flying away from her. Everything blurred, black and red punctured by light.

She slammed to the ground, her shoulder lost to agony at the impact. Her head bounced off the road, her vision a haze of specks and shadow. Her breath... gone, so hard to catch. The man had barreled into her, his shoulder dealing all the hurt like a rock-hard battering ram. Were her ribs broken or just bruised?

The massive weight pinning her scrambled to hold her legs down. The heavy breaths—hers? His? Both?

Aeley stared up. Instead of blue sky, there was darkness. From above, firm hands pushed on her chest. A foot pressed hard on her stomach, and she coughed, wincing as deep aches flared through her waist.

"Time to sleep," a voice murmured, almost soothingly. Fingers wrapped around her nose and mouth, a wet hand doused in a bitterness that became sickly sweet. Her thoughts shattered into fragments, overcome by silence.

She whispered Lira's name and everything fell away.

Chapter Seventeen

The explosives. Always those damned explosives, taking down her home, shattering the life with their father, tearing and ripping and punching holes into everything that was left... Blood, thick on the walls, splattered guts oozing down with it, drops trailed along the hallways, crusty with grit and stone and dust, all of it screaming from the ruins... and the ghosts... The ghosts that haunted always, stealing her away, stealing life despite her cries to stop, holding it back, holding it close, holding... haunting...

Aeley breathed deep, the slow crawl of an icy darkness overcoming the bloodied guards and torn corpses holding her hostage in her nightmare. Allon's face faded, but his throaty, gutting laughter lingered. Always that lingering, that inability to just let go, everything that would see them both damned in the end...

Chains rattled—a sharp, strange pull away from the darkness that sent her reeling into consciousness. The laughter was gone, banished, lost somewhere in the void. Around her, the air was moist, dank, and heavy as it filled her nostrils and mouth. She took another breath and choked on it, coughing as she struggled for air. Dragging her forehead across the ground, she fought the cruel bite of the aches surging through her ribcage. Her shoulder fared no better, its own demands for relief going unanswered. Everything hurt, inside and out, and dirt—all she could taste was gritty, stale dirt laced with a nauseating tartness that stuck to her tongue like something fuzzy and rotten.

Face pressed to the cool, hard floor, her cheek raw from a hard strike or three, Aeley worked her jaws and smacked her lips, easing into regaining her senses. Thin strands of straw danced in front of her face, but when she finally reached for them, metal cuffs entered her sight.

Shackled.

She sat up, crying out as everything in her body retaliated, a unified mass that sank and jammed and crushed her abdomen in protest. Aeley raised her hands and pulled the chain taut between her wrists.

One glance around the barred cell confirmed she was nowhere she recognized. Surrounded by dull, charcoal-grey metal and dim torchlight, she could have sworn she was in the lower levels of the Dahe estate. A guard stood outside the bars with his back to her, and the dark forms of objects hung on the wall across from him. She counted three cells other than hers, all of them small, isolated, empty save for shackles and haphazard clumps of straw. Beyond the guard, the silhouette of a staircase led upwards, most of the steps shrouded in darkness.

Even with the marred and filthy floor, Aeley considered lying down. Her body screamed for comfort and a soft mattress, but even a flat, metal floor was better than sitting...

Ugh, no. I'll never get up. I need to stand. Need to be ready for anyone who comes in—wait. The men.

She looked down. *Pants, tunic...*

Aeley sighed deep enough to anger her ribs all over again. Her captors had taken her belt and boots, but everything else remained. *At least for now. Maybe they like them feisty and dressed.* She shuddered and hoped for better, whatever *better* was.

"Hey! You!" Aeley rattled the chain. "Big guy. Mind telling me where I am?"

The guard remained still, almost like a statue, except for his one hand as it curled into a fist.

"This should be fun," Aeley muttered. She glanced around the cell again. Windowless and locked from the outside, the only way out was the door in the bars, while a set of keys hung on the wall between the guard and the staircase. There were few options for escape but plenty to taunt her with.

Smooth walls, so no climbing. The bars are too thick and too close together to do anything. The only door is locked with keys I can't get. Who needs options when you've got nothing to work with anyway? I don't even have boots. Nothing special to them, but they're gone anyway. And my knives are probably still out in the carriage, or they took them. I'm going to kill Ryler...

Assuming he was still alive.

She sobered at the thought. The group that attacked them had been ready and willing to use whatever force was needed. If she was the only target, they could have easily done away with Ryler and left him for dead, little more than necessary damage. If he was a separate target, however, they may have hauled him off somewhere else for interrogation. Any one of the cells across from her could have been his for however long she had been asleep. For all she knew, she had missed the party and he was being strung up by his toes somewhere. He would have deserved it, and *that* was where any semblance of sympathy ended.

I'd hate to deliver bad news to the Derossas and the Council, considering the mess we're tied up in, but in all the ever-loving cruelty of the Goddesses' humour, I really hope they've gone and finished him off because those bloody wandering hands of his—

"Ah, good, you're finally awake."

Aeley had never bit her tongue so fast.

Tongue, teeth, eyeballs—she wanted to rip all those damned things out of his head for choking fodder, the harder the better.

"*Ryler.*" She growled as he stepped out of the shadows, into the light near the bars by the door. Bruises darkened his cheeks and eyes, though they would never be good enough, not if this was how they were playing. The vicious chill that raced down her arms, the ice-cold rage that slammed through her—she wanted to shove every bit of *that* through Ryler's face and make him scream murder.

For now, the bastard was on the wrong side of the door, and that just grated Aeley's nerves all the more.

"Welcome to the Derossa family estate," Ryler said, his voice husky. "Looks like we've misplaced our hospitality for the day." He sneered and flicked his fingers at her. "Told you not to get me so hard. Like your punishment?"

"So I hit you in the throat—deal with it. And seriously, you think *this* makes up for *that*?" Aeley pushed up from the floor and sucked in a breath, almost hissing as she straightened.

"You should be clearer," a low voice scolded from the darkness. "This isn't for that. This is for things well before now and what's left of your future."

Aeley bit back a grumble that would have only come out as a groan. *Goddesses, no. Not you, too.*

Another shadow swept across the floor as Emon approached the bars and leaned against them, his body angled towards his brother. He took small glances at Aeley. "He likes to be dramatic, especially when he feels he's been slighted or embarrassed."

"Embarrassed? Who's embarrassed?" Ryler argued, thrusting his hand between the bars towards Aeley. "She's the one in this hole. I had her exactly where I said she'd be. It went off without any trouble. Didn't even lose one man."

Aeley dug her nails into her palms. "Good one, those lies. You're a regular ass in need of a good kicking." She snorted. "The whole 'you're paranoid' and 'you need to relax' bit—nice touch."

"Yeah, I know. Thanks for making it easy." Ryler looked at Emon. "That was risky, though, coming upstairs when we came by. You were supposed to be gone before then. What gives?"

Emon grunted. "It took me longer to find the chest than he said it would. But it was buried in the floor where he left it. I managed to get the gold out to my carriage a little after you left. No one has any idea. Though next time Allon says to get something, he needs to be clearer."

Allon.

Because of course.

She should have stuck with her instincts the first time around.

Aeley's cheeks burned, most of what she wanted to say tucked behind her strained efforts to stay in control. Fool her for believing Allon— for giving any idea of his any leverage whatsoever. She was never going to hear the end of it.

Lucky for her, she could ensure Allon never heard the end of it, either — or saw anything but a cell for the rest of his wasted life.

"Gold, huh? From that dirty, lying cheat?" Aeley snickered, if only to keep from grinding her teeth down to nothing. "What have you been doing with my brother?"

"Oh, look, she's finally cluing in. Though you've gone practically ten shades of red while we've been standing here, and I'd say you're just about ready to put your fist through my face," Ryler teased with a laugh. He turned to Emon, his face seeming to fight with itself over looking serious long enough to be convincing. "Apparently she doesn't like it when anyone talks about him. Who knew?"

Ryler stopped laughing, his gaze back on her. "Hey, Aeley — Allon. Allon. Allon, Allon, *Allon*, *Allon*!" He teetered back and chortled, banging on the bars as Aeley stormed towards him, fists aching to pummel his bruises right on through his skull. "Look at her! She wants to kill me. Oh, I'm scared."

Emon scowled, his face pinched as he swatted Ryler's head. "I'll kill you myself if you don't quit it."

"I'd take that as a threat, but I can't. We agreed we wouldn't. The family still needs us, especially with Lira being such a pain," Ryler argued.

Another chill blasted through Aeley, freezing her in place. Lira's name — his vile tone, the amount of disdain that dragged it down to a depth she hated more than the shackles... Lira was practically a goddess next to him. She deserved more than the snide contempt that oozed from his every word.

One thing at a time, she reminded herself and shook the shackles. "Hey, ass for brains, we were talking. What about my brother? Has he been making you empty promises? Bribing you to get him out?"

"No and no. He's staying right where he is for now," Emon answered. "And they aren't empty promises. He's delivering on exactly what he said. Promised us payment as a sign of good faith, and now we have it."

"From our estate?" Aeley frowned. "There wasn't anything there." She would have known— they had swept through every room in the estate after Allon's attack on Oly Valley, looking for traps or problems he had set before leaving the main house for the smaller estate. There had been nothing, not even personal effects. Everything else had been at the estate in Oly Valley.

"Funny, that, you thinking you know everything," Emon muttered. "Except that's the interesting thing about secret stashes of wealth: they're *secret.*"

"We just had to get into the estate, and since you fell for everything, we got in. Well done." Ryler grinned. "We thought Allon's plan sounded too foolish to work, but we didn't count on your version of ridiculous."

Come over here and say that again so I can slap you. Aeley crossed her arms, painfully aware of the rough metal that chafed her skin. "So all this song and dance, the raiding and ranting, terrorizing the villagers—just a cute little game of advantage and piss, then, with me as the fool in the middle."

"But, see, that's the beauty of it: all of it *was* a game." Emon drew his dark hair over his shoulder to play with the ends, denying her gaze as he examined the strands. "Every attack, every message—just pieces being played." He flicked a look up at her. "With you as the prize, actually. A fool, but a prized one."

"We were always coming for you," Ryler said. "We just had to move it faster than planned, because *someone* couldn't keep her hands off. And then you went and invited the mercenary in."

Oh, she heard the disgust there, almost as full of loathing as every reference he made to Lira.

Gren was going to kill her for this, if not strongly kick her ass.

He'll have to wait in line, though—Mayr and Pellon have the first go, and they might not leave anything behind to share.

Why had she not waited for Mayr to come home? And how long would it take for any of them to realize something was wrong? Mayr would come looking, she had every faith in that, and Pellon would never forgive her for telling him to stay at the estate instead of going with her. But how long it would take for any of them to figure out who captured her and where they were… the thought was far from reassuring.

Yeah, she had fallen too far into the trap and the punishment was real.

"Great," Aeley muttered. Her chest ached with a fierce burn, lost somewhere between searching for where her pride had dropped off and where her father's bright ideas began. "And let me guess: Allon was just raring to go along with it."

"Oh, he gave us the idea." Ryler slipped his arms through the bars and folded one arm over the other. "We have an understanding. He thought the marriage was a good way to get back at you *and* help his friends out, because he owes all of us in one way or another. He's got a lot of things you don't know about. Precious things, worth more than you can understand. And he's willing to give it all to us if we just do this one little thing."

"What? Throw me in a cell and starve me to death?"

"Hardly," Emon replied with a grunt. "One of us gets you and whatever you've got. The other gets all of Allon's wealth that he's hidden away."

"We just had to get you to take us more seriously," Ryler added. "Everyone else, too. We're tired of our family being the one that lost. A little chaos went a long way to driving you to us, though." Ryler gestured to Emon. "He thinks you were desperate to trust someone."

"More like desperate in general. That's how Lira's been all over her," Emon corrected. He glared at Aeley, a deeper, darker anger unfurling in his gaze. "Who, by the way, is as involved in this as we are."

Aeley's worries slammed to a stop.

No.

"Oh, wait, did I forget to mention that?" Ryler smiled, his teeth looking entirely too perfect *not* to punch through the back of his head and leave the whole thing spinning. "When you fall for it, you really fall and just keep heading straight to the bottom, don't you?" He laughed and shook his head. "Yeah, she's been in on it. Played her part real well, too. Had me convinced. Well, almost. You should see her face when you aren't looking. Not necessarily in your favour." Ryler feigned retching, his hands at his throat. "We've heard the stories, and she's tired of choking on it. Actually, she's just tired of choking on you."

Control snapped in Aeley, and everything tumbled out, ready to bury them. "I'll make *you* choke if you don't shut your trap," Aeley snarled, smacking the bars and holding on. "Kiss my ass, you rancid piece of—"

Emon snapped his fingers, silencing Aeley. He held his hands up before him. "Believe what you will, but before you start yelling that she's innocent and we're just criminals, you should know she's pulled the strings over your head. She's been in on it the entire time—just doing it on her own terms. She wants to be Steward and take over our family, even while my father's still alive. She's been very, *very* busy. And you know our sister: she can do anything she puts her mind to, and, apparently, her touch."

Lies!

Aeley gritted her teeth, her heart crying out to fold in on itself and hide. "I don't believe you."

Emon shrugged. "Fine, that's your choice. I just thought we'd let you know what's really going on. Why do you think she was at that initial meeting? It wasn't to warn you away from us—it was to ensure you went along with it. She knew about the marriage contract all along and didn't tell you, not until then. We know—we saw your face. She's played you as much as we have."

"Has she told you about our mother yet?" Ryler asked. "Possibly with tears and a sad face? Told you she had her poor little heart broken when she was a girl and how terrible Mother's been? Maybe mentioned something about being ignored? Forced into things she says she didn't want?" He tapped his forehead. "All from here. She was never forced. She was given everything she ever wanted, spoiled until she turned rotten. Got it into her head that she's been wronged, so she's taking it out on all of us and wants to destroy the family. She's using you to do it. And you fell for it."

"Though, hey, you shouldn't feel so bad," Emon added quietly. "We fell for it, too. I guess that makes us all fools, doesn't it? United in the downfall while our sister gets exactly what she wants."

Ryler nodded, his hands shoved into his coat pockets. "Really should have seen it coming, I guess." He sighed, a deep, languishing breath out that ended in a grimace. "Should've known," he muttered. "She was way too eager."

Aeley glared at them both, unable to keep either gaze for long.

"Yes, I know, it hurts, but honestly, did you think it was real?" Emon asked, his tone soft, not so much scolding as it was concerned. "Did you not notice how quickly your romance has come along? How fast it's fallen into your lap, maybe even how perfect it all seems? And let me guess: she doesn't talk about herself. She avoids it, brushes it off. She's sweet to you and acts like she cares, like she wants to get to know you." He smiled, almost sadly. "Maybe you've been distracted, more interested in spending time with her than doing your job. Maybe she's made you think she's clever and funny, someone who wants to listen to your problems without adding the burden of her own. And maybe she's been around you just after an attack has happened, claiming she knows nothing. I'd say it's all very interesting, full of coincidence, and fast. *Too* fast."

"And Allon—he says she played her part perfectly," Ryler said. "At the quarry, remember? You took her along to that meeting. He says she was in perfect form that day. Very believable. You had no clue."

No. Just so much no.

Aeley stared at the floor, none of it making sense. *Lira would never—she couldn't have, never…*

And yet, for being liars, they knew too much. Intimate details they never should have had.

She tried to remember the expression on Lira's face when Lira talked about herself. Had they really been lies? Had she truly strung Aeley along? "You're lying," she whispered.

"I bet she didn't tell you our parents haven't been here for weeks." Emon tilted his head to the side. "She didn't, did she? She just kept close to you, staying in the village and saying she didn't want to go home. She may have said something about not getting along with our parents and feeling like she's forced out of the house." He tapped one of the bars closest to Aeley. "But she neglected to tell you that no one's been here except for the two of us, and we've been busy elsewhere. So before you doubt us, maybe you should ask her why she lied."

"Because we're telling you the full truth, in case you didn't notice," Ryler added with a shrug. "There's no point in lying about it anymore, because you're here, exactly where we want you."

"Why *are* you telling me?" Aeley spat out, grateful for the change in subject. Right then, anything more to do with Lira was the surest way to make her vomit. She wanted to lose herself completely and punch the wall into the next fifty tomorrows, most likely breaking her hand in the process and feeling all the better for it. If her not-so-genuine relationship was in shambles, why not take her body out, too? "Since you love saying how ridiculous *I* am, let's talk about you. I think it's pretty damned ridiculous to give up everything, even when I'm stuck behind bars."

Emon chuckled. "Yes, well, that's a matter of perspective, isn't it? We simply want you to understand what we're capable of—that you're in over your head. To impress on you the implications, should we let you go."

"Let me go? Now who's lying?"

"No, that's the truth." Emon crossed his arms, the hint of a smile at his lips. "You don't have to spend the rest of your life here."

"If?"

"If you're willing to play the game. All of us can win and neither of our families will be further disgraced. We can put the past behind us and go forward together, assuming you're willing to be nice."

"Be nice? What could possibly make me want to *be nice* to you ever again?"

Emon gestured to the bars with a limp wave. "Other than being stuck here forever? A few things. We know you're pretty fond of Mayr and Haydin—all of the people who live under your roof, really, as sentimental as it is. You also seem to have something for the magistrates and people in general. Our sister, too. And you obviously value your own life, or else you wouldn't have fought so hard to keep it."

"Meaning what?" Aeley watched Emon's face, annoyed with how easily his expressions slipped. Details. She needed details.

"Goddesses, you're slow," Ryler muttered. He banged the bars, jolting Aeley back. "Pain. Loss. Death. Absolute chaos. We know a lot of people, some of whom enjoy Allon's ideas and wouldn't mind going along with them. There's a lot of grief to go around, and he's not the only one with access to things that go boom." He shrugged. "I figure we'll mess with people so bad, they'll *beg* for a new Steward. And you know, if *you* should meet a rather untimely death, guess who the people will likely turn to in order to fill in the spot? One guess." Ryler smirked and pointed between him and Emon. "That would be *us*. We'll campaign hard and say we tried to solve every problem, but you refused us."

"But that won't save anyone you love," Emon said softly.

"Mm, he's right. Listen to him." Head tilted, Ryler pressed one finger to his lips. "I really *do* wonder what it'll look like, all that carnage in that pretty estate. The walls are already red all over the place, so let's just stain them a bit more, shall we? Shake things up, make them interesting. Really watch your guards get to work and go down for the trouble."

Aeley ran cold as the blood rushed from her face. Threatening to kill her was one thing, but threatening the lives of those she cared for was something else entirely. Her family... Haydin, Mayr, Pellon, the guards, Cook... they were all she had left. She would always protect them, even if it angered Mayr to the point where he ignored her.

And the people—*her* people—they were her responsibility, those under her roof and in the rest of the tract. For years, she had worked hard to do the best she could for them. It would not end with Emon and Ryler. It *could not*.

"So why don't you just kill me now?" Aeley sneered. Over her dead body would she let them ruin everyone's lives and live to tell.

Ryler snorted and fell back. "Hardly. Notice I said it was *likely* that people would turn to us to fill in for you. It's not guaranteed they'd give it to us, no matter our promises. That's where the marriage is advantageous. We get the control without the same risk."

"And before you think you won't get anything out of it, consider how much good you can do from a marriage instead of a funeral pyre," Emon said. "Even keep us in line if we go too far. We'd be willing to entertain the possibility of being wrong, as long as you keep your mouth shut about the rest of this. You don't, we take matters into our own hands."

Aeley spun on her heel and headed for the wall on the other end of the cell. Was she a fool for considering anything other than no?

But then there's everyone else, and the punishment...

Images of Oly Valley resurfaced, the thunderous explosions, the crumbling walls. Blood and guts. She had been there once, lost among the aftermath and unable to escape the foul taste it left behind. How could she subject anyone else to that? How could she bring that suffering to people she had sworn to protect?

She bit her tongue and turned back. "I don't understand why you did this at all. You'd have the same thing if you had just stuck to the marriage contract—"

"No, not quite," Emon argued. "The marriage deal outlines only a few things to benefit our family, but we've decided we want a lot more. This is how it has to happen. We deal here, while you're in the position to be serious about it. Then, and only then, can we believe you're willing to make it work. Once you agree, there's no backing out. You're bound to your promises or there will be consequences."

"Not to mention we're doing this as a favour to your brother with a pretty good payoff," Ryler said. "He's a friend; a good friend. And we hate what you did. Instead of just handling it the way other families would have—as a *family*—you made the Council deal with it and go around pretending like you didn't put him in the position to lose his mind. He's willing to give us everything just to see you squirm, including his estate and his things, all of which reverted to your possession. You agree to this and we get that."

"So it's all about you," Aeley muttered. "Big surprise."

"No, not us: our family," Ryler corrected. "We've got a lot of fixing to do. A lot of things your parents helped break. But you wouldn't understand. Your family's had it easy."

If you call this life easy, we have very different definitions.

Ryler believed every word he said, making him dangerous enough, but Allon whispering in his ear made it even worse.

Emon tapped the bars. "No need to make a decision now. We're happy to give you all the time you need. We have somewhere to be as it is. Can't allow people to think we've disappeared, too." He beckoned his brother with one hand.

The moment Ryler stepped forward, Emon punched him in the face.

"What was that for?" Ryler yelled and stumbled back, holding his cheek.

"You need the sympathy. The head guard has to believe you and so does everyone else. Come here so I can add to it."

Ryler snarled and slapped Emon's fist away. "I've got enough bruises to make it work. I just have to play the emotional bit. Cry and sob about how *she's still out there*," he wailed before pretending to wipe a tear from his eye. "See? It's not that hard. But I'm bored now. Let's go."

Emon and Ryler disappeared into the darkness, reappearing for a few moments on the staircase. Somewhere at the top, a door slam closed.

Aeley almost collapsed, her heart all but hitting the floor without her. She wanted to do nothing more than curl into a ball and cry for the first time since her father died. *Disaster—an absolute disaster. Father would be so, so disappointed. And Lira... is any of it true?*

Aeley crept towards the back corner to the highest pile of straw and sank down, then wrapped her arms around her as far as the chain would allow. She felt used. Even more, she was gullible to a fault. The lengths the ridiculous family feud had gone made marriage seem like child's play. There was no easy way out. Either way, she lost. The only choices left were how much was she willing to lose and how.

Alone in the silence, she begged for a third option.

Chapter Eighteen

The guard's gaze slid over Aeley as if she wore nothing, a leer that left her feeling exposed and ready to burn through every obstacle on her way to freedom.

If only you'd come over here so I could punch you in the face. I'll be a real sumptuous meal then.

Aeley stretched her stiff limbs, and the straw pile sank further beneath her. How long had she been captive? Shrouded in the darkness, the most she had to track time was the single shift change of the guards.

Glancing at the guard's back, she wished for the previous one. *That* guard had ignored her, which suited her just fine, but this one had a difficult time keeping his eyes in the right direction. He was young, perhaps only twenty, and unable to stand still, inexperience dripping from him like he was a leaky bucket. Either he had received different instructions or he ignored the responsibilities of his assignment, turning to look at her with consistent timing.

I'm not going anywhere. No need to twist your neck off... unless you want me to. What I'd give for that much. I can't keep sitting here. This isn't me.

After pushing up to pace around the cell, Aeley drew her hand along the walls. No imperfection, no means of escape, even without a guard. Just a deal to bind and gag her.

I never should've asked for help. Why did I think Allon had a point? He never has a point, not unless it benefits him. And handling it on my own—I could've done that. Why didn't I just believe it and run with that whole thing? I shouldn't have listened to Lira, either.

Aeley pressed her forehead to the wall, first with a quiet groan, then a long sigh as she pulled back just enough to gently thump her forehead off the metal. Was it true, Lira's role in cornering her? She hated the heavy, sickening knot in her stomach, its various twists and tension worsening as she remembered Ryler and Emon saying Lira had lied. They could have jammed a thousand thorns into her insides, bleeding her dry, and it still would have failed to outdo the hurt tearing through her right then. She wanted to believe they were the liars, their words sharp, but strategic and false.

Except...

Despite how much she hated Emon and Ryler, they knew what had passed between Lira and her, and not just things other people could have noticed. Details. They knew too many details—

intimate, private, all of it information they never should have had.

Not unless Lira told them.

Eyes squeezed shut against the headache taking root with a piercing jab, Aeley slumped against the wall, her folded arms pinned under her head, enduring the metallic bite of the shackles. If none of what Emon and Ryler said had been the truth, she would have completely ignored them.

But there is truth to it, and that's what makes this all so sad.

Lira had burst into her life so suddenly, at the same time as the problems started. Then, as the attacks continued, their relationship skipped ahead, one step, two steps at time, carried away like leaves whipped into a frenzy by a breeze. Even though Aeley had wanted it, it was still fast, her falling for Lira so quickly and getting that lost in her. Emon was even right about how distracted she was by Lira.

Maybe... just maybe... they were telling the truth.

Aeley spun around and fell back against the wall. Arms on either side of her, pulling the chain of her shackles taut over her thighs, she tilted her head back to watch shadows flicker across the ceiling. Was this another twisted nightmare? Was she actually off somewhere else, lying unconscious in the road, making up villains to compensate for not having Allon around? Had she finally fallen that far, too deep to climb out of the darkness alone?

If only her constant full-body ache could have pissed off, leaving her to that particular fantasy.

If only the absurd ridiculousness of this entire situation wasn't real. She glared at the wall on the other side of the cell. It was real, all right, no less than what she thought she'd had with Lira. *Why can't I get over this idea that it's not what it is—what I want it to be?*

Her thoughts all but screeched the answer. She was more like her father than people realized, settling for the difficult path through life. Being alone for so long, sacrificing her life to take care of her father and clean up after Allon, all of it left her feeling empty, stuck in a dark pit with too many knives and not a single spoon to dig her way out.

But Lira made her question everything, inspiring Aeley to reach for more than drowning her nightmares in whatever decanter she could swipe and surrendering her life to everyone else. Lira was her means to fight the emptiness, a chance to be herself in ways she had forgotten. Their conversations kept Aeley honest, allowing her to admit things she never normally would because she feared judgment.

Though maybe it was the fact that Lira was always composed and calm that helped the most, and the way it reminded Aeley of her father left her smiling sadly at how fitting it all was. Aeley envied how Lira tamed the chaos in a way Aeley could only grasp at sometimes. That peace, the comfort Lira offered in living, it drew Aeley to her without any intention to let go—only get closer. Even more, Lira was easy to talk to, and she listened more than most people.

Yet Lira rarely spoke about her life, keeping secrets instead of trusting Aeley. The only time she talked about herself was when she was confronted, and especially when she was trapped. The most forthcoming she had been came only after Aeley pointed out how she said one thing but did another.

Then again, she had also never driven Aeley completely away from Ryler and Emon, despite snide remarks about their egos. If anything, she had instructed Aeley to contact them. She had also been the one to suggest the ball, encouraging them to put the entire situation out in public for everyone else to see... to pressure Aeley with. Maybe even to make a spectacle and force Aeley to stay in the middle with the decision hanging above her head, considering their families had avoided each other for more than thirty years.

If she cared as much as Aeley wished she did, would she not have run them off? Kept things secret? She had the means. All it would have taken were a few words to settle the entire matter and Aeley would have gone along with it.

There was also the question of Allon, with whom Lira had seemed all too comfortable. It was difficult to forget how he had stared at Lira like he knew what she was doing. Had they known each other the entire time? If Allon was friends with her brothers, Lira would have seen him on occasion. It was difficult to believe that she never would have met him. Why would she say nothing?

Not to mention she knew about the marriage contract and played it off. Except she had a reason, an explanation that made perfect sense. Except her brothers knew everything she'd said to me, almost like it was rehearsed, or like they've heard it over and over again. And she just happened not to be there when Ryler took me... but she was there all those times things went wrong. She also didn't look the least bit surprised to see the meeting hall had gone up in flames... and she only pushed things further while her brothers were around...

When everything was coming up coincidence, at what point did it start being a planned truth?

Aeley gripped her head with both hands to keep from shouting everything out, the rattle of chain mocking her as much as her doubts did. *No! This is exactly what they want. I'm paranoid, they're liars, and there's got to be a way out of this. They couldn't have thought of everything. If they're friends of Allon's, they can't be that perfect.*

She peered up to find the guard watching her again, his fist around the sword hanging loosely from his waist.

"What are you looking at?" she yelled.

He remained silent, but the corners of his lips twitched, a sign of his failing restraint.

"So I'm good to stare at, but you can't talk to me?" Aeley glanced at the keys on the wall. She needed to get them into the cell. *And the only way is to get him in here, except I have to do something to get his attention, and I've got nothing.*

But that lust on his scruffy face...

She wanted to scratch his eyes out if it was the last thing she did. Did he think that staring would get her to strip? Though considering the bulge in his pants, she supposed he did. Either that or it was a trick of the light.

"Come in here and try something, I'll make sure you don't see anything again," she mumbled, turning her head away. Whatever the mess they were in, whatever the lies or the truths or the somethings in between, she wished Lira were with her. *She'd think of something. Something I wouldn't. Knowing how modest she isn't on the inside, she'd probably call him over and seduce him like she did me.*

Memories of the armoury came into focus. Lira. The taste of her soft skin, the way her body curved with each touch, enticing Aeley to play, to want. It had been worth every moment, even the chance of being caught, to hear Lira moan and cry for more. Even the way she touched herself drew Aeley in for more, content to just watch...

Was *that* her third option? Could it really be that simple?

No. She glimpsed at the guard, his restlessness open for the taking, the eagerness to *do* speaking to him more than the rigidity of duty. *But I really am that desperate right now. It's either this or I make a deal that cages me for the rest of my life. And I've never been good at being quiet.*

Hastal give her strength, because she was about to hate this with every thread of her being.

"Hey, you," Aeley called. When the guard faced her, she headed for him, her steps slow as she swayed her hips deliberately. Gripping the bars, she leaned forward and tilted her head downwards to peer up at him through flickering lashes. "You've got to be terribly bored, standing around here watching me do absolutely *nothing*. I can't imagine this is any fun." She pouted and drew her hand across the skin above her tunic. "A guy like you should be out and doing things, showing off and having fun. You and that big, hard, powerful sword you're carrying. Girls like that: a man who offers them something so strong, so ready... so long and lacking for nothing but the right place to shove it in, *over* and *over* and *over*."

Aeley dropped her gaze to his groin, a crawl of a look that considered her options. She had been right about that interest burning itself through his cock—he was partway ready to take himself in hand, if not find himself a cold bath to stumble into and die. If she could just convince the rest of him...

After a swipe of her tongue across her lips, she sucked on her bottom lip and ran her hand down her chest, tugging on the laces of her tunic. "It's been a while since I had any man let me handle their weapon," she murmured, "which is a shame, because I really can't help myself when I'm holding it. I love the ups and downs, the power of the thrust, and Goddesses... that heat." Aeley fanned herself with one hand, her head tilted back as the collar of her tunic fell open further. "That moment when you give everything, when you're dying to get off as long as you can, but it can't come fast enough... My hand around you, feeding that anticipation... getting it off... coming for all it's worth..."

As the guard drew closer to the bars, she slipped her fingers inside her tunic and pulled gently above one breast. "It's such a shame that you're on that side and I'm on this one," she said quietly, "because I'm ready for it, but I guess I'll just have to enjoy you on my own... all alone... all by myself."

Aeley sauntered back to the straw pile in the corner, hands swinging with her hips, her stomach doing a dance all its own—one that needed a bucket and a sharp, forgiving drink to chase off the taste of bile and vomit. How much more could she possibly hate the words coming out of her mouth?

She sank into the straw and leaned on her side, propped up by her elbow. "I know you can't talk to me, but did they say anything about not enjoying me?" Aeley cupped one hand around her breast and bit her lip before drawing her fingers down her body. As slow as she could manage, she pulled her tunic upwards and dragged her fingertips across her exposed stomach, shivering at the cold touch.

Gag... She really needed to gag.

Licking her lips, she slipped her fingers inside her pants. The cuff and chain raked down her groin, a sickening weight as her touch crept deeper. One fingertip slid over her clit and she groaned, a soft sound followed by a louder moan as she rubbed harder.

Lira. She needed to think about Lira. The carriage ride, the armoury, all of their secret nights together since then. Every touch, lick, nip of skin, and gentle call to sink deeper, share more...

The wetness came easily with the memories, her fingers moving over and into her with less resistance, enough to have her throwing back her head. "Goddesses—*oh*—I'm so ready," she called between forced moans. "For you. I'm so—oh—*oh*—I need... yes... If only you could be inside me—so wet—"

Keys clinked. Metal rattled. A bolt slid back, followed by the whine of hinges.

The guard came for her with every thirst going in his grin, his hands at the buckle of his belt.

"Yes," she hissed. With a tug on her pants, she exposed more, pressed deeper.

His belt hit the floor, the sword clattering away.

You're a damned fool. You're going to deserve this.

Though when the keys clanged, she almost lost it, the threat of a laugh edging too close to the surface.

She sat up and threw out her hand, her glistening fingers catching his attention. "Wait. Let me," Aeley said between laboured breaths, scrambling onto her knees in front of him. Her touch was tender, gliding down his clothes from stomach to cock, with a hint of pressure that had him moaning with each pass of her fingers. At the small thrust of his hips, she peeled down his pants, freeing his swollen cock before she brushed a fingertip down its length. He shuddered, his eyes closed, one hand snaking over her shoulder.

This is going to hurt.

She rammed her head forward.

Quick, hard, with a jolt, she slammed her forehead into his cock. Before he could get too far, she gripped his shaft and twisted, sharp as she could.

He howled, his cry echoing off the walls. Hands over his cock, he stumbled back. "You—"

Aeley jumped up and ran around him, no time wasted as she flung the chain over his head, around his throat, and yanked.

The guard crashed against her, hands at his throat. "Stop—" he rasped. He struggled, choked for air, fingers curled around the chain that she held at both ends, the links digging into her palms. Feet scuffing the floor, he leaned back and forth, his fight admirable but getting in the way.

Gnashing her teeth at the strain, never letting up on her tight hold despite the pain gnawing at her fingers, Aeley dragged one hand over the other, crossing her wrists and twisting the chain as she pulled even harder. She hauled him back, battling his struggle with her own, every muscle in for the fight, every nerve ready to strip itself raw just to see him to the floor. He slapped at her, but she held fast, finding just enough slack to give the chain an extra yank into the lump in his throat before scraping the links over his skin. Her hands burned as he choked harder into silence. Pushing against him with her shoulder, she wrenched the chain into his throat as deep as it would go.

His struggle lessened. His hands weakened, fingers unfurling, his gasps over. As he slumped into her, she stumbled back and let him crash to the floor.

Aeley rammed her heel into his temple, satisfaction creeping through her as his eyes remained closed and his head swung to the other side without resistance. Dead or alive—it failed to matter. She snatched up the ring of keys first and compared each one, hoping the smaller key belonged to her shackles. Once she jammed it into one cuff and turned, the small click of the cuff's release was the best thing she had heard in a while. Shaking her scratched wrist, the cuff crashed to the floor while she removed its counterpart.

The shackles discarded, she collected the abandoned sword and its belt, hissing at the sting of her injured hands as the leather and hilt rubbed against her angry skin. After strapping the belt around her waist and attaching the key ring, she ran without looking back.

No boots, no armour. I'll have to make it work.

She rushed up the stairs to the door, then opened it slowly to peer through the crack. As she pulled the door further, she held her breath and listened.

Silence.

Aeley eased the sword from its scabbard and snuck into the hall, closing the door quietly behind her. Pressed against the wall, she rushed ahead, light on her feet as she passed empty rooms and turned dimly lit corners, searching for stairs to a level aboveground. *I'll take anything right now—*

Voices came towards her from down the corridor.

Aeley scurried back and slipped through the open doorway of the closest dark room, careful to hide just beyond the doorframe, out of sight. The voices grew louder, the words clear. Two guards, she figured, at least from the amount of chatter.

One fist tight around the sword, she controlled her breaths and waited. *Please don't look. Please don't be going to check on me.*

The guards passed the room and continued down the hall, their voices fading.

When she was certain no one else was in the hall, Aeley continued forward. *There has to be stairs here somewhere. How could they possibly go without... wait.*

The silhouette of a long staircase appeared from around the corner. *If this place is anything like home, the main floor's just up there.* The stairs were cold and dirty as she ran to the door at the top and pushed through, expecting light to blind her.

Darkness dotted with yellow light greeted her instead. *Not more cells.* Aeley squinted, making out a window frame, followed by another, and more beyond them on the other side of the long expanse of empty corridor. Night had fallen, though whether it was closer to dinner than midnight...

Even more important: where were the guards and how many? Whenever she stopped to listen for movement, she heard nothing, none of which comforted her. If the guards were anything like how Mayr trained and managed the Dahe guard, the silence could mean she was being watched from multiple corners and allowed to move around until finally being caught. *Though if Emon and Ryler are in charge...*

She had no idea what to make of them, but she also had no mind to stay and find out. Forging ahead, she stayed close to the walls. Beneath her feet, the smooth marble floor was a kindness on her scraped feet, the near-white stone a match to the numerous narrow pillars lining the corridor. Colourful, intricate tapestries hung from the ceiling and touched the floor, waving as she passed.

A flash of bright white snapped her attention to one of the windows across the corridor—moonlight, shining between clouds before disappearing behind them again, leaving her in the emptiness. If not for the fact she was trying to escape, she would have stopped to appreciate the possible beauty of the estate instead of cursing almost everything about it.

I need a way out. Any way out. I'll take any door—

More voices sounded in the distance. Boots scuffed the floor, headed her way.

Goddesses, can't I get a single chance here? Holding back her irritation's silent scream, she slipped behind one of the longest tapestries and waited.

"She should be down here," a light, feminine voice said—painfully familiar and wreaking so much havoc in Aeley at that moment. "There's no other place to hold her."

"Except a bedroom," another familiar, deeper voice answered quietly.

"Please don't. Just—don't. Let's keep going," the first voice replied, flustered.

Mayr? Lira? Aeley held her breath, fighting every instinct to jump out.

"And you're sure there's not many guards to worry about? I'm not getting killed for this," a second man said, his annoyed tone easy to recognize.

Gren.

She was going home.

Aeley stepped out into the corridor as they neared. "Looking for someone?"

The three of them stopped cold, Lira stumbling back into Mayr before he righted her on her feet.

"How did you—where did—how?" Lira moved closer, reaching for Aeley. Her hair was mussed, most of it tied back in a loose tail except for a handful of rogue curls that tangled about her shoulders. Everything about her was disheveled and ragged: the sleeves and skirt of her dress were rumpled, while a dark shawl was wrapped around her waist and tied in a loose knot just off from her hip, the entire thing skewed.

"I really don't want to talk about it," Aeley answered sharply, immediately regretting it but having no heart to take it back, not even as Lira recoiled, a flicker of pained confusion on her face. The thought of talking to her...

Yeah, right. If she's in on it, what's the point? The damage is done, the contract is moot, and we're more than over.

But if Emon and Ryler had lied…

Talking right then was impossible, especially with her head set on doubts that refused to go anywhere else. She needed time to wade through the conflicting thoughts, sort them. It would have been even more helpful if her body stopped hating her and simmered down with its aches and strains. Decisions were difficult enough without taking a step and feeling as though she was going to fall apart, even more since strangling the guard. She had more questions than answers, but she needed out of there first.

"Thank the Four you're here," Aeley said to Mayr, grabbing his wrist. "Can't tell you how happy I am to see you. How did you find me? I didn't think anyone knew."

Mayr snorted, his eyes narrowed. "Yeah, because you didn't damn well *wait for me*." He gripped her shoulders, firm but reassuring. "We need to talk about this," he said quietly, "but it'll wait until we're home. You're all right, though? We can get you out of here now?" Once Aeley nodded, Mayr pointed at Gren. "Good. And thank him—he figured it out."

"Found out these rat bastards were visiting Allon," Gren said, gesturing behind him with one of his swords. "I came back as soon as I could, but you weren't there. Then your guards came hobbling back home, said your carriage had been ransacked and you were gone. Figured we'd start here, especially after that mouthy disgrace disappeared, too, so we came looking for something useful—and there may've been something about rescuing you." He stared at her bare feet, one of his brows quirked. "But apparently we're late."

Lira reached for Aeley again. "He said it was my brothers, and I just couldn't belie—"

"We need to get out of here," Aeley interrupted, pointing up the hall as she sidestepped Lira's touch.

Mayr's confused scowl found Aeley first, then Lira. "Yeah, I know, so let's go back the way we came."

Lira frowned. "We came in through the kitch—"

"Fine. Let's get going. Gren, I'm up front with you." Aeley brushed past Lira and Mayr to follow Gren's hurried lead through the hall. "Where are they? I don't know when they visited me last. I don't know how long I've been gone."

"The day. And they're probably off boasting about Ryler's oh-so-brilliant escape," Gren replied.

From behind her, Aeley heard Lira whisper, "What did I do?"

"I don't know," Mayr whispered back.

After that, Aeley blocked out whatever else they may have said, her focus on the nooks and hallways ahead of them. There was no time to explain, despite how much she needed to. Though avoiding it altogether... "We need to be careful," Aeley said, turning the corner. "They could be—"

"At home, listening to people who really shouldn't be here."

Aeley stopped short at the husky voice, almost bumping into Gren—and all but spitting out every foul curse she knew.

Emon and Ryler.

Mere paces down the hallway, they stood with two of their guards, short swords drawn. Their dark gazes were unwavering and heavy, full of a deep, twisted loathing that Aeley would see them buried under. With slow movements, Gren withdrew his second sword from the scabbard on his back while Aeley held tight to the one she refused to let go until they were well away from the Derossas.

"Emon! Don't make it worse!" Lira yelled and rushed to Aeley's side. Just as quickly, Mayr pulled Lira back into him, shushing her as she struggled to get away.

"What? Like you?" Ryler laughed. "Or how about you, Aeley?" He tilted his head and swung his sword back and forth by his side, flicking his wrist as he played. "You should've just taken the deal. But no, you had to mess it all up and run off. Now we have to fight, and it could get messy."

"Fortunately for you, we can't afford to keep so many guards, nothing like the illustrious Dahe Stewards with all their eyes in all the wrong places." Emon sneered. "Otherwise, you'd have been caught and beaten down already. But that's just fine with me—we'll handle it right here, right now. I was bored with you anyway."

"This isn't helping anyone!" Lira shouted, still in Mayr's protective embrace. Fingers fisted, she held tight around his black bracers, some part of her understanding he had to hold her back, but the rest of her looked ready to claw his arms off just to get free. Whatever fight she may have thought she lacked, she had plenty of it right then, raring to go—and Aeley wanted to let it, just as much as she wanted to calm it down.

Emon stepped forward, his sword held level before him. "Would someone get her out of here?"

The two guards moved before anyone else could—a rush forward, light on their feet, their dark leather armour not much different than that of the Dahe guards. Gren bolted towards them, snarling as he caught their swords with both of his and forced the guards back.

"That leaves you for me and your pet for Ryler," Emon said, his gaze still on Aeley. He ran forward, swinging his sword high.

Aeley blocked Emon's strike as it came down. Not far off, in a flash of movement at the edge of her vision, a blur of colour and shadow shifted and veered as Mayr shoved Lira aside and intercepted Ryler's attack.

Too close. They were too close to the people she cared for, too close to dragging her future down further, and Goddesses be damned, they were too close to everything Allon had thrown into her life.

Done. Over. She was finished with Allon and his lackeys and everyone else who thought they could get away with whatever they wanted. However things had gone while her father was in control, however peaceful and kind and diplomatic in the name of avoiding confrontation, they were no longer, not when those graces were abused and violated and threatened. Her father's time was over; this was hers, and it came with the score of a blade, not just words.

If they wanted a fight, they would get it.

Aeley struck out at Emon, low and hard, with every intention to maim.

His sword stopped hers, his fall back and vile smirk deserving of her snarl. Emon's shoulders tensed, readied for his next attempt—only for him to shuffle forward and lunge again, quick, efficient, controlled... and completely taking advantage of her fighting style.

Aeley cursed as she narrowly avoided his strike and hit out at him, her fist grazing his head. Sparring: they had done that just the once, while Emon and Ryler were at the Dahe estate during the investigation into the Cigils. He had pressed for it, saying they were getting to know each other better to make marriage easier.

But now...

Yeah, she knew just what he had been getting to know better, and why.

Forget you, and you can damn well forget this, she seethed. Forcing him back with a sharper blow towards his neck, she sent him ducking and aimed for his knees, annoyed when he blocked the hit at the last moment. As Emon teetered with the effort, off balance just enough to use, Aeley pushed even harder, backing him away with each thrust and strike, his stumble through each move lessening as he regained control.

"This will not end well," she shouted. "Don't make this worse. Just stop now."

Emon wiped his mouth on the back of his hand and sneered. "No."

Aeley lunged again—an attack that was thwarted as their blades crossed, clanging loudly.

With the twist of his hand and a snatch to her right, Emon pulled her into him, his fist in her hair, yanking at her scalp.

Aeley cried out at the piercing burn, aimed to hit—

"Lira!" Mayr yelled.

Aeley peered over Emon's shoulder, only to be jerked back, his grip tighter on her hair, threatening to rip and tear her to pieces one fistful at a time.

Growling, she punched at him with her free hand, catching what she could but landing few useful blows. *Just one. I just need one—*

She got a hilt in the head for her troubles.

Smashed down by Emon, the breath knocked from her, Aeley groaned as her own sword skidded across the floor. A second blow to her side, a hard thrust, the back of her head one big ache—

She was face-first to the ground before she knew it, choking on air until he rolled her over.

For a single, terrifying moment, she was back in Oly Valley, convinced she was about to die.

No explosives. No scurrying lackeys. Not even a full contingent of guards. But cornered—she was there again, pinned down, held back, her life in someone else's hands, and it killed her faster than she could take a deep enough breath to save herself from falling apart.

"Not so smart, but nice try." Emon stood above her, the tip of his sword at her throat, teasing. The fine point scraped over her skin, the threat close enough to taste all the ways she would haunt his sorry excuse for a life if he killed her. "Thanks for making this so—"

Emon stopped. His mouth fell open, eyes caught in a perpetual blink. Tearing his gaze from hers, he turned to look behind him.

The knife wedged in his back glinted in the torchlight, a welcome flash of silver exactly where it needed to be.

Beyond him, Lira stood frozen, her grey eyes opened wide, both hands covering her mouth... and a gaze so full of the deepest, darkest horror, Aeley wished she could have taken everything back—the contract, the carriage ride, the awful thoughts about her. Everything gone just to see that cloud of dread wiped from Lira's face.

Gren rushed up behind Emon, his single hit to Emon's lower back sending Emon to the floor with a cry. "You're done. Time for you to join your friend," Gren muttered.

He slammed Emon down, one fist around Emon's neck. Emon's face rammed into the marble, accompanied by a sharp crack before Gren withdrew a pair of simple metal cuffs from one of the pockets of his long coat. Once the cuffs were secure around Emon's wrists, Gren dug his heel into Emon's neck, adding a twist that left Emon squirming and crying foul.

"You're so done, Lira!" Ryler yelled. Pinned to the ground by Mayr, he lay on his stomach, his cheek squished against the floor. He struggled to free his hands from Mayr's grip, but cried out as Mayr kneeled on the small of his back and pressed down, digging his knee into Ryler's spine. "You messed up *everything*! We were doing fine until you came along. Couldn't keep to yourself, could you?"

"I didn't do anything!" Lira protested.

"You got in the way!" Ryler writhed under Mayr's hold, twitching beneath the hand at his neck. "Now you've thrown a knife in his back. I told Emon we should've gotten rid of you first. *Told him* you'd be better off dead." He roared as Mayr squeezed his throat. "Piss off, and take that bitch with you," Ryler snarled, only to have his own face slammed into the floor, hard enough to bruise his forehead for days.

"What?" Lira's face paled worse than it already had. "Dead... as in kill me..." She flicked a glance at Aeley, then Emon and Ryler. "But I didn't know. I didn't do anything. I—"

"Dammit, Lira, that was the entire bloody point." Emon grunted as Gren sat on his legs. "You weren't su—"

Shouted curses echoed off the walls as Gren yanked the knife from Emon's back and wiped it on Emon's long coat, none of it gentle.

"You weren't supposed to get involved," Emon spat out after he caught his breath, blood dripping from his nose. "You, so blissfully damned ignorant, living in your own little world, playing like the traitor you are. Then Allon said he saw you with Aeley... said something was going on. When we saw you at the meeting... how friendly you were... we couldn't let you get her. We were coming for you next."

"Not with us," Ryler snarled, "not needed by us. Out the damned door you go, you filthy little whore from—"

His face smashed into the floor again, this time followed by a whimper and a turn of head into the opposite direction.

Wait.

No.

Aeley scrambled to stand, every urge to crush Emon by stomping on him raging to be let loose.

They had lied. Again.

And she fell for it. Again.

Enough to take it out on Lira. Aeley swallowed back the bile creeping its way up. *Enough to blame her when she had nothing to do with it.*

There was no denying the confusion on Lira's face—the genuine struggle to understand what was happening. The realization she had been dragged into something she never saw coming, the truth raw and cruel and breaking her heart as tears glistened in her eyes.

When she looked at Aeley, all of her turmoil and doubt seemed to search for help before she drowned in it.

Aeley froze, unable to do much more than mouth, "I'm sorry," and pray Lira forgave her. Lira deserved better than suspicions and a silent apology, and she certainly needed someone who knew better than to doubt her motives, but if Aeley told the truth…

She'll hate me for it—that I believed for even a moment she had anything to do with this. Then whatever we have, it'll be over for good. Just… over.

Even so, she deserved the truth, especially after being trapped in the lies as much as the rest of them. After being used as much as she hated to be. If Aeley laid it all out and begged her to stay, would she be forgiving?

That was a question her nerve would have to chew on for a while longer. Right then, another matter nudged Aeley's concerns: the shock on Lira's face was going nowhere, and unless Aeley's eyes were playing games, Lira was trembling, arms wrapped around herself as she stared at the floor.

Dammit. They needed to get Lira out of there, and soon.

"Now what?" Gren's voice broke through her thoughts.

Aeley glanced around, noticing for the first time that the two guards Gren had fought lay on the ground, unconscious or dead. Should she have expected less?

She cleared her throat. "We lock them up and escort them to Council. They're the warden's problem now."

And once again, I'm left to clean up the mess.

"All right. Time to go," Gren said. He hauled Emon from the floor and half-dragged, half-walked him through the hall. Mayr followed, pushing Ryler ahead. They disappeared around the corner at the furthest end.

Once the grunts and snide comments faded into the distance, Aeley dared to step closer to

Lira. "So… you threw the knife?" she asked, then grimaced. How was *that* the only thing she could come up with?

Lira smiled sadly, though the struggle to get that far played out on her face more than she probably realized, her gaze still downcast. "Looks like that lesson was better than I thought," she said, "even if I wasn't the most attentive student." Her glance flickered away, further from Aeley. "I'd say I'm sorry, but I don't make it a habit to apologize on their behalf."

Aeley shifted her feet, wanting to be even closer, but giving Lira space. "No, don't. They have to answer to it, not you. But thank you, for saving my life. Without you…" She took a deep breath and let it out, but still, a familiar feeling took hold, one that drove her words faster than her thoughts. The truth was going to spill again, whether she willed it on or not. She was going to throw her heart down for the breaking and— "There, before they showed up, I… wasn't in my right mind. I wasn't—"

"Very nice?" Lira muttered.

"If you want to call it that. It shouldn't have happened, and I'm sorry." Aeley leaned towards Lira, trying to catch Lira's gaze. When Lira lifted her glance, her confusion rivaled Aeley's fears.

The longer she stared, the more Aeley's resolve slipped. She moved closer to Lira, barely a foot between them as her words rushed out. "Everything in my head was messed up. I can't stand being trapped, and then there they were, threatening everybody and trying to force me into an awful marriage, and saying things—"

"It's fine." Lira shrugged one shoulder. "You have your reasons. Just..." She shivered and looked behind her, once more avoiding Aeley's gaze. "Can we leave? I really need... out. We can talk later, but I just... I need out. Away. From here. Permanently."

Before Aeley could reply, Lira started down the hall, leaving Aeley to stare after her. As the distance between them grew, Lira untied her shawl from around her waist and drew it tight around her shoulders, almost hiding in it.

Just how long would it take before Lira walking out became a done deal in whatever relationship they had left?

Aeley sighed and followed, her steps quiet on the marble compared to the click of Lira's boots that only quickened as they made their way through the estate. Her timing was wrong. Even if her intentions were good, apologizing right then... There was no taking back what Lira had done, throwing the knife into Emon's back, and there was no undoing what Ryler and Emon had said. If anyone understood that much, it was Aeley.

Space. She needed to give Lira the space to deal, to mourn whatever she had lost, even if it was just her sense of clarity among the chaos.

Then she needed to apologize—truly apologize—because losing Lira was never going to be a price Aeley was willing to pay.

Chapter Nineteen

They wanted her dead.

She could have killed Emon.

Aeley had been ready to forget she existed.

And her parents…

Lira snorted, sinking further into the black cushions of the carriage. Her parents had disappeared for the entire thing. *How perfectly convenient.* Though the part that hurt the worst?

They never would have missed her had Ryler and Emon succeeded in getting rid of her.

Pulling the softness of her mauve knit shawl tighter around her shoulders, Lira curled deeper into the corner, her fight having long run off. It was languishing somewhere back there on the road, unable to take shelter in what had been her childhood home but not having anywhere else to go. Alone in the darkness of the carriage, hiding behind the dull blue curtains that let in the tiniest sliver of dim light, her thoughts ran rampant, stumbling, fumbling, rolling over each other in a bid to just *run*. The irony being the carriage was one that belonged to her parents, taken from the Derossa estate along with a single wagon to cart

Emon and Ryler to Vasserey Call, all to be presented to Councilmen Severn and Cota in an impromptu prisoner transfer. She had ridden to Deros Glengale with Mayr and Gren, the three of them on separate horses that were now pulling the carriage and wagon.

The group of guards accompanying them was a new addition, too: not just Dahe guards that had arrived at her parents' estate shortly after Lira, Mayr, and Gren had gotten there, but also cuffed Derossa guards with Bareda looking grim, his hands and feet as locked down as her brothers'.

According to Bareda, kidnapping Aeley had not been on his duty schedule, nor had Emon and Ryler run the plan by him. Had they tried, he would have intervened—or so he claimed, if his protests could be trusted. Though how they had kept Aeley in the cells without Bareda knowing, without him bothering to check on why *any* guards were down in the cells to begin with, or even catching on to the possibility that *something* was amiss... that was still in question, and no amount of sputtered responses or silence helped Bareda's case. *"My guards, my responsibility"*— how many times had she heard him say that over the years?

Either way, his career as Head of the Derossa Guard was effectively in jeopardy, if not completely over. His guards were in no better shape, the lot of them under suspicion with likely only a few being legitimate culprits, though all of them would suffer the consequences to various degrees.

Some part of her wanted to care, but it kept slamming into the part of her that was too numb to care about much of anything.

Riding in the carriage alone had been at her request, though Aeley's voice filtered down into the darkness from where she sat with Mayr on the driver's box. They spoke quietly, their words fading in and out, most of them drowned out by the squeaks of the wheels and the creaks of the jostling carriage. From somewhere in the distance came Gren's gruff voice—likely telling her brothers where to shove their foolishness—but those words were lost, too, never meant for her ears.

None of it made her feel better, not a bit of comfort or relief settling down around her. She was alone in her sinking feeling, left to tread a path she had no means to walk. Everyone had their place, even if it was Emon finally rotting in a prison cell, and it left her turning in an agonizing circle, wondering where she fit.

The patter of rain on the roof seemed to agree, getting heavier as Aeley cursed and jeered at Mayr, who returned the mockery with sarcasm and laughter.

Yes, *that* was how she felt, the entire situation playing out like a scene from one of the dramatic fictions she wished she could devour from one day to the next and onwards still. It was rainy and muddy and messy, dripping with more disdain than even she could capture with words. Suddenly her little part of the world was more chaotic than it ever used to be, and she had no idea what to do with it. The answers were so far out of reach, and she had no clue when her parents were supposed to be back. Even worse, she had no answers as to where she was even going to *live* anymore, and that was terrifying. She certainly was not about to return home, not ever, but she needed somewhere to go. Somewhere safe.

Their family was ruined and she wanted out. She *had* to get out. There was no choice now, just the starkest reality.

It could have been bearable in the barest sense of the word had everything not gone down all at the same time, tied together by that damned marriage contract. Emon and Ryler had violated the contract in one of the worst possible ways. Now, Aeley would rip it up, throw it out, and dismiss Lira. They had broken the law—and Aeley would want to put as much space between her and them as she possibly could, including pushing Lira away. After all, Aeley's own brother was in prison, and she was tired of cleaning up his messes. With Emon and Ryler headed for the same fate, and maybe even Lira's parents if any criminal charges could be laid there, it was just another mess to be cleaned up. Another scandal.

That was too many scandals in such a short time, particularly for a fledgling Tract Steward, and one with so little political clout. They were also deeply troubling crimes against the republic, enough to warrant life sentences for anyone involved. The more Aeley could distance herself from those responsible, the better. The circumstances may have gained her some points with certain families, but no one would bury the news now or permanently. The gossip would follow her like a proverbial stench, no matter whose side it was on.

Aeley had never wanted the contract anyway. Now she had countless reasons to set it on fire and walk away, even if she and Lira had made a connection. At least Lira believed they had. Maybe it was as conditional as everything else was.

Sighing, Lira pushed one of the thick blue curtains open just a little, enough to watch the heavy rain pound the road, hooves and wheels splashing through the puddles, trying not to get stuck in the red mud. Her brothers had negotiated the contract with her father and Korre, and with that came a certain doubt about her father's own innocence. Just how much had he known? Approved of?

By the Four, that damned family feud. She had always known about it, having grown up hearing the stories about how awful the Dahes had been to Asha and Etalynn's rightful authority, every new telling a shallow regurgitation of the same sob-seeking tale.

She had never cared for any of it. Which family controlled what had never been her concern—just that they do right by the people and show compassion while taking care of business. But with everything she knew about her parents and her brothers...

No, they had never been the right ones to handle the Tract Steward position, even if her grandfather had served the position honourably. Honour was never a given; it was a choice, and her parents had forgone that choice, then taught the same to their children. Nurtured it. Given it every opportunity to get this far, though she did not doubt they would claim shock and surprise, crying "How could this happen?" before spinning it into a new tale of how terribly hard done-by they were. She had seen it before, how it was always someone else's fault and not theirs. It was never theirs, even if they orchestrated every last detail and brought the consequences upon themselves every moment of every day.

But Korre had chosen honour, at least in most things. Like her grandfather, he had seen the true point of being Tract Steward and understood the responsibility it demanded. No doubt it was why he had been elected, allowing for a smoother transition from one Tract Steward to another without losing the benefits of someone who put their people and duty first, not their individual desires.

Aeley had all the same potential to do as well as they had. She just needed time to get her footing, and Lira... she wanted to be the one to help Aeley find that footing. She would have given anything to be that person, even now when she had nothing much *to* give.

By the ever-loving Four, her heart still clung to the fear from earlier—how the battered and beaten guards had stumbled into the estate, yelling for Pellon, desperate to send help after Aeley. How hearing *"she's gone"* sent Lira into panic, unable to breathe.

She had worried greatly for Aeley then, and that worry only deepened as they had looked for her. The thought of losing her... it killed a part of Lira in a way she never wanted to surrender, no matter how much it hurt, because losing who she loved drove a thousand knives through her. She had so little, and had lost so much by making choices she thought were right, so to lose Aeley and what she brought into Lira's life...

Not much could be done now that Emon and Ryler had messed it all up and Lira had missed every sign, never going to the very ends of assumption when it came to how far they would go to get what they wanted.

However bad people had thought Lira was before, they were going to truly abhor her now. How could she not have seen it coming? How could she not have stopped it? Rumours would spread about how Lira was like her brothers, or perhaps even worse, given how she worked for Aeley; how they had been seen together privately. The gossips and the Grand Families alike would accuse her of knowing and doing nothing, or of being so ignorant she was unfit to be anywhere in their ranks. No matter the angle, no matter the accusations, they would be right in some way, to some degree, and she was already blaming herself for her part in it, finally seeing just how naïve she was.

Whatever the nonsense, people would spew it behind her back as usual, their spite so much worse than what they said to her face. And if by some grace of the Goddesses she were able to carry on with Aeley... it would be a disaster for Aeley, one Lira did not want to be the reason for. Aeley had enough to deal with. She had a right to be left alone, not dragged around.

If anything, Lira was tired of being the spectacle. She would be lucky if she got to keep her job.

Curled into the corner, shivering from a chill no warmth could soothe, Lira watched the rain, the fields and trees a blur in the dull grey light of dawn. She wanted to give Aeley the benefit of the doubt. Lira's hurt was mostly a storm of fear and terror and feelings she had no words for, with reason trying to pull itself together in there somewhere. Her own family wanted her dead—

how could she even begin to reason with that? It was the ultimate betrayal, the greatest punishment for being herself. She had never asked for anything, save to be left alone. There was no running away now, just the firm slam of every door in her face, denying her safety. She had a bit of money to her name, thanks to Vant, enough to find shelter for a few weeks.

Still, she had nowhere to go if Aeley decided Lira was guilty of something, whether it was true or not. She would want out of the contract, that much was given, but would she keep Lira as scribe or cast her away? Yes, Lira could ask Vant for help and possibly find more work as a scribe—perhaps appeal to Priestess Kee and the Temple of the Four, especially if no one else was willing to hire a sibling of those who had kidnapped the Tract Steward. The Temple libraries were full of tomes that would need transcribing to replace faded copies, and they added new books on a frequent basis, or so she had been told by the priests who had kindly invited her to read those tomes—a tempting offer considering she had exhausted her own book collection and had few coins to spare to purchase more. Except none of that was guaranteed, and it fixed nothing.

She wanted to stay. She wanted to be the Steward's Hand, trusted with Aeley's words and intentions. She wanted to be Aeley's in every way, not just through ideas on parchment.

Though what she wanted and what she would get were two vastly different things. In the end, she would have to reinvent herself... if she only had any idea of how to do that. It sounded so easy in the stories she had read, everything boiled down to what could fit on the pages without losing the audience.

But tangled in the longer threads of reality, she stood to lose herself. For all of the years spent defending who she was, she would have to start all over again. There was no easy way out, no devious plot twist to reverse her fortunes. There was her and a will to survive. A hope that maybe life was there for the taking should she make the right decisions.

If only Aeley were one of those right decisions. Lira wanted to hide in her surety, just for a short while, just until the world flipped right-side up again and she could meet it head-on. There was a comfort there, and an ease that came with the family Korre and Aeley had pulled together over the years. With everything else slipping away, Lira needed something to hold onto, and with her family falling further from her life, she wished someone would grab onto her and just hold on, even if by the flimsiest cuff. She could do flimsy: it left all the opportunity to grow into something of strength. She just needed someone to care enough to try. She needed to know someone saw her well enough to want it — to want *her*.

At a time when she had never felt more alone, she just needed someone to help her through the downfall.

Chapter Twenty

It was pouring, she was soggy, and by the blessed annoying Four, she had the raging urge just to hack everything to pieces with a hatchet.

No, burn it. Nothing wrong with a good burning.

Aeley huffed and eyed the worn white doorframe as she hustled up the front stairs and into the Dahe estate, her chills and sore rear grateful to be home with Lira right behind her. *All right, so maybe not everything has to go. Just everything Emon and Ryler touched.*

She shuddered, her feet sliding along the wet floor and taking her straight into the dry red and yellow-striped blanket Haydin tossed around her shoulders. Emon and Ryler were still outside, shackled down in the wagon parked on the avenue outside the gates. There was no way she was letting them get closer to the house, and Mayr had agreed, barking at them to shut their mouths when they complained.

Gren had merely grinned at the exchange, grey eyes gleaming as he settled back on the driver's box and drew up the collar of his dark brown leather long coat, ready for the rest of the journey. He enjoyed the temporary role of jailer, and she was happy to let him to it. They would need to talk afterwards about having him around more often. She suddenly had an entire list of tasks perfect for a mercenary—mostly all the ways in which he could make Emon and Ryler's lives more difficult while they sat in prison. She had to pay Allon back *somehow*. Even from the distance of a life sentence, he wreaked havoc.

Yeah, well, two can play that game.

"Come on, let's get you warm," Haydin murmured. He threw a second blanket around her and led her further into the foyer, towards the staircase, before he covered Lira with her own set of warm blankets.

Around them, guards hurried up and down the steps to Mayr's shouted orders, some falling in line behind him by the entrance to the dining room, while others rushed towards the Guard House at the west side of the main house. A hand's count of household staff joined the confusion, too, hovering off to the right side of the foyer with blankets and towels, waiting for Haydin's orders as he fussed over Lira.

"Yeah, that. What Haydin said," Mayr agreed, snapping his fingers at one guard as they passed. Just as the guard stopped and turned back, Mayr caught a white towel thrown at him over the banister of the main staircase by Pellon, who jogged down the rest of the steps, a black long coat in hand.

"You two stay here. Get comfortable," Mayr said, drying his face, neck, and arms before flicking the towel over his shoulder and letting it rest there. "Pellon, you stay put and keep a contingency on Ae and Lira. Pull whatever rank you need to, but I want Stick and Stuck on them. I'm taking another ten for the road, rotating out four. Lisreft's mine; Gates, too. And for my own bloody sake, keep Aeley from anyone we don't like. If we'd kick their ass in a heartbeat, she doesn't go near them."

The tight-lipped glare he cast her way said everything between the words, his worry still outdoing the anger. From beside him, Pellon looked just as serious, both of them staring at her as though they expected a fight.

Aeley only nodded, her fight packed away. She was too tired to bicker with anyone else. Not to mention that she'd had it coming, and they would never let her hear the end of it.

Besides... She peered at Lira over her shoulder, frowning at her sombre quiet, one that had allowed Lira to accept the layers of blue and black blankets from Haydin but kept Lira's heavy gaze from meeting Aeley's. *I messed up. I need to fix this.*

"I'm not going anywhere," Aeley said, looking at Mayr again. "Just don't let them go running off. I'd really love to see Severn give them a piece of her mind."

Mayr grinned, a dark glee passing through his gaze. "Oh, yeah, that's definitely going to happen.

Besides," he said, twisting the towel around the long, matted tail of his wet hair, "she *loves* when they just drop into her custody, all the work done. Saves time so she can cut straight to the roasting." He tossed the soaking towel at Pellon, then snorted at Pellon's catch and roll of eye before Mayr braided his hair in a tight plait. "Better with her than here, disgracing our cells. I really don't feel like wasting resources on them, and certainly not a damn bit of Cook's fine work." Mayr tied off the braid and glanced around him, muttering as he surveyed the dozen guards gathered. He sent six out to the wagon.

"Right." Mayr turned back to Aeley and Pellon. "Send Lisreft, Gates, Lilia, and Keyer out to me. Everyone else stays. We're going directly to High Council Hall, getting the bastards comfortable wherever Severn wants them, then coming back. No dallying." Lips pursed, Mayr bounced a glance between Aeley and Lira. "That applies to all assembled parties."

Before Aeley could respond, Mayr crossed the foyer and pulled her back towards the dining room, almost into the corner, his hand firm on her elbow. "Look," he said quietly, turning their backs to everyone else, "I don't know what you think Lira's done—"

"Mayr—"

"—but she didn't have anything to do with this. She was just as worried—"

"*Mayr*. I know." Aeley gripped his shoulder, digging her thumb into his arm to get him to stop talking. "I made a mistake, and I'm not about to do it again." She peered over her shoulder. "You get going. I've got a few hundred apologies to make."

Mayr frowned, glancing back. "Just make sure to take care of her while you do. She's not taking this well." He sighed and raked a hand over his hair. "Then again, it's like Allon and you all over again. The survivors get to keep the memories and the friends they stir up. So make sure she doesn't hold on to them too tight. Let her hold on to you tighter. Rouse her spirit a little and get her settled down. Don't force peace, just... encourage it, yeah?"

Aeley nodded, a sigh slipping out that matched his. "If she'll let me."

"She might." Mayr tucked stray strands of her hair behind her ear and gave a small smile. "If you grovel well enough—and I mean *grovel*. And if she starts looking like she'd rather throw a book at you than writing one with your name on it, go for the begging and pleading and bleeding knees. And get Pellon to witness it so he can tell me later, because I'd really, *really* die to see it... mostly in laughter, but, hey—"

Aeley punched his shoulder. "Shut up and get going, would you?"

"Yeah, I know," Mayr said, grinning like he was fifteen all over again and purposely getting her into trouble. "Just *gro-vel*, because anything less—"

"*Mayr!*"

He threw up his hands, laughing as he turned away. Once he took the black long coat from Pellon and slipped it on, Mayr hurried out the door, another two guards falling in step behind him.

As the door closed, Aeley took a deep, painful breath and headed back through the foyer, clasping Pellon's arm as she stopped by him. "Give us some time, all right?" She stole another look at Lira, how her head remained tilted downwards, grey gaze focused on the floor, if anything at all, not really blinking, just... somewhere else, pale fists holding blankets around her. "Two-guard team, twenty paces back," Aeley murmured, stepping closer to Pellon, "and another two after that, ten back, with two at the end of the corridor in front. Not enough to overhear everything, just keep a close eye. Same thing as before, after Allon. I'll aim to sequester, so it'll be two in close proximity; four at the ends. Either way..."

Pellon rubbed her shoulder. "Done," he said, his voice as soft as his touch. "Do what you need to do. I'll haunt the halls for a bit, get everyone in place. You need me, scream all the absurdities in the world and I'll knock some heads around."

"Thanks, Pell." Aeley waited for Pellon to issue orders to the few guards in the foyer and up the stairs before she fought for another deep breath. If only everything that rattled inside would calm down. If only she could just *breathe*, more in the principle of the concept than anything. The air came in and went out, but her chest—it hurt, once more surrendering to that awful ache that had become all too familiar since the fight in Oly Valley. Just when she thought she was getting over whatever plagued her from that mess, she was right back to it. She had hoped the nightmares could ease, but she was stacking them up again, adding fresh irritation to old wounds that had yet to heal.

But now she had someone else to think about, someone who had been pulled into that dark pit with her, and she seethed at the injustice of it all. The problems were hers. The bad choices were *hers*. Lira had nothing to do with it, she knew that, and for Aeley to even have entertained that notion was more than an insult—it was a nasty stain on a future she still wanted badly and could have very well killed.

Just another to add to the body count. If it's not dead-dead, then it's just plain old dead, and that's almost worse. No ceremony, no grand gesture— nothing to mark the disaster I've made. Even with silence I'm a bloody menace.

After a tap at her arm, Pellon headed down the corridor towards her study, two guards behind him as others took their places in the hallways, their gazes on Aeley before drifting elsewhere. The foyer freed up as more bodies left for their posts, Haydin's own staff quietly moving away. Only Lira stayed still, the growing distance between them a crumbling chasm filled with awkward intentions and things that wanted to be said—needed to be said. Yet the words played chase-and-catch from thought to thought, teasing until they laughed and ran off again.

Aeley shrugged off her blankets and handed the dampest one to Haydin, her smile strained as she received a nod in a return. With a glance at the three staff that remained, Haydin wandered around the staircase and down the hall past the kitchen, the wet blanket draped over his arm, no doubt on the way to the laundry to dry. His staff followed, their gazes flicked downwards.

Rumours would flutter about the house before long, but Aeley wanted to be well in hiding before that happened, mostly to avoid the headache of trying to correct everyone when all she really wanted was to pass out and not get up for two days. Her head was splitting, almost in competition with her chest to see which one of them could do her in first.

Maybe she should allow Lira to do the honours. Of everyone involved, Lira had the most right to it.

Stepping close to Lira, finally able to take an easier breath without feeling crowded, Aeley held out her hand. "Can we talk?"

Lira eyed the offering, her grey gaze cloudy as she flicked a look up to Aeley, then back down to her hand. Time dragged on like it had drunkenly stumbled around for relief and found every locked door along the way, but eventually Lira slipped her hand into Aeley's, her fingers cool to the touch. Even under two layers of thick blanket she shivered.

Aeley draped her own blanket around Lira's shoulders, ensuring Lira had a firm hold on it before letting go. On the withdrawal, she glided the back of her hand down Lira's cheek, partly wanting to test the clamminess of Lira's damp skin, but mostly hoping it gave some sort of reassurance. She had pulled Lira into the mess; now she needed to get her out of it.

Turning Lira around, Aeley tucked Lira's hand into the crook of her arm and led them from the foyer, down the stretch of corridor towards her study, her steps steady but measured.

"I'm sorry," Aeley said softly. "None of that back there… It wasn't fair. It wasn't right. You shouldn't have been dragged into this. *No one* should've dragged you into this. Not me, not them. None of us."

Lira shrugged. "I'm used to it, honestly."

"So? That doesn't make it right."

"No, but it's not about what's right, is it? Just what has to be done."

Aeley clenched her jaws. Lira's family had some answering to do, and not just Emon and

Ryler. There was an entire lifetime to pay for, and that included whatever they had done to Lira. But that would be just the start of it. There were entire beds of searing coal to rake their words over where the law was concerned. She would have to flip a coin with Severn and Cota to see who got to interrogate them first.

"You're not a *'what has to be done,'*" Aeley said through gritted teeth. "And it *should* be about what's right. I lost sight of that—I did—but I'm willing to admit it and fix it if I can. Your brothers..." She let out a restrained breath, heavy with irritation. "There's nothing I can say to fix that, and I don't know how to make that up to you. They'll have to live with their asinine decisions. They never should've listened to Allon, and I shouldn't have, either. Ever. Allon's self-serving first and self-important second. You said it yourself before his trial: he's chaos. That's the long and short of it."

Aeley sighed, lighter this time, mostly disappointed with herself as she led them around the corner nearest the closed door of her study. "I don't know if I'm all that much in the way of order, especially with how I was earlier, but I'd like to think maybe there's hope. If there can be." She glanced at Lira, leaving unspoken questions hanging in the air with a hint of *help me* attached to them.

When Lira said nothing, her focus on the hall ahead, her face giving away nothing, Aeley drew them to a stop in the middle of the hallway, her study just a foot away. "I'm sorry," she offered again. Taking a chance, she brushed her fingers over the strands of dark hair near Lira's throat, mostly dry, loose curls that clung to the edges of the blankets bunched around Lira's neck. "I was a damned fool—I listened to your brothers, then took it out on you, and I really wish I could take that back. I'd take all of today back if I could—well, except maybe the whole arresting them bit. That's one of the better parts. You could write stories about it, something we can put up on every sign post in Gailarin. Just some light reading."

Lira snorted, accompanied by the hint of a smile. At least, Aeley hoped it was a smile. A sneer would have been well-deserved if not completely heartbreaking.

"I'm not always smart, I'll admit it," Aeley said softly, "and I'm a fool for you. You have no idea just how far gone for you I am. I'm just so done, absolutely gone." Still toying with Lira's curls, the backs of Aeley's fingers caressed Lira's throat, taking in the heat. Lira had yet to move away—a good sign, if Aeley was lucky. "I couldn't stop thinking about you while I was locked up, and you… you inspired my escape. I was stuck, but then I got thinking about you and everything made sense after that. *You* always make sense, even if I don't always get it at first. It was you who got me out of there. Even if you hate me for whatever awful choices I made after that, just know that much. And if you want to leave…"

The words got stuck in her throat then, despite how hard she tried to say them.

The fact that Lira said nothing was almost as terrifying, though she stayed close to Aeley, her expression revealing little of what she felt.

That's all right. I can work with that. Maybe even earn my way into better graces?

With Lira's hand in hers, Aeley headed for the study—only to be pulled back by Lira, who curled her arm around Aeley's and drew them back into a stroll up the remainder of the corridor, their pace no faster than it was before. Two guards stayed ahead, tracking their movements from the furthest end of the hallway, while four guards followed them, keeping a steady distance. As Aeley peered over her shoulder, she caught sight of Stick's white-blond hair. No doubt Stuck was right beside him, silence in their wake.

"How are you feeling?" Aeley murmured, guiding Lira's hand into the crook of her arm, wanting to keep as much of Lira as warm as possible. The slight tremble was still there in her hands, though her cheeks had more colour to them. Her head was up higher, too, and still tilted, almost in contemplation. "If you want to talk about it, I don't mind. If you don't, that's all right, too. Just—"

"Betrayed," Lira muttered, moving closer, brushing hip to hip with Aeley. "Given up. I don't know what else I'm supposed to feel beyond that."

Aeley's heart sank, imagining one of her fists aimed at her own head. She could be awful when she was upset, and now Lira took betrayal away from that mistake, holding onto it and maybe not wanting to let go—

"What do you do when your family decides they want you dead?" Lira asked softly, her grip tightening around Aeley's arm, getting closer still. "When you're such a burden they'd rather you be a corpse than give you the means to be on your own, disowned and all the freer for it? Why couldn't they just let me go off on my own?"

"I don't know." Aeley sighed, confusion seeping in. Had they moved on that quickly? "Trying to control what they still could, I suppose? Reasserting what power they've managed to hold onto all this time? Either that or Allon got that idea into their head, too, considering what he put me through." She smiled sadly. "You saw how he was at the prison—it really chafes him I'm not dead. Maybe he figured they'd have better luck, especially if it hurt me at the same time. He would've loved that."

Lira nodded, her gaze lost again to whatever was in her head. "I could've killed him—Emon." She shrugged one shoulder, the blankets slipping. "I reacted, didn't really think. Usually I would've thought that kind of thing through, maybe stopped myself, but you were—and he was—and

I couldn't—" Lira sighed heavily, her shoulders dropping. "That wasn't me, and yet... it was. It wasn't about revenge. Not even about protecting myself. Just... reaching out and stopping him, that's all I wanted. Just to stop him for once. *Really* stop him." She shrugged again, both shoulders this time, her other hand keeping the blankets pulled close. "My words never meant anything to him. To any of them. I've defended myself all this time, lashing out however I could with whatever I could say, but then with him there, ready to kill you... words weren't enough. Then again... I was already dead as far as they were concerned, or close to, so I suppose there really wasn't much else to it."

"Hey." Aeley stopped, keeping Lira close as she turned to face her. "There was a great deal to it. Don't think you have to brush this off like it's nothing. It's a very big something, and I'm grateful for it, even if I don't deserve it." She kissed the back of Lira's hand and held on. "You, on the other hand, deserve a great deal better," she said quietly, caressing Lira's knuckles.

Now *that* was a smile on Lira's lips, a soft touch that faded slowly, lost to how Aeley drew them towards the conservatory at the end of the hall, with its red doors and opaque white glass...

A conservatory they bypassed completely, the staircase further down the hall taking Lira's interest instead. It was almost a shame: Aeley had been looking forward to wandering the autumn garden with her, the burnt oranges, fiery reds, and bright yellows of the various leaves and dark flowers a gentle whisper of beauty in silence.

She followed Lira without complaint, however, heading up the stairs to the first level of bedrooms and linen closets, content to carry on their stroll. Walking was good, particularly since the pressure in her chest had subsided, her breaths coming easily.

Even Lira had more spirit in her step and the strength to raise her eyes level to Aeley's, her lost look taken over by a growing clarity. From cloudy, sad grey to the pensive grey of a gathering storm, Lira's glance revealed nothing else, the secrets drawing Aeley along just as much as her feet. Would Lira stay if she asked, not just as scribe but something much more personal? Or had Aeley been tried and tested, only to fail at the first opportunity to show loyalty? Given what Lira had been through, loyalty meant more than pledging it and expecting that to do: it had to be shown, followed through, from first act to the last.

Fighting. Aeley was good at that, mostly. And if fighting for Lira was the way to get her back, then fight she would. They had started something she wanted to keep, and no brother or father or contract had anything to do with it. Lira had come with Vant and stayed by her own merits. Her virtues were her own, her choices and successes from her own hard work, and Aeley intended to keep that intact, no matter what fight the Derossas put up. If Lira wanted out, Aeley would keep the door wide open, and if Lira wanted to carry on with that something they had—at least what Aeley *thought* they had—then every door into Aeley's life was open... if Lira wanted them to be. If she wanted that life and whatever came with it.

"So... what will you do now?" Aeley cleared her throat and clenched her arm tighter around Lira's, keeping her as close as she could while they continued through the hallways. Household staff bustled past them with linens and buckets, their glances caching Aeley's briefly before flicking away. The rumours about her near-demise had started, she could feel it. It felt like insects crawling over her skin—more like fluttering, really, with nausea-inducing touches that annoyed her to no end. At the rate things were going, the history books would remember her as Steward of the Damn Bloody Pests.

Lira was silent, her footsteps faltering. "I don't know," she muttered eventually, regaining her footing as they turned another corner, headed in the direction of the main staircase that would take them down to the front foyer. "I'm afraid my current employer may not have need of a scribe with scandals to her name. I may have some free time to fill."

And there went Aeley's heart, the releases snapping as it threatened to drop straight into her stomach without a lick of apology.

"I don't know," Aeley started, forcing her feet to keep moving, "but that's not what I heard. Rumour says that employer of yours isn't interested in another scribe. Actually, she's likely to gut anyone who thinks her current scribe is anything less than what she wants. Something about speaking her mind, saving the Steward's life—the usual what's-a-scribe-to-do list of things."

"That's... quite a rumour." Lira's words were almost too soft to hear, but there was a catch in her breath, a tight grip at Aeley's arm.

"Sure, if you like those types of things."

"You don't?"

"Rumours? Not so much. I'm more into knowing the truth. Rumours just get me into trouble."

"And this trouble... a terrible affliction, I take it?"

"The *worst*. It follows me. I really need someone to keep me out of it because I can't be left to my own devices. Supervision needed, as Mayr would say."

Lira pushed into one room, the door opening with ease. "You sound like my employer. She can't stay out of trouble, either." She shrugged the blankets off and laid them over the brown wood chest at the foot of the bed.

Aeley's bed.

In her room.

Aeley slipped inside and closed the door behind her as Stick and Stuck took up their posts in the hallway.

"But trouble comes with the position, or so it seems," Lira continued, drawing her hair over her shoulder, her back to Aeley. "I hear it gets lonely. Duty is a difficult calling, always demanding more, always demanding a choice." She peered over her shoulder. "What's a scribe to do but help express those choices?"

Lira gestured behind her, fingers waving downwards.

It took Aeley several moments to realize Lira was pointing at the laces of her gown, long enough to have Lira glancing over her shoulder again.

Right... Aeley stepped up behind Lira and started on the dark blue laces. The faint pink gown had fared better than Aeley's clothes, its smooth, heavier fabric dry to the touch with only the skirt hem dirtied from red mud that had long since dried. The laces, however, gave Aeley every reason to want to cut them into tiny bits with her knife and let the gown fall as it would. They were tight. And annoying. And in the damned way.

"I suppose we're equally matched," Lira said softly, "because trouble follows me, too, and it's been a lonely calling. Maybe I need a Steward to help me figure it out, to manage it, because I don't think I can do it alone anymore."

Aeley almost choked, jerking on the laces. With a gentler tug, she pulled Lira against her, unable to resist brushing a light kiss to Lira's throat. "You do realize we're in my room, right?" Her lips lingered as she breathed Lira in, that sweet orchard scent wreaking havoc on her senses. *Too much too fast...* She wanted to drown in that scent, fall into Lira's arms and stay there, everything else forgotten. No duty, no rules, no interference. Just them, with the rest of the world kept firmly on the other side of the doors and windows and mindset.

Lira peered back, her smirk outdone by the gleam in her eyes. "You do realize we're busy, right? That getting naked takes a bit of work?"

Aeley nipped at Lira's ear and worked her way downwards, humming in agreement as Lira reached back with a contented sigh, her arm curling around Aeley's neck. "You sure about this?" Both hands slipped around Lira's waist, Aeley kept her touch light for fear of holding on too hard, the play of her breaths along Lira's neck just as careful. "You wouldn't rather just take a rest? It's been a rough day and it's not even noon yet."

The turn in her arms was so quick, Aeley stepped back to keep balanced.

Lira's kiss was even quicker still. Hard. Seeking. Not at all shy or uncertain about what she cried out for as her lips searched for relief and took Aeley with them.

Aeley sank into the touch, fingertips gliding up Lira's neck before settling just beneath her cheeks, keeping them both still — a delicate hold for difficult times, courting patience to counter the hurt. They both needed healing, with Lira having stepped too far onto Aeley's side of danger without a shield to deflect what came.

Time dares us all, but forever does not yield; as the heart of Kattal beats, so do we.

She intended to live that motto, especially now, where the fight had nothing to do with a battlefield and everything to do with shoving the world away and holding onto each other, grasping for clarity as they defended what kept them coming so close and pushed against being so far.

"Yes, I'm sure," Lira said as she drew back, only to lean her forehead against Aeley's lips. "I need the distraction. Reminders of the good things." A trail of kisses brushed along Aeley's jaw, the soft warmth of Lira's cheek pressed to Aeley's igniting better memories. "Sleep will come, but for now..."

Another kiss teased her lips, quieter as Lira undid Aeley's belt and dropped it next to the chest, the buckle clattering down the wood. Her tunic came next, Lira's touch creeping up the inside of the damp fabric, fingertips dancing over Aeley's skin, shivers in a race to catch up and play as they kept her there, happy to surrender to Lira's attention. The kiss deepened with a moan, Aeley's eyes closed to all else but the images taking over her thoughts with vivid colour and anticipation. That familiar taste of fruit and blossom to Lira's skin was faint but still a distraction all its own—

A stifled gasp caught its life and death between them as the sweep of thumb across Aeley's nipple sent everything into chaos, feeding the threat of flame and ruin through more than just her core. Maybe she should have said something more, and maybe she should have insisted they just sleep, but right then she wanted nothing more than the talent in those fingers to be somewhere else, chasing after a different set of cares.

And from the flushed look on Lira's face, there was nothing but shared determination to let loving touches wipe away the bitter sting of what had crawled out of the darkness and struck them both down. Where Lira had appeared lost before, searching the voids of life and lie for answers, she was so alive right then, clarity overcoming storm. Whatever the battle she fought on the inside, she *was* fighting, quietly taking control and leading Aeley to where she needed her to be—where she needed *them* to be.

Aeley was happy to follow, to see where it all went. Goddesses knew she was tired of leading all the time.

The first thing to go was Aeley's tunic, landing somewhere behind her, followed by her dingy, torn pants and the muddy boots she had taken off Emon after he had stolen hers. Not that she cared where any of her clothes ended up: the fire was just as good as the floor, especially when her focus was on Lira's gown. And yet, once the crumpled fabric of Lira's gown lay gathered in Aeley's hands, free to be discarded carelessly, Aeley laid it over the chest of blankets, fully intending to see it cleaned and cared for, if not completely replaced should Lira want to do a little burning of her own.

Before Aeley could turn and face Lira once more, the warmth of Lira's palms glided over Aeley's bare shoulders, stoking the need to settle in the heat between them and bed down with the peace it brought. Lira's caress slid down Aeley's arms and up again, then down her back, carefully tracing her spine over the tender bruises, their dull pain flaring slightly under Lira's touch. A kiss to her shoulder blade had her groaning every agreement, but it was the trail of kisses down her back that had her spinning around and taking Lira's mouth for her own, wanting everything Lira offered.

Hands, lips, tongues... their touches were everywhere, staying nowhere for long and lingering somewhere between calm and chaos. Lost to mindlessness as she was, they moved towards the bed. There were steps involved, she knew that much, though how many and how she had managed them was a lost cause. She even avoided smacking into the bedside table as they tumbled onto the bed, a small mercy despite her scrambled thoughts.

What she did know was that blinding hot slide of Lira's touch inside her—one finger, then two, slipping through the wetness and driving forward, Lira's thumb grazing her clit, leaving Aeley all but screaming murder at the need to come.

Lira's soft chuckles drifted over Aeley's ear, lips haunting her neck with the lightest caress before a hum played down her throat. Kisses traveled along with it, drawn out with the hint of a bite to feed the frenzy. Skin to skin, limbs entangled, Aeley sank into the cool sheets and held on, first with a clawing grip to Lira's back, then with her fists in Lira's hair as Lira's mouth moved lower. Down her chest and over each breast, Lira took the time to lavish both nipples, Aeley's focus shifting from one to the other—

She cried out, arching up as Lira stroked her clit, those slow fingers still inside her, her focus gone.

Lira's mouth journeyed further still, the shock of her tongue on Aeley's swollen everything bringing on the scream that had been raging its way up.

Aeley's release came quickly after, both of her hands still in Lira's hair, caught between stroking lovingly and gently tugging in effort to keep some kind of control on the agony ripping through her. The sight of Lira lying between her legs, tongue sinking deep, fingers even deeper with unrelenting strokes, the focus on her clit, sucking, teasing, drawing out her cries—it was the best damn distraction, so much better than locking herself in her study and brooding. There, it would have been anger, disappointment, bitterness—every reason to hate what the title of Tract Steward brought and its never-ending demands of duty.

Here, it was something else altogether, reaching beyond anger to what could have been lost. To what being Tract Steward had wrought in the line of that duty; a series of decisions that had brought them close and allowed them to get closer still. Lira could have walked at any point. She could have left them all behind and let the families crumble, or at least take each other down without her as witness. She still could, what with being thrust into the middle and expected to choose sides.

Yet she was here, not on a lonely road somewhere, looking in all directions to find a place to call her own.

"I need a Steward to help me figure it out, to manage it, because I don't think I can do it alone anymore."

Those had been staying words. A soft call to Aeley to tell her she was welcome in her life. The quiet need to know she could have a home that would never cast her out; never force her to choose between what was right and who she was.

And by all that was sacred, Aeley would meet that need with the only answer she had.

Drawing Lira up for a kiss, the taste of herself passing between them with the faintest hint of Lira's perfume, Aeley pulled her close, one leg slipping between both of Lira's. Her fingers followed, bathed in Lira's wetness as she returned the tender strokes, smiling against Lira's lips as Lira bucked and moaned. She rode Aeley's thigh hard, fast, taking all she could of Aeley's fingers as they moved inside her, pushing for more, rubbing against her clit. Fingers gripped Aeley's shoulder and hip as tightly as the rest of Lira did, her release close enough to—

Climax came in a shout muffled in Aeley's shoulder, Lira strained to stillness before shaking apart.

Aeley held her close, both arms wrapped around her, comforting her through the comedown. A sob jerked on the threads of her heart, and she hugged Lira tighter, letting her cry out whatever it was that was trying to heal. Tears moistened her shoulder, mixing with the sweat, and Lira collapsed against her, trembling with quiet sobs, her face buried in Aeley's damp hair, hiding in Aeley's throat.

When the sobs finally subsided, replaced by sniffles and a caress along Aeley's side, Lira drew back, her eyes still teary and red.

"Sorry," Lira whispered, tucking Aeley's hair behind her ear before offering a sad smile. "Not a criticism about you, I promise. I didn't mean—"

Aeley caught the rest of her words in a kiss, the apology brushed aside. "Never thought it was," she muttered against Lira's lips. "Just thought it was you being you—with me. Just how I like it."

Lira pulled away and watched Aeley carefully, brown curls in a tangled mess around her face, the ends trailing across Aeley's arm, tickling along the way.

Aeley knew that look: the weighing of how much was intentional and how much needed questioning.

"You never have to go back," Aeley said, cupping Lira's jaw. "Stay if you want to stay, but you never have to go back there. You don't have to go anywhere if you don't want to—live here, take over this room if you want, and I'll make sure you have everything you could need." She smiled, her heart lighter with the relief in Lira's eyes. "We could spend some time together, see what we can make of it."

"But what about the gossip? It'll come, and it'll follow, and you'll have to defend us until someone yields."

"Yes, and they'll just have to take it because that someone won't ever be me." Aeley kissed her again, soft and sweet, a gentle caress of lips on lips. "I'm annoying like that, and they'll just have to get used to it."

"So your answer is—"

"That they'll have to suffer their own opinions, because I just don't care." She offered another kiss, lingering on their shared breath. "Your opinions—I care about *yours*, that's it. You talk sense, they'll talk rubbish—nothing's new. But you, you can stay as long as you'd like, and I'll listen to every word."

Lira leaned forward, her forehead pressed to Aeley's. "That might be a lot of words."

"Mmm, I'm guessing so."

"Because I can talk, *a lot*, at least when someone's listening."

"Yeah, kind of figured that."

"And I read too much."

"So I'll build you a personal library."

"And I can't stop writing."

"We'll keep you stocked up in soap, parchment, and ink. Make the merchants filthy rich."

Lira's light laugh followed her down into Aeley's neck, a kiss claiming Aeley's throat. "And I think I've been falling in love with you. I'm pretty sure I'm there already, fallen straight to the bottom without an end in sight."

"Just fine with me—I've been right here, falling along with you," Aeley said softly. "So how about we try landing and find out what trouble we can get into together?"

"Safety in numbers?"

"I'll handle the safety, you handle the numbers. Everything else we'll make up as we go."

Lira shook against her, this time with laughter—the best thing Aeley had heard in days, and one of the greatest comforts she needed right then. Laughter she could do every day of her life. Tears she would find a way to soothe. *And everything else...*

They would deal with it and make it work, one day after another, moving forward even if it meant stepping back. She would see to it that the shadows scampered off, with the chain of duty in one hand and Lira's heart in the other. All else would have to fall in line or put up with the consequences.

She refused to be duped again.

If Emon and Ryler had taught her anything, it was that Kayte was right. Korre was right. She needed to pull herself together and bite back. Trick her once, that was down to her poor judgment, but never again.

She was tired of playing Tract Steward; it was time to be one, for all the pain and headache it caused, but also the good. Because right then, there was nothing but good in her arms, whispering all the kindnesses in the world, and they were everything she would follow right on down to the end.

Chapter Twenty-One

"He looks nervous," Lira whispered.

Aeley leaned against the doorframe and stared at the back of Lower's dark red hair. The last time she saw him, they had all gathered at High Council Hall for Emon and Ryler's trial and final sentencing, witnessing what Cota and Severn did best: send both brothers to prison for the rest of their lives.

That had been one month ago, three months after Emon and Ryler's arrest at the Derossa estate. Dealing with the issue had taken longer than Aeley wanted, their trial not expedited like Allon's, though given how many laws Allon had violated with dozens of witnesses and an entire estate's worth of damage, his trial had needed less investigation. Emon and Ryler's case required more evidence, multiple testimonies, and the interrogation of their accomplices.

Severn and Cota had also interrogated Lira's parents, who swore on the lives of all four Goddesses and their lovers that they'd had no role in the scheme. For their part, they seemed genuinely horrified, with Etalynn embarrassed enough to pack her things and run off to the Riaes tract in southwest Kattal for weeks on end. Asha remained in Gailarin, except the latest reports suggested his health was failing faster than what remained of his business.

Neither Asha nor Etalynn had bothered Lira since then, and that was best for everyone. Aeley had few things to say to them, none of them kind.

"What could he possibly want? And why is Vant here?" Aeley frowned and crossed her arms. "Lower talked to us at the trial."

"I don't know. Maybe we should ask him." Lira gave Aeley a gentle push into the meeting room and stepped in behind her.

Vant glanced up from his book. "Ah, good, you're both here. We can start."

Lower jumped up from his seat. His youthful face strained with worry, the flush at his cheeks almost the same shade as the pink scarf draped loosely around his neck. "Aeley, good to see you again. And Lira—a pleasant surprise." He stopped as Mayr ran into the room, hanging onto the doorframe as he swung in and rested against the wall, his sword peeking out from beneath his black leather long coat. "So it's a full meeting, then."

"Hey… I need to know things," Mayr said, trying to catch his breath. He bent over and raised his gloved hand, the snow on his boots leaving its mark on the floor. "Carry on."

"Thanks for the permission," Lower muttered before he faced Aeley, hands buried in the deep pockets of his sky-blue Council long coat. "The good news is that this isn't about your brothers, either one of you. They're gone for the rest of their lives, stuck slogging rock and being penned up. I'm assured by the warden that their visits will be supervised with names and other information recorded. We can't be too certain that they won't try something again."

"Fantastic. No more wasting our time," Mayr said.

Aeley rolled her eyes and waited for Mayr to continue with his rant. He had done that often in the last four months, ever since Emon and Ryler's arrest, especially when they or Allon were mentioned. There was no digging them out from beneath his skin, the damage they had wrought difficult to forget. Maybe with time and distraction it would get better—at least she hoped it would. Certainly her bouts of abject panic had calmed down a little, though how much of that was Lira's influence and how much was because she had learned to deal with them better... that was a question she was almost too scared to answer.

When Mayr was silent, however, giving her a quirked brow and *what's your problem* stare, Aeley smiled at Lower. "The bad news?" she asked.

"None, actually, only more good news. Well, for you, not for your father. Although he's dead, so really—" Lower held up his hands, his ears going redder than his face. "Never mind. What I mean is that the marriage deal is over. Everything I said before—forget it. Never happened. We'll just say I had the wrong document, the wrong family, the wrong everything, and move on. You're free to choose whomever you want—or no one, if that'd make you happier. Whatever you decide, we'll support." He pointed at Vant. "And put that in your notes, sir. Record it as officially said by the Councilman of Tract Stewards and Republic Leadership. It can't be taken back."

Really? Aeley glanced at Lira. "Why the change? You were adamant before."

"I know, and I recognize the error of my foolish ways," Lower said, bowing from the waist. "It wasn't my best moment. I was trying to honour your father's wishes, which I thought were perfectly good. They fooled us all, the bastards." The usual playfulness in his blue eyes clouded over with annoyance. "My fault there, in particular, considering I believed their ridiculous, foolish—" He sighed and rolled his gaze up to the ceiling. "My condolences to you both." He waved his hands. "But it's all over. With them punished and everything investigated, there's really no point in forcing something that obviously won't work. So you're free. We release you. And by we, I mean me, the official runt of the Council litter. Also, I'd like to apologize for executing the mess."

"It's funny you should say that," Aeley murmured. Reaching back, she took Lira's hand and squeezed it. "We were going to come to you with the exact opposite."

Lower's smile faltered. "What?"

"You keep forgetting there's still a member of the family left," Lira answered. She drew close to Aeley's side and raised her chin, the bright berry-purple jewels of her hair comb glittering faintly in the winter-afternoon light. "No one ever bothered to talk to me about it. And you never really talked to her about it, either."

"Talk to you? But why? The contract was negotiated and signed by..." Lower glanced at Aeley, then Lira, before peering down at their entwined hands. "*Oh.*"

"Yes. Exactly." Aeley tried not to laugh, though the look on his face... "We didn't want to spread the news faster than we could enjoy what we have. We've decided to take it as it comes, but we're leaning towards marriage. Meaning I'll still honour my father's wishes, which is just asking for trouble, I know, but I'll do it *my* way, on my time. Is that going to be a problem, now you've released me and all?"

Lower shook his head. "If it's what you want, we're not going to say anything. Well, except congratulations and happy marriage, whenever you get to it, and please don't kill each other. You know, the normal stuff." He held out his arms, a smile brightening his face. "Good news all the way around, then! Except maybe for you," he said, pointing at Mayr. "You'll have two mistresses to serve instead of just one. Think you can handle it?"

"Now that this one's stopped drinking herself to misery and the other one distracts her, I think I'll be perfect," Mayr replied with a grin.

"Well, who am I to argue?" Lower gestured to the door. "Suppose I'll see myself out, then, and let you all get back to whatever you do."

After he slipped out the door, Aeley turned to Lira. "What *do* we do? I can't seem to remember what we had planned."

"Well, you know, I think I'm in need of another lesson," Lira answered dryly, "because you *know* I can't be trusted with anything sharper than a dinner knife."

"Only if we close the door this time."

Lira leaned into Aeley, pressing a kiss to her lips. "Who said anything about being someplace with a door?"

Before Aeley could fathom her meaning, Lira rushed into the hall, her dark violet skirt trailing behind her.

"Better go or she'll start without you," Mayr said, laughing quietly. "No, I'm serious—get out before I throw you out. Keep enjoying that new life of yours. And don't break anything, not again. I'm not cleaning it up."

Flashing him a smile, Aeley ran into the hall. Lira waited at the end of the corridor, hiding behind the wall of the hallway to the right, her eyes bright as she peeked around the corner. When their gazes met, Lira grinned. She beckoned with one hand, then waved and hurried away again, leaving Aeley to the quickening rhythm of her heart and the love of the game, the promise of a happy end wrapped up in easy smiles and tender touches.

The playfulness was a reminder of the changes in their lives, not just in reclaiming peace, but the way their lives melded together under the same roof. While she still had nightmares, reliving what had happened in Oly Valley in fits and spurts combined with what Emon and Ryler's antics contributed, they haunted her with a little less frequency than before. It was not the only change over the months: as Mayr had pointed out, she even drank less, inspired by Lira to find another way to solve the problems in her head, and she breathed easier, even though worry still piled on too heavily sometimes and her chest tightened in protest.

Despite all of that, she pushed on, her attention never failing to stray to Lira, especially in the worst times. Focusing on Lira was like holding a light to the darkness: with one soft word or understanding smile, she gifted Aeley with confidence in her moments of doubt. If putting aside the melancholy and doubt meant surrendering to someone who filled her with joy and surety, she was already there, her heart, hands, and soul fully invested, ready and willing to brave everything that lay ahead.

It only gets better from here.

Epilogue

This was hers now, this life, this choice. Hers, and no one looked set to take it away, certainly not while Aeley was alive to defend the lines firmly drawn around their relationship, keeping those who disagreed with their choices on the one side while they continued building their shared life on the other.

Lira sipped her starberry mead and hid her smile behind the colourless crystal goblet, her focus sweeping over the packed ballroom, its earthy grey stone lost under the bright, festive colours of wedding decorations. Guests mingled happily, the sea of their customary white wedding attire interrupted by the touches of gold, pink, and black of the tables and chairs. The tablecloths were snow white like the chair dressings, though their runners were black, as were the fine sashes wrapped around the chairs, pinned with gold brooches and ribbons. The flowers spilling over the rims of the glass vases on the tables, however, were a variety of pinks, from the softest barely-more-than-white buds to vivid magenta bell flowers in full bloom, mixed with fern fronds and short stems of midsummer berries. Those bouquets were all for Lira, Aeley had insisted several times, and Lira had no intention to argue. She enjoyed the attention, oddly enough, touched by the details Mayr, Haydin, and the entire Dahe entourage had added to the feast. She had been married for all of an afternoon, but it still felt entirely too surreal.

She laughed quietly. *Married*: the word still stuck in the throats of some of the members of the Grand Families where Lira was concerned, yet it rolled off the tongues of others without any trouble, joined by warm smiles that were just as easy. In any event, this marriage was hers, and Goddesses help anyone who suggested otherwise.

As if to ensure no one forgot why they should keep their unfavourable opinions to themselves, several white banners with the red, black, and gold Dahe bearcat crest and shield hung on the walls—a clear reminder of whose home they were in, and why. If that was not enough, the white-clothed guards standing to attention throughout the room and the rest of the estate were a further note to keep things civil.

Though with the hard came the soft: pink ribbons with massive plaited and woven bows draped across the walls, accompanied by gold-painted lattices with cascades of various pink and white flowers arranged in gradually changing hues, and thin gold chains with dangling strands of delicate crystal charms that gave the room a subtle sparkle.

She could imagine who was responsible for that lot, but the thought of the guards fighting with the most fragile elements... she had to laugh, just a little, after having gotten to know most of them. To her understanding, the affair had been an all-hands effort, with the guards overseeing the decorations while Haydin's staff saw to the tables and food. Many an expletive had been dropped, according to her earlier conversation with Stuck, who had merely grinned, shrugged, and strutted away into the crowd, one hand on her sword and a puffy jam and cheese pastry in the other.

If there was anything Lira would remember most, it was the unseen mark of family that was imprinted over everything. A family she was officially part of now, an entire household that welcomed her as surely as Aeley had. She was rarely alone, even when left to her work and the need for privacy. The presence of nearby guards was all too familiar, their duty to watch for anything that could creep out of the corners and bring her any kind of harm—a far cry from her life before Aeley.

Even the High Council had accepted her part in Aeley's life with little objection. Since the meeting with Lower eight and a half months ago, when he had announced the contract null and void, the councilmen had let them be, save for the usual matters over governance, commerce, and resources.

What they truly thought about Aeley and Lira keeping the marriage contract in play, however... there had been a few raised brows, but no disagreement.

As far as Lira was concerned, that was best for them all. Aeley had no interest in sharing that she had intentionally, and effectively, weaponized the contract to protect Lira. Their marriage fulfilled the stipulations of the contract, but there had been no clause included as to what should happen if the chosen spouse legally disowned the rest of the family, assisted by the backing of the Tract Steward... thereby suspending the family from getting anything, as her parents had recently discovered. Lira would be the only one to benefit, and with Emon and Ryler in prison without rights to anything that belonged to the family, should her parents die, everything would fall into her hands and Aeley's, mostly as reparation.

There was nothing else to be done about it, given how Korre had negotiated the wording of the contract. Everything that was Lira's passed into the Dahe family without a scrap of advantage for anyone else in her own family—just their contractual obligation to play nice and provide what they owed when they were instructed to so as not to have everything ripped from them. Had Asha never signed the contract, he could have saved himself the consequences.

But Korre... Lira smiled to herself. Korre had bound Asha to the contract *and* Lira as much as Asha had been tied to Emon and Ryler's fate. With his sons, Asha would have shared in the spoils. But with Lira, he had successfully given Aeley the means to protect Lira's interests, turning the contract neither of them wanted into a sharp instrument of destruction.

A quiet game of calculated moves, as had been Korre's way. While he was never one for outright confrontation, that never stopped him from playing a reserved version of offence and defence.

Leaning back in her chair, her crimson dancing slippers crushed beneath her bare feet on the dais, Lira cradled her goblet close to her chest, content to watch the guests. Some milled about or danced while others were lost in deep conversation, drinks and food following wherever they went. All twelve councilmen were present, several attending with their families or other guests.

Somewhere in the mix were the other four Tract Stewards and their families. Kayte and Rosayra drifted among conversations from one side of the room to the other, pausing only to get a dance in every few songs, their gentle sway to the string ensemble paired with such loving looks that no one dared to interrupt them. Although Lira had lost track of Ulyne Forey, the Tract Steward from Lasael, she occasionally caught sight of Stewards Paloan Mahne and Erneda

Hewyth with their business faces on as they spoke to the councilmen and other officials, likely striking deals and working out issues for their respective regions, Eruelme and Riaes.

Riaes. Lira nearly chugged down her mead just to keep distracted from the ire that name awoke. Her parents were at the feast, too, hidden among the few hundred guests. She had not looked for them, nor did she care where they ended up. The only reason their presence was being tolerated was due to the request of Tract Steward Hewyth, who had asked for it as a favour, one she promised to return to Aeley anytime it was needed. Hewyth's relationship with Lira's mother was at fault, their childhood antics and close family ties keeping them connected, no matter the borders in the way or the passage of time.

To respect the necessary alliance between tracts, Lira had agreed, grinding her teeth and reminding herself she was mistress of the household and Steward's Hand of Gailarin. Both roles honoured her place as official scribe for Aeley as much as they did her marriage, placing her at Aeley's side when it came to decision making and important details. There was nothing her parents could do about either.

Fortunately, avoiding her parents had been easy: there were more than enough people in attendance to provide a screen between her and them. Still, she would have been happier not to have seen or heard about them at all. The quiet away from them had been a blissful reprieve for the last year, giving her a chance to settle comfortably without a constant struggle.

"You know, it's easier to do away with them by not thinking about it."

Lira startled, Aeley's voice jolting her from her daze.

Across from her, Aeley leaned over the table, her chin resting on her palms, propped up by her elbows near the table edge. Slashes in the arms of her wine-red tunic revealed glimpses of bare tan skin, and loosely knotted ribbons kept the delicate, airy fabric gathered at her shoulder, elbow, and wrist. Over that was a narrow bodice around her waist, dark crimson leather like her skintight pants and knee-high boots.

Lovely as it all was, Lira suspected Aeley was more interested in showing off her shiny new gold and black diamond dagger, which remained strapped to her bodice. Not that Lira minded: the dagger had been her gift to Aeley at their wedding, and the fact it was kept close was a sentiment she appreciated, but the thought of being the one to remove both the bodice and the dagger had its own deliciously delightful appeal. So did sinking her hands into the dark blonde waves of Aeley's hair and doing away with the red ribbons keeping the cascade tamed.

"I know," Lira said softly, reaching across the table to Aeley, her palm upwards. "It comes and goes, though I don't know why. It's best just to move on."

Aeley slipped her hand into Lira's and held tight, warmth seeping into Lira's cool palm. "They're your parents, Li. It's not going to be easy. But that doesn't mean you need to spend the rest of your life on it. A little bit here and there, with all sorts of good things in between." Entwining their fingers, Aeley turned their arms slightly to kiss the inside of Lira's wrist, a breath playing its own heat over her arm. "And I'd say that includes some dancing." She tugged Lira's hand. "Come on."

Lira arched one brow, setting her goblet on the table. "You hate dancing."

"Mostly. But you don't, and I love you." Aeley grinned, brown eyes full of mischief as she trailed kisses up Lira's arm. "It's a sacrifice for a good cause."

"Alas, the agony. It's bloody awful." Lira snorted as she slipped her shoes back on then made her way around the table, the skirts of her scarlet gown in one hand while she reached for Aeley with the other. Once Lira stepped off the dais, Aeley curled Lira's hand into the crook of her arm and patted it with reassurance, though the look in her eyes was far from complaining about the circumstances—more begging for a reward for her thoughtfulness, even if they had to wait for a while yet to enjoy that reward in private.

Another lively tune filtered through the ballroom as the ensemble played with vigour, and gazes followed Lira and Aeley as they strolled through the crowd. Several guards shadowed them to the dancing area, their movements slow, meant to avoid attention. Mayr and Pellon lingered the closest, despite not being on duty. They remained dressed in the same white attire they had worn at the wedding ceremony, though not with their floral crowns, which all those in the wedding party had worn. No doubt they had removed their crowns because the pink and gold flowers could get ruined while they insisted on working, especially if someone yanked on the long coils of black ribbons.

Lira matched Aeley's stride, focused on the empty space towards the middle of the dancing area. There was just enough space for them to sneak in and—

"Lira! *Wait!*"

A hand grabbed, tugged on her free wrist. Then two hands, pulling *hard*, grappling at her fingers. Demanding she stop. Commanding she obey.

She stumbled, ripped away from Aeley, her toes scraping the floor, ankle twisting.

And a gasp—such a loud gasp from the onlookers.

A snap in focus brought her gaze to her mother's, their alikeness with the same dark hair and grey eyes turning Lira's stomach.

"*Please*, I just want to talk to you." Etalynn pawed at Lira's fingers with one hand, the other jerking her closer, towards the crowd that had backed away around them.

There was a shout to let go—more than just Lira's—then cries as Etalynn refused to release her, hands moving quickly—

Everything went too fast then, more than just hands getting in the way. Full bodies swept past Lira, with Mayr suddenly at Etalynn's side, pushing her back. And Aeley—Aeley was right there with him on the other side, hands on Etalynn's shoulder and arm, forcing her to release Lira.

If only that had been the end of it.

Aeley said nothing, her hands nowhere on Etalynn as she backed Etalynn up against one of the tables, sending the few guests gathered there scattering back. With nowhere to go, trapped by shocked onlookers to all sides and Aeley in front of her, Etalynn paled and clutched at her white gown, hands and arms drawn into her chest, looking so much smaller than Lira had ever seen her.

"Hands. Off." In the quieted space, the controlled tone of Aeley's voice carried through well enough. "Not her, not here, and not ever again."

Lira jumped as a touch brushed her elbow. She glanced sharply to her right as strong hands steadied her.

Gren.

He stepped into the empty space by her side, his jaws clenched, his look asking if she was all right before he moved that extra step further, placing himself between her and Etalynn. To Lira's left stood his lover, Tracel, her blue gaze sympathetic as she encouraged Lira to lean against her and shift the weight off her aching ankle.

Casting a quick glance through the open space that had grown around them, Lira spotted Pellon and other guards as they kept the crowd back, then Kayte, Rosayra, Severn, and Cota, all of whom looked just as ready to jump into the chaos as any of Aeley's guards. Even the music had stopped.

"You are a guest in my home," Aeley continued, "but never again if this is how you go about it."

"I just wanted to talk to her," Etalynn argued, rubbing her wrist, her face still pale. "She's been avoiding me, and you—you've encouraged it. You made it happen." She straightened her back and raised her chin, though only partially. Her gaze was almost high enough to meet Aeley's, but her voice was stronger. "You took our daughter away from us. You told her to leave us behind, to punish us when we did nothing but love her, and then you cheated us out of everything. I did what I had to."

Aeley stepped even closer, one hand on the dagger at her waist, and all of the fight bled from Etalynn, her back bowed over the table.

"No, you did what you *wanted*," Aeley said, "nothing more and definitely nothing less. But that's always been your way, hasn't it? Getting what you want, not a lick of care about much else, least of all who you're doing it to." Arm outstretched, she snapped her fingers, then flicked her wrist. Footfalls sounded from behind Lira, a rush of air sweeping past as two guards joined Mayr by Aeley's side. "And I didn't do a damn thing. She's avoiding you because she's had enough—I'm just respecting her wishes. Funny what a little loving support can do."

Etalynn's grey eyes widened. She peered around Aeley to Lira, as if pleading for rescue.

Lira shook her head. There was nothing to be done. The years for that had long since passed. Everything else since had been a sliding scale of healing between bouts of new damage, playing push-and-pull with Lira in the middle, spinning in circles and putting confusion in control.

"Congratulations," Aeley said, stepping back with a half-bow, one arm held out, "you get to leave early, and with an escort, no less." With a glance at Mayr, Aeley fell back half a dozen steps, giving Etalynn space to move. "You, out."

There was a huff, a flurry of skirt, then a bark at Lira's father, who slipped out from the edge of the crowd near Etalynn. He seemed to have aged another fifteen years since Lira last saw him, his grey hair even greyer, his dull blue eyes weighted with shadow and exhaustion. Without sparing a look at Lira, Asha took Etalynn's hand and pulled her away from the table, towards the closest set of doors. Mayr and the two guards followed, close on their heels, with only Mayr flicking a glance at Lira and offering her a strained, apologetic smile.

As they passed, Lira stepped forward, leaning away from Tracel's gentle embrace around her waist just enough to stand on her own. Her ankle protested but bore the weight. "Mother."

Etalynn and Asha stopped to look back at her, their troubled gazes nowhere near as sorry or warm as she wished they could have been. Even with all the changes, some things would always remain the same.

Lira took a breath. "Leave me alone," she said, her gaze leveled on Etalynn's. "This can't happen again. I can't keep doing this with you. Just leave me alone. Just... stay out of it. Mind your own life and leave me to mine."

Whatever Etalynn may have wanted to say never made it to her lips, though the anger and hurt in her eyes screamed at the darkness between them, the void impossible to fill.

Nor did she try—Etalynn turned on her heel and hurried away, Asha behind her, the matter as settled as it could be.

Tracel hugged Lira about the waist, rogue curls of her thick blonde and red hair tumbling over Lira's shoulder. "You did good," she said, "but we need to get you resting. I'll go get my kit."

"I agree," Aeley added, scowling as she sidled up to Gren. Around them, chatter resumed, the gossip already brewing. "Our table, for now."

Tracel nodded, then rushed off for her healer's case as Aeley and Gren helped Lira through the ballroom despite Lira's insistence that she could walk, painful as it was. They relented only once she was in her chair on the dais, throbbing ankle up on the chair next to her. The feast fell back into a familiar hum of tones, while the musicians played a sweet, quiet ballad, presumably to calm the excitement.

Lira turned away. The hundreds of glances her way prodded too deeply, making her skin crawl. Even now she had to be humiliated, just when she thought—

"Hey." Aeley crouched by her side, her voice soft as she slid two fingers beneath Lira's chin, drawing their faces close together. "It's fine. *You'll* be fine. The transgression was hers; let her be the one to pay the price." She waved off the stares. "Ignore them. They saw what happened, they'll talk—and hopefully they'll keep her in line. If anything, they'll leave you be." Her touch was gentle as she gave Lira a tender kiss. "We'll deal with this," she said, her lips lingering on Lira's. "We'll always deal with it."

Lira kissed Aeley back, hard, and with a promise to thank her properly later, which only brought a gleam to Aeley's eyes that left Lira laughing. Before the rest of the ideas in her head could turn into words, Tracel appeared with her blue healer's case and sank down near Lira's ankle. As Tracel tended to the injury, Aeley stayed beside Lira, her hand in both of Lira's, watching while Gren spoke with Cota at the end of the dais. Cota looked as unimpressed as Gren did, his gaze catching Lira's with a silent need to ask questions, ones she wanted to avoid right then.

"Ah." Lira winced as Tracel finished bandaging her ankle and laid it down.

"Sorry," Tracel murmured with a grimace. She reached for Lira's hands and drew them close, her attention on Lira's arms. Bruises were trying to form, Lira could feel them, though their visibility would come later. "Just try to take it easy for the next couple days. Limit how much you're up and about, take the stairs with help, and apply cold cloths. And keep your ankle up, not down. Give it a chance to heal." She cast Aeley a knowing glance, a smile playing at her lips. "That means *careful* activity, Steward. Nothing to make it worse. Only better."

"Oh, well, when you put it that way..." Aeley grinned. "I can be creative."

"I'm sure you can." Tracel laughed as she closed her case. "Something tells me your bedside manner will be just fine. Giving. Very giving." She peered behind her as Gren returned, Cota behind him. "I'll leave you to it, then."

"Thank you." Lira smiled the rest of her thanks to Tracel before Gren nodded.

"We won't be far," Gren said. "I have a pup of a Head Guard to go talk to." He gestured to Aeley that he was keeping both eyes on her and Lira, then led Tracel away, one arm curled around her back, keeping her close as they spoke quietly.

"Well, that was… eventful." Cota offered Lira a sad, concerned smile, the jagged scar along his left cheek casting a whole new darkness over the matter. She had scars, too, none of them visible. "Is there anything I can do about it?"

Tempting. So very tempting.

Aeley's face said the same, irritation creeping in all over again.

"No, but thank you." Lira shrugged. "It's a family matter, one we can handle on our own." *For now.*

Cota's look called her out on the latter, but he said nothing. Instead, he pulled a small, brown leather documents case from out of his white long coat. Folded parchment was in his hand the next moment. "This is for you, Aeley."

Aeley snatched the letter from him faster than Lira could make sense of it.

The varied emotions that played across Aeley's face were odd, one moment confused, then pleased, followed by annoyed, only to end in her shaking her head with a laugh. "That bastard." She handed Lira the letter. "You might want to read this. It's... enlightening."

More than a little curious, Lira accepted the letter, immediately recognizing Korre's handwriting despite the scratchiness of the script.

Dearest Aeley,

Reading this means you've made your choice, and I'll congratulate you either way it's gone. If you've chosen Emon or Ryler... may the marriage work out in your favour, and don't forget to keep both eyes on them. If, however, you've opted for the independent journey, I wish you the best of luck for as long as you walk it, and with much love. You've always had a strong spirit, and Hastal will guide that, I don't doubt. Maybe She's guided you this far, your resolve tested, tried, and truly found. May your future be blessed, darling girl, and may your time be golden.

On the other hand, if you've married a certain scribe, double congratulations are in order for more reasons than I can account for in this single letter.

We never discussed your romantic inclinations, though we should've. There never seemed to be a right time to poke around in that part of your life. It seemed like something to let you keep for yourself, not have to share because your father was being nosy. In any event, I wanted to keep your options open, giving all the reason to why I negotiated the contract as I did: fully negotiable relationship matters, at the discretion of all parties and their particular needs, without any one gender specified, all of it neutral to keep you from being forced into any one action by anyone involved.

But Lira... I've secretly hoped for that match. She's had such wonderfully big eyes for you, darling girl, though she likely believes it went unnoticed. Maybe you'll have noticed by now and be making the best of the mess I've left you in. If anything, take comfort in her: she's a lovely companion with a personality to complement yours. Perhaps even temper the things to come. I've never presumed to make it happen, however: you certainly would've railed against it, and Lira... she's already had enough to shoulder. I haven't wanted to add to either case, just hoped that leaving you to work together might give you time to get to know each other, maybe become friends, perhaps even lovers as a lovely addition. *Both of you have been lonely; both of you need an ally, someone to look after and be looked after by.*

To my deepest regret, sickness is taking me quicker than I can keep up, making this the best I can do with what little I have left. Whatever your choice, I hope you find happiness. And if Lira wasn't your choice, please take care of her, whatever the state of your relationship. Nail her parents to the wall while you're at it. I failed to, choosing a quieter path with a stronger player, though Lira is stubborn like Pellon, and we both know how his situation has continued to play out. She has the same pride and dignity as he does, and she needs the same level of protection.

I know I led you into their den, but dearest, you are tough like wolfe-kind and they won't know what to do with that. Change will come with you, but for the better. The fight is yours now: do what I couldn't and turn the tide. Things need a bit of shaking up, especially with what's to come.

All my love to you both,
Father

Lira clutched the letter, her gaze skipping over the words as she made sense of it. The warm flush at her cheeks only grew warmer. She felt so exposed, her secrets mingled with Aeley's and Korre's in the same breath. Korre had seen much more than she realized.

Suddenly she wanted to cover up and hide under a mountain of blankets just to escape the raw truth that bled all over the page in black ink. She was a scribe, recording other peoples' words, their meanings. To see her own life, her vulnerabilities, captured on the page was unsettling.

'That bastard,' indeed.

Cota cleared his throat. "I have something for you, too." He drew a second parchment from his documents case and handed it to Lira.

Again, the letter bore Korre's hand, though as she unfolded the message, a small silver key fell into her lap.

Dearest Lira,

I'm sorry I couldn't be there for you, now or ever again. I'm also sorry I can't deliver this news to you in person. But you are a purveyor of the written word, so perhaps this is more than fitting.

Enclosed is the key to a handful of chests in my private collection, all of them books. More specifically, all of them original copies of rather old, terribly precious manuscripts I've kept locked away for long enough. They were collected by Renalys, Aeley's mother, and my mother, Jenaley. Both of them were historians and keepers of our family's most valuable literature, including ancestral histories and records, but also legends and other tales that have survived time and lived to tell. They need a gentle hand and a passionate spirit—someone who sees them as treasure to be preserved.

They're yours now, if you want them. A gesture of family, no matter your relationship with Aeley. Perhaps you can share them together and raise a few spirits while you're at it. The bodies may be lost, but the memories remain. The words may be old, but stories can live forever. You, of all people, know the value inherent in capturing life in such ways, and all of the meaningful directions they can lead us. Perhaps these will help you find more meaning, if not a kindred spirit.

With love,
Korre

A tear hit the parchment, smudging the ink, and Lira cursed, wiping at her eyes before more tears ruined the message completely. Even in death, he was more a father to her than her own.

Even from the Realm of the Dead, he opened doors and offered his hand to lead her through.

"This looks bad. Should I be concerned?" Aeley kneeled beside Lira's chair, one hand stroking through Lira's hair, her fingers catching on the blackish-red ribbons and strands of fiery red crystals woven throughout the loose curls and thin plaits.

Lira shook her head. No, not concerned. Liable to raise her father's ghost to give him the worst tongue-lashing a spirit could have, but not concerned.

"Just your father being himself," Lira said quietly. With careful hands, she folded the parchment around the key and gave it to Aeley. "Hold on to it for now. We can look for them later."

Aeley quirked one brow. "Sounds like work. He left me more, didn't he? Because I swear, if I get one more damned notification—"

A kiss was the best way to quiet her, and it worked even better than Lira hoped, with Cota sneaking away in near silence, save for a low, muted chuckle. Aeley, however, sank into her, both hands settled at Lira's waist, taking the hint to hold on and enjoy the moment. Because that was what they had, failing everything else: an ongoing thread of moments, some of them ones she could put words to, others…

Others were meant to be captured and tasted and lived, igniting every emotion that roiled and burned and begged for release. Some moments would bring joy, others hurt, and others still would bring every feeling in between. But in the end, she had escaped the fire of one family and found warmth in another, and everything else…

Well, everything else was the story yet to be told.

Fin

Playlist for A Question of Counsel

(Artists and songs are listed in alphabetical order)

Originally inspired by:
Florence + the Machine – Blinding
Ke$ha – Take It Off

Themes:
Bedroom Rockers – Nothing Else Matters
Beyoncé – Halo
Nikki Holland – Secret
The Glitch Mob – Becoming Harmonious (feat. Metal Mother)
UNSECRET – Till I See You Again (feat. The Powder Room)

Rest of the Playlist!
Active Child – Evening Ceremony
Active Child – Hanging On
Active Child – Johnny Belinda
Alex Clare – Too Close

Banks – Waiting Game

Chase & Status – Embrace (feat. White Lies)
Chase & Status – Midnight Caller (feat. Clare Maguire)
City and Colour – Day Old Hate

David Gilmour – High Hopes (Live in Gdańsk)
Delilah – Go

Eivør – Is It Cold Outside
Ellie Goulding – Beating Heart
Ellie Goulding – Hanging On
Emika – Wicked Game
Emily Browning – Sweet Dreams (Are Made of This)

Fever Ray – Keep the Streets Empty for Me
Fleurie – Hurricane
Florence + the Machine – Heavy in Your Arms
Florence + the Machine – Howl

Gregorian – All I Need
Gregorian – Dark Angel

Hurt – House Carpenter
Hurt – Still

iiO – Is It Love
In This Moment – In the Air Tonight

Lana Del Rey – Young and Beautiful (Dan Heath Orchestral Version)
Leon Else – Protocol
Luca Fogale – I Don't Want to Lose You

Marina & the Diamonds – Lies
MiaKoda – The After You

Nikki Holland – Skyfall (feat. Gardin of Edan)
Nonpoint – In the Air Tonight

PVRIS – Empty

Ruelle – Slip Away
Ruelle – The Other Side

Sam Tinnesz – Don't Close Your Eyes
Sarah Brightman – Winter in July
Sarah McLachlan – Fear
Sarah McLachlan – Fumbling Towards Ecstasy
Sarah McLachlan – Mary
Schiller – The Smile (feat. Sarah Brightman)
Sia – Chandelier

The Glitch Mob – Bad Wings
The Glitch Mob – Between Two Points (feat. Swan)
The Neighbourhood – Afraid
The Neighbourhood – How

Tommee Profitt – Can't Help Falling in Love (Dark Version) (feat. Brooke)
Tommee Profitt – Heroes Rise (feat. Sam Tinnesz)
Tommee Profitt – I'm Not Afraid (feat. Wondra)
Tommee Profitt – Noble Blood (feat. Fleurie)
Tommee Profitt – Onward & Upward (feat. Fleurie)
Tommee Profitt – Remembrance (feat. Fleurie)
Tommee Profitt – Sound of War (feat. Fleurie)

Unions – Bury
UNSECRET – Lay Your Weapons Down (feat. Sam Tinnesz)
UNSECRET – Never Give Up (feat. Rose Cousins)
UNSECRET – Vendetta (feat. Krigarè)
Ursine Vulpine – Wicked Game (feat. Annaca)
Ursine Vulpine & Annaca – Lovers Death
Ursine Vulpine & Annaca – Without You (Extended Version)

YUNGBLUD & Halsey – 11 Minutes (feat. Travis Barker)

The Republic Continues in
Four

THE REPUBLIC BOOK 2

Four

ARCHER KAY LEAH

One night. A second chance. The perfect match he never saw coming...

On the outside, Mayr seems to have it all: a successful career as Head of the Guard for a prominent politician, family and friends who rely on him, and the attention of beautiful lovers. But appearances are a good way to bury secrets, including mistakes he can never fix and a broken heart that never seems to heal, forever searching for the one person to share his life with.

When his last girlfriend takes him back and suggests an intimate night together with Tash, one of her lovers, Mayr reluctantly agrees. The last thing he expects is to fall hard for Tash, who is nothing like Mayr's previous lovers... and much too difficult to forget.

Tash is a secretive priest with deep, dark truths connected to a past he will never completely outrun. He keeps romance at a distance, knowing it can destroy him. Except with Mayr in his life, love might just ignore all the rules and push his limits.

But when Tash undertakes the Uldana Trials, love may ruin them both. If Tash fails, he'll likely die. If he succeeds, he must give up Mayr and break both their hearts...

(Author's note: The relationship at the heart of the story is an MM romance. There is a minor amount of MF and MMF intimacy included, but this is not an MMF poly romance.)

Author's Note

Hello, and welcome! Many warm greetings to anyone who's just stepping into *The Republic* series for the first time—thank you for giving this book a go! And if this isn't your first time around, thanks for coming back! These books don't go anywhere without readers like you. <3

So, *A Question of Counsel*... this massively expanded second edition has been on the books for a couple years now. The first edition was published in 2015, originally written as my submission to Less Than Three Press's *Damsels in Distress* collection of novellas. Though the story didn't get taken on as one of the books in that collection, it was signed on as a general release and officially kicked off the Republic series. (Though fun fact: there was a novella before that—*Rule Breaker*—which was published in an anthology, which was where Aeley, Gren, Tracel, and Allon made their debuts. That story is also being rewritten and will be republished once I can get it sorted, and it'll be The Republic #0.5.)

The original version of *A Question of Counsel* was a novella under 50,000 words, which I didn't think of expanding at the time, especially since my publisher preferred shorter works. But over the years, issues with the story cropped up; things I wanted to fix or at least play with a bit more. Then there's the little matter of where the series has ended up in terms of the over-arching storyline, which made itself known after I wrote book 2 (*Four*). That put this first book into a bit of a conundrum, seeing as it missed out on all the connections the other books are making.

Needless to say, it was time for this story to be brought up to speed! This new edition now slides perfectly into the series-long storyline, with hints of things that will mean even more later... but shh, spoilers!

Perhaps the best part of writing this edition was pulling in all of the other characters. For the first time, readers actually get to hear from Korre, who's only ever been referenced but has never gotten a say. I wanted to explore his motives and concerns, especially given how important he is to Aeley, Lira, Mayr, Pellon, and others who knew him. Korre left a lasting impression on so many characters, and even though he wasn't a fighter in the physical, militant, or aggressive sense, he fostered fighters and gave them opportunities when they most needed them. But he also made mistakes, even if his heart was in the right place, and that's all part of the story.

I also loved bringing in more of the fun personalities that appeared while I was writing book 4 (*Soulbound*), including Stuck, Rosayra, Kayte, and Cota. I got to know them well during that book, but they really wanted a chance to shine in this one. Honestly, they wanted to hijack it, and Stuck basically did just that. She's one to keep an eye on, especially as the series continues. Actually, they all are. Things are going to shake up and happen...

Finally, there was the matter of getting deeper into Aeley's head and stepping into Lira's, because there was so much there unexplored, and I've wanted to dig into their issues more for quite a while. The original touched on Aeley's PTSS but didn't delve into it, and Lira... she's had a tough go with a family that's got a serious case of narcissism happening, for which she's had to keep paying the price. She's a survivor, living with her family's abuse and trying to forge ahead with what she has, but she finally gets a say in all of this—and she also got the last word, which was so important, considering everything. This new version gives them a much more solid foundation, especially since they'll continue to make appearances throughout the series as it unfolds.

All my love and thanks to everyone who helped bring these characters and their story to life, especially with that first edition! I never knew this series was going to be a thing until I was inspired to write this story for that collection call— meaning Less Than Three Press, this one's all because of you! My deepest heartfelt thanks to Sam, Megan, and Sasha for everything the three of you gave under the LT3 banner. You changed my life so much, you have no idea just how deep that impact has gone. <3 <3 <3

Thank you also to Tan-ni Fan for editing the first edition and to Raelynn Marie for the gorgeous map—I used it while writing this! I really did! And big thanks go to Natasha Snow for the *OMG, it's so PERFECT* cover. This was our very first project together, and since then, you've been my go-to for covers. You're a goddess of cover design and it's such an amazing blessing.

And thank you, thank you, thank you to my partner for being with me through all of this. It's not easy living with an author, I know, but babe, thanks for hanging in there. xoxoxo

Finally, but never least, plenty of thanks to you, readers! It's always humbling to have you with me along the way. Thanks for being here and for spending a bit of your time on these words. <3

For more about what's coming in the series or about my other projects, stop by my website or find me on social media! I love hearing from folks, so come on by and say hi.

Blessings and peace to you all,

Archer

Also by Archer Kay Leah

THE REPUBLIC SERIES
A Question of Counsel (The Republic, book 1)
Four (The Republic, book 2)
Blood Borne (The Republic, book 3)
Soulbound (The Republic, book 4)

NOVELS
For the Clan

NOVELLAS
Heart, Lace, and Soul
Of Kindred and Stardust

About The Republic Series

Welcome to *The Republic*, high fantasy romances for across the LGBTQA+ spectrum, where love, fight, and hope are at the very core, entwined with the lives of romantic partners, friends, and families... and maybe a few lifelong enemies, too. Come step into their world where games linger and foul play is afoot!

• • •

Democracy. Family. Loyalty. Honour.
The perfect system.

Freedom. Belonging. Unity.
The perfect illusion.

With the right people and the right price, the Republic of Kattal can be brought to its knees.

Peace and security are never a guarantee when greed and lies threaten the balance. Fear and control know no bounds; and sacred tenets don't keep the monsters away. The right to choose can be a nightmare.

But for every line crossed, someone waits on the other side, ready to push back.

In justice, there is wisdom. In wisdom, there is protection. In it all, there is love. Maybe it means saving a village; maybe it means saving someone you can't live without. Sometimes it's just about doing the right thing and learning to love yourself.

Magic may lurk in the shadows.
Crime may never sleep.
But love doesn't back down.

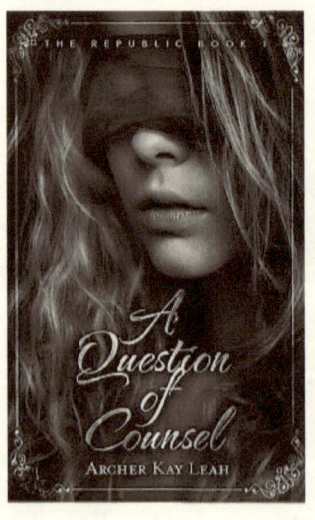 

THE REPUBLIC 3

BLOOD BORNE

ARCHER KAY LEAH

THE REPUBLIC 4

SOULBOUND

ARCHER KAY LEAH

About the Author

Archer Kay Leah was raised in Canada, growing up in a port town at a time when it was starting to become more diverse, both visibly and vocally. Combined with the variety of interests found in Archer's family and the never-ending need to be creative, this diversity inspired a love for toying with characters and their relationships, exploring new experiences and difficult situations.

Archer most enjoys writing speculative fiction and is engaged in a very particular love affair with fantasy, especially when it is dark and emotionally charged. When not reading and writing for work or play, Archer is a geek with too many hobbies and keeps busy with other creative endeavors, a music addiction, and whatever else comes along. Archer lives in London, Ontario with a non-binary partner who loves video games, composing music, and all things out there in the vast space of the universe.

Website: archerkayleah.wordpress.com
Goodreads: goodreads.com/ArcherKayLeah
Facebook: facebook.com/ArcherKayLeah
Twitter: twitter.com/archerkayleah